LIGHTFALL

THE STARCHASER SAGA
BOOK IV

R. DUGAN

WAVE WALKER
press

For information contact:
R. Dugan
PO Box 1265
Martinsville, IN 46151
reneeduganwriting.com

Cover design by Maja Kopunovic
Map by Jessica Khoury
ISBN: 978-1-7339255-4-9

First Edition: June 2021

10 9 8 7 6 5 4 3 2 1

DEDICATION

To Miranda and Cassidy.
Because this book—and this author—wouldn't be what they needed to
without your love and light.
Long live the Bookmates. <3

And to every reader who has endured something they thought would break them.
To the survivor, the thriver, the shaker of shadows and breaker of chains.
You are a tide-turner. A fate-changer.
And you are stronger than you will ever fully know.

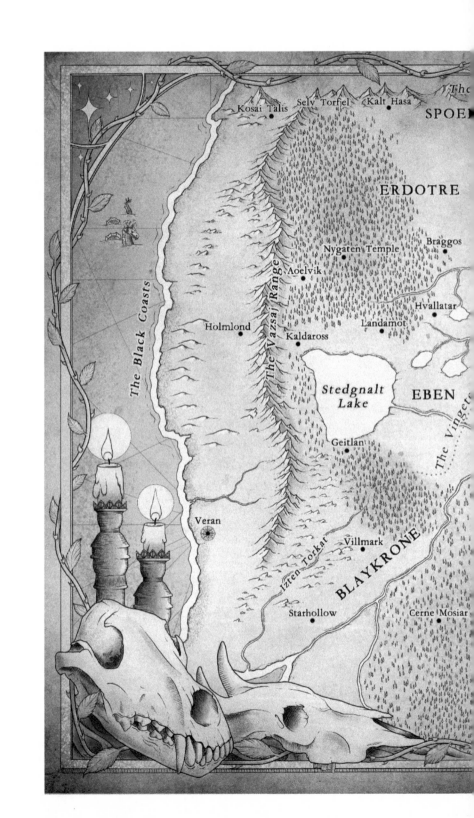

ge

ralek

NORDBRAN

Azkai Temple

KROAKEN

Felstrond

n Hatcheries

Detlyse Halet

Keltei Temple

Niort River

dom

LATAUS

VERD

The Wildwood

Soratt Temple

copr. 2020 Jessica Khoury

THE
HUNTER

OF

SECRET AND
SHADOW

CHAPTER ONE

THOUGH AUTUMN STILL reigned in the Northern Kingdom of Valgard, ice already crowned the upper passes of the Vaszaj Range, and Princess Cistine Novacek shivered in her piled-on furs every step she followed her friends up the mountain. Snow sucked at her boots, though she walked in the others' footprints: Aden in the lead, Quill at his heels, Tatiana on his. Quill's mischievous smirk held the secret of why he ripped them all from their private apartments in the courthouse and gave them wind augments to cross the distance, camping the night on this mountain's southern face and beginning this perilous ascent before dawn.

She paused, sweating despite the cold, gripping a hardy mountain shrub for balance while she sucked in lungfuls of air so frigid it stabbed her throat. It felt good in a way, a distraction from another night of restless sleep, the heaviness in her chest, the somberness that clung to her spirit, and the strange, sick sensation in her stomach.

All her life, there was a call inside her, a sweet and urgent song growing stronger after she came to Valgard. But when she first set foot on the great rune-slab lid over the well beneath the courthouse—one of the Doors to the Gods from which Valgard once harvested their mighty augments—the call went from shrill to sour. And now, deep in her core, it snarled.

Her fingertips rattled the leaves. She pushed off from the shrub, body singing with urgency, and the ice crust snagged her ankles. A gloved hand caught under her elbow, hoisting her back up when she stumbled.

"Careful," Thorne warned. "If you think you're cold now, I don't advise getting better acquainted with these drifts."

"So much for my plans to protest Quill's secrecy." She stabbed her feet more firmly into the footprints three-boots-deep ahead of her. "Ashe could tell you how effective my tantrums are."

But Asheila Kovar, her Warden since birth, wasn't here; nor was Maleck Darkwind, one of the cabal's most trusted warriors. They were in Talheim, Cistine's kingdom, where the weather was more seasonable and the world milder and full of light. She missed them, and her home, desperately.

"Princess Cistine Novacek, throwing tantrums? Surely not." Ariadne passed them breezily, throwing a one-sided smile back at her.

Thorne released Cistine's arm but didn't move away, and she risked a glance at him. His disheveled silver hair sparkled brighter than the icicles dripping from the mountain ledges, his concerned gaze searching her face. "Are you all right?"

She rubbed her arms and nodded. "Just wondering what Quill's scheming. But it's good to be out of the city for a bit."

He sighed a cold plume of breath and raised a tentative hand toward her face. "That it is." Cistine flinched at the motion, head humming with spectral sensations of a blow from a different hand, and Thorne recoiled. "I'm sorry, that—forgive me."

"There's nothing to forgive." But she couldn't draw in a full breath until she moved away from his voice and touch, from the memory stirred by his eyes and voice of an enemy more creature than man.

It was nearly sunhigh when they reached the treeline, a broad shelf of stone dropping perilously toward a thin river between the mountains, and Quill fanned out an arm. "We're here."

A lonely caw floated down from the trees; Faer, his trained attack raven, swooped from scouting to alight on his shoulder. Cistine wandered past them, brushing a hand down the bird's back and leaning over the ledge to peer at the water far below. Aden flung out an arm across her front, shaking his head. Tatiana whistled, high to low, folding her arms and cocking her weight on one hip. "Impressive view, Featherbrain!"

"If the plan was to remind us of our nominal place in the vastness of Valgard, message received." Ariadne nudged Quill's ribs. "But couldn't this have waited?"

"The view, maybe. But not this." He plundered in his pocket and withdrew a glittering globe of godlike power—a fire flagon.

The taste of what lurked within that thin glass shell blew through Cistine sharper than any mountain wind. She didn't realize she'd taken a step toward Quill until Aden's deep voice halted her. "Why are we here?"

Quill's gaze fixed on Cistine, full of lively challenge. "Because I want to see what she can do."

As the Key.

The words hung unspoken and understood; they all must've been wondering it while they fought to rescue her from Chancellor Salvotor over the past two months. No one else like her existed in this kingdom, a girl forged of power in her father's bloodline before she was born—power that reached out to the flagon in Quill's hand.

Come. The familiar call thrummed in her chest. *Come and see.*

When she laid hold of the augment, Quill's three-fingered hand tightened over hers. "Only if you want to, Stranger."

She sucked air down deeply, filling the parts of her that went hollow during captivity in a dark mountain prison. "I want to."

She took the flagon and turned, catching Thorne's eye. He lingered farther off than the others, giving her a wide berth, but his attention was focused and intense, waiting for her to need him. That look, if not his touch, still made her heart race pleasantly. When he offered his hand, she slung off her pack and passed it to him. "What do you want me to do, Quill?"

A dart of his chin indicated a peak more than a mile away. "See that mountain? Try to hit it."

"That's all? You're not going to tell me how?"

"I think you already know how."

She opened her mouth to tell him that was absurd, it took weeks in sparring and swordplay before she started to feel the last bit competent, and this was no different—yet the augment trilled in her fist, and her spirit echoed it, a melody her untrained ears knew and loved.

"Stand back," Thorne warned as Cistine broke the flagon against her armored thigh. Panic lanced through her along with the fire that it might escape her control like the lightning in Kalt Hasa when she tried to set them free. But where that lightning was vibrant and volatile, this fire purred and hugged her contours, sliding into the reinforced armor that conducted it away from flesh it could otherwise melt, sinew and bone it could sunder in any body but hers.

And then it traveled deeper.

Frowning, she shut her eyes and dove after it.

This sensation was different from the blinding few moments of escape from Kalt Hasa when she embodied light, then lightning; the fire congealed at her very center, heat flowering into a sphere, and in her mind she could wrap her hands around it and mold it to her wishes. The more she concentrated, the stronger it felt—not only a fire augment, but the wild heart of fire for which she was Named. Her spirit sang to that which was like it, a portion crafted before her birth in a ritual known only to her father and the *visnprest* Order that came before, the making that would pass down to her descendants and their descendants. A trust as sacred as the throne Cistine was born to in the Middle Kingdom.

She reached the bottom of her breath, the door in her spirit where the fire shuddered to a halt. Then she opened her eyes, focused on that faraway peak, and unleashed a sickle of flame, blazing and bellowing like dragon's breath, blasting the cabal away with audible shouts.

Fire sheared into stone, booming like thunder. With a distant crack, droves of snow, ice, and rock gave way, and half the mountaintop plunged into the valley below.

It took far too long for the echo to fade, for Cistine's racing heart to slow and the embers to stop drifting from her fingertips. Behind her, Tatiana breathed, "Holy stars."

"*Logandir.*" The name was a helpless prayer on Ariadne's lips. Aden stared openmouthed. Quill folded his hands around the nape of his neck, gaping at the damage, and Cistine's cheeks heated like all the rest of the embers gathered beneath her skin.

Thorne cocked his head. "Why did you close your eyes?"

She swallowed. "It felt different from how I thought it would, so I followed the power and molded it into the shape I wanted...like how my mother molds clay in her sculpting classes."

Quill dropped his hands, looking swiftly at Tatiana.

"Is it...not like that for everyone else?" Cistine whispered.

"To us, the power simply *is*," Ariadne said. "We channel it, but we don't shape it."

Cistine hugged herself, cold all over again. "I wish it wasn't different for me."

Ariadne's angled eyes softened. "What we see as different, the gods often deem miraculous."

"Now, that," Quill said when another clot of rock shattered from an unstable ledge and hurtled into the valley, "is going to need a *lot* of molding."

"I'm ready whenever you are," Cistine vowed.

He turned his scorched-white wing of hair across his scalp. "Then we should probably start now."

When Thorne stepped up to Cistine's side, she didn't flinch this time. She desperately needed the solidarity of his presence in the silence that followed, beholding the destructive potential of her power.

CHAPTER TWO

TALHEIM'S CAPITAL GLOWED under a banner of ghostlights and stars, flocked with sellers from the horselands of the north, the deserts of the south, the woodlands and wetlands of the west and east. Accents blended across the city plots, pinioning off symphony halls and eateries, the great circus, and the Citadel, home of the royal family.

Asheila Kovar studied that shimmering expanse of glass, marble, and stone through the fringe of her black-dyed hair, heart drumming with longing and unease.

Once, she walked that Citadel as little less than royalty herself: Warden and loyal friend to Princess Cistine since birth. She'd practically been family. Now she was less than nothing, a stranger seated on a bridge looking toward home. Choices—from the Blood Hive arena to derelict Jovadalsa to that stormy night outside Stornhaz when she threw away her prized sword, and that seaside temple where she walked away from her commander and bent the knee only to her princess—had stripped her of places to belong, friends to rely on, titles to boast in. Now all she had was a mission from Cistine, a wineskin in her hands, a new blade on her back, and a Valgardan warrior sitting beside her.

Dragging her gaze from the Citadel, she risked a glance at Maleck and found him transfixed on the assembly across the moat where a pair of vendors tied a garland between ghostpoles, the phosphorescent plants already broken open for the night. "Why are all these people gathering?"

The quiet rumble of his voice, as usual, lulled some of her specters to sleep. She passed the wineskin to him. "For Darlaska, a fete for the True God and his vassals. Our priests and priestesses encourage celebration for what the gods give. Not augments, but...our breath. Our bodies. Our kingdom. We spend a week celebrating, and at the end we give gifts."

Maleck frowned at the jutting terraces spilling from the marketplace into the moat. "We were told Talheim shunned the gods and their gifts because augmentation wasn't given to them to protect."

"Sounds like we were both wrong about the people we went to war with." Emboldened by wine, she propped her shoulder against his and pointed toward the booths. "See those pennants? The four colors—gold, green, blue, and brown? Compass points, so you know where a merchant came from and what they specialize in."

Maleck's shoulder stiffened when she pressed into him, then slowly relaxed. "The same as your royal colors."

She was just tipsy enough to be impressed he noticed. "That's right. Vendors flock for this chance. No better time to sell your wares than during Darlaska, when everyone is buying everyone else something."

"The festival is soon, then?"

Ashe snorted. "Gods, no. More than a month away still."

Maleck tipped his head, rustling the dark waves of his newly-unbraided hair. "A month of gift-buying seems...excessive."

Stealing the wineskin, Ashe drank and passed it back to him. "That's proof you haven't done much shopping with Cistine."

His gaze softened. "I imagine she's quite fond of this occasion."

"That's putting it lightly. We practically live in the marketplace from the end of autumn until Darlaska. She fills up her hollow leg with peppermint tea and I carry everything for her until I look like a pack animal."

Though this year, she likely would've carried her own bags.

Struck with melancholy, Ashe put out her hand for the wineskin again. This time, when Maleck passed it over, his gaze lingered on her face. "We've watched the Citadel for the Queen's patterns these last four days, but we've also sat on these bridges every night, and gone to the beachside dances, and surveyed the markets."

"And?" Ashe muttered.

"And I wonder why, when time is against us. Rion Bartos could ride down from the border forts and take the Queen's ear any day. King Jad and Mahasar's forces might already be in Middleton, giving us less time than ever to convince them a treaty exists between our kingdoms." Maleck spanned an arm to the sparkling terraces and stalls, and the buildings beyond. "Why all of this, knowing what's at stake?"

Because I wanted to see my home through your eyes, to know if there's anything left in it worth hoping for. I wanted you to know there's more to me than sand and steel. Because of the way you screamed my name when I closed that grate and left you underneath Stornhaz, the way you stepped between Rion and me when I came back. Because I hesitated whenever I thought of you. Because of how you're looking at me right now.

Ashe rinsed those honest confessions from her mouth with another drink. "Because if we're going to buy Cistine time fooling Jad with this so-called alliance, he'll have to believe you don't hate Talheim. Knowing Astoria's heart seemed like a good place to start."

"I don't hate this kingdom, nor do I need to know its heart to know its worth. Only yours."

God's bones, he was good. Handsome, too, in his stolen Talheimic attire. And the wine was making her weak.

Ashe stood. "Tonight's what we've been waiting for. When Solene ventures out to shop, we'll have our audience with her whether Rion's sent a warning ahead about me or not. We'll tell her what Cistine's up to, and then...Middleton."

Maleck rose, enviably steady though he'd drunk at least as much as her. "You're certain the Queen will speak to us?"

"If we tell her it's about Cistine and it could help Cyril? Absolutely. She'd do anything for them."

He nodded. "Cistine's told me of the love her parents share. She claims they're *selvenar*."

Ashe snorted. "The King and Queen of Talheim, blended hearts. Who would've thought?"

"It's not so unlikely. *Selvenar* can be found anywhere. As the tales go, when the gods forged man of stardust, there were those who were made of the same substance, drawn together across all fates that separated them."

Something pulsed deep in Ashe's core at his words, at the sketch of light on his face. She drove it away with a blow to his shoulder. "If you keep this up, I might be fooled into thinking you're a romantic."

Maleck rubbed the offended spot, cheeks coloring. "What matters is that concern for her *selvenar* may make Queen Solene sympathetic to us."

"We'll know when we see her. Come on, I know where we can sleep for the night."

She led him through unlit avenues to one of Astoria's central plazas, speckled in gold and crimson from the impressive building dominating its edge. Music filtered from every vaulted window and sealed doorway, washing the polished cobblestones with sweet melodies; lovers stopped to dance in the echo, laughing and twirling beneath the stars.

Ashe grinned at Maleck's wide-eyed stare. "Astoria's most famous symphony house. I know a way inside."

In the sliver of an alley between the symphony hall and the tailor next door, she counted sixteen cobblestones down, took as much of a running leap as she could, and climbed hand-over-hand up to the ring of loose wooden boards above the colonnade. Maleck flipped himself easily onto the ledge beside her. "Dare I ask how you found this?"

Ashe dug the knife from her boot and pried the supple wood. "By accident. When I was nine, my parents promised to bring me to a symphony, but they revoked the privilege when they caught me practicing with wooden swords. So I improvised." Smirking, she peeled the board loose. "From then until the war, I came to any symphony I wanted."

"And after?"

Sadness bore down on her gut so hard it ached. "I was officially Cadre, so I had to train. And then there was Cistine."

The short crawlspace beyond opened into a ramshackle stairwell disused by attendants. Ashe slithered out onto the broken steps, then turned back to steady Maleck when he dropped behind her. They climbed the narrow shaft, walls reverberating the deep thrum of cellos and the high echoes of brass. Ashe's pulse settled into tune with the strings when she and Maleck vaulted the staircase onto an old prop balcony cleared long ago. Only dust and shadows remained, gathered behind a thick red drape—along with the memories Ashe made in this place. "I used to stuff my shirt with candies from our flawed confection pile before I came up here. Sometimes I'd be so full after eating them, I had to wait to climb back out."

Maleck's laughter was the perfect accompaniment to the music when Ashe peeled back the curtain, revealing the edge of the dome's deep upward vault, the plush seats, and the stage far below. He drifted to the thin railing beside her, bracing his hands on the splintered wood and staring at the musicians.

Ashe leaned her head on her knuckles wrapped around the thick velvet fabric, watching him. "You said you loved piano. I happen to think Talheim's are the best."

Maleck's eyes fluttered shut and he breathed in the music. "And you...you played the violin. Why did you stop?"

She settled cross-legged, bracing her arms against the railing. "The same reason I stopped coming here. My future was as a Warden."

And now she was nothing. Until Cistine told her what to do, she wasn't even certain she had a place in Talheim anymore. It was a terrifying notion, the expanse beyond it bleak and void; her eyes burned with the uncertainty as the music swelled and sank around them.

They were quiet for a time, leaning into the melody. Maleck rested his chin on his arm, tracking the pianist's movements with a warrior's focus and a lover's softness. "I slept in a place like this before my brothers took me."

He'd told her more since they came to Talheim than ever before about the brothers who forced him into the war, the day he met her on the battlefield, and how their friend Aden's father broke rank to come for him and lead him from ramshackle Cerne Mosiar back to the City of a Thousand

Stars. He laid all that pain at her feet like an apology for being the boy in whose face she screamed her fearlessness when he came to kill Cyril Novacek more than twenty years ago.

"Whatever happened to them?" It was the last piece of the story he hadn't told her yet, but tonight she was wine-weary enough to ask...perhaps even to dream of hunting down the people who stole him and forced him into that war.

"They haunt the far north as creatures called Bloodwights." He shook his head. "And they don't belong in places like this."

Ashe settled in more comfortably beside him, shutting her eyes and focusing on the music's smooth, rising notes, the violin sweetest of all. A tear slid down her cheek as it reached its crescendo; hastily, she knuckled it away.

"If you had a violin," Maleck said, "would you play again?"

"I don't know. If you had a sketchbook, would you go back to drawing?"

"It's possible. But I can't say if happiness makes as fine art as sorrow."

"Are you? Happy?"

He stayed quiet for so long, the music became a lullaby easing Ashe toward slumber, her head resting on her folded arms against the railing. Then, "Yes. Here with you, in this place and every day since we came to your kingdom. I am happy, Asheila."

A second tear joined the first. This one, she didn't wipe away. *I'm happy being with you, too.*

The song ended, the violin's last high note keening against the velvet-wrapped walls and echoing where she and Maleck slumped against the railing, faces turned, eyes fixed on each other while thunderous applause took the symphony hall by storm.

CHAPTER THREE

THE SLAM OF blades echoed across the bronze-painted vaults and sand-scattered floors of Kanslar Court's private training hall; pain barked through Cistine's shoulders as she thrust back against the descending might of Ariadne's sword. They'd sparred since daybreak, driven by another night of bad dreams. Sweat wicked away the memory of Grimmaul's hands on Cistine's hips, but it couldn't erase the echo of his screams in her nightmares when she broke open a fire flagon and burned him alive—nor the vindictive pleasure of wishing it were real.

She dreamed of burning Grimmaul and Salvotor every night. She didn't know what that meant about her, what she became in Kalt Hasa.

Ariadne's saber cleaved against hers so hard she fell to her seat on the floor, breath pushing from her with an undignified puff. Wild, girlish laughter bounced off the curved ceilings. "Teach me how to do *that*, Aden!"

Rubbing her aching tailbone, Cistine glanced over her shoulder. Between the next two pillars, Aden sparred with a girl half his size and twice his energy, her grin revealing the gap where she lost her last tooth the day before. Catching Cistine's look, Pippet halted to blow her a kiss, and Aden swept her ankles, sending her tumbling with a furious yelp.

"Like that," he said mildly, flashing Cistine a smile. It was a wobbly effort to return it, her eyes leaping to the four-point compass pendant hanging between his bare collarbones—a last gift from his father, who gave his life to free Cistine and Thorne from Kalt Hasa. Her fingers flexed, desperate to drift to the token for the dead strung around her own neck, though that warped remnant of a rose-gold betrothal ring was only good for heartbreak.

Ariadne rested her sword tip in the sand and crouched. "Are you finished?"

Cistine scrambled up and retrieved her weapon. "Not yet."

The beat of their blades pounded out the imperfections of her sorrow, fear, and anger like a hammer on new steel. Everything Maleck taught her about swordplay during long sessions on the rock top outside Hellidom, Ariadne provoked to greater heights. Lessons of footwork and handwork and how to brace and push back flitted through her mind, kinder, cleaner, more sensible and far more rewarding than dwelling on her dreams.

Lean in, she commanded herself. *Lean in, lean in.*

Sweat swarmed her eyes and sand caked her toes; every breath shredded her throat like a blade. Finally, it stopped being Grimmaul or Salvotor on the other side of the saber, and Ariadne's face annealed back into focus.

"I did it!" Pippet's shriek of victory shattered the dark tunnel of Cistine's focus, and light flooded back in. She turned just as Aden hit the floor, groaning from a kick to the stomach, and Pippet mounted him with a foot on his chest, arms flung up in victory. "Crown me princess of the Blood Hive! I have defeated its Lord!"

An unfamiliar laugh and a pair of clapping hands stole all their attention from her, and from Aden blanching under her weight; a woman had crept up on them, dark hair and tawny skin accentuated by a deep scarlet gown. She splashed her tall, graceful form against the pillar between their two sparring matches, eyes brimming with mischief. "We have a little lioness on our hands, I see."

Aden sat up under Pippet's foot, a smirk melting the pallor from his face. "Mirassah."

"Hello, Aden. It's been a while, hasn't it?"

Pippet frowned. "Who are you?"

"An old friend," Aden said. "Very old."

"It's poor manners to tease a woman about her age, you know."

"I was referring to how long you've been creating havoc in this city." Aden planted a hand on Pippet's shoulder and pushed himself to his feet. "Though that dress is rather becoming."

"Flattery! Much better."

"You didn't let me finish. I was going to say it's becoming too bright for the eyes."

"Ah, there's the Aden I knew and barely tolerated."

Dark humor flashed in his gaze. "Not quite the preening Vassoran guard-to-be who pushed Sander into the Channel on his graduating day, are you?"

"And you not quite the posturing Tribune's son who tried to stop Quill from following us in."

"Are you *still* telling that story?" Quill's voice heralded his arrival, arm around Tatiana's waist as they wove between other sparring matches near the mouth of the training hall. "It's not even that good! I've staked my reputation on a lot better since." He caught sight of Pippet and grimaced. "Better acts of service and safety, is what I mean."

"You jumped into the *Channel*?" his younger sister demanded, fists on hips.

Quill rubbed the back of his neck and shot a glare at Mirassah. "Let's not put ideas in anyone's heads, all right?"

Aden laughed. "As long as Mira is there to pull another reckless child from those treacherous waters, I see no cause for alarm."

"I'm afraid my days of swimming are over," Mira said. "Along with any commission I might've had in the Vassora."

Aden's teasing smile faded. "You never rejoined?"

"It wasn't for me. Fortunately, I have plenty of talents besides sticking the sharp end of a blade into some brute's gut. I like to leave those easy tasks to men like you." She patted his shoulder in passing and halted before Cistine, hand extended. "I don't believe I've had the pleasure."

Gulping back her shock at how casually this stranger poked fun at

Aden—and earned no more than a withering glance for it—she accepted her hand. "Princess Cistine Novacek of Talheim."

"Ah, of course! The princess who crossed borders to save her kingdom. I've heard much about you. I'm sorry for what you've suffered."

The sorrow in Mirassah's eyes was genuine, hand gripping Cistine's like an anchor. She found herself smiling back more easily than she had in days. "Pleased to meet you, Mirassah."

"Please, it's Mira. Only one person calls me Mirassah, and that's when I've infuriated him...which is delightfully often." With a last squeeze, she let go and turned to Tatiana. "You, I do know. The girl in the beaded dress who dominated that Tribune's feast all those years ago."

Tatiana smirked. "Glad to know they're still telling that story in the elite circles."

Mira laughed. "Like a legend. I've always wanted to meet you." She glanced aside to the quietest member of their gathering. "And you must be the warrior Ariadne, the one this upcoming trial hangs on." When she nodded, Mira stepped forward to clasp her shoulder. "There are many, many women in this city who are grateful for your courage...more than you'll ever know. More than are willing to say."

Pippet barged between them. "I'm Pippet! I'm the youngest member of the cabal."

Mira laughed. "Oh, your name needs no introduction! There isn't a person in Kanslar who hasn't heard of your exploits."

Pippet blinked. "There isn't?"

Mira swung an arm around her shoulders. "Pippet the fierce, traveling with warriors across the wilds in search of the stolen princess..."

The whole cabal laughed; one chuckle, softer than the rest, came from the pillar behind Cistine. She took two steps back, eyes kept on the others. "You're being dramatic, lurking in the shadows like that."

"Guilty as charged."

Thorne entered her space like a warm breeze, carrying the smell of hard soap and sandalwood in the folds of his dark attire, and the state of his head startled a squeak from Cistine. "What did you do to your hair?" It was shorter than she'd ever seen it, a dignified, forward-feathered crop cleaning some of the wildness from his ten years in hiding.

"Preparation for today's ceremony. I thought of dyeing it fuchsia, but Tatiana refused." Laughter danced in his eyes, and for an instant she wanted to lean into him, as close as they were in that prison pantry where everything changed—for the better, she believed at the time.

She gripped the chain around her neck with all her might. *You wouldn't want to betray Julian's memory too soon.*

"Thorne!" Tatiana beckoned him over. "Come show everyone the hair!"

"I like it!" Pippet said. "What's it for?"

"His swearing-in, remember?" Quill shoved her. "And we're about to be late for it. Now, march."

She pulled his arm around her and dragged him through the training hall, chattering with Tatiana about new inventions her father was cobbling together in his shop. Aden and Mira fell into step, discussing things too quiet for Cistine to hear. Ariadne trailed them, gaze lost in thought. Cistine and Thorne took the rear.

"You were awake before dawn again this morning," he remarked—a question that was not a question.

Cistine picked up her discarded blade and sheathed it on her back. "A bad dream. As usual."

He paused, rubbing his left calf. "Do you want to tell me about it?"

"It was Grimmaul."

Anger twisted his mouth into a scowl and swept his brows together. He didn't speak again until they mounted the steps from the training hall. "I know there are things you don't want from me right now, but never forget my door is across from yours and I keep it unlocked for a reason. I'm here if you ever need me."

She wished with all her heart that the distance between needing him and having him was a straight line; but ever since he Named her, his touch tended to bring back the black skies and bloody battlefields she saw in the House of Visions, and if he said the wrong things in the wrong way, it dragged her mind deep into Kalt Hasa. "I can't always wake you. You need sleep, too."

He shrugged. "I'm too busy for it most nights, anyway."

She bit her tongue against a protest. She was in no place to tell him how to face his pain, and he was in no position to heal hers. She was a princess of twenty, him a High Tribune of twenty-eight, facing specters many people twice their age never fought. That darkness was deep, the path through it unknown.

Today, she reminded herself. They only had to survive today. And then tomorrow.

They caught up to the others at last, joined in the middle of the hall by a bright-robed, brown-skinned, amber-eyed man who slipped from a side hall to accost them. "Good morning, all!" His grin lingered longest on Mira. "Up at dawn to mingle with the dreck I see, Mirassah."

She batted her lashes at him like a blink of sunlight on steel. "Occasionally, one needs time away from you and your other lovers to remember what civilized company looks like, Sander."

"You wound me."

"I'm losing my touch if you think this is what a wounding from me feels like."

His laughter bounded along the walls, and Cistine relaxed. Tribune Sander was one of the few outside the cabal who knew she was the Key; every moment he spent in good spirits with her friends made her secret feel safer in his hands. "And how are you feeling this morning, *Banjor*?"

She arched a brow. "I feel like you had Vihar track my scent all the way here, which makes me feel like putting my knee into your groin."

"Manners, Mirassah, stars! We are among brutish, uncouth, soon-to-be-*Chancellor* company."

"It takes talent to hurl so many insults in one breath," Ariadne remarked.

Mira groaned. "Oh, don't praise him, his head already fits funny."

"Nonsense," Sander grinned. "You are the one person prettier than me in this city."

Curiosity pricked Cistine's chest. She wondered if he said the same thing to all twenty-seven of his lovers—of which Mira was clearly one. There was no accounting for taste, she supposed.

A harsh bark echoed from further up the hall, and Sander's tamed wolf, Vihar, trotted into their midst next to Mira. His nose brushed her hip, and she tapped the top of his head. "Shall we?"

They were a strange entourage: five warriors, a Tribune and one of his twenty-seven lovers, a young girl, and a princess in armor, all led by a wolf. They only held silence in common on the way to the ceremony where Thorne would finally accept the power to change injustice, cruelty, and imbalance in Valgard. When they reached the sunlit courtroom, already brimming with elites and Tribunes, Thorne paused with an apologetic smile. "The Chancellors are waiting for me."

Melancholy panged in Cistine's chest. As long as she knew him, Thorne belonged to himself, a High Tribune of the wilds with loyalty to his cabal; but today he became a leader with other authorities to answer to. He wouldn't just be theirs anymore. It felt like saying farewell, watching him enter that room ahead of them.

"Thorne!" she blurted after him. "Baba Kallah would be so proud of you."

He glanced back, eyes softening at the mention of his late grandmother. "Thank you. I'm honored you're here to witness this, Cistine."

Then he was gone, passing a pair of podiums and a wooden fence at the center for the dais where four men waited. Sander gestured after him. "So, the Chancellors. Bravis of Traisende and Maltadova of Yager, I hear you're all quite familiar with."

Cistine swapped smiles with Tatiana. No one but the cabal knew women made up Yager's true ruling body, their influence kept secret by archaic laws forbidding them from the Judgement Seat.

"Those other two strapping men," Sander went on, "are Valdemar of Tyve and Benedikt of Skyygan. I'm sure you're aware of their animosity toward Kanslar's former Chancellor."

Cistine's skin prickled watching the men fix Thorne with hungry, furious stares. She could only imagine what went through their minds.

Thorne's father had held cruel sway in their Courts. Did they fear his son would continue that tyranny?

Movement stirred through the bustle, coming toward them, and Sander groaned low in his throat. "And these are my fellow Kanslar Tribunes. Marcel of Spoek, Enar of Lataus, Gunther of Unsverd, Hafgrim, soon to be *officially* of Blaykrone, Njal of Eben, Tadeas of Erdotre, and Vaclav of Kroaken."

It took effort not to think of them as the people who voted to have Thorne whipped and nearly stripped of his title a decade ago. They were potential allies now; Cistine had to treat them as such. "It's a pleasure to meet you all."

Marcel scoffed, licking at the thin mustache perched on his sneering upper lip. "This is the company you keep now, Sander? Outlaws, Hive fighters, children, and Talheimics?"

Sander's gaze hardened. "A new day rises in Kanslar, my friends. I think it's best we all acclimate, don't you?"

"Salvotor will not forget what you did, placing his son on the Judgement Seat. There's a special place in Nimmus for traitors."

"Then you should be very careful how you serve our new Chancellor."

Marcel's eyes traveled around the cabal, lingering on Tatiana. "I remember you...the tinker's daughter. That armor suits you better than the stitched-together old thing you wore to the Tribune's ball."

She shrugged. "What can I say? Toppling tyrants looks good on a woman."

"Indeed." Marcel's eyes flicked to Ariadne. "Even if she must lie and entrap men with her body to do it."

Aden started forward, and Mira caught his arm, fixing Marcel with a level look. "I doubt any woman in this courtroom, or indeed in this kingdom, needs half a wit or a flirt of her lashes to topple *you*."

His gaze narrowed right back. "I didn't realize we sank to allowing invalids into our courtrooms."

Sander's mouth jumped open this time, but Mira spoke over him. "I suppose we're both fortunate full acumen is not required here, hm?" She glanced at Sander. "Don't you men have somewhere to be?"

Shoulders smoothing, he led the Kanslar Tribunes away, tossing a parting grimace at Mira. She fluttered her fingers after him, then turned to Ariadne, all traces of humor gone. "The things you've endured and the valleys you climb from are not weapons in any man's arsenal. Don't give him ground in your story."

Tight jaw relaxing, Ariadne nodded.

"Why did he call you an invalid, Mira?" Cistine asked, prodded with curiosity's familiar barbs.

"No reason that matters to prudent people." Smiling, she slipped away into the crowd gathering at the fence.

Pippet craned her head back, peering up at Quill. "What did that mean? What he said to Ari?"

Quill clasped his sister's shoulders and pressed a kiss to the side of her head. "It means we have more work to do in this city than just removing Salvotor from power."

Tatiana fell into step with Ariadne on their way to the fence. "Are you all right?"

"Yes. They're only words, Tati." But her hollow gaze told a different story.

Bravis, the acting Chancellor, waved a hand to quiet the room. "I know we're all excited, but since Traisende's time is doomed to controversy from start to end this time, why don't we get this over with as quickly as possible?" A smattering of chuckles crossed the room, most uneasy. "As no doubt everyone in Stornhaz and half the territories knows by now, Chancellor Salvotor of Kanslar Court was disbarred from the Judgement Seat on charges of defiling a *visnpresta*. Pending his upcoming trial, Thorne's retention of the High Tribune's title makes him Chancellor over Kanslar. We've reviewed the records provided by Tribune Sander and find no reason to contest this swearing-in. However, given your absence from Stornhaz for the past ten years, Thorne, the Courts request you undertake tutelage in matters of law and leadership. Do you accept these terms?"

"I do," he said.

"Hallvard, present the Book of the Law." The Traisende Tribune stepped around the dais, tome in arm, and Thorne laid his hand on the ancient cover. "High Tribune, do you swear to uphold this Law in word and deed, to improve upon it within your legal rights and ensure those in your Court do the same?"

"I, High Tribune Thorne of Kanslar Court, solemnly vow before the Courts and the gods that I will administer justice without partiality. I will do right by man and woman, rich and poor, common and elite...by Valgard and all its allies." Judging by the murmurs around the fence, that last bit was not a standard of the oath; but it warmed Cistine's core just the same. "I will faithfully and fairly perform the duties of my station as Chancellor for as long as they are mine to uphold."

Hallvard produced a dagger from the scabbard at his hip and striped Thorne's palm in one light, brief stroke. A flash of cold hissed through Cistine's body with the memory of iron fingers clamped around hers, guiding a knife in six diagonal slashes across Thorne's chest.

It's all right, it's all right, Wildheart.

His voice towed her back into the courtroom. "—this oath before all the people of the Northern Kingdom. And may the gods themselves strip me of my title if I fail."

There was no cheering when Thorne's hand slid from the Book, leaving a scarlet stripe on its face. Bravis regarded him pensively. "Many years ago, your father stood exactly where you're standing and made the same vows. In the end, they meant nothing to him. I caution you to remember that legacy."

"I accept your word of caution, and I give you one in turn." Thorne's voice dropped. "*Don't* condescend to me. I'm not my father. We're finally free of his influence in the courtroom...let's not bring him back by finding his face in the shadows."

Nodding curtly, Bravis waved Hallvard away. "Take your seat on the dais, Chancellor Thorne of Kanslar Court."

Though her hands hung like lead, Cistine forced herself to start the room clapping; a few were slow to join in, but the tension eased when Thorne reclined in the seat, spreading his arms on the rests.

When the applause quieted, Bravis addressed him again. "You must choose a High Tribune to succeed you. You have a day to deliberate."

"I don't need it, the choice is clear. Tribune Sander, step forward." Mutinous glares from the other Tribunes followed the preening man like a foul stench to the base of the dais. "Do you solemnly vow to serve as legal counsel to the people of Valgard and to me? Will you always remain faithful to examine the complaints, concerns, and charges laid before you, betraying no defendants, victims, or accusers through bias or personal opinion?"

"I vow it," Sander said, eyes shining.

"And do you swear to uphold the anonymity of the Courts with every subject, to discuss Kanslar's private matters with no one—even your twenty-seven lovers and your trained wolf?"

A ripple of laughter surged through the room, and Sander repeated, dryly this time, "I vow it."

"And do you resolve yourself not to be swayed by reports of malice, intimidation, hatred, prejudice, or affection as it pertains to the cases brought to you, affirming the innocence of all persons until proven otherwise by the due process of our laws?"

"I am resolved, solemnly and absolutely."

Thorne flashed a brief, crooked smile. "Then before all the witnesses in this courtroom, I name you High Tribune Sander of Kanslar Court."

The applause was immediate but brief this time, led by Mira and trailing off when the Chancellors rose, shook Thorne's still-bleeding hand, and retreated into conversation among themselves. He descended through the gate, and the cabal hurried to meet him, Cistine in the lead. "Congratulations, Chancellor Thorne."

His eyes glinted with humor. "Kanslar appreciates Talheim's unfaltering support and vote of confidence, Princess Cistine."

Quill whooped with laughter, clapping him in an embrace, and the others swarmed in with congratulations. Pippet even jumped on Thorne's back and hugged her arms around his neck. But his eyes lingered on Cistine, his smile wider than she'd ever seen, and that glee in his face, that joy, the victory and desire—

Look at you, Wildheart.

Chills scraped down Cistine's arms, burrowing into her hips so sharply her excitement choked and died. Fear puddled in her core and pangs of nervous energy fluttered along her limbs. Her feet raked against the ornate marble floor, taking her away from them.

Thorne frowned, straightening until Pippet slid down from his back. "Cistine?"

"I'm sorry, I have to..."

Run.

Sander pushed through the crowd and cuffed Thorne on the back, freeing her from his gaze. Her breath rushed out, and she nearly sagged. *I'm all right, I'm all right. I am not broken.*

"Meeting with the Chancellors," Sander spoke above the courtroom chatter. "They have some matters to discuss with you."

"Tell them I'll be there shortly." His gaze still shredding into her defenses, Thorne nodded to the cabal. "Today is yours. Celebrate however you like. Ariadne, Aden, I want to see you at dawn in my room."

With quick, parting embraces to their newly-named Chancellor, the cabal slipped out. Quill knocked Cistine's shoulder in passing, his gaze sharp, missing nothing. "Training."

"May I see you tonight?" Thorne called after her.

Though it tested the last inch of her self-control, Cistine pretended not to hear him as she followed Quill from the courtroom.

CHAPTER FOUR

LIGHT POURED THROUGH the glass dome of the acting Chancellor's sanctum, warming the round table and the men seated there. Each had a stack of papers before his seat, which would soon become Thorne Starchaser's latest problem.

"I know how taxing the day of swearing-in can be," Bravis began, "so we'll keep this brief."

"Two things you ought to know," Maltadova said. "We have our best warriors hunting for Devitrius. As the head of your father's personal retinue and an agent operating in other Courts under false names, his testimony could be vital in this and other trials. Unfortunately, he's eluding us...we think with the help of your mother."

Thorne expected nothing less from the woman whose greatest mercy was ignoring him completely and greatest betrayal was holding him still while his father belted his back. Only one thing surprised him. "You let her leave the courthouse?"

"We didn't realize she was gone until it was too late," Valdemar admitted.

"Rakel has acted as your father's stewardess for some time," Maltadova added. "He dispatched her on an errand while he was still in Kalt Hasa, through Devitrius. She vanished along the way and has not been seen since."

Thorne spread his shaking hands on the table's edge. "So my father is in chains, but his two greatest supporters are not only free, but untraceable."

Bravis grimaced. "We hoped you might help us with that. Is there anywhere they might go?"

He pondered a moment, then shook his head. "Nothing comes to mind. My father didn't keep me privy to most of his dealings, especially with them."

Benedikt cut in eagerly, "Well, what of the spies in our Courts? Your father's refused to call them back or tell us who they are. Perhaps they can help us find where Devitrius and Rakel have gone."

Thorne drummed his fingers on the table. "There might be one solution to both. My father kept ledgers that could us tell his trusted locations and the names of his spies. I can take them and start deciphering once he's taken to trial."

"Why delay?" Valdemar demanded. "What can he do if we tear his rooms apart for them now?"

"I'm not certain, and that's what worries me. He has too many loyalists left in this game, too many ways to strike if he grows suspicious." Pain lanced through Thorne's calves, and he dug his bootheels into the stone floor. "I won't risk harm coming to my people."

"To say nothing of the rest of us," Benedikt muttered.

Thorne shot him a glare. "I've lost my grandmother and a man of my cabal to this hunt already. I won't risk the ones who survived. If you take issue with that, feel free to confront my father's schemes your own way."

Benedikt started up with a growl, and Bravis snapped, "Both of you, enough. We will take Thorne's advisement on this matter...he knows his father's mind better than any of us. But you'd do well to remember, Thorne, it is not the Chancellor's way to think only of those he deems important."

Thorne receded, muscles twisting tighter with shame. "Granted. And speaking of what's important, I have a matter of my own to broach before we adjourn." Bravis nodded him on. "The Bloodwights are on the move in Oadmark."

Valdemar's jaw flickered with tension. "They've been flitting about on the borders for some time."

"This is different. They're capturing Oadmarkaics."

"Children?" Maltadova demanded.

"Among others."

Bravis scratched his bearded jaw. "Anything having to do with the former Order is cause for concern. But with everything else at stake, I can't spare the Vassora to investigate now. Once Salvotor is condemned and his threat removed from over our heads, we'll look into this matter. Until then, we keep watch and keep our focus."

Thorne fought not to scowl. Dangerous a gamble as that was, he understood it; the more they divided their focus, the more gaps they created for Salvotor to slip through. And with the last twenty years laid out before them, his father proved the more pressing threat.

He stood, flexing the tension from his legs. "I should go. Apparently I have studies tonight."

Lips twitching, Bravis shoved the nearest stack of papers toward him—old laws and new rulings to review. "Indeed you do. And we'll see you and the Princess soon to address those treaty discussions she's so eager to start."

"Alliance with Talheim," Valdemar scoffed. "I can't believe we're even entertaining the notion."

"Their princess was integral to Salvotor's arrest," Maltadova reminded him. "We ought to at least hear what she proposes."

Thorne shot him a grateful smile, fully aware the words were Chancelloress Adeima's as well as his. Gathering the reams of paper, he let himself out.

It was a long, lonely walk back to his room, his legs aching with every step, but to his amazement it was not empty when he arrived. Cistine sat at the dining table, two teacups before her and a book of truncated epics open in her lap. She looked up sharply when he shut the door.

"This...is a surprise," he admitted, sliding into the empty seat across from her. "How did it go with Quill?"

Her smile was smaller, more tentative than the broad grins he took for granted during the summer in Hellidom. "Well enough, I think? It's still strange, learning how to wield augments. But he's a good teacher."

Thorne cut away a spurt of jealousy that with Quill, she had no qualms of closeness. He would thank the gods every day that there were still friends she didn't recoil from. No matter how desperately he wished he were one of them, he couldn't make her suffering or joy about him.

"What did the Chancellors want?" she added.

Between gulps of the rosemary tea she poured for them both, Thorne told her of the reports, the spies, and the speculation that Rakel was loose in the wilds with Devitrius.

"*Rakel?*" Cistine banged down her teacup. "Salvotor's stewardess was your *mother?*"

"Much to her regret." Thorne smiled humorlessly, polishing off his cup just to avoid her eyes. "And now I have to hunt her."

"Well, when you have those ledgers, would you like help deciphering them? I know my family's cipher isn't quite the same, but maybe with that foundation—"

"I'd be grateful for your help."

Smiling a bit easier this time, she gathered her feet onto the chair and balanced her teacup on her knees. "We'll find those spies together. I know we will."

Chest aching, he spun his empty cup and watched her. "Can I ask why you wanted to run from me today?"

She blanched, dragging her lip between her teeth. Then she set aside her tea and circled her knees with her arms. "You looked at me too long. It reminded me of the dinners in Kalt Hasa."

Thorne sucked back a curse. So many things reminded her of that place, and him most of all. Some days it felt like everything about him was wrong...that *he* was wrong for her. "Cistine, maybe we should—"

"No. I can't let him win, I can't let him chase me away from what I want." But desperation tinged her voice like she was trying to convince herself.

You don't want this, he was tempted to say. Healing would come easier if she wasn't bound heart-to-heart with a man who stared too long with eyes too much like his father's, whose voice and face carried the damning nuances of her former captor's. She didn't want him to touch her, to look at her, to even whisper her Name.

He *was* wrong for her.

"What about you?" She changed the subject while he struggled for words. "The swearing-in, and now your mother...that must feel awful."

He shook his head, returning his cup to the tray. "I shouldn't have told you any of that. You carry enough of a burden already from my family."

"Your hurts and scars don't scare me. You should know that by now."

But it wasn't *his* scars he worried about this time. Shaking his head, he rose and grabbed a cloth to wipe the condensation from the table, keeping his hands busy when they threatened to shake again.

You're all wrong for her, boy.

"Thorne?" Cistine balanced her elbows on the table, chin in her hands, a tentative smile on her lips. "I'm so proud of you. I hope you know that."

A sigh blew through him, loosening his tense shoulders. "I do." He faced her, resting his haunches on the table. "I'm proud of you, too. The Chancellors are truly interested in what you're going to present about a potential treaty."

She caught her breath, and he wanted to bang his face against the table. Yet again, he said the wrong thing. "When?"

"After the trial's commencement, I imagine." He smoothed a hand through the air. "We still have plenty of time."

But her gaze darted feverishly again, refusing to be calmed. "No, we don't...I need to write down my appeals and the counterpoints for any arguments they might have And I should start now...there's so much to do." She snatched up the tray and bobbed an oddly-formal curtsy. "I'll see you soon."

"Cistine." Her name slid out of him, anguished, and she turned back at the door. "Thank you for the tea."

She raised the tray. "Any time you want to gossip about your family history, I'll keep the kettle warm."

In her absence, Thorne sank to the floor and buried his head in his hands, overwhelmed and enraged with himself.

Wrong, wrong, wrong. He was doing *everything* wrong by her.

He was still sitting like that more than an hour later when the door opened again and Quill's voice reached him. "Saychelle and Iri just arrived, they're in..." he trailed off, a frown in his silence. "Thorne?"

"I'm coming." Cursing, he reached back for the edge of the table, stiff and shaky from sitting so long on the floor; his calves loosed a throbbing pang sharp enough that he buckled.

Quill was beside him in a flash, one hand on his back, the other on his chest. "You're all right, you're all right. Steady, *Allet.*"

Gripping his friend's shoulder, Thorne scowled. "Just stiff."

"Right." There was nothing convinced in his tone. "You know we're all here if there's anything you need?"

Turn back time, then. Make it so Cistine never met us. Give me the courage to kill Salvotor and face the second death before it came to this. "I know."

"All right, good." Quill shook him lightly, then let go.

Thorne straightened, breathed deep, and brought his armor back around himself. "Where are they?"

"Ari's room. Tati's hunting her down."

Thorne beckoned him with nod out into the corridor where the cabal's rooms all lined up—his at one end, Aden's at the other. Ariadne had already arrived at her closed door, the murmur of a dozen Vassoran voices wafting from beyond it; but she didn't enter, just hovered, then turned anxious eyes on them when they approached.

Quill shoved a cinnamon stick between his lips, halting beside her. "I know it's been ten years and everything's changed, but she's still your sister. If Pip and I were separated like that, no matter for how long, I'd want to see her. She'd want to see me, too."

Ariadne nodded, eyes glinting. As one, they entered the plain, pale room, blue ghostlight washing from the tabletop and mantle, painting stripes over the *visnpresta* Saychelle, her mentor Iri, and the Vassoran guard securing the room. Thorne's stomach clenched at the sight of them the same way it did when he laid eyes on Saychelle in Keltei Temple, the first time in ten years looking at the woman he used to love.

She deserved better. Through this trial where she would testify as witness to her sister's suffering, he hoped to offer her a shred of that.

Everything fell silent when Ariadne whispered her sister's name. Saychelle whirled to face her, and all at once no one else mattered. There were just two sisters, one clad in robes and one in armor, one silver-haired and one black as night, meeting halfway through the room to grip each other's arms.

"You've grown," Ariadne remarked, looking her over.

Saychelle's lips twitched. "I would hope so, after all this time."

"I didn't mean your height." She swallowed audibly. "Thank you for risking everything you've built of yourself to bring Salvotor to his knees."

"I'm not doing anything for that *bandayo*. This is for you, Ari. All of it, my place in the Order, this testimony I'm giving, everything...it's always been for you."

The last word was barely out of her mouth when Ariadne pulled her into a crushing hug, and Saychelle flung her arms around her neck, burying her face in her sister's shoulder. Quill grinned, and Iri's eyes brimmed with tears; but though Thorne wanted to be happy for them, reunited at long last, dread settled in his bones instead.

After tonight, there was no stopping the barreling forward of the trial. These sisters would face Salvotor in the courtroom, and there was little telling what Nimmus he prepared for them in his confinement, with nothing to do but scheme and plot against the Courts. Against Thorne's cabal.

He hadn't protected either of them when Salvotor attacked them a decade ago. And he wasn't certain he could protect them now.

CHAPTER FIVE

FROM THE ROOFTOPS above Astoria, Ashe passed Solene Novacek and her Warden detail, moving swift as a shadow.

Every year, the Queen started her Darlaska shopping in the West Market, broad and glamorous with an agate fountain spanning its middle. Four streets and six alleys branched from the edges, and Ashe lunged across the narrowest one, scrambling up a shop's sloped roof and draping herself against the spired pinnacle. She spotted Maleck easily below, though his attire was nothing like he usually wore: snug trousers, polished shoes, and a dark vest fitted to his chest and sides, stark white sleeves clashing with the red cravat and trickster's tophat slanting on his unbraided hair. His posture completed a look of casual innocence, elbow propped on the side of a flower cart at the second street's mouth. It had taken some threatening looks and finesse to secure the trappings, and more than that to convince Maleck it was all necessary.

Now he stared her down, finding her as easily on the rooftops as she found him in the crowd. She flashed a grin and patted her cheeks, mouthing, *It suits you.*

Free me from this, his gaze pleaded.

She propped her shoulder to the spire, shrugging, and he tugged his cravat and fixed her with a glare. Fluttering her lashes, she pulled her gaze away from that painfully well-fitting suit to the mouth of the street where the entourage of Wardens slipped into the crowd.

This time, she signaled outright. *Here they come.*

With a swift nod, Maleck was on the hunt. Ashe crouched, arm looped around the spire, and watched the scene unfold below.

The Queen entered the market like a gust of summer air, warming the chilly vendors and customers with her ready smile and calling men and women from the crowd to shop and speak with her. Ashe couldn't help a small, sad smile. Though only seven years separated them, she'd longed to see Solene as a mother when hers was always disappointed at best, ashamed of her at worst. Solene, on the other hand, had called Ashe God-sent and gifted when her violin's sweet song lulled a fussy newborn Cistine, or when she took the princess to play while Solene fulfilled her queenly duties.

But after today, she might just be the latest in a long string of people to look at Asheila Kovar with betrayal in their eyes.

A timely cloud rolled across the sun, caressing Ashe's face with shadows. On the corner of her vision at the market's edge, a woman peeled away from a stall side and glided after the Queen with casual grace. Six paces away, she knocked down her hood, bearing her feathery red hair and angular features to the weak daylight.

The Wardens were on her like wildfire. Two gripped her arms, yanking her away from Solene; a third grabbed her chin and backed her to the fountain, looking into her bright brown eyes. Then they bundled her away in a flurry, no doubt demanding where she came by a Cadre uniform and what she wanted with the Queen.

Ashe held Maleck's gaze across the market, her despair reflected in his eyes. Rion's word had already reached the Wardens, then; anyone who looked like Asheila Kovar, redheaded and in Cadre attire, was not allowed near Solene.

Tears stung the tip of her nose. She cursed and scrubbed them away, and Maleck's face softened, his jaw unknotting. Then he straightened, smoothed his clothes, and chose a soft pink rose from the cart as the Queen and her escort drew near. When a gap broke in the crowd, he stepped forward, half-angled in the Queen's path, and offered the rose with a bow, one arm tucked behind his back. "A gift from your *selvenar*."

Solene stiffened at the word, taking the rose gingerly, sunlight whispering on the note wrapped around its stem. By the time her entourage moved on, she was already reading it, and Ashe was already moving. She'd wasted too much time distracted by the Wardens' reaction; now she lunged recklessly from rooftop to rooftop, flipping over the ledge into the third alley and landing on the cobblestones with buckled knees, bouncing upright to face the narrow mouth just as the Queen slipped inside.

"Asheila." A thin stripe of danger edged her gentle voice. "This cloak-and-dagger isn't like you. Something must be very wrong if you're following me from the rooftops and sending a lookalike to test my guard."

A sheepish smile wrung across Ashe's lips. "How much do you know?"

"I know orders came from the northern forts two days ago, which my Wardens burned before they increased the watch at my doors and windows. And from their reaction to that woman in the market just now, I suspect those orders had something to do with you."

Shadows shivered along the cold alley walls, and Maleck alighted on the rooftop, keeping watch for Solene's guards. His presence was a surprising beacon of strength for the next words that came from Ashe's mouth. "Rion sent those orders. He stripped me of my title...he doesn't want us speaking."

"He's back from the North?" Solene pulled nearer, jaw feathering. "Then where is my daughter?"

"Still in Valgard." Ashe flashed her palms for peace. "The rumors you've heard are true. Cistine, Julian, and I went to treat with them for an alliance to thwart King Jad."

"How did Cistine know about the threat from Mahasar?"

"That was my fault. But sooner or later she would've learned. It seems like everyone has by now, what with the King being in Middleton. Even Darlaska can't quiet the whispers."

Solene didn't deny it, but her face remained stern. "And whose idea was it to travel north?"

"Cistine's. I went along to keep her safe."

"*Is* she safe?"

"She is." And Ashe truly believed it now, though it was an understanding hard-won through her own mistakes, face-to-face with her specters. "She sent me to ensure you hear that...and to bring you this."

She drew Cistine's note from her pocket, written in the same cipher that drew Solene into this alley. She flicked it out and the Queen caught it, unfolded the creases, and read silently. When she looked up again, her eyes narrowed. "What is Rion going to tell me differently from this?"

"That Cistine's being held against her will, most likely. That you need to send every available Warden who's not in Middleton to retrieve her."

"And you don't believe I should?"

Ashe shook her head. "Cistine is there because she wants to be, and we both know dragging her home would betray her trust."

Solene folded the cipher down to its smallest square, her gaze fixed over her shoulder toward the market. "I knew we couldn't keep her away from Valgard forever, no matter how much Cyril hoped. She's always had that longing, just like him."

"Because they're both Keys?"

Solene swung around to face her, wide-eyed. "Does she know?"

Ashe nodded. "Why didn't you ever tell me? How could you expect me to really protect her if I didn't know the truth about what I was protecting her from?"

"Because we were afraid. We hoped if we controlled every whisper about Valgard, Cistine would never wonder about it. Then we tried to extend our bloodline so that if Valgard ever learned the truth, there would be so many Novacek children they would only have to spill a few drops of blood each to open the Doors. But that...well, you know." Solene laid a hand to her plump middle. "So I tried to prepare her to defend herself with the bow. Cyril coddled her so she would never want to leave. But I still feared this time would come."

"Maybe it's not something to be afraid of. It might be just what we need." The words hung strange on Ashe's lips, but she forced herself to keep speaking. "Cistine's spent months building trust with the Valgardans, and with the Writ of Nobility from Rion, she's on the brink of securing a real alliance. She sent me to convince Jad it's already in place."

"To discourage the threat of war," Solene breathed.

Ashe stepped toward her. "If we let this play out, I know she'll come through for us. We just have to trust her."

Though the depth of the Queen's breaths suggested she fought not to cry, her voice was steady when she said, "Cistine is a brave and powerful girl. More powerful than she knows. You may be right...just like her father, she might turn the tide for us all." Quietly, she added, "Though gods only know how she's managed to negotiate thus far, she never had much time for politics."

"She's had a good teacher in Valgard." Ashe cast a glance at the rooftops. "Several good teachers, actually."

Solene squared her shoulders. "When I take Rion's report, I'll bear this in mind. I'll bear in mind, too, that Cyril sent him away for a reason seven years ago. The Bartos family does not always have sound thinking in matters pertaining to Valgard."

Ashe's chest clenched. "Then you're letting her stay?"

"She's of age. It isn't my choice." Solene's crisp tone clashed with the dampness in her eyes. "I love my husband and daughter. I'd rather see us allied to Valgard than at odds, with their lives at stake. I only have one condition: you get to Middleton as quickly as you can. These peace talks with Mahasar are not progressing well so far. And I fear..." The mask of the calm ruler fell away, revealing the anxious wife beneath. "I fear for Cyril facing that madman again. Jad's promise of retribution was especially against him. If Cistine's plan succeeds, she may save more than our kingdom. She may save her father."

Ashe swallowed a swell of fear. "I'll leave straight from here. Thank you for hearing my report—and for believing in Cistine. She needs our support to make this treaty possible."

The Queen's eyes shone with tears. "I know you're right. But to give it is to lose my daughter's heart to the North."

Ashe had no answer for that; in some ways, she already had.

The moment Ashe rounded the alley corner, Maleck descended beside her, stripping off his cravat. "I see where Cistine inherited her bearing. And her fire."

"You should've heard them arguing during archery lessons." With some base level of disappointment, she watched him shed the vest, unbutton his shirt cuffs, and roll the sleeves to his elbows. "Ready to leave?"

His eyes flashed to her, strangely soft. "Would you believe me if I said I would be just as content to stay here for a hundred winter nights?"

Ashe kicked his haunch. "Hopeless flirt."

"Quill claims I don't know the meaning of the word."

"Because you've never flirted with *him*."

While Maleck chuckled and strode ahead, Ashe hesitated, looking back—a twist of worry in her chest.

Even hearing her title was stripped, Solene had offered no guarantee of a place for her when this was done. Whether or not they succeeded in Middleton, Ashe had no promises of a future with the royal family.

But even so, she had to go.

CHAPTER SIX

Tatiana Dawnstar breathed in the sweet smell of freshly-laundered linens, skin prickling deliciously where a powerful arm circled her waist and a three-fingered hand rested on her hip. Distantly, a fire crackled in the hearth, and husky snores stirred the ringlets at the nape of her neck. But whatever Quill was dreaming about, his body wrapped around hers in the sheets of *their* bed, in *their* apartment, it couldn't possibly be better than what she was waking up to—what she'd dreamed of having and never let herself hold until it was almost too late. She tucked herself more firmly into his curves, squeezing her eyes shut against the memory of fever-bright mornings, icy plunges, and mountain heights.

Faer's low, sleepy bleat from the armoire was the only warning that peace as they knew it was over.

The door banged open and a gangly body hurtled into the mattress, slamming into their knees and driving them both up into the nest of pillows, waking Quill with a shout. Curled against their entangled legs, his sister beamed, wild brown eyes dancing under a mess of dark hair. "Good morning!"

"*Pippet*, stars, how many times have we told you not to jump on us when we're sleeping?" Tatiana ground her palms into her eyes.

"I know, I know, but Tati, get up! *It's snowing!*"

"What?" Quill pinched the bridge of his nose, eyes screwing shut. "You woke us up for that?"

"*It's snowing, Quill.*" Pippet stretched the words into nearly-unintelligible syllables. "Already! I can't believe it!"

He flopped back into the pillows. "*I* can't believe I used to take sleep for granted."

Pippet shook him by his bare shoulders. "Can we go sledding? Can we build snow people? Can we have a *snowball fight?*"

"Can we wake up first?" Tatiana yawned.

"Fine, if you *hurry!*"

Faer took wing from the armoire and landed on Pippet's head, an effective distraction while Tatiana scooted backward and ran her knuckles along Quill's cheekbone. "Rise and shine, Featherbrain."

"I'd rather stay here with you." Eyes popping open again, he hooked one arm around her waist and sat himself up with the other in one fluid motion, towing her back to rest against his chest. "I'm getting used to letting other people stand watch while we get some well-deserved rest."

Tatiana snuggled under his chin, watching Pippet and Faer chase each other around the room. "We only have ten years to catch up on."

"More than ten years to make up with *you*, Saddlebags."

Shivering at the morning rasp of his voice, she craned her head back and kissed the stubbled line of his jaw.

Pippet dodged Faer with a deft swivel and a laugh, flinging the thick blue drapes wide and letting in the unmistakable brilliance of a snow-heavy day. "Even in the mountains, it doesn't usually snow this early! Can we go out and play *now?*"

Quill sighed. "Not today."

"Why not?"

Tatiana braced her hands on his thighs and sat up, flashing Pippet a half-hearted smile. "That trial everyone's been talking about starts this morning."

Pippet deflated with a huff. "I forgot." She chewed her lip a moment, then brightened. "Can I go into the city, then? There's some girls from my class who invited me to go shopping!"

Tatiana's *yes* blended into Quill's *no*, and Pippet cocked her head.

"If you take Faer," Quill amended, and Pippet whistled for him, darting out into the hall.

"What was that all about?" Tatiana asked.

"She just started at that school the day before yesterday." Quill's anxious eyes followed his sister out. "Isn't it a little soon for her to have friends?"

"Just because she's barely had a chance to make them before doesn't mean she can't."

"I know, but what if they don't really care about her?"

"What if this is about us, you mean?" Tatiana twisted to search his face. "Don't you think she's lived in our shadow long enough?"

He groaned, dropping his forehead to her shoulder. "You're right. I'm just not used to this being our life now."

"It's not all bad." She inclined toward him, then paused where their breaths mingled. "Take this, for example. We still don't have to be in that courtroom for another hour."

"Plenty of time." The last word was lost as his mouth covered hers.

They convened in the same courtroom as Thorne's swearing-in, but everything felt different today; not only the tension in the air among the elites and Kanslar's Tribunes gathered at the fence, but the placement of the seats on the dais beyond it—one for each High Tribune.

"A Chancellor's trial is unusual, so every Court has a say," Thorne was explaining to Cistine when Quill and Tatiana pushed through the crowd to join them, disheveled and slightly late; Aden shot them a dry, knowing look. "Bravis chose Tribune Eskil to do the questioning. If he's still anything like he was in school, we're in good hands."

Cistine shoved her hair behind her ears. "But this all seems so pointless! We know he's guilty...in Talheim, he'd already be hung."

"This isn't Talheim," Aden said. "Salvotor has his right to a fair trial the same as any Valgardan. If we overlook that, we're no better than him."

"I know, it's just...*him*."

"It's the harder way," Thorne agreed. "But it secures my place on the Judgement Seat and ensures his lies and schemes die with him when the sentence comes down. I'm asking you to have faith in my kingdom the way you've had it in me."

She eked out a smile, and Thorne returned it, parting to join the other Chancellors beyond the fence. Tatiana leaned on the sleek railing, surveying the milling elites and Tribunes.

He and Aden were only half-right. No one in the Courts was impartial when it came to Salvotor; the trial was an excuse to pass judgement on a thousand wrongs, not just one, and that *bandayo* had to know it. Which meant he was plotting something truly sinister to escape a decade of imprisonment or worse for what he did to Ariadne.

This wasn't a trial, it was a battle.

Cistine stiffened suddenly, paling so fast Tatiana's stomach turned. Lips parting around a shaky breath, the Princess swung toward the door.

Salvotor arrived silently, sending forth a billowing malignance from between his Vassoran escort, suffocating all talk before him. The sunlight caught the glittering ripple of reinforcements under his skin while he searched the crowd, hungry gaze landing on Cistine. His shackled hands lifted, fingers wiggling in a mocking wave. Quill cursed under his breath as the Vassora marched Salvotor forward, the people parting to let him pass, giving him everything he wanted: the trappings of a king for a man in chains.

Thorne crossed paths with his father at the fence, and the look between them raised every hair on Tatiana's body; then he took his place among the cabal while the guards threaded Salvotor's chains into a ring on the pure iron table moored to the floor.

"Where is the defendant's representation?" Bravis asked of no one in particular.

"I will represent my own case." Tatiana wanted to claw Salvotor's face off the second he opened his mouth. She'd forgotten in just a few days how much she hated that voice.

"Of course you will. Let it be noted by all in attendance that the accused has chosen to represent himself." Bravis sat in the Chancellor's Judgement Seat, the High Tribunes settling around him. "Chancellor Salvotor stands accused of defiling a *visnpresta* acolyte, the penalty for which is disqualification from the Judgement Seat and a decade's imprisonment. How do you plead?"

"Not guilty, naturally."

"Do you wish to face your accuser?"

"I do."

Ariadne's shoulders peeled back, her tight, sleek braid swinging as she strode to the seat below the dais, facing Salvotor. If trials could be decided on looks alone, they would need no more proof than the heat of her glare; but Salvotor met it without flinching. "If I may, Chancellor Bravis, I would like to voice a concern."

Bravis's lips formed silent words that looked like, *Must you?* But all he said aloud was, "Yes?"

"The matter of my alleged crimes is a delicate one, purely Valgardan. I question the Court's decision to allow the Talheimic emissary to preside over it and would request her immediate removal from the courtroom."

The focus shifted like a storm's cold wind away from Salvotor and onto Cistine, riddling the air with uncertain murmurs. No one made to accommodate Salvotor's demand, but the balance of power in the courtroom danced along a knife's tip.

Cistine gripped the railing in shaky fists, her eyes trained on Bravis. "I understand Chancellor Salvotor's reservations, but seeing how he held me captive for two months, Talheim has a vested interest in whether he faces imprisonment or walks free. Unless Valgard's Courts would prefer to deal directly with King Cyril on the matter of my imprisonment."

This time, the murmuring had nothing to do with her and everything to do with her father's reputation. Even Bravis grimaced. "Given the circumstances, I see the merit of allowing Talheim's emissary to attend. Eskil, the trial is yours."

Rugged and unkempt, bright red hair curling over his muscular shoulders, Tribune Eskil seemed better-suited to carrying out the executions of the convicted than trying them for their crimes; but his buttery voice was as made for these quiet halls as Quill's was for storytelling. "High Tribunes, by the testimony of the accuser and the witnesses, as required by law, it is clear beyond a doubt that Chancellor Salvotor premeditated the crime for which he stands trial. He lured a *visnpresta* acolyte into his own dwelling, defiled her, disqualified her permanently from the position to which she long aspired, then drove her from the city and buried all accusation made against him. Every step was a calculated attempt to subvert the very laws which he swore to uphold as Chancellor. This crime and the misappropriation of evidence outright disqualify him from his title. To that end, we seek full recourse if the accused is found guilty."

"Noted," Bravis said. "Salvotor, how do you counter?"

He stood, chains clinking loudly. "Esteemed High Tribunes, it is with great humility that I stand before you today. Tribune Eskil's statements were meticulous, and I applaud him for that. Unfortunately, the picture he's painted of this trial is quite different from the truth.

"You will hear a tale in this courtroom of a woman and a villain, but what took place was truly between a man and an ambitious, clever girl whose aspirations reached far beyond her humble origins. She was of accountable age on the night in question which has now cost me a life's hard-won reputation and my title...and it differs wildly from the story told ever since. For all my mistakes, I am not guilty of the heinous act for which I was stripped of my livelihood, as the evidence and testimonies will prove. All I ask is that the Tribunal afford me the same unbiased trial as any person, even one without the history of service and sacrifice I have made for Valgard." He dipped his head. "As one mitigator of justice to many, I thank you for your *impartial* adherence to the law in this matter, the same law I've always upheld—and that will verify my guiltlessness in the face of these threadbare accusations."

He returned to his seat, and Bravis rose. "The High Tribunes will reflect on these opening remarks. Today we adjourn, awaiting witness and victim testimonies."

"That's all?" Cistine hissed while the crowd broke apart.

"Litigation is a long process," Aden said.

"It's not just *long*, it...how can Salvotor just *lie* like that?"

"Opening remarks are irrefutable," Thorne explained. "It's the nature of a trial. Don't worry. He hasn't convinced anyone."

Tatiana hoped that was true. But when she watched the Kanslar Tribunes stalk out, Salvotor's gaze trailing them hawkishly, she wondered if conviction mattered half as much as intimidation...and just how far the former Chancellor would go toward achieving one if he knew he'd never have the other.

CHAPTER SEVEN

MIDDLETON LAY ON the far side of the Calalun Peaks, an arduous ride slowed by torrential rain. Ashe spent most of the treacherous ascent laid out against her horse's neck, weaving with its movements so they didn't slide back down the incline. At least her Valgardan armor kept her dry, face shielded by the scarf Maleck gave her when she left Hellidom.

Her mount lurched at last onto the edge of a flat game trail weaving along the mountain face, and she twisted in the saddle to find Maleck climbing below, his own mount laboring under his greater weight. She smirked. "I think you might move quicker if *you* carried the horse!"

He craned his head back to shoot her a baleful look. "We are not all graceful as assassins and light as blades."

She braced her arm on the saddlehorn. "I think you missed your calling as a poet."

"And you as horsewoman." His face twisted as his mount's hooves splayed, seeking purchase on the slick ground. Ashe's stomach lurched so hard it tore her out of the saddle, boots stomping the rocky path.

"I could've been a horsewoman, actually," she called while Maleck navigated his mount toward surer footing, "if my father's father hadn't left the northern lands for a life in Astoria. I might've grown up riding barebacked on the plains instead of...well, you know."

"Riding to war as a girl?"

It was almost dizzying to think of; she would've been a child of the open horizon and the wind, knowing the royal family only by rumor and respect, the war something that happened to other people—and she would've never known Maleck. He might have perished at Rion's hand, crippling Thorne's cabal long before it even began, only because a redheaded girl would never scream at him that she was unafraid.

The smallest flame of pride and purpose flared in her chest, then sputtered when Maleck's horse lurched nearly even with her and skittered sideways on the slippery rock. She lunged, gripping a tall pine in one hand and snagging its bridle with the other. "*Get off the horse.*"

He leaped down without pause, and for a heart-stopping moment, backslid on the exposed rock. The panicked shout of his name jammed into the backs of Ashe's teeth; then he slammed his hand down, bare fingers ripping against the stone, and with one mighty leap he was in front of her, his hand on the reins as well. He was so close, his heat sliced through the rain drumming on Ashe's numb skin. Teeth gritted, she blinked water from her lashes and gazed up at him—one of the few men she had to crane her head to look at. He stared right back, motionless except for the laboring of his chest pushing against hers, crowding into her senses like every other part of him. For a dizzying instant, her world was cedar and charcoal and steel, finding green flecks in his hazel eyes like secret notes in a symphony.

The horse surged suddenly, dragging Ashe up the incline back to her own mount. Maleck was right behind them, taking the beast's cheek strap and soothing it with quiet murmurs.

"Walk the horses?" Ashe panted.

He peered back down the steep incline, paling. "Yes. I think that would be best."

The rain eased with the silent hours that followed, the clouds scudding on above the empty game trail, and in the dim salmon glow of sunset they rounded a bend in the path and finally emerged on a rocky outcropping beside a waterfall. The stone ledge dropped into a timbered valley between slopes, the river from the falls snaking to a distant lake with a city sprawled along its shore.

"Middleton." Ashe halted, squinting at the distant pike wall and sprinkling of ghostlights within. "It should only be another day or so."

"Then we camp here tonight," Maleck decided. "It's dangerous to navigate these slopes in the dark."

They untacked the horses and tied them off near the falls where the grazing was best. Ashe built a fire with what dry wood she could salvage while Maleck vanished into the trees to hunt. It was quiet, domestic, contrasting sharply with the unease boiling in Ashe's core.

Cyril and Jad both awaited in Middleton, and tonight she didn't know which she was more reluctant to face. Jad was an enemy, but Cyril held the power to rip away what remained of her identity. He might not even accept her help when she marched into Middleton with the same Valgardan who crept into their war camp all those years ago to kill him.

Cursing, she broke a branch over her knee and added it to the pile. She should've brought someone else. Aden. Tatiana. Quill, even. Anyone who hadn't personally tried to assassinate the Prince, now the King.

Sitting back from the kindling, Ashe chafed at the necklace she'd grown almost too used to wearing in the last few weeks: the starstone gifted from a Valgardan stranger who died claiming the gods intended it for her, that it served some greater purpose. Though she gave up hoping there was anything like that for her the second Rion stripped her title, she couldn't bear to throw the stone away. It would just be one more betrayal, and she'd done enough damage.

Besides, touching it was somehow a comfort.

Maleck returned at last, slinging four mountain hares down by the kindling heap and crouching next to Ashe. "I'll help you skin these."

There was blood on his hands, too much to come from a hare. Ashe lurched forward, frowning. "What did you do to yourself?"

He glanced down at his hands, then blinked. "I suppose I skinned them when I dismounted from the horse."

Muttering under her breath, Ashe retrieved bandages and the waterskin from her pack. To Maleck's pointed look, she said, "I'll refill it in the river.

Now give me your hands."

He turned his palms up, knuckles resting on her knees. She rinsed the wounds three times and took stock of the damage, a good deal of skin shorn clean off by the stone. At the simple brush of water, the lacerations opened up again, blood curling down his wrists. "How have you *not* been complaining all this time?"

Maleck watched unblinking while she cleaned the wounds a fourth time, then pried gravel from the scrapes with her fingernails. "I don't always feel pain. Or notice things that matter."

He'd told her and Cistine something like that in the mountain camp of Villmark, but she hadn't imagined it would distract him from wounds like these. "What made you like this?"

His fingers flexed slightly. "Augments."

While she bandaged his wounds, he told her more about what his brothers did to him—of power not wielded like a weapon but ingested like strong herbs, and how it changed people from the inside out. Memory sparked while he talked, an ember quickly fanned into flame. Ashe lifted her hand from his and settled it carefully over his heart instead. "That scar I saw the night Thorne found us in the meadow, that wasn't from any flagon you wielded in battle."

His hand slid over hers, holding it to the ridges of scarring palpable even through the reinforced threads—and to the wild beating of his heart beneath. "Perceptive as always, Asheila."

Warm breath wafted against her face, playing havoc with her pulse until it matched the unsteady cadence of his. "Show me."

When she dropped her hand, he undid the ties and clasps of his armor, stripping the collar and buttons open until the cratered mark showed through, branching from his heart almost to his shoulders and disappearing toward his navel. Ashe spread her fingers against it and forced herself not to recoil. The first time she saw this scar, it was all the reason she needed to hate him; she'd looked at his wounds and seen an enemy, not the scars from being forced into a war he never wanted.

The war she chose for herself was chosen for him.

"I'm sorry for what they did to you. What we all did to you."

Maleck's fingers slid under her chin, raising her head until their eyes met. "You didn't do this. You set me free from this."

"But I hated you for it. I would've killed you that day in the meadow if Thorne and Cistine—"

"But you wouldn't kill me now. The only way I have survived these past twenty years is to live now, not then." He released her chin and moved to button his shirt, but Ashe stopped him, both hands on his wrists and her gaze on his. Then she bent toward his unmoving, unbreathing chest, until every beat of his pulse brushed against the tip of her nose.

She pressed her lips to his scar, over his heart.

Maleck's breath tumbled out in a rush. He caught her face in his hands, tilted it up, and slanted his head, pausing in a silent question for permission she gave with a swipe of her tongue along her lips.

Then he kissed her.

His mouth tasted of wild waters and pine, like he'd stopped to drink while he hunted, and his touch was both fierce and awestruck. When a soft growl of delight echoed from his throat, Ashe broke before him, curling forward on her knees, hands burrowing into his shoulders and climbing the sides of his neck, then scraping down, fingertips rippling over his collarbones, across his scar.

His body tightened, fighting a wince. And even with her mouth tangled in his, even with the taste of his lips spinning her head like a blow to the skull, clarity stole every breath she hadn't given to him.

He stopped when she did and didn't fight when she withdrew. Panting, they stared at one another, firelight guttering across their faces, and she saw her own miserable face reflected in his eyes.

She was no princess with treaties and purpose, no fighter clawing back from shadowy depths for those she loved, not even a Warden with title and rank to speak of. She was still in that pit others ascended from, and if she held any tighter to him, she'd drag him down into the depths with her— the traitor who sentenced old women to painful deaths and led hateful warriors onto Valgard's soil without thinking twice, ushering one of

Maleck's own specters back into his path.

She couldn't do this. Couldn't be this with him.

She pushed herself to her feet. "I'm going to check the horses. Start skinning the hares if you want."

Rasping the starstone against its chain, she slipped from the firelight to their mounts, lifting their legs, checking their hooves for rocks, feeling their muscles for heat and tenderness—and silently begging her wits to come back and her racing heart to forget the taste of Maleck's lips.

There was no point in wanting this. It wasn't fair to him.

Cursing, she braced her arm around her mount's neck and squinted along the neighboring peaks, giving her eyes somewhere to look other than back toward their small camp, wondering if he was watching her, too.

That was when she spotted the vague, distant smolder haloing a ledge halfway across the valley.

Suddenly, it snuffed out.

Ashe's scalp prickled and she snaked her arm from around her horse's neck, gaze skipping east.

A second fire flared—then died.

She bolted back to their camp, skidding on the wet grass. "Mal."

"I saw it." He'd shifted position, blocking their fire with his body. "Should we change course and investigate?"

Ashe looked to the east scoop of the valley, then west again. No other fires kindled. Slowly, her racing pulse steadied and sense broke through. "At best, it's hunting parties taking different halves of the valley. At worst, Jad has spies camping here. In either case, we still need to reach Middleton."

Maleck nodded. "Then we keep the course."

There was no sleep for Ashe that night, watching the valley for another spark that never came. And through the restless hours of the dark, waiting until it was bright enough to sanely risk the clefts on horseback again, all she tasted was water and pine.

CHAPTER EIGHT

CISTINE HOVERED IN her closet doorway, gazing at the racks of sparkling dresses inside. She ought to choose something modest and commanding for today's meeting, like the burgundy gown she wore in Veran the last time she treated with the Chancellors; but she couldn't tear her eyes away from the assortment of plunging necklines, tight waists, and sheer skirts. Her skin prickled with the chill of stone walls and her ears echoed cruel rankings in tune with her clamoring pulse.

She jumped at the sound of Thorne's voice through the bedroom door. "It's time, Cistine. Are you ready?"

"Come...come in!" Her voice cracked.

The handle jiggled. "It's locked."

She smoothed her sweat-soaked palms on her thighs and hurried to the door, flinging it wide to greet five armored warriors smiling in the hall. "What are you all doing here? Shouldn't you be patrolling or training?"

"As if!" Tatiana snorted. "Today is important for us too, you know."

Quill brushed through the doorway and dumped himself on the foot of the bed. "All those *tortuous* mornings waiting for you to catch up on our runs, pushing you through your exercises, listening to you complain..."

Cistine's ears went hot. "Thank you for that."

"All worth it," he concluded with a crooked grin, "to see you treat with the Chancellors."

One by one, the others came inside, Ariadne pausing to search Cistine's face. "Are you ready?"

"I have to be."

Aden propped himself against the wall, arms folded. "The trick is to remember that underneath their robes, they're no better than Viperwolves. If nothing else, appeal to their base nature rather than their political one."

Her stomach ground with nausea at the thought of how low she might have to stoop to reach that nature. "I...I need a few more minutes."

Thorne's brow creased, eyes flicking to the open closet. "Take all the time you need."

She dashed inside, slammed the door, and chose a gown by touch alone, changing in the dark and jerking down the long sleeves to disguise her battle armor beneath. Then she ducked out, shut the door, and leaned against it— stiffening when sunlight edged the light-purple skirt and high, frilled collar.

"Well, that thing is hideous," Tatiana remarked, "but that's good, I suppose. Give them a reason to value your words over your appearance."

"Tactful as ever," Ariadne deadpanned. "She looks perfectly fine."

"How would you know? You only wear one color: black. You're as hopeless as Thorne!"

His mouth twitched up and he motioned with a tilt of his head for Cistine to follow him into the hall. "Remember, you already have Kanslar's full support. That will stand in your favor."

"Of course." She hated the brush of skirts against her legs while they walked; she hated that *this* was how she had to present herself.

"And it isn't all of Talheim you must make them believe in," Thorne added. "Only you. And you are enough, Cistine. A princess worth fighting beside."

For once, she wanted to take his hand, but she wasn't certain her fingers would cooperate. He seemed miles away, not mere inches, when they crossed the courtyard and mounted the broad steps into the courthouse market. The moment they passed through the doorway, that sick, uneasy feeling returned, a sense of impending calamity bearing down on the bright-lit chamber. She almost stumbled over her skirts when the floor pulsed against her flats, rising and sinking like drowsing breaths.

COME, it growled. *COME AND SEE.*

Thorne's hand brushed the small of her back under the guise of herding her toward the mezzanine, but his face was grim, jaw ticking with concern.

She couldn't let herself be a distraction today. This was too important. Lengthening her stride, she led the way through long, bustling halls to the Chancellor's sanctum where she first laid eyes on Salvotor. Its new circular table was already occupied; Chancellors Maltadova and Bravis nodded to Thorne, while Benedikt and Valdemar watched with the same glowering intensity as at his swearing-in. But when their eyes alighted on Cistine, Thorne became nothing.

She was the commodity. And she felt like it.

She would've cared less if Chancelloress Adeima were present, some feminine strength to prop up her wobbly courage. This felt too much like a meal in Kalt Hasa where her body was the coveted course.

But this was not Grimmaul and his men; these people were not Salvotor. She was not a prisoner and she was not above or beneath them.

Thorne drew out two seats, and Cistine lowered herself into one, tugging the Writ of Nobility from her sleeve and laying it in the center of the table. "Thank you for seeing me today, Chancellors. My name is Princess Cistine Novacek. I'm here as Talheim's official emissary, and this Writ grants me power to treat with you in full station."

It took an eternity for the Chancellors to examine the Writ. She wished Thorne would say something, shatter the silence, make a joke. Her head felt puffy, her upper lip tingling when Bravis finally set the Writ aside. "Traisende will hear the words of the emissary."

"As will Yager," Maltadova said.

"Skyygan is intrigued," Benedikt admitted.

"Tyve has some concerns," Valdemar said.

Cistine bore down on the inside of her cheek, shooting a glance at Thorne. He held fast apart from the curl of his fingers against his thigh.

"Why should we listen to the proposal of a daughter of war?" Valdemar went on. "Talheim only offered us peace after months of bloodshed. Whole towns were burned and hundreds displaced in raids, many of whom died in the tundra. And the peace they *did* offer, with their knives to our throats, was strictly on their terms. Why should we care for this Writ of Nobility? What *nobility* does Talheim claim to have?"

Cistine took quick, shallow breaths to brace against the blow of his words, but that only made her face numb. "I am *not* blind to the wrongs my kingdom committed against Valgard."

"Then you're foolish to even *think* of seeking a long-standing treaty with us."

She almost burst into hysterical laughter. How had she ever believed a trunk full of books and baubles would convince these men to stand with her? The resentment in Valdemar's eyes was undimmed for twenty years; the war might as well have happened yesterday.

And how could she blame him? She hadn't known about all the burned towns and displaced people in the tundra.

But she couldn't go down that path. Talheim needed aid *now*. And it was in her power to claim it—or lose it forever.

"Consider that Talheim could attack Valgard right now because of what one Chancellor did to its princess. But I choose to hold Salvotor *alone* responsible for that, and I hope you'll show me the same courtesy," she said, and Valdemar shifted. "Hear me as a princess who was born after the war...and as the future ruler of Talheim. Either you'll meet with me as the Queen then, or you can meet with me as the Princess now, but I promise you the Princess is *much* more eager to negotiate a treaty. So, will Tyve hear my proposal?"

Valdemar's eyes flitted to his fellow Chancellors, as if years of Salvotor's influence in his Court made him reticent to decide without another opinion. When nobody offered one, he muttered, "I will *hear* it, yes."

A wave of dizziness washed through her at his mutinous tone. No alliance would come easily from him—from any of them. But with Ashe and Maleck likely in Middleton by now, time worked against them. It all rested in her hands.

The room tipped and spun, her pulse raging in her ears. She slowly peeled herself to her feet to address them, but the moment she was upright, nausea corkscrewed in her stomach. Light rippled against her dress, the creases flashing lavender like lightning, the high collar choking her. She gripped the table's edge, knees buckling.

Run.

She wanted to flee from this room where Salvotor once ruled, where his face broke her knuckles and she learned too late the man she was treating with—because Thorne hadn't told her the truth before it was too late, and she came here thinking this would be so simple, but Ashe was gone, and Baba Kallah died, and Julian, and Helga, and Kristoff—

Run.

The Chancellors stared through her dress, through her armor, to the battered, naked prisoner beneath—a Talheimic enemy against Valgard's best interests. They'd already marked her as their foe.

This was impossible. She couldn't do it.

"Chancellors, forgive me, I..." She clapped a hand to her mouth, bile burning against her lips.

Thorne shot to his feet. "*Princess.*"

She flinched away from the sound of his voice, nausea twisting her stomach, that awful feeling cresting within her like the world was going to end and she was trapped in the middle of its dying. "I have to go."

Then she fled.

The sobs came with the pound of her feet down the mezzanine steps to the market and didn't stop all the way through the courtyard and into Kanslar's wing, the world blurring in a violent haze. She stumbled against her door and slammed it open, bringing four figures to their feet all at once.

The cabal had waited for her. She almost turned and ran from them, too, but there was nowhere else to go. The halls weren't safe. Nowhere was.

Bawling with frustration, she kicked the door shut and yanked at her clinging sleeves, staggering toward the closet. "This gods-damned *dress!*"

A heartbeat later, Quill's arm looped around her waist and his knife slit the dress clean from top threads to skirts, the tip barely grazing the dip of her spine. Tatiana dragged the bodice, leaving only her armor behind. Bereft of the fabric's chokehold, Cistine broke down where she stood, and Quill settled her gently on the floor. "Breathe, Stranger, we've got you."

And they did. Ariadne and Tatiana held her hands, Aden's fingers stroked her hair, and Quill's arm was still around her from behind, the other supporting them against the floor. But it didn't help; she shook, she sobbed, and vomit pulsed in the base of her throat.

"I'm sorry," she choked. "I'm so sorry."

"Don't apologize." Aden's voice might as well have been his father's, a haven of comfort in a dark place. "This is nothing to be ashamed of."

But she *was* ashamed. And terrified.

Which bad feeling was which—her memories of Kalt Hasa or the sense of doom hanging above her like a sword on a string? The scream of her nightmares or the scream from the Door always under her feet? And which sensations were real, if any were?

There were treaties to be negotiated, peace to be claimed. She had a kingdom to save, and she was unfit for any of it.

You are not broken, she chanted to her fractured pieces. *You are not broken, you're all right, it's all right.*

But her heart didn't believe her.

CHAPTER NINE

THORNE COULDN'T MOVE from the table, leashed by the quiet among his fellow Chancellors in Cistine's absence. Their faith in her already teetered at the brink, showing its weaker seams. Whoever broke the silence first would decide the future of this tenuous treaty.

Cistine was already gone. She might want him with her now in her panic, or she might not; but she *needed* him to stay.

"She'll be all right." His voice brought their attention back to him, a lesson he learned well in Kalt Hasa: better he bore the brunt of their focus than her. "This is a wound inflicted by my father. We all carry scars like it."

Valdemar scoffed. "A frightened girl hardly inspires confidence."

"You allowed my father to intimidate his way into your Court. You have no place to hold her in contempt," Thorne growled. "She came to Valgard searching for peace, and he showed her the back of his hand. If you expected her to emerge unscathed, if you believe *any* of us would, then *you're* naïve."

Valdemar scoffed, slumping back. Bravis, in contrast, sat taller. "Thorne, you understand the doubt this casts over these talks. You summoned us around notions of united kingdoms, stronger together. What does it serve Valgard to ally with a broken princess?"

"Cistine Novacek is *not* broken. She's had barely any time to recover from what Salvotor did to her. I've seen enough of her strength before and since to still believe Valgard is safer and stronger in alliance with her kingdom than standing alone."

"It's served us so far," Benedikt argued.

"Has it? If not for my cabal, you would be living under Salvotor's reign rather than trying him in a courtroom," Thorne said. "Look around you. All we do is hoard our augments and fight with one another. It's time we had something else to occupy our attention...like an alliance that would benefit our kingdom for years to come."

Valdemar drummed his fingers on the table. "You believe Talheim has some knowledge to our use?"

"I've already learned things I never thought possible before I made peace with their princess."

Thoughtful silence trickled in. The Chancellors all looked at one another, except Maltadova, who studied Thorne with calm, compassionate eyes.

"We'll discuss how to proceed," Benedikt said at last. "But we make no vows."

His tone closed the subject and shut Thorne out of it. He'd already made Kanslar's support of Talheim clear, so he had no part in that discussion—and no place in this room anymore.

Anger pounding in his temples, he stalked from the Sanctum and shut the door. The outer hall was deserted, not a single Vassoran guard in sight; so it was perfectly safe to spin on his heel and punch the wall.

Aden stood guard at Cistine's door when Thorne arrived, eyes falling at once to the bloody whorls across his knuckles when he strode down the hall. "What happened, *Mavbrat*?"

"Politics." Thorne wiped his hands on his pants. "How is she?"

"Resting. The others went to dispose of that dress and find food. She asked me to keep watch."

"I'm not surprised. She sees Kristoff when she looks at you. Even in Kalt Hasa, he made her feel safe. You make her feel safe now." Unlike him, whose likeness to his father only signified danger.

Aden's eyes narrowed slightly. "What happened in the meeting?"

"I don't know. It could have been the stress, the way we were seated at the table, something one of them said..."

"She mentioned the dress."

Lavender. The color of lightning. Guilt kicked Thorne's chest so brutally his heart skipped. "Julian."

Aden measured him with the same piercing stare that always compelled him to reveal his mischief-making and feats of daring, no matter how well-kept. "Don't envy the dead, Thorne. She carries his ring, but you hold her heart. You're still her choice...and I think you always will be."

He wished that felt true—or like it was the right thing for her. "Do you think I should go in?"

"She asked me to ensure you would." Aden clapped him on the shoulder. "I'll see how the others are doing."

Cistine was curled up tightly on the bed when he entered, facing away from him, stirring slightly when the door clicked shut. After a long moment, she whispered, "I ruined the negotiations, didn't I?"

He sat at her dining table, peeling off his boots and rubbing his throbbing calves. "I did what I could. They're deliberating now."

She rolled over to face him, eyes pink from weeping. "Thank you for trying. I'm sorry I ran away."

Thorne walked to the bed, gripping one of the corner posts and leaning around it to search her exhausted face. "Do you want to sleep, or find a distraction?"

She dropped her gaze, fingers floating to the chain around her neck. "I was thinking of training, actually. Would you like to join me?"

He blinked, giving outlet to the punch of surprise in his gut. "I thought—wouldn't you prefer Quill?"

"Not today. He doesn't know...everything. What it was like, what we survived in that place." Her throat heaved in a harsh swallow. "You do. You were always with me."

Throat tight, he offered his hand, stomach lurching when she let him draw her upright. "I'd be honored."

They walked to the training hall in silence, and with every stride Cistine's steps grew firmer, her shoulders straighter. In the dimness of the familiar brown stone walls and amber ghostlight below the courthouse, her gaze crystallized. When they took up their practice swords, her hands no longer shook.

When she attacked, Thorne was lost in her.

They dueled barefoot through the lonely vaults, every clang of steel the echo of the cabal's essence: dreamers and victims forged into warriors and survivors, pouring out their pain through striking fists and slamming blades until the world made sense again. Cistine dominated the steps of this wild dance, relearning old strokes and adopting new ones, a flicker of a smile tugging her lips and coaxing one from Thorne in turn.

At least this helped—this familiarity, this release. He hoped they'd always have it, like rain-slick rocks and mountain heights.

All at once she lunged through his guard, locked their sabers, jabbed her knee between his, and hurled him against one of the pillars. He froze when she pressed in, knuckles digging into his sternum and full weight balanced behind the blade. Her abdomen jerked against his in rapid pants, and her smile burned like the sun. "Pinned you."

He loosened his grip on the sword. "I'm at your mercy, *Logandir*."

Her gaze dropped and her head tilted, the press of her body shifting as she leaned into him. Her eyes fell to half-mast, her breath wafting against his lips, and his heart thundering, wondering if she would dare—

"Your warriors spoke the truth. You do fight all your enemies with the blade, whether they stand before you or within you."

Thorne and Cistine yanked apart as Chancelloress Adeima swept into the room, tall, aristocratic, and fierce as a lioness, her brown skin warm in the tawny ghostlight. Her compassionate gaze settled on Cistine. "Tatiana and Ariadne gave me entrance to find you. Are you well?"

Her jaw shifted. "I don't know how to answer that today."

Adeima nodded. "Yager understands your pain better than most, which is why I told Maltadova I would deliver the Courts' decision about the treaties myself." Her gaze swept between them. "They will meet with you again...on condition."

Tension splintered through Thorne's calves. Cistine's eyes widened. "What *condition?*"

"That you would find a way to face your specters so today's outburst does not repeat." Adeima raised a hand when Cistine opened her mouth. "This is not punishment or proof of anything, it is what the Courts deem necessary for these treaties to proceed. There is not a woman in Yager who begrudges your pain. That you choose to stand before us so soon after what you suffered shows courage beyond measure. I hope you will accept this condition, not for your kingdom's sake, not for ours, but for yours. You deserve to be well."

Cistine sucked in a breath through her nostrils. "I'll try to do something about it."

"Take time to deliberate if this is a requirement you can meet. The Courts await your word." With a dip of her head, Adeima strode for the steps, and Thorne gritted his teeth.

There was another conversation that needed having—one he'd put off too long for fear of his own shortcomings. But after she offered this compassion, this understanding not only to his *selvenar*, but to him, he couldn't let her go.

"Chancelloress." Thorne jogged after her, falling into step when she slowed. "I owe you an apology. I'm sorry I haven't come sooner to make it."

"It's been a difficult few months. What do you wish to apologize for?"

"For not upholding my part of the bargain we made in Veran. I hope my failure to deliver the witness from the Black Coasts doesn't change Yager's choice to stand with Talheim against their southern foes."

Adeima glanced back at Cistine. "We do not judge women on the actions of men. But we do not give our support lightly to anyone, Thorne. We will watch carefully how she faces these trying times."

"That's between you as rulers." Thorne dipped his head. "Just tell me how *I* can restore Yager's faith in my Court."

"There is one thing." Mischief twinkled in Adeima's eyes. "Until now, our solitude in the belief that women ought to sit on the Judgement Seat has kept us from proposing the law that would legalize it. But now that Kanslar has a sensible Chancellor again, we need to sway only one other vote to pass such an amendment."

"You want me to talk to Bravis." Thorne tipped his head. "Why not bring this proposal yourselves?"

"It would seem disingenuous if it came from us, seeing as we will be the first to place women in power."

"Cunning as ever. All right, I'll speak to him when I can."

"We will see." With a fleeting smile, she departed, freeing a snarl in Thorne's chest; that was one wrong mended, at least. And hundreds more to follow.

He wandered back into the hall to find Cistine cross-legged on the floor, practice sword jabbed into the sand and brow pressed to the grip. The weary bend of her shoulders shoved a blade through his heart.

"You don't have to do it if you don't want to," he murmured, leaning his own blade against a pillar. "We can find different terms they'll meet on."

"I need help, Thorne." She stared through the empty doorway where Adeima vanished, lashes lined with tears. "I'm barely sleeping. I'm never hungry. I hate dresses. *Dresses!* And I just have this awful feeling, all the time, like something terrible is coming." She slid her fingers back through her unkempt hair. "I wanted everything I have now so badly, the treaties, this chance..." Her gaze flicked to him, a silent conclusion that sent his stomach into somersaults: *you.* "But I can't enjoy any of it with all this chaos tangled inside me."

He knelt slowly at her side. "Cistine..."

She shivered, then groaned, dropping her saber with a dull *thunk* and dragging her hands back through her hair. "Even your *voice* makes me think of him! And if it's not you, it's Kalt Hasa, and if it's not that, it's..." She broke off so abruptly, it raised the hair on the back of his neck. After a long, tenuous pause, she slowly shook her head. "I can't do this anymore, but I don't know where to start changing things."

Quiet memory nudged deep in Thorne's mind. "May I see your hand?"

Hesitantly, she offered it to him. He brushed her knuckles with his thumb, turned her palm over, then tapped it four times.

"When I was a boy, my family all lived in one apartment." He gritted his teeth against the memory of silver and scarlet doors, forcing himself to focus only on the old calluses on Cistine's knuckles from beating on Quill. "Baba Kallah and I shared rooms next to each other. When Salvotor truly wanted to punish us, he'd separate us...sometimes for days at a time. But we found a way to speak to each other, a pattern of taps on the wall between our rooms. Salvotor never deciphered it, even though it was simple enough for a boy of five to understand."

Her soft laughter brightened the vaults to their uppermost reaches. "Show me?"

He tapped the center of her palm four times. "We asked this question often: *are you all right?*" One tap. "*Yes.*" Two more. "*No.*" Five taps. "*You are not alone here.*" Six taps. "*I am proud of your strength.*" Seven taps. "*All will be well, I promise.*"

"What does three taps mean?"

Heat crept up Thorne's neck. "I love you."

A blush spread across the bridge of her cheeks. "*Oh.*"

"Some nights I would lie awake after he belted me, listening to a pattern of three knocks from her room, over and over, until I fell asleep."

Cistine turned her hand over, fingers hovering at the blue headwaters of veins gathered in his wrist. Then she tapped six times—firm and deliberate. "When I can't talk to you, we'll do what Baba Kallah taught you...taught *us*. We'll find peace together, somehow."

Though he was desperate to press a kiss to her brow and wrap his arms around her, he only tapped her arm once. Then he drew her to her feet. "I think I know where to start...someone who can help. Ariadne, Saychelle, and Aden are counseling with her already for the trial."

Cistine blinked. "No one told me they were doing that."

"It's their choice how much to say." He shrugged. "They tell me this sort of work is harder than training, harder than anything else they've done. But it can help if you step into it with all your heart."

"I will. I have to, for Talheim's sake. And for mine." She drew her bottom lip between her teeth, brow scrunching. "Do I know this person who's helping them?"

Thorne fought not to smirk. "As a matter of fact, you met her here when I brought her to assess Ariadne and Aden."

Cistine stared at him, then broke into laughter. "*Of course.* I should've guessed it was Mira."

CHAPTER
TEN

NERVES BUZZING, TATIANA hurried through a dark and unseasonably-warm winter rain that washed away Pippet's beloved snow. Part of her felt like a traitor, leaving the courthouse after Cistine's nervous fit, the others trading shifts guarding her door and Ariadne's; but she hadn't visited her father since they commandeered his augwain to slam through the courthouse gates, and the letter he sent asking her to visit tonight held a flavor of urgency she couldn't ignore. Not after everything she'd put him through.

Anxious energy sang in her fingertips when she entered the lower-level room of her childhood home, rife with her tinker father's half-finished inventions. His inking device was set out from the rest and looked freshly-used. Breathing in the smell of oil, grease, and metal-workings, she fumbled with her buttons. "Papa, it's me! I got your letter!"

"*Don't* take off that coat!" Morten tripped on his way down the stairs, a cloth-wrapped bundle tucked under one arm, sweat beading on his brown skin. "We're late as it is!"

"Shocking." Tatiana yelped when he hooked his hand under her armpit and spun her back out the door. "Slow down, will you? Where are we going? I thought we were having dinner!"

"We'll be eating there." He hugged her around the shoulders, dulling the edge of his hurry. "I know it's short notice, but I wanted you to meet some friends I've made."

"Friends? Since when do you have time for friends? The shop is your whole life!"

"Well, things have been slow since the summer." Summer—when the cabal's bandit raids along the Vingete Vey came to light, tied back to all of them. Rage and shame bristled up Tatiana's spine, nearly muffling her father's next words. "But with all this free time, I've met other tinkers. We meet and discuss the trade every other week or so. I want you to see everyone!"

She peered up at his eager face, grinning despite the rain. He didn't even sound this thrilled when she and Quill told him they were *valenar*. "Papa, what in *Nimmus* have you gotten yourself into?"

"You'll see!"

He guided her to halt before a patchwork of buildings where prosperity elbowed out poverty. Tan, russet, and blackwood wattle-and-daub homes vaulted from the cobblestones, this one in particular offset by bright burgundy ghostlamps blazing in the windows. Music wafted from within; shaking the rain from his head, Morten opened the door.

The home was broad and deep, two open levels burning under ghostlight and the glow of a broad hearth along the far wall. On every surface, stuffed into corners and balanced preciously on shelves, were creations like nothing Tatiana had seen before: strange timepieces and odd harnesses, skeletal frames outstretched with leather strung from their boning like bird's wings, cog-and-wheel machinations that tooled around the room under the inhabitants' feet. The music resonated from an artfully-crafted cabinet in the upper gallery, plunking on a wide disc slowly turning in the center. The people were as peculiar and magnificent as the inventions, variegated in complexion, gender, and status, the only thing alike about them the sleepless bruises beneath their eyes, their worn hands and singed-off brows, and the excitement in their chatter.

Morten squeezed her against him. "Welcome to *Heimli Nyfadengar*."

The Tribe of New Birth. The Old Valgardan name made Tatiana's spirit soar, stretching her grin wide. "These are all inventors?"

"Every one!" Morten guided her forward, raising his chin in greeting to a few who shouted his name. "I found them, or rather they found me, after I finally managed a sale to an elite. An *elite*, Tati! I replicated the design of a flagon but with acrid powders instead of augments, and this woman gobbled them up. She's Vassoran, you see, and—"

"*Formerly* Vassoran." A short, well-muscled woman stepped into their conversation without invitation, smile knife-sharp. "Some of us are made to give orders, not take them."

Grinning, Morten turned them to face her. "Kadlin, this is Tatiana. Tati, this brilliant woman is the head of Stornhaz's first inventor's guild."

"And hopefully not the last!" Kadlin's handshake was welcoming, though her eyes retained that steely glint. "So, you're the daughter I've heard so much about. Morten tells me you're inclined to inventing and repairing."

"Among other things." Tatiana returned that wolfish grin. "And those things have taken precedence over the past decade."

"Pity! From what I've seen, the arts run deep in your family." Kadlin winked at Morten, and he straightened his spine and smoothed his clothes. "I'll fetch us some drinks while you make yourselves comfortable. Tatiana, any preference?"

"No alcohol for me."

Morten squeezed her shoulder, the smallest touch bursting with pride.

In Kadlin's absence, Tatiana nudged him. "So, *this* is what you've gotten into? Shameless flirting and showing off?"

He swatted her on the rump. "Is it so wrong for a man to seek recognition for his talents?"

"Oh, it was absolutely your *talents* she was recognizing." Tatiana fluttered her lashes, then danced away when Morten swiped at her again. Something knocked into her ankle, and she glanced down at a cog-and-wheel machine thunking into her boot. Grinning, she picked it up and popped its belly hatch, studying the tightly-wound gears inside.

"Excuse me!" a high-pitched voice shouted. "That's *mine!*"

Tatiana arched a brow at the boy no older than six or seven years skidding to a halt beside her. He put out both hands, and she surrendered the device. "And what do you call...this?"

"Its name is Vohrun. It makes deliveries. And it's mine."

Tatiana crouched on his level. "And who are *you*?"

His cheekbones pinked. "Athlis."

"Well, Athlis, I think Vohrun makes a good deliverer. And an excellent ankle-biter." Tatiana ruffled his hair and straightened again.

"Athlis is our youngest member," Morten explained as the boy scampered away. "His mother died this past year of bloodcough. He's given up schooling to make deliveries for some of the shops. Little Vohrun was the only friend he had before he found us. Now Kadlin pays his board."

"It's the least I could do. He's a brilliant boy." Kadlin insinuated herself in the conversation once again, beckoning them to a low table where she poured three cups of clean cider. "So, Tatiana, tell me about yourself."

She shrugged. "What's there to tell? I've lived in the wilds for the past ten years. I'm handier with a blade than any tool these days. I helped my friends depose Chancellor Salvotor." Kadlin's brows rose. "What about you? You're wealthy for a former Vassoran guard."

"Tati," Morten chided.

"It's all right, Mort. It's curiosity that makes tinkers and inventors of us." She flashed Tatiana another sharp smile. "My grandfather helped design the first augwain. I'm sure you can imagine, he didn't lack for mynts. Nor did his daughter, or his granddaughter." She gestured to the length of herself. "He taught me his craft—that was my passion. When I grew bored of beating people's faces in and being told how best to do it, I swept up my inheritance and began *Heimli Nyfadengar*."

"Well, I love what you've done with the mynts."

Kadlin cackled. "So do I! Your father mentioned you've done some designing yourself since you returned to the city."

"*Papa!*" Tatiana groaned.

"What?" he said. "Is it some great secret now?"

"Yes, it is!" She shot a desperate glance at Kadlin's intrigued face. "It's nothing. Just some sketches I made one night, I don't even have them with me—"

Morten picked up his parcel from the floor, uncapped it, and unfurled the contents on the tabletop: Tatiana's first new design in a decade. Humiliation heated her neck. "*Really*, Papa?"

"I thought they were inspired!" he argued.

Kadlin surveyed the clumsy drawings, her fingertips tracing the sketches Tatiana made the night they returned to Stornhaz; merely being in her childhood home had reawakened the craft in her, setting her fingers tracing outlines of dreams while the others slept in her father's loft. "Are these what I think they are?"

Tatiana dragged a hand through her curls. "They will be if I can sort out the structure."

Kadlin's eyes flicked up, all traces of aloofness gone. "The hinge joints, you mean?"

"More like how they'll function in practice. Designing them is one thing. Controlling them..."

"Another matter entirely." Kadlin bit the side of her thumb. "Let me think on this. When the guild convenes next, will you arrive early and dine with me? I'd like to help you if I can."

Her generosity stoked Tatiana's suspicion. "What makes you so interested in helping us?"

Kadlin's stern expression softened. "Not to steal your invention, I assure you. Morten is a good friend, and you a bright mind. I can hear it in your questions, see it in that frown. I think you could have a place with us, and I'd like to help you decide that." She tapped a nail on the drawing. "This is where it starts." Someone hailed her from across the room, and she rose. "Think on it. And if you choose to dine with me, come at sunset a week from today." She flashed a smile just for Morten, then sauntered away.

Tatiana rolled the drawings and stuffed them back into their case, scowling. "You should've warned me this was why you brought me along."

"I knew you would refuse."

"That was my choice to make!"

"Tati. Do you prefer pride or success? Because you can't have both. I'm not clever enough to sort this out with you, I've been poring over these sketches for weeks. But Kadlin..."

The way he spoke her name, the way his voice hitched, coaxed Tatiana's eyes back to him. She found not only joy, but sorrow in his face. "What's wrong?"

Morten's gaze swept the room. "Do you see a future in this, Tatiana?"

She studied the collection of smiling dreamers and creators from so many corners of life, supporting rather than competing; the people who'd helped stitch her father back together after she abandoned him.

Fixing things was in her blood—a tinker father, a medico mother. Was there a future in this for *her*?

She shook the notion away. "I like the concept, and I might come by with you again. But joining it's not for me. I belong with my cabal." Even if there was far less to do now that Thorne had Vassora to order around.

Morten patted her knee, the sadness lingering in his eyes. "That's all right. Whatever you choose to be, I'm proud of you."

She drew her legs up onto the sofa, leaning her head on his shoulder. Together in silence, they watched these people bantering and smiling, full of joy that came from a united purpose.

Deep in her core, an aching emptiness began to fester.

CHAPTER ELEVEN

Ashe and Maleck rode into Middleton tired, saddle-sore, and without one word exchanged between them about what happened on that valley ledge. The Wardens welcomed them inside the pike wall, where broad markets and cobblestone plazas gleamed in late daylight, ringed with stone buildings stretching out to distant farms and fisheries. Like Stornhaz, the only way in and out was by gates, the wood pikes doused every evening with water to protect against flaming arrows. At the mouth of the valley, set against the mountains' sweeps, Middleton was the last line of defense should trouble arise from their southerly neighbors.

"It's well-fortified," Maleck said. "But the pike wall..."

"It's stood for centuries," Ashe grunted. "We know what we're doing."

Maleck marked her defensive tone with a sideways glance. "The blood of an Eldur asp from the Sotefold is flame-retardant and poses little risk of mildewing the wood."

"How in God's name did anyone learn *that*? Who was spraying snake blood on their walls?"

A flicker of a smile. "Eldur asps trace their lineage back to a draconian bloodline. The same blood cools the dragon's veins so their fire doesn't consume them. Such a glaze could help fortify this city even further."

No doubt its people would appreciate that. Wary eyes peered from homesteads and storefronts while they made their way up the broad, pennant-fletched street toward Lord Dorminger's estate, and no one smiled.

But no one accosted them, either. Rion's reach didn't extend this far yet.

After minutes of walking on foot, their horses left at the communal stables, they reached Dorminger's manicured stone home—twined red ivy and creeping kudzu carefully cultivated for visual appeal, windows glinting in their gilded settings, outer turrets at the barbican gleaming like smoky jewels. Three Wardens descended the terraced gardens and sauntered to meet them.

"That can't be Asheila Kovar!" one barked. "Last time I saw you, you were such a skinny thing you could hardly lift your own sword!"

She scowled. "I promise I can lift it now, Arnost, so let's leave the jokes and reminiscing for another time, shall we?"

"If you insist." Gray-haired and grinning more than any man who fought in the war had a right to, Arnost halted before them, appraising Maleck with unhostile eyes. "And who is this? A new recruit?"

"No," Ashe said, at the same moment Maleck said, "In a sense."

They swapped glances while Arnost guffawed. "Well, he's a bit older than we like to start them, but with that build I'm certain we could make use of him. Borek, Jolana, inform the king his daughter's Warden has arrived."

Paranoia warned Ashe there was metal in those words, and quiet gloating. Arnost knew more than he ought to.

"So, what of these rumors?" He cast an arm around Ashe's shoulders and led her down the steps to the estate's circular front path and fountain, Maleck at their backs. "Rion ran from this place like his ass was on fire months ago, and now there's all this talk that you and the princess and that lordly son of his went missing, that you were never at the Bartos estate to begin with. What's that all about?"

That Arnost knew any of it painted a vivid picture: Rion had been bragging, certain the small retreat to the coast would be the beginning of Julian and Cistine's courtship—likely ending with his son as King.

How right and wrong he was. About all of it.

Ashe shrugged away her melancholy. "You pampered old men crammed in here waiting to retire are worse gossips than Cistine."

Arnost gave her a shake. "Maybe if you behave yourself, you'll have the chance to be pampered here, too."

The estate's front doors burst open, and Ashe fought not to cringe when Cyril Novacek descended toward them, decked in plated leather armor to blunt a weapon at close range. That told her all she needed to know of how the peace talks were going; one look at his furious face told her the rest. He halted before them, gaze cutting from Ashe to Maleck, and once more she battled back a wince. Cyril was little more her elder than Solene, yet a father's rage burned in his eyes. "Inside. *Now.*"

Even Maleck, with nearly five inches' height over the King and twice the musculature, scurried up the steps like a chastened child.

All the same wingbacked sofas and armchairs took up the same sitting rooms as during Ashe's last visit, all the same tapestries and trinkets dotting the stone halls Cyril led them through, arriving at last in a spacious suite on the second level between the turret-towers. It was clearly Dorminger's room, dominated by a portrait of the redheaded family above the fireplace, but for now it belonged to Cyril—the desk arrayed with his papers, his swordbelt propped against the bedside, his favorite books on the mantle, pillows stuffed under the covers to the height and shape of his Queen's body and a second blanket tousled at the foot of the fireside sofa.

"Are you finished assessing my living habits?" His furious tone ripped Ashe's attention back to him, settled behind the desk. "Because if it *pleases* you, Asheila, I'd like to discuss my daughter's whereabouts."

For the third time, throat just as dry as the first, Ashe told Talheim the story of its princess: the war-council and the birthday celebration, the fabricated estate visit and the ship that carried them north. She told him more than she had Rion or Solene—of bandit raids and training, journeys and revelations. Lightly, she touched on Siralek; on Julian and Cistine, what they'd become and what became of them; all culminating in the Writ of Nobility in Cistine's hand and her plans laid bare.

72

By the end of it, Cyril sat forward, elbows on the desk, hands folded to his mouth; when she told him Cistine was staying in Valgard, he slowly kneaded his temples.

Silence reigned. Maleck shifted his heels, hands folded behind his back, anxious eyes darting from the King to Ashe like he might have to leap between them. But if it came to that, Ashe would tell him to stand down. Whatever Cyril had in store for her, she deserved no better.

Finally, the King said, "How imminent is the threat to Cistine where she stands now?"

"No worse than the threat to you, facing Jad." Cyril warned her off with a scowl, and she amended, "She's surrounded by people who'd lay down their lives in a heartbeat to protect her. She's even safer there than here."

Which meant that now, regardless of where Ashe was, Cistine would be all right.

Another corner of her heart crumbled at the notion, widening the chasm in her chest.

Slowly, Cyril stood, fingertips braced on the desk. His haunted gaze traced the door, and urgency nipped Ashe's skin. With one word, he could empty the city and send men to the north—and destroy everything. "You aren't going to retrieve her, are you?"

"If I was, I'd have done it already." Cyril dragged a hand through his russet hair. "Solene sent a letter. It arrived days ahead of you."

"You already knew everything I just told you?"

"Not in detail. I wanted to see your face while you told it, to know what was really true." He circled the desk to stand before her, and Ashe steeled herself—only to recoil in surprise when he took her shoulders. "And to see which parts hurt the worst, so I'd know what to say and what not to."

Heat swarmed her eyes, and she ducked her head.

"So. Valgard." Cyril released her, reclining against the desk. "Tell me why they sent one of their warriors with you. I know what you are," he added when Maleck started to speak, "I know you used to be an augur. I spent enough time with the Order in that gods-forsaken mountain, performing the ritual. I could sense the power writhing on their bones. You feel the same." Maleck's face showed no change, though the words must've struck deep, clumping him together with his brothers. "Now that we all understand one another, I'll ask again: what is a Valgardan doing here?"

"This is Maleck. He's my..." Ashe trailed off. Friendship was too cursory, and anything deeper risked breaking the barriers she carefully stacked between them after that moment of weakness on the cliff.

"I am her ally on a mission from Princess Cistine," Maleck intervened. "While she instills friendship and trust between our kingdoms, we've come to convince your enemies in the south that an alliance already exists."

"So you've come to lie to Jad az-Rashar." Cyril shook his head. "If he discovers that, every careful step we've taken to build peace between the Middle and Southern Kingdoms will crumble. I can't allow it."

"The alliance isn't a lie," Ashe protested. "Cistine *can* do this. It's just a matter of time, and time is against us."

"We do not deceive," Maleck agreed. "The alliance is real, merely...unsigned."

"Knowing Jad, it's the signing he cares for."

Ashe shrugged. "I can forge Cistine's signature, then."

Cyril pinched the bridge of his nose. "Sometimes I wonder if assigning such a dangerous woman to my daughter's personal guard was the best or worst decision of my life."

Ashe's faint spurt of amusement guttered. It was something he wouldn't have to wonder ever again once Rion arrived. "Maleck and I are cut from the same cloth, we can convince Jad of anything. We just need to keep the peace talks going until Cistine brings us the signed alliance, or intimidate him into making a peace treaty before she finishes her work."

Cyril's gaze lurched between them. "You truly believe you can peddle this lie to the Mad King of Mahasar, that warriors from opposite battlefields twenty years ago are the face of a new alliance between the Northern and Middle Kingdoms."

Ashe glanced at Maleck, loosening her grip on her heart and freeing a hint of what she felt that night on the valley ledge: heat and wonder and desire. "Not only *can* we. We *will*."

Maleck held her gaze steadily. "For Cistine, for her kingdom, for all of you, I will do whatever I must."

Cyril crossed his arms. "Why?"

Maleck wrenched his gaze to the King's stony face. "Your daughter came into my life when I knew nothing but darkness, and she was light. She and her Wardens gave me a reason to live. Purpose. Hope. I had none left before I knew them." His gaze flicked back to Ashe, then returned to Cyril. "For her, I will lie and cheat and fight to my last breath. I owe Talheim my life in more ways than I can say."

Cyril studied him, eyes deep with thought. "During the war, I captured a man who wanted to do nothing but speak with me while we dragged him with us to the City of a Thousand Stars. He told me of *valenar* and *selvenar* and your governing constellations. I knew from the first pot of wine we shared at the fireside, speaking of our loves back home, that my father's war wasn't as simple as we were taught. So I'm willing to test this tenuous truce you offer. But if you betray us, if you threaten these peace talks in any way or harm my people, I will show you justice that will make my father's campaign in the North seem merciful. Do I make myself clear?"

Maleck dipped his head. "Utterly."

"Good. Then go find Dorminger. He's a beef of a man with hair redder than Ashe's, you can't miss him. Tell him I sent for him."

Ashe's pulse drummed in her wrists and knees. This was the moment she dreaded—holding the King's undivided attention. It was an effort not to make some excuse to slip out on Maleck's heels, particularly when he glanced back with a silent question in his eyes. But she had to ignore it, holding her head high before her King.

The door shut, and they were at last alone.

"Do you know who that man is," Cyril said, "*what* he is?"

"A former augur and acolyte, I know. But he hasn't wielded augments in twenty years, and we don't have any with us."

Cyril chuckled and shook his head. "Of course." He returned to the desk and stacked his papers, solemn again. "The whole affair is dangerous...letting Cistine stay and negotiate. Letting you and this *Maleck* deceive Jad. But you've caught me on a desperate day."

Frowning, Ashe propped her hip against the desk. "How bad?"

"Reports are flooding in...the border fort sackings stopped when we first invited Jad, but they've started again in the past fortnight. Weak jabs, testing our mettle."

Fury knotted Ashe's shoulders. "Where is Jad now?"

Cyril cleared enough space to unfold a map on the desk and circled a plot with his finger. "Our scouts place his camp to our southwest, near the Caves of Camere at the coast of Blacklake." Far from the Calaluns where Ashe and Maleck spotted those signal fires, but the realization was little comfort. "Why they chose somewhere damp and rocky is beyond me. It's as different from Mahasar as possible. But then, Jad's built his reign on wily, unpredictable maneuvers."

Ashe bent beside him, hands splayed on the desk. "It's a good two hours on foot from Middleton to Camere. He may be testing to see if you'll attack while he's on the open road."

"It's difficult to say, which is what worries me. I don't like an enemy without patterns." Cyril rubbed his bearded mouth. "He never negotiates for the same thing twice, and whenever we reach an agreement for peace, he goes away for a day and changes his mind. Asks for land, then asks for cattle, then asks for rations for his starving people."

"If there's nothing he truly wants, why is he dragging out the charade?"

"I think he does want something, but he's testing how accommodating we'll be. So it's likely his real demand will knock our legs from under us."

"Or he's biding his time to muster an army powerful enough to defeat us."

Cyril leaned back, frowning. "If you're right, then both sides are playing for time, not peace. And that is a dangerous game."

The door swung open and Dorminger and Maleck strode in, the ruddy Lord with an arm around Maleck's shoulders and a sheepish yet mollified smile lighting the depths of Maleck's eyes. Ashe stomped her heart flat when it lurched at the sight.

"Ah, there she is! Asheila Kovar!" Dorminger rushed forward to embrace her. "Lucie and Alena still speak highly of the time you taught them knife-throwing. Such fond memories!"

Ashe couldn't help a smile of her own. "Where are those two mischief-makers, anyway?"

The Lord released her, sterner when he stepped back. "I sent them away with their mother to our lands in the north. Just a precaution."

"Dorm, these two are my honored guests," Cyril said. "See to it they have accommodations in the estate."

"You need a few less influential friends, Cyril. Between all the Lords you've invited, the Cadre, and my own servants, I only have one room left."

Ashe stiffened and Maleck paled.

"I'm jesting, of course," Dorminger cackled after a vicious beat. "There's a room in the east wing and one in the west, find a servant and they'll escort you there. In the meantime, Your Majesty, if I might have your ear?"

"If you'll have the rest of me, too. I'm afraid it doesn't detach easily. Ashe?" Two steps nearer to the door, she looked back, meeting Cyril's warm gaze. "Welcome back."

Melancholy washed over her. Until that moment, she didn't realize how badly she wanted him to say welcome *home*.

CHAPTER TWELVE

WORD REACHED MIDDLETON the day after Ashe and Maleck did, by way of a Mahasari messenger at the pike gate: Talheimic autumn with its hard rains and bouts of chill disagreed with King Jad's body. He would be delayed for some time at Camere.

Agitation drove Ashe to Middleton's well-stocked training rooms before dawn each day, one of a dozen people pummeling grainsacks with knives and fists, imagining each one was a Mahasari Enforcer or Jad himself. Every session was another reminder that she was here, in some ways, under false pretenses, and the camaraderie she shared with these Wardens over waterskins and well-aimed blows a charade. They welcomed her now, but if they knew what she felt toward Valgard, toward the former augur whom they avoided in the halls, they'd treat her no better than Rion did.

Frustrated with herself and with them, she forewent practice one morning and sought out Maleck instead. At least the strangeness with him was navigable, a melody she knew her piece in.

She found him bent over a newly-purchased journal at one of the long tables in the dining hall, the only one sitting there despite the crowded room. Whispered orders had trickled down from Cyril through Dorminger that he was not to be harmed, but no one offered a hand of friendship, either. He was always alone if he wasn't with her.

She banged down her bowl of porridge and slid onto the bench across from him. "What are you writing?"

He hastily flipped the journal shut over his wrist. "I'm not."

"Then Valgard must have some interesting uses for fountain pens no one's taught me yet." To her surprise, his cheekbones colored. She studied that interesting splash of red across his skin, smiling. "Maleck, are you *drawing* again?"

"Possibly."

"Let me see." She fluttered her fingers. "Please?"

"No."

"Maleck, really, what's the worst I could see?" She wiggled her brows. "Is it *naughty*?"

He groaned. "Asheila."

"Show me your scandalous sketches!" She rose from the bench, balancing on one knee and reaching for the journal. Maleck slid it away from her, then hefted it high out of her grasp, and she paused with her hands braced on the table. "Do you *really* think holding that above my head will stop me from taking it?"

"Consider if you really want to do this, here, in front of these people."

It hit her like a battering ram—where they were, and with whom. Not in the forest anymore, not on rooftops in Astoria where no other eyes could see the ease with which she teased him; and though the Wardens and kitchen staff kept to their own meals at separate tables, her well-trained senses told her they were watching, too, gathering gossip to turn more and more hearts against her.

Slowly, she slid back into her seat. "Fine, keep your secrets."

Maleck flipped the journal shut and changed the subject. "Rumor has it Jad's been seen moving about the Caves of Camere and some of the lands beyond in fit physical condition."

Ashe didn't bother asking how he heard. "But no word yet when he plans to grace us with his esteemed presence." They both bent over their porridge, arms curled around the bowls, heads close together. "The Wardens are restless."

R . D U G A N

"And the townspeople have begun boarding their windows. Whatever the cause for this delay, nothing like it has happened since Jad first made camp in Camere weeks ago."

"Why do I have the feeling it has something to do with us?"

Maleck's frown bored against hers. "The signal fires?"

"It could be. We're the aberration. We arrive, Jad delays." She stirred her chunky porridge, pondering the safer points of that night in the mountains. "Maybe we should investigate after all."

The dining hall doors hammered open so loudly half the room jumped. "*Asheila Kovar!*"

Anger ripped down Ashe's spine, digging jagged claws into her hips and lifting from of her seat. "Well, he got here faster than I expected."

What surprised her more than the sight of Rion Bartos storming toward them was the simmering disgust it evoked. Had her opinion of him truly changed so much in so little time? Or was this merely the rebellion of spirit before she fell to her knees and begged him to take her back, to give her a sense of belonging and purpose again?

It was almost exhilarating not knowing; nearly as exhilarating as the adrenaline singing in her veins when the Commander halted before her, flanked by Rozalie Dohnal and Viktor Pollack, his best below what Ashe once was. Judging by Viktor's gloating smile and Rozalie's scowl, things might have changed on their long journey back from Valgard.

What hadn't changed was Rion's fury. Arms crossed, nostrils flaring, he filled up every hollow inch of Ashe with his fire. "I want to know how you reached her first."

Ashe raised a brow. "By *her*, I assume you mean *the Queen*. As for the *how*, I'll let you speculate."

Viktor inclined toward Rozalie, hands in his pockets, whispering in her ear; she shrugged him off, gaze fixed on Ashe. It was impossible to interpret that look, but there didn't seem to be any resentment behind it.

Unfortunately, Rion had enough for all three of them. "You undermined me, spat in my face, and lied to the royal family. I'll have you in the stocks for that."

"She told no lie," Maleck cut in. "Only preempted yours."

Viktor's hand fell to his sword as if he just now noticed Maleck was there. Rion's broad shoulders tensed, eyes narrowing with hate. "You again."

"*Meszaros.*" Maleck bent his chin without taking his eyes from Rion.

"What is this Valgardan *filth* doing in the halls where our King resides?"

"Strange how that proximity didn't matter as much to you when you abandoned Cyril on the snowy tundra to take a piss and left me to save his life twenty years ago," Ashe snapped.

Cursing, Rion lunged for her. Maleck's boot cracked against the table's edge, slamming it into the Commander's hip. He stumbled sideways, and Viktor's steel ripped from its sheath as he leaped across the table at Maleck. Ashe hurtled after him, kicking him onto his seat mid-leap and bloodying his nose with a blow.

"That was for Pippet." She drove her boot into his ribs. "And that was for Aden."

Clutching his hip, Rion straightened and drew his sword. "Get that *thing* out of the King's dwelling, or so help me, I will remove it in *pieces.*"

"You couldn't kill a boy of fourteen with that blade," Maleck said. "I doubt you'll survive the humiliation of trying again."

Ashe swung an incredulous look at him; his posture hadn't altered, his gaze still fixed on Rion, yet the faintest cruel smile turned his mouth.

He was *taunting* him. Maleck, who always drove in like a shadowed blade, not one wicked gleam on his edge before he struck...he was toying with *Meszaros*. Ashe couldn't reconcile the shift, couldn't imagine why Maleck, alone and friendless except for her, would choose now to goad an enemy. And *this* enemy, of all people.

"What is going on here?"

The thunder of King Cyril's voice choked any hint of a fight from the air, setting Rion, Viktor, and Ashe crashing back on their heels and loosening Maleck into his full height.

The King strode to join them, no less imposing even with a porridge bowl in his hand. He halted beside Rozalie, gaze snapping between them all. "Rion, I didn't know you'd returned. Welcome home. Since when don't you come to me *first* after a mission?"

Rion grimaced. "I was made aware Asheila Kovar arrived ahead of me."

"You say that like it's anything new."

Ashe winced, but to his credit, Rion merely angled his blade toward her. "I was going to remove the infestation before I came to see you."

"Infestation." Cyril's eyes flicked to Maleck. "I take it no one bothered to tell you this man is under my protection."

Viktor's eyes widened. Rion's jaw clenched. "And I take it no one bothered to inform *you* what escapades Asheila was involved in back in the North. How she holds their interests over ours now."

"That's not true."

The soft rebuttal came not from Ashe, not even from Maleck, but from Rozalie. Rion fixed her with an icy stare. "Are you contradicting your Commander's report?"

"I'm telling His Majesty that Asheila Kovar never holds anyone's interests above Cistine's," Rozalie said. "If she sent Ashe, then they're working together like they always have, because they love Talheim with everything they are. If they think we need a Valgardan here to save our kingdom, I'm willing to have a bit of faith."

"If you're so inclined to faith, go serve in a temple," Viktor snapped. "This isn't a matter of gods, it's a matter of swords."

"You would know, Viktor, your sword *is* your god."

"Enough," Cyril ordered. "Ashe and Maleck told me why they're here and what they hope to accomplish. It's a risk, I know, but I agree with Rozalie...it's one I'm also willing to put faith in."

"I see." Rion's voice smoothed, but there was a subtle shift in his bearing, the planting and posing that always preceded his hardest blows. "And did Asheila also bother to tell you I stripped her of her title for misconduct? That she no longer has a Warden's commission serving the royal family?" The indifference in his tone, like the loss of her was no more cutting than the dismissal of a trainee after a fortnight, bladed straight to Ashe's core.

She was nothing to him now, if she'd ever been anything more than a prop to his hate.

Cyril's gaze landed sharply on her. "She didn't mention as much, no." Another beat of silence, too heavy. "But Warden title or none, if we can convince Mahasar of an existing alliance between our kingdoms, we may save thousands of Talheimic lives. It's worth the risk."

"This is madness," Rion snarled. "This whole plot, it's a joke."

Cyril's eyes narrowed. "Don't forget whose idea it was to entreat the North for help, *Brother*." Rion looked away, and Cyril beckoned to Ashe and Maleck. "Both of you, with me. Pollack and Dohnal, report to Dorminger. Rion, wait for me here."

Ashe slid over the table to walk behind her King, shooting a glance at Rozalie, who tossed her blonde hair over her shoulder to hide her face from Rion and mouthed, *Dinner?*

Ashe nodded, then escaped the dining hall.

Cyril led them to the nearest bench down the corridor and sat, porridge bowl on his knees, looking up at Ashe and Maleck. "Which of you wants the privilege of being honest with me first?"

Ashe opened her mouth, but Maleck was swifter. "I tried to kill you as a child."

Cyril's brows vaulted. Ashe ripped her hands through her hair, staring at Maleck, but he didn't spare her a glance.

"I was...not myself," he went on. "Forced to become something I couldn't bear, something I will never be again. But Asheila saved you from me. I'm not certain Rion ever told you that. When nothing and no one else stood in my way, she did. And she woke me from the place I'd gone. I fled rather than finishing you, and Rion followed."

Cyril frowned. "Into Cerne Mosiar. I remember...he was gone for so long, I feared him dead."

"Not dead, hunting. He butchered his way through the swamplands, killing every Valgardan he met on his way to me. My...friend's father found me and helped me escape. I had not seen Rion Bartos in twenty years, but our paths crossed again when he came to Valgard."

"I understand how painful that history is. But you're not to antagonize my Commander in these halls, is that clear? We present a unified front, Talheim and Valgard...that goes both ways, regardless of how you feel toward each other." When Maleck nodded, Cyril's gaze flicked back to Ashe. "What about your title?"

"I wouldn't let Rion use a Valgardan child as bait against their Chancellors," she muttered. "Not that it ever would've worked, anyway. He was spoiling for a fight, and it wasn't one I was willing to let him have."

"He is your Commander."

"Apparently not anymore." She rubbed a chill from her arms. "I'm sorry I didn't tell you before."

"While I wish you'd been honest with me, what I told Rion is true: titles don't matter to Jad, only the face we present. And it *will* be unity." Cyril finished his porridge in three swift bites and climbed to his feet. "I'll speak to Rion. He's going to keep his prejudices to himself from now on, and we'll have peace in this house. We won't give Jad a single crack to slither into. Understood?"

Ashe and Maleck snapped their heels together and nodded.

"I have a question," Maleck said when the King turned away. "Can you restore Asheila's title?"

Cyril pivoted back, looking at Maleck long and steady. "It's within my power, yes. But I won't do it."

Ashe's heart plummeted. "Why *not?*"

"Because I officially made Rion my Commander again the moment I joined him here in Middleton. It's his right to declare who is Cadre and who isn't, and if I undermine him it will only fissure our ranks more."

"Then I'm not Cistine's Warden."

"In title, no. But in deed, I doubt you're capable of being anything else."

His words stung as badly as his refusal to give her any place in his household. He didn't know how badly she hurt Cistine from Siralek, how her princess might not even want her anymore. Without the King or Queen's blessing, she had nowhere to go.

She bowed and turned away before they could see the emotion threatening to break loose across her face.

"Ashe," Cyril said to her retreating back, "I don't do this only for the sake of unity or these peace talks, but for yours."

Of course he saw how Rion looked at her, and surmised the torture her life would be if he instated her back into the ranks against the Commander's wishes. She'd be made to suffer day and night for what she did.

Suffering there or suffering with no place to belong; either way, Asheila Kovar was doomed to pain.

She managed to avoid Viktor and Rion all afternoon, escaped Maleck's undisguised attempts to find her at her chamber door, the training room, and on the grounds, and dodged whispers and glances in the corridors until nightfall when scents of beef and lentil stew drove her back to the dining hall. Rozalie waited there, perched in the same place Ashe and Maleck ate breakfast, her feet on the bench and her seat on the tabletop. She'd dressed down in a tunic and trousers—a small gesture of kindness that she didn't flaunt her rank and title.

She leaped to her feet the moment Ashe entered. "Why don't we go to a vendor for supper?"

Rion and Viktor would arrive soon, then. Ashe spanned an arm to the door. "After you."

They passed through the estate grounds in silence, offering nods to Arnost and his men. Ashe tried to count it as nothing when their eyes and whispers followed her and Rozalie up the broad stone steps out of sight.

Under dusk's cool light, they ducked into the first shop they found still open and purchased bowls of pork, dumplings, and pickled cabbage. Rozalie broke the silence while they waited, leaning against the serving counter with arms crossed and eyes averted. "I tried to delay us as much as I could, but I think Rion was growing suspicious at the end. There's only so many times you can feign a headcold or a lame horse before it becomes a pattern."

Ashe snorted. "I appreciate what you did. Not just biding time for us, but today in the dining hall."

Rozalie took her bowl from the vendor and handed Ashe hers. "I was surprised not to see Aden with you."

A pang of missing pierced Ashe's stomach. "He's in Stornhaz with Thorne and the others."

"Then those rumors, about you two—you know—"

"Not true."

"Ah." Rozalie followed her down a short slope to sit beside the pond at the city's center, where ducks paddled and children skipped stones. "Then that man today..."

"Also not true," Ashe lied.

"I didn't say there were any rumors."

"But we both know there will be."

"That's the least of your problems now." Rozalie speared a chunk of pickled cabbage and gestured to Ashe with it. "Rion promoted Viktor as his second the moment we left Keltei Temple. He's telling everyone he gained the rank by exposing you for the rat-rutting traitor you are."

Ashe stabbed her pork moodily. "Are you sure you even want to be seen with me? It could hurt your reputation."

"I've lived my whole life with a poor reputation. Most people don't look favorably on former brothel workers, whether they were in the trade by choice or not." She crunched on the pickled cabbage and spoke with her mouth full. "Besides, if this was the *King's* idea, then as far as I'm concerned, you share His Majesty's mind. I'm not going to argue with that."

"Thank you, Roz."

She swallowed and shrugged. "You know what they say: you can tell the tree you're eating from by the fruit you bite into. You don't stand to gain anything by keeping this up unless it's really what Talheim needs. And as for Viktor and Rion...the way they spoke about you after the temple, I can see why you slept alone so often while we searched for the Princess. I spent my share of nights outside the firelight, too."

Ashe didn't bother to ask why she stayed on with the Cadre given that. Adrift between kingdoms, belonging nowhere, was a pain she wished on no one and wouldn't have inflicted on herself if she knew how it would rip this gaping hole in her chest that never stopped bleeding. "Where are the others?

Symon, Petra, Andrej..."

A mischievous smile stretched Rozalie's mouth. "They may have fallen suddenly ill with uncontrollable bowel discomfort at the northern forts."

Chuckling, Ashe nudged Rozalie's shoulder. "Thank you. For all of it."

"It's the least I can do after all you've done for me...and what I did in Valgard." Rozalie finished off her portion, set her bowl in her lap again, and spoke down toward it. "How...how is Pippet?"

A painful smile dragged across Ashe's face. "She was healing well when I left. Happy to be with her friends."

"Good. I'll never stop being sorry for what we did to her." Regret gleamed in Rozalie's eyes. "Whenever I think of her now, I just see my sisters, and I don't know how I ever let it go that far. Children are children, no matter which kingdom they come from, and thinking otherwise is how you build brothels for little girls. All it takes is one compromise."

"Careful, Roz. If you keep talking like this, there's no telling what Viktor will call *you*."

She knocked her shoulder against Ashe's. "Those jealous little bastards can call me whatever they like, so long as I still get to call myself your friend."

A fraction of the weight lifted from Ashe's chest. "I'm willing if—"

She broke off, gaze snagging across the pond. Rozalie followed her stare and tensed.

On the opposite shore, where a cluster of willows brushed the water, a shadowy shape slipped between the fronds. Eyes flashed in the murky light, framed in the contours of a swaddled cloth and heavy brow—then vanished.

Ashe set aside her bowl and beckoned Rozalie with a jerk of her head. Stealthy as wildcats, they prowled around the shore. Ashe signaled the children to leave, and with one look at her hands on her knives, they obeyed. The last ripples of their movement still teased the water when Ashe and Rozalie ducked into the willow grove.

It was difficult to see in the twilit gloom, and a faint reek hung on the air, balsamic and harsh. Ashe and Rozalie separated, taking the grove inch by inch, parting fronds with their steel and searching for a hint of that cloth-wrapped face and flashing eyes.

"Ashe, come look at this."

Nerves bristling, she pushed through the foliage to reach Rozalie, crouched in the damp soil at the base of a tree. Her fingers traced the perfect imprint of a boot, oddly-shaped with a pointed toe and broad heel.

Ashe ran her hand over the willow, flaking off crumbs of pebbled loam from its bark, then swiveled to peer through the fronds at the opposite shore—empty now except for their white bowls glinting in the dead grass. "They knew we saw them, so they went up."

Rozalie straightened, dusting off her hands and craning her head back. The tops of the trees were empty and still. "Viktor? Maybe Rion sent him to watch us?"

"Let's hope so," Ashe said.

There was no need to discuss any grim alternatives. Not yet.

CHAPTER THIRTEEN

HANDS UP, STRANGER!"

Cistine caught the globe of water Quill threw to her, straining to hold its shape. For days they'd kernelled out this water flagon and tossed it back and forth, just as they did with fire and wind—every time a different augment, each one a different strain. Today she could barely remember how to keep the water from running loose over her fingers.

"I know it's hard." Quill watched the water shiver in her palm. "Moderation isn't as easy as letting it all out at once like you did on that mountain. You'll get better with practice."

"So much for everything being innate." Cistine lobbed the globe on the sandy floor, the splash echoing through the empty chamber. Usually she enjoyed the solitude of her early-morning sessions with Quill, but this morning everything felt too empty—inside and outside of her.

He raised a brow. "You're in a mood. Bad dreams?"

"As usual. And I'm meeting with Mira today."

Quill walked toward her, palms offered silently. She started pummeling, losing herself in the familiar cadence, bobbing and weaving through the chamber with him; it might as well have been the rock top in Hellidom before everything went wrong, when the world and her mission made so much more sense and Baba Kallah, Julian, and Helga were still alive.

Before she ever met Kristoff. When she felt *whole*.

Sweat dripped into her eyes and her heart thundered in her ears, muffling the echo of a familiar caw carrying through the chamber. Faer swooped to roost in one of the wall niches, ruffling his feathers; Ariadne entered behind him, smiling at the headlock Quill held Cistine in. "Having a productive morning?"

"Depends on what she does next," Quill grinned.

Cistine snapped her heel into his stomach and squirmed free, scrambling to her feet. "Is it time?"

Ariadne nodded. "Aden's session just ended."

Taking Cistine's offered hand, Quill surged upright. "Aden's shut up like a steel trap about everything. What does Mira have for him that we don't?"

"Perhaps a solution for his pain that doesn't involve fists or ale."

"I resent that. We also have gambling and *Voitaja*."

"Careful. Pippet's watching your every move now. You wouldn't want her to learn your methods of coping, would you?"

Quill winced. "Point taken."

Cistine left them bantering, retrieved her coat, and tied up her hair with shaking hands. So much could go wrong today. What if she went into hysterics or panicked, and there was nowhere to run? Worse, what if she could coax out no feeling at all? What if Kalt Hasa had made her a husk, every emotion just playacting, and that truth became clear today?

Faer settled on her elbow, talons squeezing, and she planted a kiss on his head, the smell of damp wind and saltiness in his feathers bringing some warmth back to her tingling face.

They parted ways with Quill near Kanslar's dining hall, his whistle bringing Faer to roost on his shoulder and his parting clap on Cistine's back full of breezy reassurance. Then she trailed Ariadne through the long corridors to Sander's room.

She hadn't known the man long, but she recognized his taste everywhere: in the sheer banners imported from gods-knew-where, the hearth arch plastered with gold, the cedar chests and tabletops aligned with precious gemstone boxes and candle dishes of every color. Paper screens portioned out the parlor sides, and Sander's lovers came and went from behind them, sheathed in fine silk, moving as quick as drawn blades winnowing past shields. They offered no smiles, only dipped chins and cautious glances that reminded Cistine of how the Six first looked at her when Kristoff brought her to their card games.

Her hands trembled and sorrow burned her throat.

"Ah! Ariadne, Cistine." Mira rose slowly from the sofa near the fire. Despite the uncommonly-warm day, she was bundled in layers, skirts parting to reveal trousers when she met them halfway through the room. "You'll have to pardon Sander's entourage. Changes in season make them cranky."

"I can't imagine *why*." One woman, pale in skin and hair, rounded a screen just to shoot a pointed look at Mira.

Mira rolled her eyes. "This is Hana. You'll want to avoid her, she bites."

"Only those deserving."

"Then go gnaw on Sander's leg, will you? He's been bothering Thorne all morning." Mira returned to the couch and nodded to an adjacent door. "There's refreshments in the dining room if you'd like, Cistine."

"She can stay," Ariadne said.

"Are you certain?"

"That's the reason I've come back to Stornhaz, isn't it? That my pain would help others escape theirs." Ariadne settled onto the sofa across from Mira. "If my story can help in any way, I'll tell it until I'm hoarse."

Mira reclined on the sofa's corner, spreading one arm along its back and the other down its velvet side; even when Cistine lowered herself shyly beside Ariadne, Mira's gaze was only for the former acolyte. "Have you given thought to what we discussed last time?"

"Why I can barely sleep and why I was more angry than glad to see Saychelle? Yes, I have." Ariadne played with the hoops of her handguards. "I think I fear, not the trial itself, but what comes when it's over."

"Which is—?"

"That's what I'm not sure of. I see my cabal drifting down different

R . D U G A N

paths: Thorne as Chancellor, Quill and Aden as teachers, Tatiana into her father's arms, Maleck on his own journey away from us, and Cistine..." her gaze flicked sideways, full of unexpected sorrow. "She's bound to another life."

"And you feel left behind?" Mira prompted.

"That isn't the word for it." Ariadne sat forward, palms pressed together. "Ever since I was small, the only thing that ever mattered to me was serving the True God. When I worked in my parents' flower shop, that meant being the brightest light people saw. As soon as I was old enough, it meant becoming a *visnpresta* acolyte. I dedicated everything I was to teaching people of his kindness and compassion, the gifts he and his vassals gave us. When Thorne and Saychelle began Sillakove, I thought *that* was my calling...to free the people absolutely from tyranny, to live and worship a cause higher than any Court. Higher than themselves.

"And then this happened to me." She gestured down the length of herself. "And after some time, I realized it was the True God's will I bring Salvotor to justice, even at the tip of a sword. Everything since then was in service to that purpose. And when it's finished, I don't..." she hung her head with her hands slumped between her knees. "I swore an oath that if he made use of me one last time, to change my grief to glory and my suffering to victory over the man who ruined my future, I would do whatever he demanded. This trial, my testimony, they are all I have left to give. How will I serve him afterward? In what capacity could he possibly want me when not even the temples will take me back? When my sisters will not look my way anymore? I have lived all my life by his voice telling me my purpose, and when I've served that...what if he no longer speaks to me?"

Mira hummed, fingers dancing along the sofa's wooden frame. "Is that the sort of God you think you follow? One who will leave you cold and empty when you've fulfilled his will?"

"It's what the temples do to those who no longer serve a purpose."

"And the old Order enslaved children. Is their way always the way of the gods?"

Ariadne hesitated, then slowly shook her head.

"It's only natural that your training as an acolyte would instill the belief that the practices of the temples reflect the heart of the gods, but I would challenge that. We are all imperfect people striving to be better. *Visnprests* and *prestas* are no exception, and their conduct is not always the will of the one they serve."

"Then what is his will?" Ariadne demanded. "I need *something*, Mira, some hope to look forward to. Some light beyond the darkness of this trial."

"Why don't you ask him?" Mira half-smiled. "I can tell you the kingdoms need wise counsel, but that doesn't mean you're called to do it. Or that we lack for guards who cannot be bought by ruthless Chancellors— but that doesn't mean you should become Vassora. Just because there's a question in the world doesn't mean you are its answer." She inclined, earnest in every angle, gaze full of passion. "What you seek, you will find, if you seek it with all your heart."

"And what if I'm afraid to know? Perhaps I will like what I learn even less than what I assume."

"Only you can answer for certain whether it's worth the risk." Mira reclined again. "So. Tell me more about your sister and Iri's arrival."

It went that way for more than an hour: Mira unspooling truths from Ariadne like a weaver artfully hemming a tapestry, and Ariadne, always the most private of the cabal, opening angles Cistine never saw before. Like a forbidden tale cracked open in the dark, she came aware of the pain, fear, and hidden resentment lurking in her friend; how she yearned for the ease with which her sister moved through the world, temple doors open before her, arms embracing her, possessing everything that was once Ariadne's— the calling, the future, even the love of her old mentor. How she bristled at the city's eyes on her, condemning her or praying for salvation. And the weight she carried, knowing the trial she feared to face held the future of her kingdom in the balance. Valgard waited with held breath for the very moment Ariadne most dreaded: when the sentence came down.

Mira's calm never wavered. Nothing Ariadne said seemed of any shock to her, as if she already guessed every word that might come from her mouth. Answers met with nodding and humming, then more questions, then conversation like two old friends discussing matters over supper.

Finally, when Ariadne was hoarse from talking, things came to a lull. Mira sipped the tea Hana brought with generous heaps of sugar, smiling over the porcelain rim. "Think on these questions we've posed today, Ariadne. Ask the True God what comes after. He may not answer at once, or at all, but sometimes voicing it brings healing of its own."

Ariadne dipped her head. "I'll do that."

"And I'm here, whatever comes of it." Mira's eyes skipped from her to Cistine, bringing a nervous flush from her hairline down her neck. "Would you give us the room for now? And leave the door open on your way out."

With a glance at Cistine, Ariadne rose. "I'll be nearby if you need me."

A trill of panic almost made Cistine say she needed her *now*; she didn't want to be alone with this almost-stranger. But Mira's steady gaze suggested this conversation demanded privacy, so she bit her tongue, fidgeting while Ariadne slipped out. The moment her footsteps faded from the hall, Mira said, "Now that you see what it's like here, will you stay or go?"

"I have a choice?"

"*Always.* I take no unwilling people under my counsel, no matter how much their families or Chancellors plead and threaten and bribe me to."

Cistine cocked her head. "Why not, if you can really help them?"

"Because if *they* don't seek my help of their own volition, whatever good I can do is only temporary...their desire is not to heal, it's to please, and change precipitated by pressure can't withstand the storm. I've learned that the most difficult way." Mira tapped a finger over her heart. "Change begins when *we* choose light over whatever darkness hunts us. I've had to rise from my share of shadows, not because anyone begged me to, but because I grew tired of living in the pit. Are you tired, Cistine? Are you ready to rise?"

She risked a glance at the open doorway. To accept Mira's help was to accept that she was broken, that she'd lost; that for all her defiance and scheming in Kalt Hasa, Salvotor really had beaten her. She'd claimed her freedom but forfeited her sanity.

That was what he wanted her to believe.

She hurried across the room and shut the door, then returned to the couch facing Mira, hands gripped tight in her lap, spine straight like she sat on Talheim's ivory throne. "Where do we start?"

Mira grinned, dimples carving her cheeks. "Tell me what made you so angry you beat your knuckles to bruises."

Cistine glanced down at her hands, surprised to find they were indeed turning angry reddish-purple. She'd forgotten to wrap them before she punched Quill's hands. "Everything, I suppose."

"It was always Sander or Aden for me when I was training to be Vassora. They liked to tease me and challenge me to fights in front of everyone. I would pummel grainsacks in the barracks until I had no strength left in my arms. I'd even dream about it sometimes, those pesky nightmares where you swing a blow with *everything* you have and it still lands like a soft wind."

Cistine laughed. "I know exactly what you mean!"

"I don't think I've ever told Sander about that...how I used to dream of punching him." Chuckling with her, Mira stretched out her legs over the opposite arm of the sofa. "What do you dream about, Cistine?"

She swallowed, skimming her thumb over her bruised knuckles, and shook her head.

"How would you feel if we traded one another a question for a question?" Mira offered after a beat.

A reluctant smile tugged Cistine mouth. "I've always liked that game."

"You go first, then."

She looked up from her knuckles. "Why did you leave the Vassora?"

Mira gazed into the gilded hearth crackling high despite the heat pumping through the windows. "I had...an accident. It was no one's fault, but things haven't been the same since. The guard was no longer a path for me anymore, like the *visnpresta* Order is not for Ariadne. But it's always been my purpose to help people, so I found other talents I could use besides my blade."

"I'm sorry. I know how terrifying it is when you feel like the thing you were born to do might be taken away."

"Do you mean losing your crown? Or nearly losing your life in Kalt Hasa?" For a long moment, they stared at one another. Then Mira added,

"Tell me in your own words. Take all the time you need."

Cistine bore down a steeling breath and made her mind like a fist, rolling her body forward, with determination centered and squared, into the blow—not toward herself or Mira, but toward Salvotor and all the things he did to break her, to lock her away in silent fear.

With a deft strike, she opened her mouth and let the truths spill out.

Cistine hardly noticed when the sunlight brushed low along the walls, when Sander's other lovers brought soup for lunch, then pork sandwiches for dinner, or when Ariadne silently returned. She talked and talked, and whenever she was tempted to stop, a conjuring of Salvotor's sneering face loosened her tongue again.

She told Mira of cold walls and dark stone, the balcony above the chasm, the Wound and the bathing chamber, the prison, the dining hall, and the hewn room. She told her of the people—leering Grimmaul with his cruel mouth and crueler touch, the quiet prisoners with only thin strands of defiance left in them, the Vassoran guards divided between their loyalties; of Dain's bashful smiles, Krusar's harsh laugh, Selanus and Suandi like twin tempests, Markvard's quick wit and Baldvin's unerring brashness.

When dusk hushed the world, she told Mira of Kristoff: of nobility clawing through nearly two decades of harsh stone and ruthless hurt, of a man with a compass around his neck who carried in his heart a dead *valenar* and two boys now grown into men.

"I'm alive because of him." Her knee pressed tight to Ariadne's as she bent forward and gripped the sides of her neck in both hands. "But I don't feel like I'm really *living*."

"You're afraid to disappoint him?" Mira asked.

"I'm afraid I'm not honoring the sacrifice he made. He could've fled with us if he really tried. He could've seen Aden and Maleck again." She hadn't even let herself feel the deeper ache of missing him until now, another pain she shut out just to survive.

"But he didn't flee. He placed your worth above his wants." Mira tilted her head. "Do you feel you have to *do* something to be worthy of that? Or are you just worried about honoring his life?"

Cistine wiped her wet cheeks. "I've never wondered before."

"No need to answer now. But think on it." Mira stretched a kink from her back, and Cistine startled upright at the soft pop, realizing only then that Hana had built the fire back up and it was *late*, utterly black beyond the windows.

"Have I been talking all this time?" Embarrassment colored her cheeks. "Mira, I'm—"

"Don't apologize. Thank me," Mira said. "Apologizing unnecessarily will only make you feel inadequate. Don't apologize for my time, thank me for it."

Rubbing the heat from her face, Cistine said, "Thank you for listening. I thought if I talked about Kalt Hasa, it would make it easier to remember, and worse because I'd remember new things. But it's not like that at all, it's..." She spanned her hands, searching helplessly for the right word.

"Lighter," Ariadne offered. "Because others carry the weight with you."

Cistine nodded. "But without the nightmares."

Unease coiled at the base of her spine, reminding her just how unexpectedly those bouts of panic could arise, but Mira interrupted with another question. "Tell me which season is your favorite."

A storm of memories blew through her: gentle spring rains tapping her bedroom window in Astoria, everything budding to new life, her fingernails caked with fresh dirt; summer birthday galas and late evenings of firebug catching, hot hours of training on the rock top and rainstorms in the lower mountain crags; dark, moody autumn afternoons as heat and chill made war, the last gasps of summer dying out in puffs of copper leaves while the whole world smelled of cinnamon and pumpkin, and then—

"Winter," she decided.

"Why?" Ariadne asked, brows drawn together.

Cistine grinned. "Because of the snow fights and spiced hot milk and plenty of time for reading and games. And I love the smell of the hearths in the Citadel, especially that first time when they burn off all the dust. Besides, the hush after a good, heavy snowfall...there's nothing else like it."

Mira's eyes darted to Ariadne.

"Ice skating," Ariadne murmured after a moment. "And dancing in the snowbursts, the kind where the sun still peeks through the clouds. Then your skirts and socks are soaked, so you dry out by the fire with a cup of hot cocoa and nothing to keep you company but books to read and papers to write."

Smiling, Mira picked up her sandwich. "It seems you two have a bit more in common than trauma and stubbornness. And what is your *favorite* part of winter, Cistine?"

She didn't know how this woman always sensed when there was some stone unturned. "Darlaska."

Ariadne cocked her head. "What is that?"

Cistine told them of the festival of gifts honoring the gods' love for people, spinning out her vivid memories of silver garlands and gold wreaths; the sea's saltwater aroma mingling with the balsam and cedar from the vending booth; the ghostlit dapples splashing along the ice-crusted cobblestones and the frigid air cut by ringing fiddles and laughter from hundreds of mouths throughout the city.

Her city. Her people, for whom she was here, for whom she endured all of this...because they deserved every drop of sweat and blood she could shed to protect them.

When she talked herself breathless again, Ariadne squeezed her knee. "No one ever told us Talheim gave gifts."

"There's plenty we didn't know about each other." Cistine gripped her wrist gently in turn. "But you know, if it *really* will make you feel better, I could give you a gift for—"

Just as the words left her mouth, everything crystallized. Different thoughts all ran together, weaving into one beautiful tapestry of light and color, snow and cinnamon, silver and gold, laughter and joy.

"Why are you grinning at me like that?" Ariadne demanded.

Cistine leaped to her feet, too giddy to sit still any longer. "No reason!"

"Wait a moment, Cistine," Mira laughed. "I have an assignment for you: practice describing Darlaska to yourself whenever your mind needs to retreat. And don't stay at the surface...go deep. Tell yourself the way the ghostpoles glint on the snow. Describe the gifts on the carts, the taste of the tea you buy. Paint it broadly, then add detail. Can you do that?"

Cistine cocked her head. "Do you really think it will help?"

"Yes. There are other things that may help, too—an anchor, something you can touch or hold to remind yourself where you are, and that you're safe. Think on what that could be."

"I will," she smiled. "Thank you again for listening."

"It's what I do best," Mira winked. "Goodnight, both of you."

Ariadne dipped her head and slipped from the room; Cistine was close on her heels, but another thought tugged her to a halt on the threshold, looking back. "Mira?"

"Hmmm?" She'd turned her gaze to the fire, but swiveled now on the sofa, paying Cistine her full attention.

"What do you think I could do about...bad feelings? Not about anything specific, just a sense I can't shake."

Mira rolled her lips inward, a thoughtful frown sketching her brow. "I always try to find the root of a feeling before I start to solve it. After all, pain from a broken bone and a broken heart come from different places, though they often hurt the same. You need to know what feeling you're facing before you know how to address it properly. You can't put a bandage on a broken heart or talk away a broken bone."

"I suppose that makes sense." Cistine tapped her fingers on the silky wooden doorframe.

Mira was silent for a moment, then added gently, "If you'd like, we can discuss this at your next visit. In the meanwhile, I'd seek the source of whatever you're feeling. We can begin there."

Relief peeled her shoulders back slightly. "I think I can manage that on my own. Thank you, Mira."

"It's my pleasure."

Cistine ducked from the room, tugging the door shut, and turned to face Ariadne who waited in the hall, watching with solemn, narrowed eyes.

"Are you all right?"

"For now, at least, and that's better than anything since Kalt Hasa." Cistine blew out a long breath. "I should go back to my room."

"Wait, *Logandir.*" Ariadne's sober tone halted her halfway down the corridor. "I want you to know my heart hurts with yours for everything Salvotor made you endure—and for how you stood fast, not only for your kingdom, but for ours. Chancellors and Tribunes might debate what Talheim would suffer for Valgard, but that is no longer a question in my mind. Its princess laid down her life for us. I will never forget that and I will never stop being grateful for it."

Tears stroked Cistine's lashes. "Well, I had a good example to follow."

They embraced in the quiet, legs licked by shadows, the moon's thin beams tumbling from windows high above; and in that dim pocket where no other eyes saw, the bond between them, always tenuous, grew another cord of understanding.

"So," Cistine sniffled when they pulled apart. "Ice skating?"

Ariadne laughed. "Go to bed. I'll see you in the morning."

She ducked from Ariadne's grip and made her way back to the bedchamber corridor alone; but for once, she didn't mind the long, lonely quiet. Her heart was lighter than it had been in some time, and the thought of sleep didn't make her so uneasy.

It wasn't until her hand touched her door that she heard the weeping.

CHAPTER FOURTEEN

ROSEBUSHES SLIT OPEN Thorne's bare arms as he plunged through the undergrowth, bleeding and gasping, every inch of him throbbing; but he didn't care about any of it. Nothing mattered except reaching her.

He burst into the open, skidding to a halt on Spruce Harbor's shore where Stornhaz's craggy skyline met the cavern walls of Kalt Hasa. Waves licked his legs, the salt burning like fire as he watched the small skiff sail away from him, carrying Cistine to her death. His father's cruel laughter rent the air.

"*No!*" Thorne's voice shattered around the shout. "Let her *go*, let her— *Cistine!*"

It was already too late. Blood pumped from her stomach around the handle of Grimmaul's knife, tears of agony streaming down her face. She screamed for him, the cracked sob breaking his heart with it; he waded in despite the hopelessness, the current towing against him, whispering cruel truths with every ebb and flow.

You'll never reach her. You'll never fix this. You will never be enough.

"Thorne."

Disbelief jerked him to a halt, treading water as he swirled around to face the woman on the shore. She gazed at him with soft, sorrowful eyes beneath a heavy-lined brow, the wind in the cavern-harbor barely stirring her silver hair. Desperate, he held her stricken stare, torn between his two greatest loves—one moving away from him, the other already gone. "Baba, *help me*! Help me save her!"

"There's nothing I can do." Baba Kallah's eyes held the familiar sadness of their last farewell. "This only ends one way. Either you stand alone, Starchaser—"

Cursing, Thorne plunged forward into the waves, kicking out for the skiff. Fear bore him forward on its own current until his fingers caught the splintered wooden edge. He hauled himself aboard, pulling Cistine into his arms, hands plunging uselessly into the tide of blood. This time it was only him, and the current spoke true.

He was not enough. He couldn't save her.

"Or you fall together." Salvotor's gleeful voice spoke above them as he stepped around the skiff's mast, dagger in hand—and brought the blade down through the top of Thorne's skull.

Agony shot from his head down through his shoulders. The breath rushed from his chest all at once. He felt his own heart stop beating.

"*Thorne!*"

He thrashed awake to hands on his shoulders, pinning him down. His father's hands. His father's *blade*—

In one deft movement he was up, slinging the dagger from under his pillow and flipping himself and his attacker, bringing his weapon sailing for their unguarded neck.

A scream broke around his Name—just like in his dream.

The knife halted mid-arc. Thorne blinked wildly, bringing to clarity the face beneath his: hickory hair spread out on his pillow, mouth agape, green eyes wide.

Horror unlocked his fingers from around the knife's grip. He hurled it into the corner of the room and shoved himself away from her, shakes plunging from his stiff shoulders all the way through his knees. "*Cistine?* Stars—*stars*, I thought you were..."

It didn't matter what he thought. He'd *attacked* her.

She propped herself up shakily among his pillows. "You were having a nightmare."

"That's no excuse, I could have *killed* you."

Bile climbed his throat. He rolled from the bed and ducked into the bathing chamber, kicking the door shut, plunging to his knees and vomiting into the chamberpot. With every heave, he saw her lying terror-struck beneath him, his knife cleaving toward her neck; and he *felt* his father's dagger cleaving into his head, bone giving way beneath it, the sudden silence in his chest when his heart stuttered to a stop.

This only ends one way.

He curled his arm across the bucket, shuddering and spitting, resting his forehead against his wrist.

Either you stand alone...or you fall together.

The door squeaked open. Featherlight footfalls padded on the stone. Then Cistine's hand slid down his back and her forehead touched his spine. "It's not your fault. I have them, too."

Her brow bumped his back five times. *You are not alone here.*

The spike of a different heat through his muscles made it difficult not to turn and ask for permission to taste those words on her lips. Instead they knelt together in the dark, neither one moving or speaking, until the last dregs of nausea faded and Thorne shifted to sit cross-legged. Cistine moved with him, hand falling from his back. "Do you want to tell me about it, or do you want a distraction?"

"I'd like to go for a walk." The one escape he never had, trapped in the apartment with his father.

"I'll go with you."

He could scarcely believe she wanted to. But she accepted the armored jacket he offered her from his closet, and they left the courthouse together.

The night was molten dark, crusted with stars and cold enough to sting despite the day's earlier warmth. They wandered aimlessly for a time, basking in the freedom forgotten in Kalt Hasa. Fresh air had never tasted sweeter, but memories still stabbed Thorne's calves, twinging in the muscles even when he stuffed his hands in his pockets and elongated his stride to escape them.

Cistine matched his pace effortlessly. "Do you want to hear about my meeting with Mira today?"

He nearly choked on relief. "Please."

She told him about her recounting of Kalt Hasa and the coping methods Mira counseled her to try. Her tone was steady, peaking only twice with nervous energy; then she slid effortlessly into explaining the festival of Darlaska—something that made her shine the way only books usually did.

"And I was thinking," she added, almost shyly, "maybe the cabal could celebrate Darlaska together. We could decorate Kanslar's wing and the garden, and exchange gifts. If that wouldn't be strange."

"Not at all," Thorne said. "It might even help prove to the Courts our kingdoms are more alike than they seem."

She grinned up at him, the easiest smile he'd seen in weeks. "Thank you."

"You don't owe me any thanks." His hand twitched, yearning to touch her, but he restrained himself. "I'm proud of you. You've taken these steps into those dark places, confronting the shadow my father casts. It's not an easy feat."

"How did *you* do it, after you came to Hellidom?"

Thorne towed a hand through his hair. "Baba Kallah and I spent hours, whole days, even, discussing what happened. What was done to us. There was a place we would go, a small cabin south of Hellidom. We would spend days talking...or not talking. I'd hit things. Break the walls. She would cry and scream. Then we would go back to the Den and be calmer for a few months until it boiled up again. So we would go back."

Cistine gaped at him. "Baba Kallah *screamed*?"

"The worst Old Valgardan obscenities." He smirked. "She taught me words I wouldn't repeat in Tatiana's presence, even."

"Teach me." Cistine's eyes sparkled. "I want a repertoire of things to call Talheimic Lords under my breath when they undermine me."

He arched a brow. "Don't you think your kingdom will have a low enough opinion of my influence over you *before* I teach you to curse like a Valgardan warrior?"

"It can be our secret."

Chuckles plumed from him, easing the tight knot in his chest. "Someday. I'll make you Baba Kallah's successor, the most prolific foul-mouth in the Three Kingdoms."

Cistine giggled, too, but sadness stamped her eyes. "How long did you and Baba Kallah keep going back to that cabin?"

Thorne squinted up at the stars. "Five years. When Aden left, I couldn't disappear anymore."

She looked down at his knuckles, still bruised after their meeting with the Chancellors. "Maybe you need to hit things again. Maybe it will help with…everything."

"I've tried. I've trained with Aden. I've trained alone. I've pummeled the walls in my room until my knuckles bled. It doesn't help. I think because it was never about the blows, it was Baba Kallah."

"Because she knew. She walked in that darkness with you so you could find the light together."

And now he felt alone, adrift like a skiff in bitter water, even with his cabal around him.

Not enough. You'll never fix this.

They traveled another block in silence before the way became familiar, a recognition that jolted Thorne from ten years of memories and misery. He hadn't come this way in so long, but if hazy recollection served…

He threw out an arm. "Wait. I want to show you something."

They hurried along the street, Thorne leading rather than meandering now, to a plain, towering building bereft of all but a few scattered windows high above. He halted outside, a relieved smile tugging up his heavy mouth. "Here we are."

"A prison?"

"The opposite." Thorne reached around Cistine's shivering frame to open the door.

With a shriek of delight, she dashed into the library full of lazy, winding staircases and open balconies on every level, brushed with moonlight through windows artfully placed to avoid fading the pages and covers of the uncountable, musty-smelling books.

Cistine bolted to the center of the tower, turning a wild circle with her hands clapped to her mouth. A joyous laugh escaped between her fingers. "This—holy gods, look at this place!" She beckoned with a roll of her hand, leading him up to the second level where sparse shelves grouped loosely around tables and couches and signs demarcated the varying sections. "How many books are here?"

"Thousands. So, roughly a week's worth of reading for you."

She jutted her tongue at him and tore books off the shelves while he lit a ghostlamp on the nearest table, spilling ultramarine light across the chairs, sofas, bookcases—and along Cistine's feet and face.

They froze, eyes meeting, memories crowding in the space between them. Thorne's mind was a chaos of dark pantries and ghostlight, the heat of Cistine's hands on his scars and her hips in his grip and how her mouth tasted when her tongue danced with his.

She swallowed audibly. "I'm going to read. Do you want a book?"

"I doubt I could retain anything right now." Thorne went to one of the fainting sofas and sprawled on it, tucking his arms behind his head. "You're welcome to read aloud if you like."

She pulled out a chair at the nearest table and opened one of the epics. Clearing her throat, she started to read: "There was once a warrior named Valstagg, who dwelled in the kingdom of Oadmark, with fifty wives and twelve hundred concubines, each of whom was..." she trailed off, and Thorne fought not to laugh. "Oh. This is a very filthy book."

The chuckles finally burst out of him. "Aden used to read that opening at his parents' supper table. Kristoff hated it. I've never seen someone so skilled at smacking a book out of another person's hands."

"Of course he was." Cistine set the volume gingerly aside, smoothing her palm over the cover. "I miss him."

"So do I." Thorne rocked his head to the side and looked at her, book shut, ghostplant sap tacky on her fingertips as she drew whorls on the tabletop.

Then she scooped up the stack of books and came to the sofa, and

Thorne drew up his legs to give her room to sit. "You sleep. I'll keep watch."

"And if I have another nightmare?"

"I'll dump the ghostplant on your head, and you can attack that instead."

Another reluctant laugh rose in his throat, then quieted when she tugged his feet into her lap and opened the book across his ankles. "What are you reading now?"

"About portends. Where they come from, what they mean."

"Portends. You mean visions of the future?"

She was quiet for a long while. Too long. Thorne fell asleep never hearing her answer.

CHAPTER FIFTEEN

GHOSTLAMPS THREW LONG shadows across the hallway outside Ariadne's room, snagging Cistine's heels with their dark fingers, but she pressed on regardless—pushing through every scrap of hesitancy. She had to...all her reading in the library the night before had proved useless.

She needed a *visnpresta*. Or three.

Pausing at the door, she balanced the tea tray on her hip and rehearsed her questions one last time before she knocked. The catch-chain slipped and the door drew open, revealing a pale, round face looking as weary as hers felt. Ariadne noted the tray, the tea, and Cistine's halfhearted smile, and sighed. "It's not even sunrise yet. Did you sleep at all after we parted ways last night?"

"No," she admitted sheepishly. "I was with Thorne at the library." They'd returned to the courthouse less than a half hour ago—Thorne to his bedchamber to prepare for the day after a short, restless sleep on the couch, Cistine to Kanslar's private kitchen for the tea, and then here.

Arms folded, Ariadne cocked her weight on the doorframe. "Is this something to do with what Mira gave you to work over?"

"No, not really. I actually have a question for all of you...it's about augmentation."

Ariadne hesitated a moment longer, fingers drumming on the door, then drew it wider and beckoned Cistine inside.

Despite the early hour, Saychelle sat at the table, arranging a bouquet of flowers, and Iri curled in the chair before the hearth, reading. Both wore battle armor in place of their airy robes from Keltei, the unexpected sight bringing Cistine to a halt, her grip turning white-knuckled around the tray.

"Safer now that the trial's begun. One never knows where danger might spring," Iri greeted her wide-eyed stare.

"As if we needed one more reason for nightmares." Saychelle snipped off a pair of rose stems too short, scowling.

"Saychelle, put the roses away," Ariadne said sharply.

She blinked, looked at Cistine's tight, rattling hands, then hurled the roses into the burning hearth and started on a bouquet of daffodils instead.

Ariadne pulled out three more chairs at the table. Iri joined them while Cistine poured the tea. "You said you had a question for us?"

"I hope it's for you," she admitted. "I don't know where else to go. Not even books have helped so far."

"Your greatest fear," Ariadne said wryly.

"We're listening," Saychelle sighed.

Cistine looked around at them, one by one, and tossed up a final silent prayer. "I've been having this...strange sense ever since we put Salvotor in chains."

"Panic?" Iri probed. "Anxious thoughts?"

"I thought it was just that at first, but I think it's something else." She dragged her lower lip between her teeth. "I have this terrible feeling something is coming. It's like all the weight of the kingdoms is coming down on me, and sometimes it reminds me of a call I've heard most of my life. From augments."

Saychelle tapped her nails lightly against her teacup. "So it's something about your nature as the Key."

"Maybe?" Cistine shrugged helplessly. "That's what I was hoping the books, or all of you, could tell me."

"Unfortunately, I'm not certain we can help," Iri admitted. "Few remain who were part of the Order when your essence was forged, and those who do aren't the same after what they endured. It's not a widely-discussed subject, you can imagine."

"Of course. But is there *anything* you can tell me?"

They were silent for several long moments. Then Saychelle tipped head and cleared her throat. "Well, the old epics do like to wax eloquent about what happens when nature shifts out of balance. Strange migrations, plagued crops, odd weather, creature attacks, that sort of thing. I wonder..." she broke off, glancing at Ariadne.

"Our armor is forged of the elements of our world. Nature braided together with power," Ariadne picked up her sister's thought effortlessly. "Perhaps *your* power is more a part of the nature of the world than we know, and you feel it shifting out of balance."

Cistine clenched her fingers around her teacup. "Meaning what? I've looked at those epics...they mentioned foresight and portends from the gods, but those were all visions. Nothing about feelings like this."

Saychelle's lips puckered. "Maybe not, but it's always described the same way, did you notice? *Nazvaldolya.* The end of all life as it's known."

Bitter dread churned in Cistine at that word. "But that's just speculation."

"Well," Iri said hesitantly, "there might be one way to know for certain. There was a prisoner we were told of, who was taken after the war against Talheim. A *visnprest* who didn't escape the Courts' judgement. He would be knowledgeable in these things, I suspect."

Cistine sat up straight. "Where can I find him?"

"I don't believe that's wise, Cistine. He'll tell you nothing without demanding a price."

She swallowed a sizzle of fear at Iri's uneasy stare. "It's my choice whether that price is worth paying."

Iri's eyes skipped to Ariadne, silently pleading. When her former student didn't speak, she huffed out a harsh breath. "If I tell you, swear you will think long and hard, and choose *wisely* what to do."

Ariadne glanced at Cistine. "We will council together before we take a single step."

Iri brushed a hand down her face, the last bout of silence bringing all three women sitting forward in anticipation.

Then she told them of a man named Vandred.

Thorne was mercifully still in his rooms when Cistine and Ariadne burst inside, a barrage of lawbooks spread between him and Aden at the dining table. One look at their faces, and he was on his feet. "What is it?"

Ariadne shut the door and leaned against it, arms folded and eyes dark as storms. "Tell him, Cistine."

She fought not to bristle at her friend's furious tone. "I need to leave."

Thorne's eyes widened a fraction. "If this is about last night..."

"I promise it's not." Cistine went to his bed and leaned against the corner post, rubbing her face with both hands. "I need to be honest with you, Thorne...I'm not just having memories of Kalt Hasa. There's this feeling like the world could cave in around us at any second, like we're always a half-step away from death or war. It's worse every time I'm in the courthouse...whenever I'm near that Door."

Aden braced one arm on the table. "It could be about the trial."

"I'm not so sure. Ari, Saychelle, and Iri agree this likely has something to do with the Key."

Frowning, Thorne propped himself on the table's edge. "How do you mean?"

Ariadne sighed. "It's possible Cistine is sensing...an imbalance in the world."

"But you aren't certain?"

"No one is, because no one's ever studied a Key before," Cistine said. "But Iri knows of someone who might be able to tell us more."

"Then we should speak to them," Aden said.

"I agree. But he's a prisoner in Detlyse Halet."

Thorne halted in the motion of straightening from the table's edge. "*What?*"

She groaned into her hands. "You don't have to tell me how reckless it sounds, but I don't know what else to do! I *have* to find out for certain what these feelings mean."

"Much as I despise the notion, she is right," Ariadne grumbled. "The voices of the gods are never to be ignored. This could be a gift...a warning beacon."

"This man you seek in Detlyse Halet," Aden said slowly, "I take it he's from the former *visnprest* Order?"

Cistine nodded. "Iri says he was captured fleeing Nygaten Temple after the war. He's the only one who might help, for a price."

Thorne crossed his arms and looked at Ariadne. "You support this?"

"I support Cistine making her own choices based on what she thinks is right. Do I like it? Stars, no. But the Key's problems are unique. To answer these questions may require equally unique methods."

Thorne sank his chin to his chest, staring at the floor, and Cistine's pulse hammered in her wrists. She didn't know what she would do if he begged her to stay away from that place where she already didn't want to travel, answers be damned. But when he dragged his gaze back to hers, it was bleak with resignation. "If this is what you think is best, then you have my support."

Ariadne's breath rushed out. "Then I'm going to pray."

She stepped out and slammed the door behind her.

Cistine hugged her middle. "Will you come with me, Thorne?"

He came to stand before her, and she held her ground against errant memories when he rested his hands lightly on her arms. "I want to, but I can't. There's too much to do here, and Ariadne's testimony is tomorrow. I can't be absent for that." He raised his gaze briefly to the roof, then looked over his shoulder. "Aden."

He stiffened. "You'd entrust me with this?"

"*I* would, if Cistine will have you."

Relief gushed through her. "You're sure you can spare him?"

"It won't just be sparing. Aden needs chances to prove his mettle as the sort of Tribune he could one day be."

Cistine gaped between them. "*Tribune?*"

Thorne shrugged. "He's schooled in it. He was in the line of succession before..." Thorne broke off, rubbing the back of his neck, and Aden studied the tabletop. "Besides, I don't trust the other Tribunes. Only Sander's proven he holds Kanslar's interests over his own. Marcel in particular has made it clear to anyone who will listen that he maintains my father's innocence, and I doubt it's an act...he was always cunning and ambitious."

"Not to mention he's testifying as a character witness for Salvotor," Aden muttered under his breath.

"There's also that," Thorne said wryly. "I intend to remove him from his position as soon as possible, but I want someone prepared to take his place when I do. My hope is it will be Aden."

Cistine smiled around Thorne at his cousin. "Well, I'd be honored to have a future Tribune escort me."

Aden rose, stretching a kink from his back. "I'd best prepare, then."

He slipped out quickly, shutting the door—giving them the privacy Cistine both feared and craved. Thorne braced a hand on the bedpost above her head and looked so deeply into her eyes, her knees nearly buckled. "Swear to me you'll go safely and come home swiftly, *Logandir*."

The anguish of uncertainty in his voice made her stomach weightless. "I will, Thorne. I give you my word."

CHAPTER SIXTEEN

ASHE KNEW IT was time the instant Maleck shook her awake from strange dreams of wind and the clouds, the feeling of flying leaving her body weightless in the sheets. When her eyes opened to his scarred face looming above her, blotting out the modest light from the west-facing window, she said it with him: "Jad is here."

She had never risen so quickly in her life, stripping off her thick muslin pajamas on her way to the dressing screen in the corner, wearing nothing but the starstone now. "Throw me my armor, Mal." Valgardan battle threads soared over the screen and clattered on the floor at her feet. She poked her head out to glare at him. "Really?"

He stood with his back to her in a sea of her discarded pajamas. She didn't have to see his face to know he'd gone scarlet. Rolling her eyes, she yanked on the threads Disa gave her in Cerne Mosiar; she supposed it was the better choice, another confirmation of the alliance between their kingdoms, though she'd elicit the most hateful glares imaginable from the likes of Rion and Viktor—maybe even Cyril as well.

But what did it matter? How much further could she really fall?

"I'm decent." She stepped around the screen, tying her hair under the armored cloth he gave her with her old blade, Echelon. "Are you ready?"

Maleck nodded, offering his fist. "It's time to win safety for our kingdoms, Asheila."

Smiling grimly, she bumped knuckles with him.

Rozalie waited for them in the arched stairwell outside the west wing where she and Maleck met Ashe before breakfast every day. There was something gratifying in the thawed ease with which they exchanged nods and fell in behind her now, flanking her down the steps.

"The King is already in the meeting chamber with Dorminger," Rozalie said. "Lord Rion's gone to the pike wall to escort Jad."

Ashe cast her a look. "Is this your first time seeing the Mad King?"

"Rion swept me up to go north on his way through Astoria. It's my first time in...this." Her waving hand indicated the thunder of hushed voices, the humid stamp of dread on the air, the darting gazes from Wardens and servants moving like dancing shadows through the halls.

Ashe cuffed Rozalie's shoulder. "Mine, too." She'd been a child when Prince Cyril and Rion rushed into Mahasar to rescue their loves against King Ivan's strict orders, and the stories had intoxicated her battle-hungry mind. Less than a year later, she ran to Valgard on the Wardens' heels to fight for a kingdom that now no longer wanted her. Heaving shut the hungry gape of that wound, she added in a whisper, "Any luck at the pond?"

Rozalie shook her head. "I've questioned everyone we saw there that day. No one else noticed anything."

The more time passed, the more that incident felt like paranoia cast in Jad's long shadow. In any case, it was a problem for tomorrow.

Ashe led her friends through the bleak estate to the lower-level meeting rooms, the broad, dark hall lit by flickering torches—a small concession for Mahasari comfort. Ashe despised the dim amber glow against the dark stone walls, reminiscent of Siralek's catacombs with trouble always lurking nearby.

They'd crossed barely half the corridor when Viktor strutted through the plain wooden door at the end to meet them, eyes flicking between Ashe and Maleck, then settling on Rozalie. His lip twitched in the beginnings of a curl, but he reined himself at the last instant. "This is how things go: we wait outside and receive Jad, his Enforcers, and the Commander. We follow them into the chamber. We take our seats—him and his people on one curve, us on the other. Rat-rompers on the King's left, Lord Rion on his right."

There was the jab Ashe waited for. "And where does Rion's second sit? On *his* right in case his boots need licking?"

Viktor arched a brow. "You used to have better insults. Anyway, once the pleasantries are exchanged, we discuss the so-called *treaty*."

Ashe drew so near, she could smell the morning on his breath and see her irate face reflected in his hooded gaze. "If you do anything to jeopardize this, I'll teach you everything you ever wanted to know about the Blood Hive. Slowly and *painfully*."

Viktor snorted. "I wonder what the King would say, hearing how little unity means to you." He snapped around on heel and barked at the milling Wardens to line both sides of the hall—Ashe and Maleck on one, Rozalie on the other, guided by a snap of Viktor's fingers like calling a dog to heel.

Ashe cracked her knuckles, and Maleck grazed her side. "Calm."

"How?" she hissed. "How in God's name can I be calm around them?" One shrug, and his whole face wiped clean of emotion. She blinked. "You almost make it look easy."

"Chasing their approval leads to nothing, as a wise woman once taught me." He held her stare while the last Wardens clattered into place down the line. "We answer to the True God for what we are, and no one else."

The door at the far end of the corridor yawned open to punctuate his words, weak light spilling down the dark stone. Rion's harsh voice guttered the torches along both walls. "Make way for the King of the South."

At the familiar one-note whistle from Viktor, Ashe dropped to a knee, arm across her chest, genuflecting to the man who would happily dance over her peoples' bones if he had his way. Teeth grinding, she listened to the march of Mahasaris moving down the hall—formation flawless, steps locked together so it sounded like just one large man stormed down the corridor.

She stiffened when the first pairs of boots passed before her—broad-heeled with an ornate, angled toe.

Her gaze snapped up and met King Jad's.

If she hadn't known him for what he was, he would never have turned her head. A plain man, curly-haired, mustached and bearded, dressed in plated armor over russet skin. It was the eyes that betrayed him, bottling madness like an augment flagon—too glassy, too wide, too dark, and fixed on her face as he passed.

The hair on Ashe's arms quivered and time slowed to a trickle, holding her captive to the pitiless energy in his stare. Then he turned slowly to face ahead, and Ashe dropped her chin, watching every pair of angle-toed boots tromp past in linked cadence. Two by two, the Wardens fell in behind them, entering the meeting chamber. When Ashe rose, catching Rozalie's eye straight across, her friend nodded grimly.

Maleck slanted to walk beside Ashe and Rozalie. "What's the matter?"

"One of the Enforcers was in the city recently. Rozalie and I spotted him near the pond shore."

"The shoes," Rozalie murmured "They're the same."

Maleck's jaw clenched. "Then they have a way in and out besides the pike gate."

Tomorrow's problem had become one for today.

The meeting chamber owed its light to more candles and torches, and hearths crackling on opposite walls. Ashe scowled when Maleck held out her chair, but slid into it all the same. Once the creak and scrape of moving seats quieted, Cyril sat forward, hands folded. "Welcome back, King Jad."

"Thank you, thank you, yes. I feel welcomed." A vein of cruelty tinged Jad's high, harsh voice. "Though your weather leaves something to be desired."

Cyril's jaw ticked, and he scribbled down a note on the parchment before him. Ashe peeked over his shoulder to read the tiny, cramped script in the royal cipher: *I'll see about changing the weather, Your Eminence. Why bother conquering a kingdom whose climes would drive you straight back to yours?* "I regret our rains postponed this meeting. I've deeply anticipated hearing your response to our latest proposal."

"Of course you have! Who wouldn't? I see your loyal watchdog has returned. I trust all is *well*, yes, after he fled so suddenly?"

Cyril raised his eyes from the parchment, jaw settling. "Your concern is appreciated. All is well. So, you've considered our terms?"

"Yes, the offer, of course. Fifteen miles of land surrendered along the border." Jad drummed his long, unpared fingernails on the table, a demented clicking like spider legs. "I think not."

Ashe grimaced, but Cyril showed no flicker of surprise. "Isn't that what you wanted?"

"It was, it was. But as I lay ill and shivering on my pillows these past few days, I thought of something *else* I'd like, oh yes, something much more profitable than a few leagues of land." His gaze danced with wild amusement. "These are *my* terms: give me your daughter's hand in union, and I'll withdraw the men from our border."

For the longest heartbeats of Ashe's life, no one moved or spoke, half a table's worth of Talheimics and a lone Valgardan warrior linked in their horror and fury while they stared down the grinning King of Mahasar.

Then Cyril said, slowly, "Peace and unity through marriage."

"It is the way of kings from olden times, yes? Are your princes and princesses not for ransom as ours are?"

"You speak of ransom lightly. You have no children."

"And you no princes." A deft, cold blow that landed true with a flash of pain in Cyril's eyes for the memory of his stillborn sons. "So the girl will have to do. These are my terms: Princess Cistine's hand in marriage, and I will withdraw from the border. After *all*, how could I *ever* bear to strike my beloved's kingdom? We will be family, Cyril." A sleek, simpering smile. "If you send for her now, I'll withdraw all but my most trusted Enforcers this very day as a show of good faith, you understand?"

This was what he'd been waiting for, this loathsome bastard, this absolute gods-damned *snake*. This was the real demand he wore them down for. Ashe's body begged to lunge across the table and wrap her hands around his throat.

Slowly, deeply, Cyril breathed, gathering his composure. Then, more dangerous than the glint of any blade unsheathed, he smiled. "I'm afraid I can't send for my daughter. She's in the North, enjoying the spoils of

Talheim's newly-forged alliance with the Kingdom of Valgard."

Absolute, deadly stillness swallowed the room. The fires trembled in every bracket and hearth. Jad's armor creaked as he shifted, hand curling into a fist. "I misheard you."

"You did not." Now Cyril was truly grinning.

"Talheim and Valgard are sworn foes from long-ago times."

"Times change. In fact, you'll notice one of Valgard's warriors is a member of my trusted council, speaking on behalf of his kingdom here. Maleck?"

He revolved his burning stare to Jad. "Talheim's King speaks true. Princess Cistine Novacek of Talheim is a friend to Valgard, strong and loyal. She proved her good will during a summer learning our customs. Our Chancellors signed a treaty of friendship with her at autumn's end."

"Talheim confirms. I was there at its signing." The lies Ashe and Maleck rehearsed morning, afternoon, and night rolled easily from her tongue. "It's a treaty of trade and commerce with one small, crucial detail."

She cast Maleck a wicked smile, and his lips tugged up in response. "That, should either of our kingdoms face the threat of war, the other would come to its aid."

Jad paled, perhaps recalling the same stories Ashe heard as a girl: the fearsome warriors of the North, capable of breaking a man's spine in one hand or twisting a fighter's head clean off his shoulders. An entire kingdom of death-gods, all but a few trained from childhood, wielding the power of the world's elements in one hand and blades of unbreakable steel in the other. They'd only been defeated once: by the kingdom with whom they'd apparently united. War against Talheim was one matter, war against Valgard another; but to incite conflict with both, when they had each other's survival at heart...even the Mad King was not mad enough for that.

"Proof," Jad said. "I would see this treaty for myself."

Maleck reached into his pocket. "The first document remains in the vaults of the courthouse in Stornhaz, the second in Astoria's treasury. But you may have this." He drew the forgery Cistine wrote before he and Ashe departed Stornhaz, which she and Thorne signed and on which Aden,

Maleck, Quill, and Morten forged the signatures of the other Chancellors—and on which Cyril himself placed his signet. He sent it rolling down the table into Jad's flexing hands. "I assure you, it replicates the original to the last letter."

Pride flared in Ashe. Maleck didn't speak like a man scarred by cruelty and war, like an outcast who lived in the wilderness for a decade, bearing the suspicion and resentment of his people; he sounded like an emissary made for gilded halls, equal to a king. Even knowing the deception they spun together, Ashe could almost believe him and that forgery, that the alliance they spoke of would one day be true.

Jad's marble-bright eyes danced across the page. "This...changes matters."

"Yes, I thought it might." Cyril clasped his hands on the table and sat forward again. "Here are *my* terms, Jad, and you may think on them as long as you like: there isn't going to be a war. I am not giving you a scrap of my forefathers' land, a single zalto, or my daughter's hand in marriage, gods forbid. She's too much woman for you to handle anyway. So, this is what I offer instead." He voice dipped. "Mercy."

"*Mercy?*"

"Yes. Mercy that I won't pay you back a blade to the chest for suggesting I give my daughter to you after you once stole my wife from me. Mercy that I'll allow you and your men to march from Camere all the way to the border with a minimal escort, as my own show of *good faith*. And mercy that I will consider signing a treaty like this one with *you* once my anger's cooled."

Gripping the treaty in a tight hand, Jad flicked wild glances from Cyril to Ashe and Maleck and down to the paper. "How do I know this man at your table is even Valgardan?"

Maleck settled, a deep, shuddering breath lifting through him. Then he rose, stripped open his armored shirt, and laid bare the twisted scar across his chest.

Swears went up all around the table, not just from the Enforcers. Rion's gaze blackened with hate. Viktor spat on the floor. Rozalie's hand flew to her mouth. And Jad blanched utterly, jaw slack at the proof of every story about those godlike augments and the damage they could do.

"You will not find any Talheimic wearing these scars," Maleck said with vicious quiet. "These are the markings of an Azkai acolyte, a child forced into slavery to the Valgardan temples. More than twenty years ago, I earned this scar, and this one," he traced his smallest finger over the notch cleaving his brow and below his eye, "in the war against the Middle Kingdom."

"And yet you profess to ally with them?" Jad breathed. "Valgard, the kingdom with no king, entreated to the Middle Kingdom with butchers for royalty?"

Rion started to rise, but when Maleck dropped his hands to the table, the whole room stilled. "It's true, Valgard has no king. But Cistine Novacek is my queen, and we *will* fight for her name." He let the silence hang for several heartbeats, then took his seat again. "Decide now if your grudge is worth the Nimmus you will face if you cross that line."

Under the table, Ashe pressed her knee to his. She knew what that simple gesture cost him; he'd trembled merely to show her that scar in the Calaluns. But for Cistine, for her kingdom, he laid it all bare.

At long last, Jad said, "I will return to Camere and dwell on your proposal."

"You do that." Cyril gave the other king the courtesy of being first to rise and first to leave the room. In his absence, the Talheimics gazed in silent awe at one another.

Rion, predictably, was the one to break it. "Too easy."

"I agree," Ashe admitted, ignoring her former Commander's vaulted brow. "He's regrouping."

"We do hold a small advantage," Maleck said. "The burden of proof lies with him. He could assume I am lying, that I am not Valgardan, or that the treaty is not real. But does he dare risk war against two kingdoms on guesswork?"

"Maleck is right," Cyril said, and Ashe shook her head at the sheer strangeness of hearing him speak those words. "Jad's greatest struggle has always been to convince his people to fund and fight in a war. Mahasar is a spread-apart kingdom, its cities mostly self-governed by their magnates. If I lacked diplomacy, I'd tell Jad his title is just decoration."

"That's why he hasn't attacked us outright," Rion agreed. "He needs us to make the first move, incite the battle in a way he can twist for Mahasar's pride and drum up support. Otherwise he won't have an army large enough to defeat us."

Maleck cocked his head. "It will be more difficult than ever to convince his people if they are to face not one opposing army, but two."

Cyril flicked him the smallest smile. "Precisely. And the more he manipulates and schemes, the more tenuous his hold becomes. Mahasar is a wilder kingdom than either of ours. If Jad pushes too hard, his people will push *him* out rather than go to war for his ambitions."

"But we can't underestimate that madness, either," Rion growled. "There's no way of telling which idly-spoken thought could give Jad his leverage for an army large enough to break down our border."

"It will not come to that," Maleck assured them. "Not with the might of Valgard at your backs."

But that might was not guaranteed them—not yet. Ashe and Maleck had to maintain the ruse until Jad tucked his tail and fled.

Nerves humming, she stood; the others followed, Lord Dorminger looking between Ashe and Maleck with a new glint of respect in his eyes, Rozalie squeezing Ashe's shoulder on her way to speak with Rion, who stared Ashe and Maleck down with such a look of knowing as if he could see every thread that bound them all the way from that first snowy night on the tundra to the cliff in the Calaluns.

Ears pulsing, Ashe stepped away from the table. Maleck took her elbow swiftly but gently, eyes full of warmth. "Well done today, Asheila."

God help how her traitorous heart leaped at those words, even with half the attention in the room on them.

Ashe cursed herself aloud when she slipped into the dim hall. She shouldn't be swayed by casual touches and pretty eyes while her standing in Talheim was so fragile. Rion and Viktor would spin it a thousand ways, and what future would she have when the woman of stone and steel became nothing more than the sugary, soft creature her parents dreamed of, melting away under someone's touch?

What future do you have now, woman of stone and steel?

Scowling at the vicious thought, Ashe swung around the corner into the next hall and walked straight into King Jad.

His hands locked around her throat without a moment's warning, spinning and slamming her against the wall so hard the wind spewed from her lips.

"This alliance is a *sham*." His spittle flecked her face, wet breath souring what little air Ashe could bring in with heaving, stunned lungs. "I do not know its purpose or how you *managed* this ruse, but I will find the truth, oh yes, I'm going to find out, you miserable little Talheimic *hasac*, and when I do, I assure you I will break it in pieces." His fingers contracted, shooting fresh pain into her wheezing chest. "Then I shall ride roughshod over every last inch of your precious, pedantic *kingdom* until its oldest woman and smallest child *beg* for—"

"*Jad!*"

That voice was like a thunderclap hurtling off the walls, and Jad flinched, peeling his fingers from Ashe's throat. Her knees buckled and she sagged, sucking in breath while Maleck stepped between her and the Mad King, grazing his hands over the hilts of Starfall and Stormfury strapped to his shoulders.

"*Walk away.*" Maleck's fury made everything plain: if Jad didn't leave this corridor now, he would never leave at all.

His gaze flicked from Ashe to Maleck, lingering over the hidden scar on his chest. "Mark my words, I will find you out, little worm." With a snap of his dark cloak, he vanished down the hall.

Maleck turned to Ashe, hands gentle on her neck. "Let me see."

"I'm *fine*," she rasped, avoiding his gaze. "He startled me is all. I can handle him."

Distress lined Maleck's eyes. "He was lying in wait for you."

"I don't care what he was doing, I don't need you leaping to my defense! I'm not your damsel to save."

"If it's only damsels that ever need saving, I suppose I'm greatest among them." His thumb brushed every tender spot Jad squeezed, and Ashe hoped it was his pitiful attempt at joking and not his cold, soothing touch that freed the groan from her battered throat. "It is never weakness to be helped by those who care for you."

Boots stamped stone, and Cyril jogged into view with Rion behind him, sliding to a halt at the sight of them: Ashe leaning against the wall, Maleck's hands on her neck, bruises blooming already under her skin. The King eyes widened. "We heard shouting. What happened?"

Face hot with humiliation, Ashe snapped free of Maleck's grip. "*Nothing.* Just a friendly conversation."

She walked away from her King, her friend, and her former Commander, all their gazes blazing on her back; all drawing different conclusions of how helpless Asheila Kovar had become.

CHAPTER SEVENTEEN

Aden's wind augment carried them to the Isetfell foothills in far east Kroaken—half the flagon spent for the journey out, the other half to return. Cistine didn't mind walking the rest of the way into the deep twists of stone at first, relishing the blue sky above, another warm break in the early-winter chill; but the further they went, the sick feeling churned up in her stomach again to match the damp, mildewed fog creeping between gnarls of rock.

They were so close to learning what all this uneasiness meant, but the nearer they came to those answers, the sicker she felt. She lengthened her stride to keep pace with Aden, studying his face to give herself a distraction. "Thank you for coming with me. I know we're not really friends yet, but I'm grateful anyway."

Aden kept his gaze ahead. "Thorne was right...I need these opportunities if he's ever going to consider me for Tribune. Besides, Mira believes facing obstacles encourages recovery."

"Is your recovery part of becoming a Tribune, too?"

He nodded. "There are a thousand men better suited for the position, but I'm at least the better choice over Marcel. If I can hold the line long enough for Thorne to find a truly fitting Tribune, then all this will be worth it. Even Mira's prodding questions."

"For what it's worth, *I* think you'll make a good Tribune." She offered a tentative smile, and he matched it. "Can I ask what you discuss with her?"

"Things that aren't meant for your ears. For anyone's, in fact, which is why we don't meet in the courthouse. Sander's other lovers always seem to be around her there."

"They do, don't they?" Cistine fingered the dagger strapped at her waist. "What do you think of him having twenty-seven lovers?"

Aden studied her for a long moment. "I think he must be masterful at doling out his time, since none of them ever appear jealous of each other."

So, he'd noticed, too. Tucking that observation away, Cistine changed the subject. "Where do you and Mira go?"

"You'll have to wait until this Darlaska Thorne mentioned to find out." She blinked. "He told you about that?"

"The moment I joined him in his rooms after you two spent the night in the library. He was more than enthusiastic about the notion."

Heat floated across her cheeks. "He's so good to me, sometimes I feel like I don't deserve it."

"Because of how you feel when you look at him?" When her gaze darted up, he added, "I can see it in your eyes."

She huffed with frustration. "I'm tired of seeing Salvotor when I look at him. I don't want to pull back anymore."

Aden was quiet through several minutes of winding, rocky terrain, toying with the pendant at his throat. "Has Mira taught you about anchors?"

"A bit. You?"

"Briefly. Have you found one?"

Her fingers drifted to the betrothal ring tucked in the front of her armor, then fell away. "Not yet."

Aden halted. With one swift snap, he broke the cord of his compass-pendant and held it out to her.

Sucking in a breath, she shook her head. "I can't take that! Kristoff gave it to *you*."

"Which makes it mine to give away." His gray eyes were solemn. "I'll never fully know what you both suffered in that place, but you needed one another then. Maybe you still do."

"But—"

"I may not be my father's son in any ways that matter, but in this, we're one." He gripped her wrist, sprang her fingers apart with a press of his thumb, and coiled the cord in her palm. "Take it. Make it your anchor. And remember my father was willing to die for you and Thorne, for the world you'd make together. Never squander that."

Though protest lingered on her lips, she knotted the cord around her neck, still warm from Aden's skin. "Thank you."

"You're welcome." He offered a last half-smile, turned up the path, then cast out his arm with a low curse.

Ahead, the mist cleared, revealing the end of the pass—a high stone wall with a round slab in its face, etched in Old Valgardan runes.

Detlyse Halet.

Palms clammy at the sight of this mountain prison, Cistine followed Aden to the door. He drew a flagon from his satchel, wafting a citrus-and-spice sensation of growing things across Cistine's senses; then he smashed it against the runes, and the earth augment broke the door down into a crumbled heap, laying open a path paved with shadows straight into the mountain. Aden stepped over the rubble and glanced back at her, ghostly green light dancing from his armor threads. She pressed her thumb to compass's worn ridge and entered the Lightless Pit behind him.

Harsh white ghostlight flared ahead and a gaunt, pallid man hurried toward them, colorless hair swaying around his waist and a blade in his free hand. "Who goes there?"

"Warriors of Kanslar Court," Aden said. "On a mission from the Chancellor. We've come to see your roster."

"You have proof?"

He drew a scroll from his pocket and tossed it underhand to the old man, who caught it effortlessly around his sword's hilt. "Sealed and signed by Chancellor Thorne himself."

"Thorne? I thought Thrand was Kanslar's Chancellor."

"Not for decades. His son, Salvotor, was just deposed for a trial."

"Strange times, strange times." With a jerk of his head, the old man led them into a small, rounded chamber. Cistine clutched Kristoff's pendant harder while the overseer situated himself behind his desk and peeled through a stack of papers there. "Why have you come?"

"Court business." Aden picked up another ghostlamp from a haphazard stack on a table near the door, examining the plant inside.

"I see. Who is it you seek?"

Cistine cleared her throat and finally forced a word in. "Vandred."

His piercing eyes lifted slowly to her face. "Vandred has not had visitors in nearly twenty years."

"Well, now he has two." Aden's tone closed the subject.

The overseer drew a sheaf from the mound of papers and held it out to Cistine. "Fifth level. Here is the map to his chamber, and here is the key." He selected it from the ring on his desk and pressed it into her hand. "Be careful not to provoke him. We've not had guards here since a small incident a decade ago. Whatever becomes of you, becomes."

"We appreciate the warning," Aden said flatly, and led the way back into the mountain's shadowy paths.

Cold sweat gathered in the dip of Cistine's back and the pits of her arms. The clean, cold scent of bare rock was too familiar, scraping her throat with every breath. Valgard's love for sealing its most valuable prisoners inside mountains would be her undoing.

They spun down level by level, Aden's breathing as hoarse as hers, the weak ghostlight striping his face with lines of dread.

"Are you scared?" Cistine whispered, afraid to coax an echo from the stone walls.

His hand rattled, setting the ghostlight swaying, "Something like that."

A distant moan turned to a high-pitched scream. Cistine flinched, bumping into Aden, and his hand wrapped around her arm by instinct, pulling her behind him. Even after the sound faded, they didn't move.

"That could've been Quill a decade ago." Aden's voice was as shallow as his breathing. "I sent him here. I sent them all to Nimmus."

Cistine tugged away, looking up at him. "You didn't mean to. You were just trying to save your father. I know what that's like." A flicker of Julian's face swirled through her mind like mist, and she closed her eyes. "Some people will do anything for their parents."

"But in the end, I never had him back. I betrayed them for nothing." His back hit the wall, and when Cistine opened her eyes, she found him rubbing his thumb over the deep creases in his brow.

She touched his arm. "You didn't have to come. I could've found someone else."

"Not one of the cabal." He shook his head. "Besides, self-sacrificial stupidity runs in my blood."

"On your father's side?"

He chuckled sharply, pushing upright and offering his arm. "The sooner we're through with this, the sooner we can leave."

It felt safer when her hand was tucked in the crook of his elbow, but she could still barely keep from running when they reached the fifth level with a single door set deep in the black stone.

The moment the way evened out, she heard singing.

Every hair on her arms and nape stood at attention. That rotten, festering feeling returned, rattling her hand while she jammed the key into the lock. When it gave, Aden gripped her shoulder and half-turned her to meet his eyes. "You're *certain* you want to do this?"

"Yes." Though her trembling voice betrayed her. "I need answers, and only he can give them to me."

There was nothing of note inside the cell, not even any light before Aden brought theirs inside and Cistine shut the door swiftly at their backs. But the prisoner made no move to sprint toward escape; he rocked on a bedlike stone shelf across the cramped, narrow cell, bent knees nearly brushing his ears. His singing was a cold rasp, Old Valgardan syllables crooning in the semidark.

"You're Vandred, aren't you?" He stilled at Cistine's question. "A former *visnprest* of Azkai Temple."

Vandred raised his head slowly, ashen hair cascading around sunken cheeks and blind eyes the color of spoiled cream. "Well, well...what are *you*?"

What. Not who. Cistine swallowed a jab of fear. "I want to know about the Keys you made."

"And you suppose this information will come for free?" His smile bared cracked teeth. "If I tell you what I know, you must tell me what you *are*."

"That's fair." No different from lying to Salvotor to save Thorne's life.

"Marvelous." Vandred slid from the shelf and spidered toward her. "What do you wish to know about the *Keys*?"

She stepped back from him, keeping some distance. "Do they possess...precognition?"

"Possibly. But is precognition not merely instinct? Isn't that what raised the hairs on your body just now?" He paused, cocking his head. "Tell me what you feel in the darkness."

Cistine crouched slowly, drawn like a lure down to his level. "Something is coming. I don't know what it is, but I can feel it. It's everywhere, when I'm awake, when I'm asleep. But I don't know if I can trust that feeling...if it's real."

"An ill-begotten instinct is as only as real as the moment that begat it."

Cistine stilled, remembering the instant she stepped onto the Door under the courthouse, the impacting ringing through her body, her bones, her very essence.

What if it hadn't just rung through her? What if she'd woken something at the brush of her boot against that lid, at the joining, however brief, of Key and lock and Door?

A single word jolted inside her like lightning: *Nazvaldolya.*

Her breaths rattled from her chest. "How do I stop it?"

"Who says you can? This only ends one way."

The entire room shivered into sharp relief as if time itself slowed, his words the echo of her corrupted Dreamwater vision. "*No—*"

"It is time for you to answer my question." Vandred's lips peeled back from his teeth in a ghastly leer. "What *are* you?"

Cistine lurched to her feet and spun toward the door. "Just a *visnpresta* acolyte who's curious about the former Order."

"No. *You* are a Key."

Hand on the door, she stilled.

Aden knocked her arm away, yanking the door open while she spun back to face Vandred. The former *visnprest* unbent to his full height, rounded shoulders and bent neck grazing the roof seven feet above. "I was there when your bloodline joined to the Doors. I know precisely why you ask these things. So tell me, what do you sense now, Key?"

They were already out in the hall, door clanging shut behind them, when she realized what he meant. "Aden, stop! Can you feel that?"

The creeping sickness intensified; terror and illness braided together in her chest.

Danger wasn't just coming. It was *here*.

His grip tightened on her arm. "We're leaving. *Now*."

They dashed through the corridors and up the stairwells, Vandred's parting laughter muffled by the shrieking toll of panic in Cistine's head. Aden thrust her ahead of him over the door's rubble, shouting a warning to the old man inside as he whirled back to rebuild the stone barricade with what remained of the earth augment. Cistine backed away, sloughing the cold and the feeling of the stone prison from her arms, but it did nothing to quiet her terror.

Come, the breeze sighed. *Come and see.*

She fell on her heels, catching Aden's gaze when he turned from the door. Something in her face made him blanch.

COME AND SEE!

Icy darkness spilled through her like plunging under fathomless waters as the wind roared down the pass, shattering Detlyse Halet's door again. Aden's hand snagged hers, yanking her in a pivot, and they fled for their lives.

Dusklike gloom and hurricane winds ripped past them and tears whipped from Cistine's eyes, her vision glowing white-green where lightning flashed and thunder wailed. Illness spilled into the pass like black tidewaters, soaking her body with fear, tugging her hand against Aden's.

"*Hold on to me!*" He yanked her up beside him and struck the pass on his knees, shielding her between him and the stone wall as all the thunder piled on top of itself in a single, world-ending roar.

This was death, this was breaking, this was *Nazvaldolya*—

Then the wind banked abruptly, screamed down the pass like a flame sucked behind a shut door—and vanished, taking the sickening feeling with it. Cistine's ears rang in the sudden silence, and when Aden leaned back, she peeled her face from the stone to look wildly around them.

The hardy shrubs shivered still; above, the sky was blue again.

"Are you hurt?" Aden panted.

She gulped air and ran a hand over her cheek, rashed from the stone. "Not badly. What was that?"

"Nothing I've ever felt before." Aden struggled up and offered his hand again. "We're going back to the courthouse."

"But...the old man, the prison..."

"Look at me," Aden growled, and she stopped blinking past him down the pass, meeting the storm in his eyes. "This is not for us to do. We'll report to the Chancellors and have them send the Vassora."

Cistine didn't argue again as he broke what remained of the wind flagon. Her courage felt thin as a sheer gown too narrow to wrap around her shaking, petrified body; she didn't want to spend another moment in this pass, with its mountain prison and that cackling, seven-foot abomination and whatever evil still trickled down its walls, whispering after them.

Come back. Come and see.

CHAPTER EIGHTEEN

Pride STIRRED THORNE'S blood, warmer than the midday sun pouring through the courtroom windows, when the time came at last for Ariadne to take her seat in the testimony chair across from Salvotor.

They'd spent all night preparing for this, and watched the sunrise that morning in quiet companionship and unspoken prayers. He trusted his strategist was as prepared as possible, the words readied on her knife-sharp tongue, her spine steeled and straight. All that was left now was to let the truth pour out.

Tribune Eskil planted himself firmly between Ariadne's seat and Salvotor's table. "For the benefit of the Court, will you restate your name and place in the proceedings?"

"My name is Ariadne," she said. "I was the victim of the attack for which Chancellor Salvotor stands accused."

"In your own words, would you describe the night of the event?"

She fixed her eyes on some indistinct point beyond the cabal, all clustered at the railing. "Ten years ago, I was nearing the end of my acolyte training. The night Kanslar's constellation rose, I was summoned to Chancellor Salvotor's apartment."

"And what did you encounter there?"

"The Chancellor was lying in wait for me—"

"Objection," Salvotor cut in. "That is a leading phrase."

"I'll allow it," Bravis said. "It's her assessment. When you're telling *your* side of the story, you can choose to use less-leading language."

Thorne gritted his teeth. Salvotor was no fool; he knew Bravis wouldn't correct Ariadne. It was a well-timed interruption to break the momentum of her account.

"The Chancellor was lying in wait for me," Ariadne repeated, much more quietly. "He entrapped and defiled me. When I struggled, he struck me on the head until I was too dazed to escape."

Beside Thorne, Tatiana gripped the railing in both hands and rocked her weight against it, lips cutting back from her teeth in a vicious scowl. On his other side, Quill's knuckles pressed to his mouth—likely the only thing holding a curse inside his clenched jaw. Thorne's own stomach swooped with rage and shame.

He'd left the apartment minutes at best before that vicious attack. What if he'd just stayed just a little longer? What if he'd been there to step between them?

"Afterward," Ariadne went on, "he dragged me through the streets still unclothed and bleeding, and nailed me by my hands to the door of my friend's home. He left me there as a warning to—"

"Objection," Salvotor interrupted. "Conjecture."

Bravis nodded to Ariadne. "Let's not speculate on intention."

"What was the result of this action?" Eskil asked.

"It disqualified me from the Order," Ariadne said. "All carnal relations, consensual or not, are forbidden."

"To the best of your knowledge, is that detail well-known outside the Order? Would the accused have known his actions would result in your disqualification?"

"I would hope he knew, seeing as he is a Chancellor and there is a law about this."

Eskil's lips twitched. "I have no further questions."

Salvotor dominated the ensuing silence gleefully, arranging and consulting his notes. Thorne's body sloped with hate, his fist aching around the smooth railing while his father rounded the table to stand before Ariadne. "When you came to my family's apartment on the night in question, what did you expect would happen?"

"That I would be given my dispatch to one of the temples."

"Is it common for a *visnpresta* to receive her dispatch in a personal meeting with a Chancellor?"

Ariadne was too still for too long. "No," she said at last.

"What is the *common* practice for dispatches?"

"The Chancellor addresses the acolytes and gives them each a scroll with their assignment."

"Then for you to expect some sort of preferential treatment that night went against the very fabric of your Order's oldest institution. I would hope you knew this, seeing as you were an acolyte and there was a certain way of doing things." He inclined slightly. "Or are you not being truthful about the circumstances of your visit that night?"

"I stand by my testimony."

"As would I, if I sat in your seat. What a flawless victim you make: cruelly lured to my apartment, mercilessly attacked, stripped of your future." The courtroom, perfectly baited, held its breath when Salvotor paused. "Of course, there is another possibility. Perhaps you came to my apartment seeking an assignment of your own choice, to the temple *you* selected. And perhaps you offered *yourself* as incentive for this favoritism...a secret kept between a young *visnpresta* and her Chancellor."

A sliver from the fence bit into Thorne's palm. His teeth locked together so tightly his jaw ached.

"And then, perhaps, when I refused you, because I *wouldn't* compromise that most sacred of all laws, you sought to take vengeance through false accusations of defilement."

Ariadne slammed her hands down on the armrests and shot up from her seat. "That was *not* how it happened, and you know it."

Salvotor raised a brow. "All I know is I never laid hands on you."

"You defiled me and nailed my body to a door!"

"So you say. Which brings me to the second point of contention:

Tribune Eskil has yet to present a medico's assessment of this so-called *assault*."

Ariadne yanked up her sleeves and turned out her palms, baring her scars. "Here is all the proof you need!"

"And am I also to be accused for the cut that bisects your left brow? What of the mark on your neck? Where is the *evidence*, the medico's report?"

"I had no time to visit a house of healing after you drove us from the city."

"Another accusation for which you have no proof."

Ariadne seethed, chest heaving, glare branding him with ten years of hate. "I was not there that night to incur favors. I came for my assignment, and you *ruined* my future."

"Hearsay and conjecture." Salvotor stacked his papers again. "This entire trial has been a sham, an utter insult of the laws to which Valgard is beholden. It is my solemn opinion that this case ought to be dismissed and those who accused me should stand trial for libel and slander."

"Not so fast, Salvotor," Bravis said. "We have yet to hear the witness accounts. They may yet corroborate the victim's testimony."

Salvotor stilled. "Of course...the witnesses. I *very* much look forward to facing them in this courtroom."

It was a mercy Bravis adjourned then. While the High Tribunes rose to disperse, Ariadne shoved away from the seat and stalked out through the gate. She didn't glance at the cabal, not even when Quill shouted her name. Thorne moved swiftly after her, pushing through the crowd.

She hadn't gone far. Tucked in a small window nook two hallways from the courtroom, she laid her hands on the sill and gazed out over the walls, apartments, and gardens below, trembling with rage when Thorne slipped in behind her.

"How dare that *bandayo suggest* that I—that my *intentions* were..." she broke off, spitting with fury and shaking her head.

Thorne pocketed his hands and slumped his shoulder to the wall. "It's a clever defense. Salvotor knows no one in that courtroom will ever see him as a paladin of good, so his only hope is destroying *your* character."

Ariadne whirled to face him, and to his shock, there were tears in her eyes. He hadn't seen her cry since they left Stornhaz, not even during those long first months when she sequestered herself in her room, unwilling to garden or read or spend time with anyone but Tatiana. And not even when Baba Kallah died. "I didn't go to him for favors. My intentions may have been overeager and misguided, but they were *pure*."

Thorne lurched upright. "Ariadne, *stars* above, I know that. I saw you struggle to walk after that night. I watched Baba Kallah bind the wounds on your hands. I will *never* doubt you."

"I wouldn't blame you if you did." She rubbed both hands down her face. "Somehow, when he suggested it...for a moment, *I* wondered, Thorne. Why *was* I there? Why did I ever believe *he* would grant me a special assignment, knowing how he treated you? But when those summons came, I didn't think twice...I went to meet him anyway. Was I naïve, or did I truly have some ulterior motive?"

Thorne rested his hands on her shoulders. "Look at me." She didn't, so he shook her gently. "*Lightfall*." At the murmur of her Name, Ariadne's gaze shot to his face. "Do you know why I gave you that Name? In the story of the four Wayfinders, there was one named Lysfalla. *Lightfall* in Old Valgardan. The Gentle Spirit of Truth." He squeezed her shoulders. "Of everyone in the cabal, I trust your wisdom most. I trust your prayers. And I *trust* the reason you went that day. He will never make me doubt you. Don't let him make you doubt yourself."

Ariadne was quiet, arms slack at her sides, gaze fixed on the floor. But the stiffness slowly dissolved from her shoulders.

"Go speak to Mira," Thorne urged. "Be with your sister and Iri. And remember that today was a triumph. The people heard the truth, and they won't forget your courage."

Ariadne shrugged him away. "It's difficult to think of it as victory when I hear myself tell that story and remember I was wronged not just by him, but by the Order." Her eyes leaped to his, her smile hollow. "It hurts as much now as then, how my sisters abandoned me because of that law. They wouldn't stand by me now. In their eyes, I am as guilty as him."

"You don't need them. You have a family that loves you. We will stand by you always."

"I know. But no family, however precious, can replace another." She brushed past him, trudging down the hall on the long journey to Mira's quarters, and Thorne turned to watch her go. Fleeting words of comfort died on his tongue, clogged his throat.

But in his mind, a faint notion began to form.

CHAPTER NINETEEN

SNOW FELL, ERASING the memory of the morning's warmth, when Cistine and Aden rode the barge inside Stornhaz's sheltering wall at nightfall. Only then did Cistine take a full breath and release her iron grip on her dagger, flexing her cramped fingers. Aden slumped on the prow, wrists on his cocked knees, head bent with exhaustion from the two augments he spent that day.

They docked near the courthouse and made straight for Kanslar's wing. Outside, Cistine slowed, laying a hand on Aden's arm. "You find the others and tell them what happened. I'll send Thorne to the Chancellors."

He nodded, and they parted ways: him toward the parlor the cabal often haunted, where they drank the night of Salvotor's interment; her toward the Vassora on guard, who directed her to find Thorne in the training hall.

Inside its dim, warm confines, she found him fighting alone against a circle of grainsack targets. Hands wrapped and knives strung across his chest and hips, front and back, he flipped, swiveled, and hurled his blades with deadly precision; he seemed oblivious to all but the whisper of weapons unsheathed and palmed, then the satisfying *thud* of impact near the inked-on center of every target—whether head, chest, or groin.

Cistine slowed to a halt, forgetting her fear for the first time since the pass. She'd seen this mortal accuracy before, when Thorne stepped between her and the pack of Vassoran guards in the Izten Torkat. There'd been no hesitation to defend her even then, with nothing but quiet questions and dangerous curiosity between them; just as he fought to save her in Kalt Hasa, when it was only them and Kristoff against Salvotor's cruelty.

He fought for her kingdom now, fought in her name, battled his own shadows and nightmares to reach her. In the face of his determination and might, the sense of darkness, danger, and the fear of him fell back, stroke by stroke, cut by cut, still screaming his name.

Thorne. Thorne.

"*Thorne.*"

He halted and swung to face her, his chest jerking in rapid pants. "Cistine. You're back already?"

She shoved between the grainsack mannequins and ran to him, and he hurled down his knives and came to meet her, arms engulfing her, the air adorned with the smell of sweat, sandalwood, and leather from his skin.

Safety, her mind chanted. *Safety and home.*

For once, her body believed it. He was shelter, a shield against the darkness outside Detlyse Halet.

"Cistine, you're shaking." Thorne's voice rumbled in his chest. "What happened out there?"

She held tighter to him and didn't stop trembling for a long time.

An hour later, the cabal gathered by the hearth in Thorne's room. Cistine curled on one of the small sofas next to him, digging her toes into the thick velvet armrest and looking anxiously at her somber-faced friends. "Someone say something before I get sick."

Sitting at the fire beside Tatiana, Ariadne offered a tight smile. "You made the right choice not to investigate that attack."

Cistine wilted. "So, you *do* think it was an attack."

"Not only that." Thorne's tone was as dark as his stare, leveled at the flames. "I have an idea who instigated it."

"Rakel and Devitrius," Aden said, slumping more heavily against the wall beside the mantel.

"Why?" Quill scoffed from his perch on the back of the other sofa, boots buried in the soft cushions and Faer swaying on his shoulder. "What would they stand to gain from raiding the Lightless Pit?"

"I'm not certain. It's just too timely to be coincidental, with Ariadne's testimony happening the same day," Thorne said. "It could slow the trial to a crawl, which is why I'm sending the Vassora to investigate before I broach the matter with the other Chancellors. Let's get the measure of this battlefield before we march onto it."

"I can lead them," Aden offered. "Make certain they know what we saw and that their investigation is thorough."

Thorne grimaced. "Much as I hate to send any one of you back there, there's no one else I'd trust to do it."

That ended their short, unhappy conference, the others trickling out with whispers among themselves and grim, parting smiles for Cistine. She met Aden's gaze when he shrugged up from the wall. "Be careful."

He nodded and slipped out, leaving only Cistine and Thorne, who turned to face her on the sofa, elbow braced on the wingback and temple propped to his fist. "Do you want to tell me what you learned out there?"

"Hardly anything." *And nothing worth what came after.* "Vandred implied my bad feelings are tied somehow to when I stepped on the Door under the courthouse."

Thorne frowned. "Then maybe you're feeling the unrest in the heart of our kingdom, with the trial and everything else happening at once."

A seam of relief opened in her chest. "You don't think I'm sensing the future?"

"I'm no voice of authority on the subject, but I do know you, and how sensitive you are. It's possible your power as the Key is ringing in tune with everything that changed when we put Salvotor in chains."

"Then the thing Iri and Saychelle told me...*Nazvaldolya?*"

"I don't know, but I hope there's no calamity on our horizon worse than what we're already facing." Thorne stood and wandered to his dining table, heaped with books and journals taken from his father's room the day the trial commenced. "I can help you look deeper, or we can concentrate on the trial and treaty and your healing for now and deal with the rest after."

She watched him, mulling over their options. In the end, it was almost a relief to let herself speak the words. "The trial and treaty come first. Anything else about these feelings, I'll take it as it comes."

"A wise decision, I think."

"Well, a princess must decide which crises to handle first."

Thorne chuckled. "Sometimes I forget you're not a queen yet. I've known lifelong rulers with less steel in their spines and wisdom in their hearts than you."

That heart was bursting with relief when she joined him at the table. Today's venture to Detlyse Halet was her longest time apart from him since Kalt Hasa, and she hadn't realized how much comfort she still found in his presence until she'd tasted that mountain cold seeping into every warm place he filled with his unwavering strength.

He tilted his head, holding her stare. "What is it?"

Blushing, she averted her gaze to the journals on the table. "Have you had any luck yet with these?"

"I wish. My father's cipher is clever. I haven't even begun to crack it."

Cistine laced her fingers together and stretched her arms out until they popped. "Precisely what you need me for! I haven't forgotten my promise...we'll find his secrets together."

"Cistine, I wish you'd tell me what changed today."

She let her arms fall, meeting his desperate gaze, and realized with a pang of guilt how unfair this all was. She asked him to Name her, then regretted it; she pushed toward him, then pulled away. And today she ran to him and hid in him, when for weeks hiding *from* him was easier.

He deserved the truth, even if it was difficult to articulate.

Slowly, she sank into one of the table's chairs. "I let Salvotor make me forget what it meant when I looked at you. What I felt when you came out of the Black Coast mines or I saw you on that roof in Geitlan. Or...even when you came back for me that first time here." Tears slid down her cheeks—not the hot, raging ones of panic she shed so often these last long weeks, but healing and soft, like spring rain. "Maybe I helped him twist it. Maybe I was angry with you and I didn't even know it...about fighting him when you said you wouldn't, and what happened to Julian because we all went."

Pain flashed in Thorne's eyes, and he dropped heavily into his own chair like his legs gave out. "Cistine, I'm so—"

"I'm not finished," she interrupted. "Even back then, when you went to fight him, you were protecting us. *That* was what I let myself forget. You cared so much about keeping *me* safe, you hated yourself for it after Baba Kallah was gone. And then you still stepped into Nimmus just to be with me, whether I lived or died. Whether *you* lived or died." She slid her palm along his stubbled jaw, past his temple, to cup his ear and sink her fingers into his hair. Carefully, she brought their foreheads together. "I forgot that whatever wilderness I'm in, being at your side is where I'm safest. I know my place, I know what I want, and I'm going to take it all back. Starting with this."

She slanted her head down and met his mouth with hers. Static sparked between them, Thorne's warm laughter brushing her lips at the sensation; but he didn't move or touch her, his mouth pliant, completely at her mercy.

Beneath the darkness of her scrunched-shut eyes, bluish ghostlight danced. His bedroom's cold draft licked her limbs, and her pulse stuttered. She started to pull back, and Thorne gave way as well.

It's not over when you're beaten, it's over when you surrender.

Kristoff's warning crashed through her memory, freezing her in place. If she surrendered now, she might never come back to this—to Thorne.

She gripped Kristoff's compass in her fist until every groove stamped her skin, drawing strength from a better memory of a stone pantry and ghostlight. She'd let Salvotor beat her down from the prison of his apartment these last few weeks, pushing her to the brink of giving up what even Kalt Hasa failed to destroy: the world she and Thorne promised to build together.

He'd almost convinced her to surrender it of her own volition.

With one last squeeze of her anchor, she came back to the warm room, the hard chair biting into her hips and Thorne's face still cradled in her hand, their mouths hovering an inch apart while he waited for her to decide.

And right then, she did.

She gripped the back of his head and slid her tongue along his lower lip, and he leaned in like she craved, one hand braced on her seatback and the other on her leg, kissing her with such talent she forgot there was a man named Salvotor or a place called Kalt Hasa or a single wound left over from it. He kissed her precisely the way she needed, his mouth an open door through which she escaped to the safety he always provided.

When she finally leaned away to breathe, there were tears on both their cheeks. His hands flexed on her knees and hers gripped the thudding sides of his neck. "You are a princess of *many* talents."

She giggled unsteadily. "I don't suppose this one will convince the other Chancellors to treat with Talheim."

"Well, *I'm* convinced about plenty of things at the moment." He brushed the hair from her forehead and settled back. "But if we keep this particular talent between us, you won't hear any complaining from me."

"*I'm* about to complain that you aren't kissing me anymore."

She bent forward, but his thumb brushed her lips, halting her. "I want this, but slowly. I don't want it to be just a way to defy my father."

He was right; he deserved better than to be a weapon she wielded against the specters crouching at her door. Anything worth having—a crown, a kingdom, a treaty, and love—was worth building up on the proper foundation.

So she kissed his cheek instead and pulled a ledger from the top of the stack, opening it with one hand and resting the other on Thorne's thigh. His snaked below her hair, callused fingers gently massaging the stiffness from her neck and shoulders, then tapping at her nape six times. *I am proud of your strength.*

She tapped it back to him, heart full to bursting. And side-by-side, they began the hunt.

CHAPTER TWENTY

I T WAS STRANGE to return to Kadlin's home without Morten to buffer the conversation, but he was so full of smiles about the whole affair, Tatiana was almost more excited than nervous when the steward ushered her into Kadlin's grand peach-and-mahogany dining room. For the first time since the Tribune's feast when she swore to make fashionable threads a precedence in her life, Tatiana felt underdressed, even in the fine silver-and-purple silks she bought that morning.

Kadlin sat alone at the table under a row of hanging ivy baskets, a scroll at her elbow and a wine goblet in her hand. When Tatiana entered, she rose, the pine-green folds of her evening gown shimmering in the bright white ghostlight. "Welcome, Tatiana! The cook is preparing duck soup and fritters, I hope those are to your liking."

Tatiana shrugged. "After ten years of missions with unseasoned meat cooked on a spit, anything is a delicacy."

"I didn't even expect you to come," Kadlin admitted while Tatiana took a seat and filled her water glass. "Morten says you've been consumed with matters at the courthouse."

"Well, there is the pesky issue of the trial."

"Of course. Salvotor, that stars-damned *bandayo*." Kadlin covered her mouth with her fingertips, staring into her goblet. Then her gaze returned to Tatiana, solemn and weary. "My family hails from Blaykrone. My parents came to Stornhaz when I was young, but our relatives stayed behind. During Kanslar's past season, I received letters daily from cousins and siblings, nieces and nephews still living there. They needed so much aid, I had to sell a great deal of my things to meet the costs. So you can believe me, I want that man sentenced as badly as anyone."

Tatiana swirled her goblet and sat back, searching for a lie in Kadlin's face. "Well, let's pray we all get what we wish for."

Kadlin smiled as the doors opened and servants appeared, toting dishes of steaming soup and plates of fritters, but she didn't speak until they were alone again. "If you wouldn't mind, I'd like to hear more about you from your own mouth." She bit into a fritter and pointed to Tatiana with the jagged half. "Morten's told me plenty of stories, but they're all a decade old. I want to know about your adventures, about that *valenar* mark on your hand. And who your invention is really for."

A slow smile crept across Tatiana's face. "All my favorite subjects."

The tale spun out of her between bites, her place in Sillakove Court and her bond with Quill entwining in life's unpredictable tapestry. Kadlin interrupted occasionally to ask questions about their journeys through Blaykrone, about Geitlan at the shores of Stedgnalt Lake and faraway Starhollow and the Izten Torkat—all the miles she journeyed in the territory they both loved.

There were no questions at all when Tatiana told her of Oadmark, the Vassora, and Hrob Lake. Cold pierced through the tall windows, nipping her fingertips with the memories of the ice-masked slope where Quill laid his soul bare before her and kissed her goodbye. Then she paused to fill her cheeks with lukewarm broth.

"I can't even imagine," Kadlin broke the heavy silence. "The pain you endured for each other's sakes and for Talheim's princess."

Tatiana shrugged. "She's our friend. We had to go, no matter how dangerous it was."

"Now, that courage and compassion Morten has told me of in detail."

Riotous laughter thrummed through the floor, and with a jolt Tatiana realized it was dark outside; *Heimli Nyfadengar* had already convened in the home's lower level. "Should we—?"

"Hardly. They're all such friendly gossips, I doubt they've even noticed I'm not around." Kadlin folded her cloth napkin off to the side of her plate. "Besides, I wanted to ask you something away from those itching ears, and now that I've heard your story, I know you're the right one to ask."

Tatiana bristled at the subtle tremor in her voice. "What do you want to know?"

"It's less a question, I suppose, and more of a confession. Several weeks ago, something very important was stolen from me...a schematic for a priceless invention. When your father mentioned your talents were more well-rounded than mere inventing, I thought I should ask for your help tracking down the thief."

"That's what the Vassora are for."

"Yes, I've gone to them." Impatience touched Kadlin's voice. "They insisted it was below their station to go sniffing about for scraps of parchment even when the victim of the theft was an old friend. But you and I know otherwise."

"Do we?"

Kadlin sighed. "Therein lies the issue. The schematics weren't mine to lose, they belonged to your father."

Tatiana's fist bent her dessert spoon. "You *lost* my father's invention?"

"Temporarily, I hope. I was reviewing the schematics at his request when they went missing. I hope to recover them before he notices what an inordinately long time it's taking."

Tatiana stabbed her pudding, pushing it moodily around her bowl. She would've agreed in a heartbeat if this happened in Hellidom, and even now her heart clamored for the thrill of the hunt—to catch a thief and pay back at least one of the many who'd stolen her father's creations.

But she knew better. "I'm sorry, I can't. I have enough on my mind already with the trial. I have to be there for my cabal."

Kadlin smiled sadly. "Well, it never hurts to ask. I'll approach the Vassora again. Perhaps I can keep them from laughing me off the courthouse grounds again if I remind them I once outranked them." She slid the starched scroll beside her toward Tatiana. "This is for you. I wanted to give it after I had your answer, so you wouldn't think I was buying a favor."

"So, what is it now? A bribe?"

Kadlin snorted. "You must get that suspicious vein from your mother. Just open it, will you?"

Bitten with curiosity, Tatiana took the scroll and unrolled it away from her dishes, soaking in its contents until a blur of tears stole her vision.

"I hope it's not too forward," Kadlin said hastily. "I couldn't stop thinking about your sketches, they were keeping me up at night. After I spoke to my contacts, it became clear how the joints ought to fit together. So I drew a few schemes of my own."

Tatiana grazed her fingertips over the drawings. "This will really work?"

Kadlin slipped from her seat to stand behind Tatiana's, leaning over her shoulder to trace the sketches herself. "So long as the muscles are fit, yes, the shaping and bindings should do the rest." Her fingernails weren't as finely-pared and lacquered as at the last gathering; charcoal and lead gathered in the beds, and the paint on the corner had chipped.

A tinker's hands. An inventor's.

"I can't pay you for this," Tatiana said. "I don't have a trade, I just guard the witnesses for the trial."

Kadlin squeezed her shoulder. "Consider it my pleasure as a fellow inventor. And perhaps...a parting gift."

Tatiana frowned. "What do you mean?"

Kadlin rounded the table to stand before the broad span of windows, leaning her brow to the glass. "Blaykrone lies in ruin from Salvotor's cruelty, struggling to limp on after a harsh autumn without aid. I've given much thought to how I could be of help. What good is a single coin to crushed villages with decimated crops, their landscapes reshaped by rockslides? They need minds built for design and people who can help not only rebuild what was, but dream up better ways to survive in the future."

Tatiana slid her chair back from the table. "You're going to Blaykrone."

"Yes. And most of *Heimli Nyfadengar* is going with me."

Tatiana's heart stumbled. "*What?*"

"Don't worry, your father isn't leaving you. He loves you far too much to part with you again. But most of the guild have no profession, either because they've retired or they never had one to begin with. We leave as soon as winter thaws."

Tatiana had no words for the kindness of these people—or the heartache her father kept secret, staying for her while his new friends, his new life, went on without him.

Kadlin sniffed deeply and wiped her eyes, straightening from the window. "I suppose I helped you not only out of kindness, but cowardice. I care very, very deeply for your father, but I can't bring myself to tell him now. So I thought I could show him by helping what he loves above all things, even more than creating or fixing the world."

Tatiana rolled up the scroll and bound it, then joined Kadlin by the window, offering it back to her. "I can't...this is too much. It's inspired."

"The inspiration isn't mine, it's yours. You had the vision and heart to do this, I merely saw the machinations that would bring it to life." Kadlin pressed the scroll back to Tatiana's chest and held her gaze without blinking. "That is what *Heimli Nyfadengar* is built on...the belief that all new stories and great designs begin when two or more join hands over visions ordained by the gods." When she withdrew, Tatiana didn't let go of the scroll. "Leaving this home and those who will not journey with us to Blaykrone will be the hardest thing I've ever done. But I *can* go, because no matter what happens, I trust what matters most within the *Nyfadengar* will continue now that you're home."

But are you? her mind whispered. *Are you home?*

For a thrilling instant, she indulged where that question could lead her—to leave Stornhaz and the cabal and journey with her father, Kadlin, and this guild to Blaykrone, to start a new life. It was the exact sort of risk the Tatiana of old would relish.

But she was not only Tatiana Dawnstar now; she bore the *valenar* mark on her palm. Her family was more than Morten, it was Quill and Pippet too. She couldn't leave them behind, and they would never go; Pippet wouldn't want to leave the school she loved already, the new friends she made, and Quill would never walk away from Thorne.

But still, her heart wandered. It wondered—wageless, aimless, tradeless here in Stornhaz; or free, mind and body and imagination, in Blaykrone with her father and people like them?

"What if," she said carefully, "my father did go? What if his reason for staying here changed?"

Kadlin studied her the same way Ariadne often did—seeking out the depths beneath her bluster. "Then I would say that wherever we settle, there would always be a place for him. And for anyone he decided to bring along."

She was a traitor for opening that door and daring to ask, but a quiet corner of her heart still sang at the reply. And perhaps it was because of Kadlin's unassuming generosity that she said, "About your thief. Let me see what I can do."

It was painfully late when Tatiana finally returned to the courthouse, slipping into her and Quill's room to find he wasn't alone; Faer roosted on the armoire and Pippet slept under her brother's arm while he thumbed idly through a children's book.

Tatiana stashed the scroll quickly behind their weapon rack, then shut the door to catch his attention. "Riveting read?"

He glanced up. "This is the good part. Does the clever fox catch the hare, or does the wily hare escape into his burrow? I can't believe she fell asleep during this fascinating literature."

Grinning, Tatiana toed off her boots and climbed into bed on his other side, nudging the book out of the way and sliding her cold toes under the cuff of his pants. "Well, *I'm* riveted."

"Mm. That makes two of us." He brushed a kiss to her lips. "How was dinner with the elite?"

"Revelatory." Quietly, she relayed everything Kadlin told her that night—except about the scroll. That was still her secret to keep.

"Stars, I feel sorry for Mort," Quill muttered. "First Dataelina, then us, now *Heimli Nyfadengar*. The man just can't keep anything he wants."

"I may not be the one abandoning him this time, but I still feel guilty," Tatiana laid her chin on his chest. "He'd go with them if it wasn't for me."

Pippet stirred, wrinkling her nose. "Who wants to live in *Blaykrone?* Stornhaz is better! Schools and vendors, and ta—tea houses and *shops...*"

"How long have you been eavesdropping?" Tatiana scolded.

"A while. Since you mentioned the fritters."

Quill flicked his sister's ear. "Well, Blaykrone is *our* territory, Hatchling, don't forget that. This cabal will always defend it."

Pippet stuck out her tongue lazily. "Even *Cassaida* is leaving it, she said so in her last letter."

"She's taking her family to Hellidom," Tatiana reminded her. "That's practically an extension of Blaykrone thanks to us."

Quill smirked. "I'm glad she's going. Hellidom could use its grain mistress back with the winter rations in effect. They don't have Baba Kallah to make sure everything's distributed right this year. They don't have *us.*"

Tatiana's throat stung at the memories of winters past: bundling in her best coats and scarves, making bets with Quill about who could chop more wood for the fires and who would have to pluck Tariq's children off yet another rooftop when they forgot their fear of heights and climbed up to check the flues. Still, it was a gift to be in this warmth with Quill and Pippet and most of the cabal. The only pieces missing were Maleck and Ashe, and she would be satisfied once they returned.

She had to be.

Pippet tucked herself closer to Quill, looking at Tatiana across his chest. "I'm glad Morten isn't going. I would miss him. I'm tired of people leaving. Helga, Baba Kallah, Julian. And Ashe and Maleck." She blew out a long, weary breath. "I just want our family to stay together from now on."

Quill bent to kiss his sister's hair. "So do we. Listen. Why don't we take Faer on a hunt tomorrow, take your mind off things?"

Pippet fidgeted. "No, that's all right, I don't want to. I have...school things. And I promised my friends I'd go play."

A shadow of hurt crossed Quill's face. "Right. Makes sense. I'll just take that bag of feathers by myself."

Pippet wouldn't look at him. "I'm sorry."

"Don't be." But that sadness stretched on into silence, deeper and heavier with every heartbeat, until Pippet sat up.

"I'm going to bed. Goodnight."

"Goodnight, Hatchling," Tatiana called after her.

"I love you," Quill added quickly.

"I love you, too." Pippet threw him a half-hearted smile, whistled Faer down from his perch, then slipped out.

Quill sat up and bent forward, elbows to his knees, cradling his head in his hands. Tatiana slid her hand along the slump of his back. "She's allowed to have friends, Quill."

"I know. It's just...she's never seemed so close to being grown before." He voice was husky, wistful. "I missed so much of it, Tati...all those summers when seeing me was the best thing that ever happened to her. Now I finally have her here, and she'd already rather spend time with her schoolmates than her brother."

"At least we have that festival Thorne and Cistine mentioned. Darlaska," Tatiana offered. "She'll have to join us for that."

"True. She's so excited about the presents, she's already begging me for weapons and books." Quill scrubbed a hand through his hair. "Since when did she stop wanting dresses, though?"

Tatiana planted a kiss on the back of his shoulder. "I know everything's changing, but *this* isn't. I'll always prefer your company, if that counts."

"You know it does." He swiveled to kiss her brow in turn. "Listen, about Mort. He'll be all right, he has us. We'll be all the family each other needs."

She nodded against him. "Actually, speaking of family, I was wondering if you could help me with something. It's about Papa."

He drew back and tilted her face up. "What do you need?"

The way he asked sparked a flaring ember of excitement in her core. "How would you feel about helping me investigate a theft?"

CHAPTER
TWENTY-ONE

ANGER BOILED IN Ashe for days, low and deep. She barely slept after her vicious encounter with Jad, devoting her nights to training, reading, and sharpening steel rather than to the nightmares lying in wait whenever she shut her eyes. She needed this false treaty behind her so she could face the problems crouching beyond. Living in the space between what she pretended to be for this charade and what she would become afterward blunted her sharp edges day by day.

"You look awful," Rozalie remarked on their way to the meeting chamber the morning Jad finally returned from Camere. "Are you all right?"

"Fine." The word was raw, her sinuses aching. Everything ached.

"Maleck says you're not eating, that you barely sleep—"

"I don't need you and Maleck reporting to each other about me."

Rozalie shrugged. "Well, you won't talk to us yourself."

Ashe pinched the bridge of her nose, squinting in the harsh light from the windows they never had the decency to curtain off. "We have enough to worry about between Mahasari spies finding a way into our city, Jad's schemes, and the other Wardens causing trouble. Worry about *that*. I can manage myself."

"Can you?"

Their arrival in the meeting room preempted her scathing retort, and

Maleck rose from his place at Cyril's left to greet them. The fact that he of all people so casually arrived ahead of them, took his seat beside the King he once tried to assassinate, and held casual conversation with these Talheimics, stoked her temper into the hottest flame.

Apparently she had no use even as his defense against men like Rion. He was welcomed at the table where they rejected her.

"Good morning?" Wide-eyed, Maleck watched Ashe yank out her seat beside him and sprawl into it, scowling across the table.

"That depends on who you ask," Rozalie said dryly. "But I think it's a good one, thank you, Maleck."

Ashe fought not to roll her eyes and interject snidely that if Rozalie and Maleck were on such pleasant terms, perhaps *she* should sit next to him and Ashe could sit three seats down, further disgraced than she already was.

A small part of her knew she was being unfair; not everything happening in this place was about her. But it was easy enough to silence that common sense; after all, she'd done it plenty of times before.

Jad joined them just as he had the last time: late, vicious, and ending all conversation with his arrival. Ashe fixed her gaze on him, warning with a half-lidded glance that she was not intimidated by how he cornered and threatened her.

He held her stare, unblinking, for far too long and with far too satisfied a smile. Then he looked at her king. "I have consulted with my advisors, and we have reached a decision. Clearly I will not tangle up in the affairs of Talheim with Valgard at its back. If this unbreakable treaty truly exists, well, it would be worse than foolish of us to make demands of your kingdom, wouldn't it? No, that would be *madness*."

Chills slithered down Ashe's spine. Maleck and Rozalie shifted subtly on either side of her.

"Yes, as long as there is love between these two kingdoms, Mahasar sees no room in the marriage bed for a third," Jad continued. "It's a shame, really, such a waste. You could have married mind over might for lovely Talheim, *but then*, you've always preferred the strong arm over the subtle thought, haven't you, Cyril? You and that whoreish wife of yours."

Rion snarled, but Cyril silenced him with a cut of his hand.

"Someday, you're going to face an opponent you can't beat with a blade, no matter how sharp," Jad purred, "and you're going to have to think *very hard* about how to best a man cleverer than you."

"I'll learn when I find one." Cyril's smile carved like a dagger. "If you hope to goad me into misconduct with threats and taunts, Your Eminence, you'll have to try harder. I learned from my father's mistakes, and I owe it to Talheim's new allies not to drag them into a war for the sake of my pride."

Rion cast him a quick, unhappy glance, but Maleck visibly relaxed. Ashe's annoyance spiked at both men for no reason she could name.

Jad's eyes skittered back and forth like a pendulum. "I suppose that concludes our business."

"I suppose it does. Mahasar will withdraw from the border?"

"Oh, yes, of course. We wouldn't wish to provoke our allied neighbors, would we?" Jad's gaze found its resting place with Ashe again. "After all, Valgard has proven itself *exceedingly* willing to leap to the defense of its weaker friends in the Middle Kingdom." Ashe bit the inside of her cheek so hard she tasted blood, and Rion scowled. "Now, should anything go...amiss with this treaty, at any time, Mahasar's offer for the princess's hand still stands. I know I'm generous beyond reason, no need to tell me. Just remember what I'm willing to offer. How badly we all desire peace."

The grim steadiness froze into terrifying rage on Cyril's face. "You can trust I will never forget *that* offer, Jad."

The Mad King smiled, twisted and indulgent. "Not that it matters, does it? What you won't forget. Because you have all the allies you need. Perhaps you should make Wardens of one or two of them, hm? Round out your ranks with capable, strong, *true* warriors—"

The room echoed with the scrape of Ashe's chair shoving out, the clap of boots on stone as she lunged to her feet. "Do you have something to say to me, bastard?"

"Asheila!" Rion barked.

Jad puckered his lips. "Such insolence from those at your left hand,

King Cyril!"

"You're one to talk!" Ashe spat. "Cornering one of the King's own in a hallway, spewing threats—"

"Ashe, enough," Cyril warned.

"I did no such thing!" Jad shot to his feet as well. "You dare accuse a foreign royal who came to your kingdom under the banner of peace?"

"Don't lie to them, I have the marks on my throat to prove what kind of *royal* you are!" Sense begged her to stop, but the reins had finally snapped loose from her furious tongue. "You lying, disgusting, gods-damned—"

"*Kovar!*" Rion roared. "Sit down!"

"She speaks the truth," Maleck glared at Jad. "Don't forget who found you with her in that hall."

Jad's brows wagged. "You would defend her, of course. Your new *ally*. Nothing can ever tarnish that treaty, yes? Not even the infamous brutality of Valgardan warriors."

Maleck stared him down, dangerous tension bristling in his shoulders. "Are you implying what I think you are?"

"I imply nothing but that even King Cyril's finest *hasacs* need brawny men to leap to their defense." Jad cocked his head, first one way, then the other, measuring Maleck carefully. "Unless this accusation of bruised throats is all some cleverly-concocted tale to shed shame on Mahasar."

Maleck kicked his chair back and rose as well. "She is *not* lying."

"*Sit your ass down!*"

The shout burst from Ashe's lips, quieting the whole room—even Jad. Maleck blinked at her, unmoving.

"*Sit down*," she repeated. "Stop intervening, stop fighting my battles for me. I am *handling* this!"

"Valgard will not sit idly while its honor and the honor of its allies are threatened," Maleck said.

"This is not about Valgard and Talheim, this is you and me and your gods-damned sense of—"

"*Enough!*" The thunder of Cyril's voice yanked Ashe from her exhausted rage, snapping her focus to the Wardens gaping wide-eyed around them, Jad smiling faintly, and Maleck gazing at her with inscrutable emotion raging in his face—and to the King's eyes, full of displeasure.

"A word, both of you," he growled. "*Privately.*"

Jad was not the only one smiling when Cyril stalked from the table. Rion's lips barely twitched, but from him, it was as good as a smirk.

Cyril banged the door shut and whirled on Ashe and Maleck. "That was disgraceful. The pair of you...there aren't *words* for that display."

"Forgive us," Maleck said. "But he *was* lying."

"You have more to learn about diplomacy than I thought if you really believe a ruler's lies need to be shouted across the table." Cyril gazed at Maleck with something that hadn't been there since the day they arrived: mistrust. "You haven't once raised your voice in this house. Now you're crying for blood."

"He hurt her."

"I know she was hurt, I was in the hall that day." That suspicious stare lingered, then swiped to Ashe. "And you. I *know* you know better. I'm disgusted with your behavior."

Every word was a blade piercing straight to the heart. "Cyril, I—"

"*Your Majesty.* I'm your *King*, though I've never been embarrassed to call myself that before." He pivoted to the door, snarling over his shoulder, "Get out of my sight, both of you, and pray to the gods or the stars or whatever you hold faith in that I can salvage this. Any lives lost or battles sworn from this outburst are on *your* heads."

Face burning, Ashe turned and walked blindly from the disappointment in his face, from her own humiliation forever stamped into every person's memory in that room. She didn't even realize where she was going until she reached Maleck's chamber, and he followed her in and shut the door behind them.

Then she whirled on him, rage exploding again. "What in *God's* name is wrong with you?"

The mask of calm slid back onto his face, but not before hurt flashed in his eyes—as if he had any right to feel *hurt* after he destroyed her strength in front of the King, her former Commander, and Mahasar's beating heart.

"I defended a friend, as allies do."

"You made me look like a soft-hearted fool who couldn't defend herself—like I needed you to rescue me from Jad. *Twice!*"

"Where is the shame in that? Why do you fear *so much* to ask for help?"

"I'm not *afraid*, I'm *furious*! Do you realize how tenuous my position is right now? I don't have *anything* left after this! I thought it couldn't get any worse, but then you keep undermining me and taking away the only thing I have left...my gods-damned pride!"

He raised his hands for peace. "That was not my intention."

"I don't care what you *intended*! Cyril thinks I'm a disappointment, you should've seen how Rion looked at us when we left that room...I had *nothing*, Maleck, and now thanks to you I have less than that!"

"Why does *that* matter so much?" He lurched away from the door. "Why do you concern yourself with the opinions of those who care so little for you, rather than those who would lay down everything to keep you safe?"

She scoffed, crossing her arms "Like who?"

He stared at her, unspeaking.

Chills pierced the fog of rage, digging into Ashe's skin. "Maleck. What are you saying?"

A humorless smile quirked his lips. "You don't know the depths I sank to, searching for you. The dazes that overcame me after Cistine and I traveled to Jovadalsa. The nightmares I had in Stornhaz that frightened even Ariadne. I went back to the places I feared most to find *you*."

"Well, you shouldn't have done that!"

"Why not? You don't believe you were worth it? Every risk, every moment since? Even in these meetings, in this place?"

"No! I'm *not* worth losing yourself over!"

Maleck burst forward, gripping her shoulders and backing her against the wall. "If you believe I'm not already lost, that I don't lose myself again whenever I look into your eyes, then you aren't as perceptive as I've always believed."

Her mouth dried. The air rushed from her lungs. "*What?*"

He cursed lowly, not harshly, his grip tightening. "Why do you think

I do any of the things I do here? Why I can't help taunting *Meszaros*? Why I stepped into the Mad King's path, why I risked *everything* we came here to do? It's all for *you*...because they hurt you, belittle you, threaten and intimidate you, and I can't *bear* it. I'd sooner wreck every promise of peace between our kingdoms than watch these men tear you down."

Terror sliced through Ashe's veins. "Don't. Do *not* do this." He couldn't want her this badly, couldn't do this to himself—to *them*. She was too busy falling to pieces without that look in his eyes stealing the last of her strength.

"It's already done." Maleck released her and slid a hand through his braids, staring at her in wonder and shock and *reverence*. "I *love* you. I have loved you since I was fourteen, before I knew your name, before I knew the truth of how magnificent and fearless you are. I will live and die loving you, Asheila Kovar, and I am not afraid of that. I'm not afraid of anything I must do to keep that love alive."

Ashe stared at him, the words glancing by, her heartbeat lulling into something dangerously calm and close to not feeling anything at all.

"Get out."

Maleck's brow tightened. "Did you not hear what—?"

"I heard you. Now get *out* of Middleton. Leave. The mission is over, you did your part. I got what I needed from you. We're finished."

She despised herself for every word, for the lies, for the pain dancing in his eyes. "Asheila..."

"*Don't*. You said it yourself, if you stay, you'll wreck the peace we were sent to build. I can't risk you ruining more than you already have. *Leave*."

He reached out to her. "Asheila, *please*—"

She jerked out of his reach, freeing one tear down her cheek. "Don't touch me, you gods-damned *augur*! Get out of this city! Go *home*, Maleck!"

The only gift she could offer him after he laid his heart before her was to loosen his grip, to cut him free before she finished her descent into darkness; before he broke with her at the bottom of this pit she'd fallen into.

But perhaps this was breaking. This moment, and that look on his face like she'd gutted him.

It was so quiet, she heard footsteps tapping in the hall and the moan of wind in places where the estate didn't fit together quite right. Then Maleck stepped past her, gathered his pitiful belongings from the bedside table, and slowly laid them in his satchel.

Giving up. Leaving her.

She didn't wait to hear what furious parting words he might have for her. Like a coward, she left his room for hers, walking quick and sharp all the way across the estate and gulping breath to keep the tears at bay. She went to her room and slammed the door, then stepped straight out onto the balcony. Bracing her hands on the railing, she watched Maleck emerge below, stride down the path, up the steps, toward the city; watched until the pike gate lifted, then lowered again. Until the stormy sky blurred.

This was the best thing for them; that he went home where he was loved by those who deserved his tender heart, and she remained here, where she'd begun her breaking, and finished this. She would make up some excuse for his absence, hinge it on his loyalty, draw his devotion to Valgard in broad sweeps. She'd sing his praises all the way to the end of her plunge. And when she broke, it would be alone, where the shards wouldn't cut others and leave them bleeding.

She backed away from the balcony, pulled the doors closed, and leaned against them, squeezing her eyes shut and covering her mouth to muffle sobs that ached to form his name.

I feel it. I know what this is. I love you, too. I'm not afraid.

But he deserved better than yet another lie. So she swallowed the tears, took in a deep, fortifying breath, and turned to go tell new lies to her king, to explain where Maleck went.

She turned straight into a blow instead.

The punch shattered her nose, flinging her through the glass balcony door, thick shards slicing her scalp and hands. She crashed into the railing, knocking out her breath. A kick swept her legs from under her and a fist dragged her head down and bashed her temple into the stone.

Darkness stole her from the world.

THE PRISONER

OF

SCHEMES AND STORIES

CHAPTER
TWENTY-TWO

THE WIND AUGMENT swiveled over Cistine's knuckles, fitting like a second sheath of skin. She could almost see the currents eddying, the distant call strumming her muscles, quieter than ever since she visited Vandred—as if it knew better than to roar again and reawaken her bitter unease.

Maybe Thorne was right; maybe it was just her spirit aching with the world's pain.

"All right." Quill's voice snapped her from her reverie. "Stop staring at the augment like that. Give it here, Stranger."

She flicked him a grin. "Why don't you come and take it from me?"

"You know that's not possible."

Jutting her lip in an exaggerated pout, she clasped her augment-girdled hands behind her back and sidestepped him. "Well, you may just have to fight me for it anyway."

Quill lunged at her, renewing the storm of kicks and hits that marked their morning thus far. Combat with augments required more thought, more balance, even greater awareness of where her body was and the space it occupied, and that precision chased out ciphers and dark storms and impatience from her overcrowded mind.

The trial's next session loomed the day after tomorrow. Yesterday,

Aden and his contingent had returned from Detlyse Halet with a report that kept the entire cabal from sleep. And today, Thorne and Cistine would deliver it to the Chancellors and discuss the treaty again.

Nervous energy sang through her next volley of blows, and Quill parried each one, effortlessly matching her unspoken need to pour worries into this fight. He and Tatiana had returned the night before from some hunt on behalf of an elite woman, and the concern for that battled with the strain of Aden's report, bright in the shadows of his eyes.

He needed this as much as she did, so she baited and teased him, letting the augment drive her thrusts harder and quicker—almost too quickly for him to block. In minutes, he was smiling, leaning his whole weight into their sparring.

"Sooner or later, you'll have to yield!" he crowed, deflecting her left and right hooks and kicking at her middle. "You're the one with noble duties to perform. I could do this all day."

Cistine stuck out her tongue and feinted. "After watching you chase Pippet every night after school, I doubt that, *old man.*"

"All right, that was uncalled for!" Quill caught her next punch, twisted his fingers around her wrist, and pivoted behind her, pinning her elbows to her sides and her back to his chest. His frame covered hers as he hunched over, laughing in her ear. "Yield!"

"Never!" Cistine shrieked, squirming against his iron grip. He blew hot breath on the back of her neck, turning her screeches to squeals as she bucked in his arms. His laughter and hers shook through her whole body, loosening what pressure remained, and her cheeks ached from grinning when she bent her head and chomped down on his wrist.

Cursing, Quill released her, and she thrust the wind against him, sending him skidding back against one of the pillars. A hand shot around it, twisting his arm up behind his back; he went down in a spiral, sweeping a kick toward his attacker—bringing Thorne crashing down with him.

Cistine laughed at their brief, violent tussle. In seconds Thorne had Quill pinned, a knee to the small of his back and both arms laced at sharp angles near his waist. Smiling, Thorne looked up at Cistine. "Good morning,

Princess."

"Chancellor." She dipped her head, face hot with the memory of their parting kiss outside her door last night, the thrill of her back against the wall and the triumph that she'd guided him to do it and never once felt out of control.

Thorne sprang up and offered a hand, towing Quill to his feet. "If we don't leave now, we'll be late for the meeting."

"I'm ready." Nevermind that there was dust caked in her armor or that her hair had come undone from the many braids Tatiana wove into it while they listened to Aden's report the night before.

This was who she was. The Chancellors could have her or leave her, but she was not stepping before them in a dress again.

Thorne pulled a sugar-crusted yeast roll from his pocket, tossing it to her as they walked with Quill toward the steps up from the training hall. "You're going to need this."

Inhaling the warm scent of powdered sugar from the crust, Cistine was inclined to agree.

She was still licking crumbs from her fingers when she and Thorne reached the door to the Chancellor's sanctum fifteen minutes later, and he took her shoulder. "I'll go first. We don't want them suspicious about how we arrive everywhere together."

"Fair enough. I'll give you two minutes' headstart."

She took the solitude to rebraid her hair and straighten the loops and seams of her armor, battling down the weight that dragged her heels from the moment she entered above the Door. It was only a slab of rock, and she was determined: a princess couldn't be ruled by a rune-littered lid far below her feet.

After exactly two minutes, she squared her shoulders, breathed deeply, and shoved open the doors.

Five pairs of eyes swung to her, and she descended the staircase holding each of them in turn, trailing her hand along the banister—a grounding habit from every birthday celebration and royal ball she attended in Talheim, one Mira had encouraged her to try again. It anchored her in the room and reminded her of her place as royalty. This was where she belonged.

"Princess Cistine," Maltadova greeted. "I trust you're recovering well?"

"I am. Thank you for your concern." She sat, placing the Writ of Nobility on the table, and nodded to Thorne.

"Before we begin the negotiations," he said, "I have a report you'll all want to hear. You know Aden paid a visit to Detlyse Halet several days ago on my orders. He returned with an unfavorable report." His gaze flicked to Cistine, reawakening the stomach-dropping fear from the night before. "Detlyse Halet was destroyed, every level collapsed, the overseer slaughtered. Not one prisoner remains, nor is there any sign they perished in the attack."

Benedikt swore. Valdemar's face drained of color. Maltadova slowly sat forward, balanced his elbow on the table, and covered his mouth with one hand. Only Bravis remained calm, but his eyes raged. "Who and why?"

"I wish I knew, but given it happened the day of Ariadne's testimony, I suspect it's joined to the trial somehow."

"Swift to conclusions," Benedikt muttered.

"One could argue that to *not* question the obvious shows a penchant on Skyygan's part to assume Salvotor's innocence. I wonder why?"

"The argument could also be made that you're swinging at shadows," Valdemar said. "There are other enemies in this kingdom than just your father who could profit from criminals set free. Devitrius, for example. Or your own *mother*."

"Two objections against Salvotor's hand in this," Maltadova said, "made by the two Courts who cowered before him. Curious."

"Let's not turn this into a search for blame at this table," Bravis said.

"But it *could* be Devitrius leading them," Benedikt scowled. "It would be just like him to orchestrate something on his old Chancellor's behalf."

"Whoever the culprit is, we know this about them," Thorne said. "They're powerful augurs working outside the Courts."

Bravis nodded slowly. "This must be dealt with immediately. I'll send Tribune Reinn to oversee an investigation of Detlyse Halet."

"Should we postpone the trial pending an investigation into Salvotor's involvement?" Benedikt asked.

"If this *was* his doing, then a delay of trial would give him exactly what he wants," Maltadova argued. "I say we proceed as if we know nothing about Detlyse Halet. Let Salvotor sweat in his shackles while we conduct a thorough search for the guilty parties."

"And then, gods willing, we'll find evidence to accuse him for this crime, too," Bravis agreed.

Maltadova nodded. "I will send Tribune Haji and his *valenar* Zoya to assist in the search, if you'll permit it. They are both capable scouts, and Kroaken is Haji's territory. He's familiar with all its hiding places."

"If anyone can find their trail, it will be your Hunters. Have them ready to depart at dawn."

Neither Benedikt nor Valdemar offered assistance. There was such a clear divide at this table: Bravis and Maltadova, tentative but hard-won allies of Sillakove Court through their years-long stand against Salvotor's advances; Benedikt and Valdemar, estranged by their submission to him; and Thorne, who carried the burden of his father's legacy, setting him apart as the untrustworthy boy at a table of men.

How could they expect Valgard to unite with Talheim if they couldn't even unite among themselves?

Cistine shook the thought away. If unity was lacking, she would have to unite them herself—with help from the silver-haired Chancellor watching her across the table, subtle encouragement in his eyes.

She clasped her hands. "Talheim's prayers are with you for a quick resolution. I wish I could offer aid or insight from my own kingdom, but, as I tried to express before I fell ill at our last meeting, we're currently embroiled in dangers of our own."

"Ah, yes, your treaty proposal," Bravis said. "Are you truly prepared to present this time?"

Cistine bit her cheek. "I am."

"Then let us hear it."

With a last glance at Thorne, she addressed them. "Talheim is facing a threat from the southern kingdom of Mahasar. For the last few months, King Jad has been rallying support for a military campaign at our shared border." Fear for her people closed her throat—the same fear that provoked her to make the journey to Valgard in the first place. "He's a madman. He beheaded his own father and laughed while his city burned. He promised to end my family and take my kingdom, and now he almost has enough support to try."

"I fail to see what concern that is of Valgard's," Benedikt scoffed. "Talheim was no better when it marched into *our* borders and slew *our* men. I say the gods are just!"

"This is not a matter of the gods," Thorne said. "This is men making war for their own selfish reasons. We're no better than they think us if we ignore the plight of innocents."

"There are no innocents in the Middle Kingdom!"

"Talheim didn't start this fight," Cistine argued

"Talheim has shown us its battle-readiness firsthand," Bravis said. "Much as I'm reluctant to admit it, your father forced a surrender without a single augment in his arsenal. Forgive me if I fail to see how he cannot do the same to Mahasar."

"Maybe you're right," Cistine said. "Maybe we do stand every chance of winning, given time. But if it comes to a battle, hundreds of my people will die before we push Mahasar back behind their borders. As Talheim's Princess, I'm concerned with preventing bloodshed, not just minimizing it."

"Spoken as a true idealist," Maltadova said.

"I'd rather be idealistic for trying to save lives than realistic for deeming them a worthy loss."

His brows rose. "And what part do you expect Valgard to play in all this?"

She took care to meet each pair of eyes, leaving none of them out from her next words. "I'm not asking Valgard to fight. My prayer is that it won't go that far. All I want you to do is sign a treaty that makes us allies, and stand with us to send a message to Mahasar that if they cross the border, it will be not just a threat to Talheim, but to Valgard. And that the North will not be trifled with."

Bravis rubbed his jaw. "If this Jad is as much a madman as you say, he may use such an alliance as an excuse to march against *us* once he's trampled your kingdom."

Cistine bristled. "Then you'd hide behind your border while Talheim fights a war for you?"

"As I said," Benedikt enunciated coolly, "well-deserved."

"You're looking at this the wrong way," Thorne argued. "Before the war, we had no need to look outside our borders...the gods provided everything we needed through augments. But someday those will be spent, and what then? We better our chances if we offer a hand of friendship to Talheim before we reach that tipping point."

"What does Talheim have to offer that we could make use of?" Valdemar scoffed. "They don't even have augwains!"

"And neither do we." Thorne's voice lowered. "Sometimes I think we forget that. We're still living like life as we know it will go on forever, but augments are no longer an infinite resource. Someday, perhaps even in our own lifetimes, we'll live in a world without them...something no one at this table has ever known. But Talheim knows no other life *but* that, and I truly believe we have much to learn from them." He met Cistine's eyes, and her heart skipped. "Think of it: if we trade our might in battle for resources and knowledge of how to conduct our kingdom when augments are gone, we secure both our futures with no concern that *we* may have to face Jad and his warriors ourselves someday when there are no flagons left."

Cistine's heart thundered with glee. This was a battlefield they had rarely taken before, only in dark rooms below taverns and fine parlors full of warrior women, but she loved it. She loved to see Thorne on it, clothed in wits and cleverness rather than armor; and she loved to let her own tongue dance and move around his, like practiced steps on rain-slicked rock.

She shifted in her seat and tugged her hair away from the back of her neck when Maltadova sat taller. "Chancellor Thorne makes an interesting point. King Jad may be emboldened by a victory against Talheim and press further north."

"Or Talheim can spend their own blood putting him in his place, and it never becomes our affair," Valdemar retorted.

"Either choice poses a risk to Valgard," Thorne said. "But only one of those risks guarantees Jad thinks twice about crossing *our* border."

"It would also serve both of our kingdoms in trade and travel," Cistine added. "Chancellor Thorne is right, we have so much to offer one another. Talheim is willing to negotiate trade routes by ship and land."

"The trade agreement would vary," Bravis warned her, "commensurate with how much blood we spent fighting *your* enemy in the South."

"Talheim is prepared for that, too." Really, she hadn't considered that at all, but it seemed fair: the more Valgard lost, the more they hoped to gain. And given how much their kingdom suffered in the last war, she was feeling generous.

"We must discuss this with our Tribunes," Maltadova said. "We will have further questions, Princess."

"Of course. Your kingdom is your primary concern. I understand that. But I ask for the same courtesy in return," Cistine said. "Talheim doesn't have a lifetime to wait. Jad is inside our borders now, conducting peace negotiations with my father. It would be ideal for Valgard to show its support at that meeting." Nevermind what would happen to Maleck and Ashe, already feigning such support, if Jad ever learned they tricked him.

"Valgard respects Talheim's position and the pressure it puts you under," Thorne said. "We also respect the sacrifices you've made to present your case. We'll take all that into account in our deliberation."

Cistine nodded to him, then to each of the Chancellors. "Thank you for your time."

"Wait a moment," Bravis said when she rose. "It would be better if you helped present this proposal yourself. There is a feast being held soon in honor of Thorne's swearing-in, an opportunity for the Chancellors and Tribunes to dine together and honor this new season for Kanslar. Join us, and you can speak to the Tribunes yourself."

A feast. In a dress. With Tribunes and Chancellors and Vassora present. There was no doubt this was a test, feeling out her rough edges and testing her conduct.

She caught Maltadova's eye, and some of her tension melted away.

Yager Court would be there, its array of hidden female Tribunes on the arms of their *valenar* and *selvenar*. She wouldn't be alone in a room full of men like another meal in Kalt Hasa; she would have allies and friends, support on all sides. "It would be my honor, Chancellor Bravis."

Smiling, he reclined. "Then we'll see you there at the beginning of next week."

Head high and heart pounding, Cistine escaped the room. At the first branching hallway, she twirled around the corner, pressed her back to the wall, and cupped her hands around her mouth, letting out a harsh burst of breath. "*I did it!*"

She could hardly wait to tell Mira and the others. It was *working*; she was carrying the weight and negotiating like a real emissary.

She still stood there, frozen in shocked delight, when Bravis led the Chancellors past, all muttering among themselves about the trial's continuation. Thorne trailed them, and no one paid any heed when he stopped and let the distance grow between them.

Then he swung around, strode back to the hall, and lifted Cistine from the wall with both arms around her waist. For a time, they didn't speak; simply held each other.

"Stars, you were brilliant," Thorne said at last. "If the choice were mine, you would have Valgard at your back *today*."

Her cheeks burned with hectic heat. "I thought I did reasonably well, all things considered. My hands were disgustingly sweaty, though."

"No one would ever know." Thorne cradled her face between his palms. "You were born for moments like this. You were born to change the stars for our kingdoms."

Cistine gripped his wrists and guided his hands down from her face. "We'll see just how many stars I change at this feast. Why didn't you mention it before?"

He winced, pulling away to lean against the other wall and rub his calves. "Because I was hoping to contract some crippling illness before *I* had to go. I've never liked Tribune feasts, I always envied Quill finding excuses to leave them."

"I think it could be fun."

"Even if it isn't, now that you'll be there, I'm certain we'll make our own." Thorne glanced over his shoulder as a door clattered deeper in the hall. "I should see to the preparations for the trial."

"And I have counseling." Cistine thumbed the compass pendant hanging over her heart. "Your room again tonight? With the cipher?"

"I'm counting down the seconds." He pressed a kiss to her lips, then left her standing in the hallway, giddy with relief that she'd redeemed the disaster of her first meeting with the Chancellors.

CHAPTER
TWENTY-THREE

WELL DONE TODAY, Cistine." Mira smiled at the end of her report, pouring steaming cups of pumpkin tea for all three of them. "Valgardan feasts are quite a treat. This will be the perfect time for you to practice what we discussed with Darlaska."

"I was thinking that already," Cistine grinned. "But I'm glad I have a few more days to practice first."

Ariadne drew her bare feet onto the couch and picked up her cup. "At least one of us is making progress."

"You both are," Mira chided gently. "Cistine sees hers now. I suspect you'll realize yours fully after the trial's end."

"I hope so. I'm tired of feeling jealous about my sister's bond with Iri or the flood of letters she receives from Keltei Temple."

"Because no one ever tried to find you?" Cistine asked.

Ariadne nodded, a flicker of pain darting through her eyes. "I thought I was above petty jealousy and envying what my sister has. But I suppose I'm the same resentful creature I've always been."

"We are all jealous of some things," Mira said. "I'm sure if you speak to Saychelle, you'll find she envies something about *you*."

"Not even she's that foolish," Ariadne laughed humorlessly.

"I'm not referring to what was done to you. But you have a family of strong warriors, a blade in your hand, and the courage to confront Salvotor. I suspect she admires that. Craves it, even." Mira smiled at Ariadne's stunned look. "Though your life isn't the story you wanted it to be, that doesn't mean it can't inspire others."

They were quiet for a time, sipping their tea, deep in thought. Cistine pressed her feet against Ariadne's in silent solidarity, and her friend pushed back.

"So, Cistine," Mira's amiable tone sparked the usual flutter of nerves as the subject shifted to her. "I hear you're still not comfortable wielding lightning augments."

Latent terror zipped along Cistine's fingertips. "Who told you that?"

"Let's see, how did it go? Quill told Pippet, who told Aden, who told Thorne, who mentioned it to Sander, who told Hana and Eyva, who told me."

Cistine groaned. "This entire courthouse is full of gossips!"

Ariadne nudged her thigh. "Your sort of people."

She swatted her foot away. "If they *were* my people, they'd be afraid to tell each other my business!"

"Why is this such a secret?" Mira asked. "Plenty of people prefer certain augments over others. I'm told Quill has a penchant for the theatrics of fire."

Cistine's mouth ticked in a reluctant smile "But it's different for me. It's not about what I prefer." She thumbed the ring strung around her neck. "Lightning was how Salvotor killed Julian."

"The boy Sander burned." The grief in Mira's eyes echoed her lover's, a memory of the injustice which thrust him wholly to Thorne's side. "Would you like to tell me about him?"

It startled Cistine how much she did. Everyone she spoke to about Julian already knew him—sometimes they knew better how he died than how he lived. But Mira had never met the cocky Warden-in-training, the unhappy suitor, the scowling boy walking in his father's shadow and wearing his prejudices like a shroud. "He was..." she slid the ring along its chain, "loyal. Kind. Opinionated. Stubborn and bold and clever."

"Handy with a blade," Ariadne added. "And he had quite the mind for linguistics."

"You noticed that?"

Ariadne shrugged. "We may have hardly spoken, but he had presence. There was no denying it."

Wet laughter struggled up her throat. "Maybe that's the best way to describe him. Julian Bartos had *presence*."

Mira stirred a lump of sugar into her tea, eyes never straying from Cistine's face. "And how long was he in your life?"

"All of it." She could coax little volume to her voice and couldn't speak at all the damning words that would've followed: *And never again*.

"If you had it all to do over, what would you do differently? What do you suppose would've made a difference for him?"

"Battle armor. Salvotor's blow wouldn't have killed him if he had threads like ours."

"He didn't want them?"

"No, he wasn't fond of most things from Valgard."

Mira nodded slowly. "It can be difficult to accept when someone's choices make the difference in their own death. It's uncomfortable to speak ill of the dead, but we come to a place where we must accept their fate was partly in their own hands."

"But *I* was his princess. I should've told him he couldn't come with me unless he had armor."

"Would he have listened?"

Cistine pondered it for a moment under the weight of Ariadne's knowing stare. "No," she sighed at last. "And that was always the problem between us. He loved me, but he didn't know how to listen to me."

And with that, the floodgates opened and the words poured out of her; she told Mira the whole story of the boy from Practica who traveled to a land he feared to save his father.

Cistine wasn't surprised restlessness gripped her for the rest of the day, or when it edged into that dark feeling in the pit of her stomach again. She slid an apology note under Thorne's door after a listless supper, shut herself in her room, and didn't sleep that night; instead she wrote questions and conversation-starters for the Tribune's feast, keeping her hands too busy to touch the ring dangling between her breasts.

The only benefit to a sleepless night was that she was the first one in Kanslar's private dining room at dawn with a bowl of oatmeal and syrup glaze, sitting at the table of her choosing, staring through the glass dome at the garden where snow from two days ago melted under the warm sun. Her mind danced over today's trial, the Tribune's feast, and Julian. Melancholy burned beneath her sternum.

Footsteps drummed down the hall, jolting her from her wandering thoughts. Pippet skidded into the dining hall, dressed in a thick wool dress, a knit cap, and mittens. When she caught sight of Cistine, she paled. "Oh! What are you doing here? No one's ever awake this early."

A tired smile crawled across Cistine's mouth. "Believe me, I wish I weren't. Where are you off to in such a rush?"

Pippet toed the floor. "Nowhere. I mean...to build a snow fort."

Cistine folded her arms. "Is that the truth?"

"Where else would I be going?"

Where, indeed. Pippet had crept around in the garden every now and then since the first day of Salvotor's trial, sometimes with Vihar or Faer in tow and sometimes not, but rarely this early. "Well, with it being so warm today, I doubt you'll be building any forts. Why don't you sit with me?"

Rebuke flared in Pippet's eyes, but she threw herself down in the seat across from Cistine. "*Fine.* Now what?"

"There's always training if you're bored."

"Aden is going somewhere with Mira even though he *just* got back." Pippet scowled at the steadily-melting snow. "I miss Ashe. She would go out and do things with me."

"I miss Ashe, too."

Pippet's eyes turned to her again, irritation fading into curiosity. "What's that?"

Cistine was chafing the betrothal ring absently against her neck. "It was a...a gift. From Julian."

Pippet gathered her feet onto the chair and wrapped her arms around her knees. "Do you miss him, too?"

"Every day."

"So do I. He taught me to play card games Quill didn't want me to learn. And he never treated me like I was too young to know about things." She plucked at the knees of her tight-fitting trousers. "I miss Helga when I think about Julian. They really liked each other. Did you know Ashe taught me a lullaby to sing when I miss her too much? Do you think if I taught it to you, it would help with Julian?"

Pressure burst from her chest, half a sob and half a laugh. "Oh, Pippet. I'm not sure that would help."

"Well, what *would* help?"

"I don't know. Maybe if I could make sure no one else ever died the way he did."

"I heard Ashe telling Aden about what happened while we were traveling. It was an augment, wasn't it?" Pippet rested her chin on her knees. "So you just have to make sure everyone has armor on all the time."

"Well, they'd still have to bathe and change clothes. No one can wear armor *all* the time, not even me. Not unless it was—"

The thought landed suddenly like an arrow aimed true. A flash, a flicker of memory, another terrifying moment when she watched someone she cared about threatened by an augment he had no protection against: a chain dancing with fire, coated in a black, inky substance.

Cistine shot up from her seat. "Pippet. You are the cleverest, most *brilliant* girl in all the kingdoms."

Pippet beamed. "Am I?"

"*Yes*, and you and I are going hunting. How do you feel about libraries?"

"I've never seen one."

"Well, you're about to."

They left the courthouse for city streets full of slush puddles turning to liquid under the warm sun, jogging all the way to the towering monolith of paper-and-ink that held life's answers inside its cool confines. When they entered, Pippet dropped Cistine's hand, gaping open-mouthed at the rows of shelves on every level. "*This* is a library? It's the most wonderful thing I've ever seen!"

Cistine shot an apologetic look at a cluster of elites nearby and wrapped an arm around Pippet's shoulders. "I agree. Would you like to see the truncated epics? Stories of adventure? There's one I think you'd like, I found it when Thorne first brought me here. It's about a lost princess found by her family on the battlefield, and a struggle between life and death and the gods..."

Once Pippet was curled in an armchair with the storybook, Cistine stepped far enough away that peace enveloped her, tinged with bright, vivid excitement. Breathing in the familiar scent of old books, contentment warming that hurting place in her chest beneath the betrothal ring, she perused for the titles she needed. To her relief, most were written in the common tongue; book after book slid off the shelf, joining the stack in her arms, revealing the true benefit of training: the ability to carry more books.

As she pulled down yet another thick volume, flipping it open between her hip and the shelf to study its contents, a strange prickle danced down her neck—the uneasy feeling of being watched.

She snapped the book shut again and glanced up. Bright, amused eyes the color of a cloudless sky watched her through the gap where two books were missing.

"Thorne!" she yelped.

"Imagine meeting you here, of all places." His face vanished, and a moment later he rounded the end of the bookcase, a modest stack of books under one arm, surveying her much-taller heap with brows raised. "Why are you reading bestiaries?"

"Why are *you* stalking the gardening section at sunrise when there's a trial happening today?"

"I have a strong sense neither of us is going to answer these questions."

Cistine's ears heated. "Not yet."

"Not yet." He relieved her of half the stack. "Care to join me?"

"For now. I brought Pippet along, but I think she's going to be occupied for a while," Cistine grinned. "I gave her that adventure tale I found the other night, the one about the lost princess."

"Stars help us all. She's going to spoil the ending for Quill and he'll be inconsolable about the end for days. I know I was."

Cistine checked his hip with hers. "Never underestimate the power of a well-written death."

"I prefer life." He nudged her right back. "I missed you last night. Did you sleep?"

"Not really," she admitted. "But I made some winning arguments for the Tribune's feast."

"I can't wait to hear them." Thorne greeted Pippet with a kiss to the head, and she growled him off, turning the page and burying her nose back in her book. Laughing, Thorne and Cistine settled on one of the broad sofas across from her; he positioned himself so she couldn't read the spines of his books.

"Who knew horticulture could be so mysterious?" Cistine teased.

Thorne shushed her. "I'm trying to read."

She found that utterly distracting. He had a certain way of gnawing absently on the inside of his cheek when he was engrossed in something. It was almost impossible to keep her attention on the bestiaries, particularly when her search proved fruitless. He was much more interesting than her failures at the moment.

"Your stare is distracting," he remarked at last.

Cistine rolled her eyes. "I suppose I'll just have to move to another couch, then."

She pulled her legs from over his lap, and he laid his arm across her knees gently, trapping her in place. His eyes flicked up from his book. "Staring challenge. The one who smiles first has to tell the other what they're researching."

Cistine folded her arms. "Fair."

They gazed at one another in silence, and she let her focus wander, admiring the shape of his brow and nose, those devastating eyes, the shorter crop of his hair—and his lips.

She sucked in her cheeks and focused on his eyes again. He tilted his head slightly and blinked in a lazy challenge, then poked the tip of his tongue between his teeth, eyes rolling toward one another.

Cistine burst out laughing, and Thorne grinned, blinking back to focus. "That's it. The truth now, *Logandir*."

"Oh, here!" She pushed the latest book toward him. "I want to know more about that beast you told me about in Kalt Hasa...the Atrasat. I have a plan, but I need to know if it's even possible with the properties of that blood. You said it was like ink?"

"It is. Let me see those." Cistine dumped the entire stack into their laps, and Thorne studied the spines, licking his thumb and turning pages. At last he offered a small, thick book to her. "This may be what you're looking for."

"Finally! Thank you!"

"Anything to keep you from looking at me that way." He flicked her earlobe, and she laughed, batting his hand away.

"Who ever thought I'd find someone more distracting than a book?"

"That may be the highest compliment you'll ever pay me." Thorne settled back, draping one arm behind her and holding his book open with his other hand. "Now, may I please read in peace?"

"*Apologies*," Cistine whispered.

They passed the time in silence now, buried in their respective books; but Cistine couldn't fight back a smile when his fingers stroked absently through the ends of her hair.

CHAPTER
TWENTY-FOUR

K ADLIN'S HOME LOOMED through another early-winter night, the first time Tatiana and Quill had peeled away from the cabal in days. While they waited for the steward to answer their summons, Quill holstered his thumbs in his belt and whistled lowly, looking over the wealthy home. "Mort's made some powerful friends since we left."

"Not powerful enough to avoid losing his inventions, apparently," Tatiana grumbled.

Grinning, he propped his elbow on her shoulder. "He does that well enough on his own."

She reached out to pinch his side, then jerked back when the door opened. Kadlin, not the steward, greeted them with a warm smile. "I hoped it would be you! I was afraid you'd forgotten about me."

"Not forgotten. Just been busy." Tatiana gestured to Quill. "This is my *valenar*. He's good at finding things too, so I thought I'd drag him along to help, if that's all right."

"The more, the better." Kadlin shot him a calculating look. "You're Quill, aren't you? Corvus's boy. I was assigned to his guard years ago."

He sketched a dramatic bow. "You have my sympathy."

Kadlin laughed. "Oh, I *like* this one. Why don't you two come inside?" She sidestepped, and they entered, passing flocks of servants bustling and cleaning as they made their way to the staircase offset in the room's left corner. "*Heimli Nyfadengar* meets again tomorrow. Everyone is mustering their inventions together to sell what we can and pay our way out to Blaykrone."

Tatiana's gut clenched. "Is there anything I can do to help?"

Kadlin smiled over her shoulder. "You do enough to grace me with your presence and allow me to steal your father's company every now and again before we go. Not to mention why you're here tonight."

Tatiana's feeble smile dropped away when she caught Quill watching her from the corners of his eyes.

Kadlin ushered them into her personal gallery, a high-roofed room with drapes drawn. The pine-and-gold walls housed a maze of cases and pedestals displaying artifacts: weapons, books, baubles, and some inventions Tatiana had no name for. "My treasures," Kadlin said. "Some I've designed myself, others were bought or given as gifts."

Tatiana's heart warmed that this woman stowed her father's plans among her treasures. "You didn't want to pack them away yet?"

Kadlin peeked at the servants in the hall, then shut the door and lowered her voice. "I've left everything untouched since the schematics went missing...a vain hope that someone would think seriously on this and want to look more closely at things as they were that night. But...well. You're here now."

Quill wandered ahead, hands in his pockets, drawn straight to a particular display case. "This *armor*."

"Do you like it?" Smirking, Kadlin joined him. "A gift from the Vassoran guard when I joined the ranks. Threaded with real gold, you can see. Lightweight but durable. And excellent for blinding enemies in the daylight."

Quill grinned. "I could use something like this."

"Wouldn't fit you, I'm afraid." Kadlin chucked him gently on the shoulder. "You're too tall and not well-endowed enough."

Quill laughed. "One of my few flaws, I'm told."

Tatiana rolled her eyes. "So, where did you keep my father's schematics?"

Kadlin led them to a thick case full of scrolls and gestured to the top nook. "Up there, out of sight. How they found them is beyond me."

"Was anything else taken?" Quill asked.

"Nothing."

Tatiana exchanged a glance with him. "Do you know how the thief got in? How they left?"

"No, unfortunately. They were *quite* good. Not a window unlatched, not a sign of entry anywhere."

Quill's brows furrowed. "Odd."

"Unsettling." Kadlin glanced at the door. "The only people I bring into my home regularly and leave unattended are the *Heimli Nyfadengar*. That's the other reason I hoped you'd look into this before we departed. If the thief is one of us, I don't want them in Blaykrone."

A shiver capered down Tatiana's spine. "We'll do what we can."

"Leave it to us," Quill agreed, skimming his hand down her back.

Kadlin cast a sad look between them. "I'll leave you to it. Call for me if I'm needed."

Tatiana tried to hunt rather than browse, though it was difficult. There was so much to look at, contraptions and weapons and small devices—even dresses that shifted color whenever she changed angles. One in particular held her stare, a white gown whose red-and-gold hem caught fragments of blue like fire when she circled around the base.

"You like her," Quill remarked while they perused the room. "I don't know if I've ever seen you take to anyone that quickly. Not even Cistine. Not even *me*."

"Wonder of wonders," Tatiana teased halfheartedly. "She's like me. Like my father."

"And she's leaving." His eyes caught hers through a glass case full of needle-thin knives. "I'm sorry."

She forced a shrug. "That's life. People leave. Let's just worry about investigating this room."

"I know something else we could investigate."

LIGHTFALL

Before she fully registered that wicked tone, Quill took her shoulder and turned her against the case, his mouth finding hers. For a moment, she allowed for the distraction he offered because he knew her sorrow so well, the heat of his mouth tugging her mind away from her melancholy. But there was another fire burning low in her stomach, stoked with the brush of his touch that promised love, that promised to lay the world at her feet.

So when they broke apart, while he was still breathless and smiling, she looked into his eyes and asked, "What if we left with them?"

Quill cocked his head. "Left...with Kadlin's guild? Left *Stornhaz*?"

"Yes."

A beat. "For once, I can't tell if you're joking."

She sank back against the glass and looked up at him. The ghostlight smoothed the contours of his straight nose, his full lips, his creased brow, and stars, she loved him; she'd known it for years, but somehow it seemed clearer now, on this hunt—just the two of them. And what if it was always just them? "I mean it. We could take Pippet with us and make a life of our own. In Blaykrone, with *Heimli Nyfadengar*."

"Dragging Pippet away from school?" Quill's hands fell from her hips. "Not even dragon scale armor would protect us from her fury."

"She'd learn to love it. There are other schools, other friends. We could build a future somewhere quiet where no one will ever bother us."

Quill frowned. "Tati, you can't be serious. We gave up everything for this."

"Exactly. Your parents are dead, Helga is dead, Julian and Baba Kallah, even Kristoff, *again...you* nearly died, too! And now what—trials and thieves and more pain? Is this the peace we earned?"

"The peace comes after it's finished. We can't leave the cabal, not like this. Maybe, once the trial is done, we can see what comes after..."

Hopelessness choked her. There was nothing coming after, and they both knew it. Pippet would grow more attached to her school, to her friends, and matters among the Courts would only become more complex over time—especially if Cistine had her way with the treaty. Thorne would want them more, need them more.

She ducked under Quill's arm. "We have work to do. This thief isn't going to just turn himself over."

"Tati..."

"I heard you, Featherbrain. Let's just do what we came to do."

Resignation hung in his silence, but his piercing look warned her this wasn't the last they'd speak of it, no matter how much she wished she could choke the words back. It was foolish to even say it out loud in the first place.

They searched long into the night, the room silent, their eyes and minds on the task. But they found no trace of a thief, not even a broken window latch or a bootprint or a scuff.

As if whoever took the schematics had simply vanished through the walls—or left through the front door as a welcomed guest.

CHAPTER TWENTY-FIVE

ASHE WOKE WITH a start, her bellow of rage deafened on a soiled rag stuffed in her teeth, arms bucking against the pulsing slice of twine around her wrists and ankles. Hunger and thirst punched through her stomach, every muscle and nerve frayed with lack of nourishment.

She knew all these sensations at once, knew them far too well.

She was someone's prisoner again; she hadn't even had the opportunity to fight back this time.

Mind strafing in memories of carts and deserts and catacombs, she heaved up on one elbow and squinted at the world: a canopy of shedding branches above her head, rust-colored leaves scattered around her in the rich blue tones of twilight, the chill on her skin not only from lack of food but also the dampness of Talheimic autumn.

Outdoors. Unsheltered.

Light kindled near her feet, a gentle cluster of silver-blue threads in a jar carried by a man who held a wineskin in his other hand. "Ah, there you are." His voice was low and musical, richly accented with rolling syllables. *Mahasari.* "You've been asleep for a while. Welcome back."

He set down the jar, shifting the tacky hair from her brow. She slammed her face into his hand—the closest she could come to biting him—and he snatched it away, grinning. He was beautiful even by that strange light, tan, sunken-eyed, and smirking, bearded with a thatch of dark hair; lovely and cruel like a serpent. "You must be famished. If I remove that gag, care to join me for a drink?"

What she wanted was to spit whatever he offered into his face, kick his legs out from under him, and wriggle to freedom. But she wasn't certain she had the strength for half those things; they'd starved her too well, bound her too tightly. She'd never get far.

Frustration and despair burned her throat. She couldn't do this again, be a prisoner forced to perform for her captors. She would rather die. How long had she been gone, and Cyril not found her yet?

Tormented with the thoughts all stabbing into her aching head at once, she panted into the gag and made no sound. There was something strange about her captor's smile, small and charming but utterly void when he removed that gag and yanked his fingers away from her dull, desperate snap. "Talheimic gratitude. Predictable."

"Which bit am I expected to be grateful about?" she croaked. "You dragged me from my room, you've kept me tied up here for gods-know how long—"

"Four days." He offered the waterskin. "Drink?"

Her mouth foamed, but she clung to the last fibers of her dignity until he gripped her by the collar, hauled her up, and forced the waterskin to her lips. She seized the opportunity while she gulped to also take in her surroundings: trees, stones, and broad slopes painted against one another, their edges a soft emerald-and-onyx. Distantly, the silver light of a river glinted under the full moon.

She was in the Calaluns.

She swallowed more greedily, relief coursing through her tingling limbs. She wasn't so lost after all; she could find her way back to Middleton from here. If she was too weak, too injured to crawl once the shock wore off and she could feel her limbs again, Maleck would find her. He'd seen the signal fires, he knew where to search for Jad's treachery—

But Maleck was four days gone. He didn't even know she was taken. And they never told anyone else about the fires.

As that first ringing note of despair found its mark in her chest, something crashed into place behind it: numbness. Resignation.

Middleton was a speckle in the distance, glowing at the heart of the valley. Four days, and no one had found her this close to the city.

The man took his waterskin back, hanging his wrists from his knees. "Better?"

That wasn't the word for it. The water's sweet taste was almost mildewed but not unpleasant, burning deliciously through her body and coaxing life back into her limbs—and best of all, quieting the ache in her chest, the memory of Siralek, the despair that this time not even Maleck searched for her. She'd finally severed that tenuous thread between them, pushed him so far he'd never look back again.

She couldn't remember why that mattered. Why it hurt so badly when she watched him ride from Middleton. There was a word for it, not in the common tongue, but it evaded her.

The man followed her gaze to the distant city. "They're not looking for you. Not one patrol, not one scouting mission, *nothing*. They don't care what happens to you." Of course not. Why expend the resources for a disgraced Warden, a murderer of grandmothers and nannies, a traitor and a disgrace to kingdom and King and Princess? "I'm the only friend you have. So why don't you tell me your name?"

"Asheila Kovar." Her voice scraped over the arch of her tongue.

"Pleasure to make your acquaintance, Asheila. I'm Kashar az-Kyrian. I have some food here for you, but first, I thought we might discuss your allies down in the valley."

Clamminess skittered through Ashe's arms and legs, driving out that moment of comfortable warmth after the drink. Slowly, she shook her head.

Kashar held up the skin. "More water?"

Ashe drank greedily this time. A delicious hum filled her head, almost like spirits but so much better.

"That's it. Now, what of this so-called treaty between Valgard and Talheim? Is there any truth to that rumor?"

Despite the comfortable warmth that settled over her like a blanket, a small, needling stab of dread found its way inside her chest this time. The sweetness on her tongue turned saccharine. She wrenched her lips from the bottle, glaring at Kashar. There was something here, he was doing *something...*

His eyes narrowed. "You *really* want to tell me the truth about this treaty."

She did, and yet... "The treaty is real."

Bent forward over his knees, so close the smell of boiled meat and sweet dates wafted against her face, Kashar growled, "Is it?"

"The treaty is real." She wanted desperately to tell him the truth—that it was a sham she failed like everything else—but that dread in her heart refused to let the confession through. "The treaty is real, it's real, it—"

Kashar fisted his hand in her hair and wrenched her head back, forcing the wineskin to her mouth. "Tell me the *truth, hasac!*"

She choked and sputtered, fighting to seal her lips against whatever was in the water that made her want to believe everything he said, to let him persuade her that he was her friend and she should tell him everything, tell him the treaty was a lie—

But it wasn't. Not all of it. Even after she struck out with all her might in fear, even after Maleck left her, there was still a thread between their kingdoms. A bond between augur and Warden, unshakeable, unbreaking, because of what he was to her and she to him. What some part of her knew ever since that night he stepped between her and Rion outside Stornhaz; on the bridge, looking at the Citadel, hearing him tell the story of people formed of stardust, all their pieces aching for each other across land and fate; when they stood on that rain-soaked slope in the mountains, when he kissed her beside the fire.

The reason she forced him out of Middleton, out of her heart.

With the drink soaking her tongue, she couldn't fight it anymore. It cracked through every defense, breaking down the walls she threw up to keep it out all this time.

Selvenar.

The word was a note strummed into the dimness of her mind, that void raging at the edges with poisoned sweetness.

Selvenar.

It joined them together. It blended her heart to his.

Selvenar.

She screamed the word into herself, raised it high like shield and sword, and pushed back the bludgeoning might of Kashar az-Kyrian and the doubt and despair he forced into her. She held her ground against the tide of whatever strange Mahasari concoction coursed in her veins, planting her feet in that one truth he couldn't take from her.

"The treaty is true!" she shouted. "It's true, the peace is true and the treaty *is real!*"

Because it was. For her and Maleck, it always would be.

The wineskin emptied all over her face, and she retched and gagged as Kashar flung her and the empty skin aside. He lurched to his feet, any hint of kindness gone. Only darkness remained, and he looked so much like Jad it snapped Ashe back to the truth of this moment.

Captor. Enemy. Danger. He was not her friend, never her friend.

"I hope you like the feeling of drowning," he seethed. "It will be your entire miserable life from now until your end. We will do this every day until you yield or stop breathing."

He stalked away, and Ashe sagged, sucking in her breath, fighting to quiet the panic raging in her body.

Selvenar. The word echoed through her, softer and yet stronger than any drug. *Selvenar.*

She'd chased Maleck off, set them both free; but there was no escaping that tether, the truth that would keep her from ruining Cistine's secret and damning her kingdom.

So Ashe clung to it, clung to *him* like a lifeline in a raging sea. And held on.

CHAPTER TWENTY-SIX

DAYLIGHT POURED THROUGH the courtroom windows, but Cistine still struggled to stay awake. The walls pulsed slightly under the strain of her aching vision, and she jumped when a gentle elbow dug into her side. "Long night?"

She offered Tatiana a tired smile. "Long year, really."

"Fair." Her friend pushed a mug of warm tea into her hands. "Is that why you look like Faer kept you up squawking in your ear all night?"

"I was at the library until late, actually. And I couldn't stop worrying about today."

"You could've joined Quill and me for cards. We didn't sleep much, either." Tatiana leaned into the wall, jaws stretching around a yawn.

"No luck with that thief?"

"None. And Pippet was out late, too, we heard her come in two minutes before midnight. I thought Quill was going to have a nosebleed. There's no sharing a bed with him when he gets like that."

Cistine frowned. "Has Pippet's behavior seemed...odd to you lately?"

"No more than you'd expect from a girl her age who's gone through what she has. Why?"

Before Cistine could answer, the courtroom doors opened and the cabal entered—Thorne leading, Quill behind him, Ariadne and Saychelle side-by-side, and Iri and Aden bringing up the rear. Thorne opened the gate to the dais, taking Saychelle's elbow and murmuring something in her ear when she passed him. She nodded, and with a fleeting smile, he let her go.

The time had finally come for her to take the witness's seat and give the testimony that, gods willing, would bring their enemy to his knees.

The prospect knotted Cistine's core with anticipation—and dread.

Salvotor swaggered in behind them between his guards, relaxed like he was the free man and Saychelle the prisoner on trial. She seemed to feel it too, shrinking back slightly in her chair while the guards clipped Salvotor's long chain to the table.

Bravis brought the room to order with a wave. "Eskil, you may begin."

While the Tribune took Saychelle's oath of honesty, Cistine watched Thorne's grim, unhappy face and wondered how he must feel, seeing the woman he once loved standing witness against the man whose cruelty tore them apart. She couldn't imagine if she and Julian were forced into a separation only to see one another in these kinds of straits ten years later.

But there would be no ten years later for them. There was no future at all with Julian in it because of the man smirking at Saychelle like a famished predator, hands folded on the table.

Cistine's own hands became fists. Quill squeezed her shoulder.

"*Visnpresta* Saychelle," Eskil's voice drew her back to focus, "please make your testimony."

"That night," Saychelle paused, clearing her throat. "Forgive me. That night, when my sister was...when she was attacked. I was...there."

"In the Chancellor's apartment?" Eskil asked. Saychelle nodded. "Was anyone aware you were present?"

"Thorne—" Saychelle flushed, "I'm sorry. The High Tribune, Salvotor's son, he was aware, yes."

"And was he also in the apartment?"

"No, he slipped out first. I..." Saychelle linked her fingers tightly in her lap, gaze flicking from Eskil to Salvotor and back again. "I was meant to leave through the window."

"But you didn't?"

Saychelle shook her head. "As I was gathering my things, I heard a...a commotion from the main parlor. Shouting. Things breaking. I thought perhaps the Chancellor and his wife were having an argument—"

"Objection," Salvotor interrupted. "Speculation without relevance."

"I'll be the decider of that," Bravis said.

Saychelle drew her augment-shocked hair behind her head, draping it across her opposite shoulder. Her skin glowed with sweat. "It was a moment before I recognized my own sister's voice. She was...begging the Chancellor not to touch her. She called him by name several times."

"Did you *see* what happened?" Eskil pressed.

Saychelle bit her lips together and took deep breaths through trembling nostrils. Her brow crumbled and her gaze averted when she nodded. "I opened the door to see if I was truly hearing what I thought I was. And I saw him...what he was doing to her..."

"Did you intervene?" Again, Saychelle shook her head. "Why not?"

"I was terrified!" Her voice cracked. "He was *defiling* my sister! I had no means to defend myself and no strength help her."

"Did you run?"

"I hid in the bedroom closet until it was quiet. When I came out to find her, there was...there was nothing, only blood and her robes left behind. I escaped through the window."

Eskil consulted his papers. "What happened after the incident?"

"My sister left Stornhaz. I stayed behind to help my parents at their shop whenever I could leave my bed."

"You were unwell?"

"I felt responsible for not intervening. I tried to bring attention to her suffering by telling anyone, *everyone* who would listen, but it only..."

Salvotor stretched, long and leisurely, folding his arms behind his head. Saychelle's gaze turned swiftly to him, then dropped toward the floor.

"I only brought suffering on myself," she murmured.

Thorne tipped his head. Ariadne frowned.

"Would you describe this suffering?" Eskil said.

"I was attacked. My parents lost their shop. We were threatened, stalked, made to suffer every day until I finally fled to save all our lives. I escaped to Keltei Temple, where Ariadne's mentor lived. She'd written to me many times, offering support and council." She flicked a shy, genuine smile toward Iri, standing on Thorne's right. "I've served as a *visnpresta* ever since."

Eskil nodded. "And is the perpetrator of your family's suffering in this courtroom today?"

Saychelle didn't look across the table. "It was Chancellor Salvotor."

Eskil had barely bowed and stepped aside when Salvotor rose. "You say my son knew you were in our apartment that day. Why was he so knowledgeable of your whereabouts?"

Saychelle glanced at Thorne. "We had considered swearing the *valenar* oath. We were discussing it that day."

"And yet you were also in training to become a *visnpresta* at the time. I see you hoped to have the best of both lives."

"I planned to leave the Order back then."

"Your dedication to your vows is inspirational, truly. So, you and Thorne were little older than children at the time...impulsive, and with every intention of forging the *valenar* bond." A generous, thoughtful pause, "Tell me, are we to believe you are yourself celibate?"

A hot flush warmed Cistine's cheeks. Color rose in Thorne's neck and ears, too.

"The High Tribune and I never joined," Saychelle muttered.

"Of course you would say that. To claim otherwise would make him fit to stand trial himself, and disqualify you from the Order that has sheltered and cared for you for ten years...ever since, as *you* say, you failed to save your sister."

"Objection!" Eskil snarled. "Badgering!"

"I'm merely using the *visnpresta's* own words." Salvotor rounded the table to lean on its far edge, inclining toward Saychelle with almost friendly ease. "I don't believe you hid out of terror that day, Saychelle. I believe you chose to hide because of your guilt. You and the High Tribune were engaged in illicit activities in my apartment, and you feared you would lose your place in the Order if you were found there."

Saychelle's gaze darted to Iri, imploring. "That's not—I told you, we weren't—"

"Let's consider your account." Salvotor lurched back upright. "If this was in fact the truth and not some aggrandized slaughtering of my reputation, it would mean you chose to *hide* rather than be caught joining with my son. You sacrificed your own sister to keep your selfish secrets."

Saychelle shook her head wildly. "I didn't mean to abandon her!"

"But if what you say is true, then abandon her you did!"

Cistine flinched. Thorne's head snapped around, his eyes boring into hers, and she gazed back at him, helpless, horrified. That tone—that inflection—

She pressed her thumb into Kristoff's pendant. *Streets of silver and gold, snow falling, scents of cider, spruce, and linen, the vendors filling Astoria's market during Darlaska...*

"These accusations of stalking and attacks against your family are already proven false." Salvotor's voice twisted with nasty pleasure as he lifted a stack of papers from the table. "I present, for the review of the Tribunal, the true cause for your family's loss of business as reported upon their return to the town of Skiodalar in Kroaken territory." Eskil brought the papers to the High Tribunes as Salvotor went on: "Decreased revenues and the rising cost of goods...which no single Chancellor can be held responsible for. As for any attacks *you* suffered, those are the unfortunate risks of living in a city this size. Unsavory characters abound."

His voice echoed through the courtroom like dark stone walls. Thorne gripped Cistine's hand and squeezed. *You are not alone here.*

The uncomfortable stab of pressure broke her frantic trance, and she forced herself to breathe deeply, diving deeper into a better memory.

Children running through the streets, the waft of pastries on the air, ghostlamps stranded across every square and plaza...

"Now. Here is what truly happened." Salvotor's voice, dangerously quiet, shredded the illusion of Darlaska she struggled to build in her mind. "You hid in my apartment while your sister and I argued over her attempts to seduce me for a commission of her choice. When *she* found you sulking in the shadows, she threatened you. You helped concoct a lie about some heinous act you saw and how it frightened you, because if you exposed her truth, she would expose yours. In the end, she and the man you joined with fled the city and abandoned you. So you perpetuated the lie as a means to live with your grief, knowing you mattered so little to them. Now you testify as a witness in these false claims to crawl back into their good graces."

"That's not true!" Saychelle shouted, snapping partway up from her seat. "High Tribunes, *he's lying*! It wasn't consensual—"

"Sit down, you are not addressing them!" Salvotor shouted, and she toppled back into her seat.

"Thorne, do something!" Cistine begged.

Eskil barged forward. "Salvotor, back away from the witness!"

The Chancellor bent lower instead, and Cistine stopped breathing. She knew what he felt like that close—how foul his breath was, how dark his eyes became. "Little liar, did you think I wouldn't find you out?"

Saychelle's brutal scream ripped through Cistine's chest like a blade. Thorne let go of her hand and shoved her toward Quill. "Get her out of the room. Aden, go!"

He was already moving, vaulting the railing and hauling Salvotor away from Saychelle with an arm around his chest. By the time Ariadne and Tatiana reached the witness's chair, Saychelle had vomited, sobbing with panic and crumbling to the floor. Thorne sprang over the gate, stepping between the women and his father as Salvotor ripped free of Aden's brawny grip and jabbed a finger at him. "I want this man arrested for laying hands on me!"

Thorne brushed Aden behind him as well and slammed a hand into Salvotor's chest. "Back away!"

"Cistine, let's go," Quill growled in her ear.

She struggled against his hold. "Don't let them punish Aden!"

"They won't! If anyone's going to be whipped for this, it's Salvotor." He spun her away from the chaos and pushed her hair out of her face. "You need to *go*, Stranger. This wasn't just for her."

Their gazes locked, and Quill nodded sharply.

"Get out." He ran and leaped the railing, landing shoulder-to-shoulder with Aden and Thorne. Salvotor held up both hands at their unified front and finally retreated.

Of course he did. The damage was already done.

Cistine tore from the courtroom and ran all the way to Kanslar's wing, to its most ornate halls. She didn't slow until she burst into the familiar chamber, panting and gasping, Mira's name a sob on her lips.

Vihar picked up his head, pointed ears flaring when she stumbled through the door; Mira, Hana, and two of Sander's other lovers, Kendar and Elsin, looked away from the game of cards they played by the fire. One glance at Cistine's face, and Mira was on her feet. "Hana, door. Elsin, bring tea."

No one questioned the authority with which she commanded them—like a queen rather than a lover of equal status. Cistine collapsed on the nearest sofa, clutching her throbbing temples, and flinched when Mira's fingers closed around her wrists. Her large, dark eyes filled with concern, searching Cistine's face.

"What happened? Was it the trial?"

Cistine forced a nod, neck stiff, arms and legs spasming with the urge to keep running, all the way back to Talheim, to Mahasar, further, even—wherever she had to go to escape Salvotor forever.

Mira settled on the sofa beside her, rubbing her back. "Will you tell me? Or should I go find Sander and ask him?"

"Already here." Spice wafting from the folds of his robe, the High Tribune strode across the room, swung Mira's vacated chair from the card table, and sat straddling it, facing them. "Thorne sent me to ensure you were well."

Of course he knew she would come to this place of safety he helped her find, with Mira forever waiting to open the door.

Cistine's fear and mounting rage reflected against Sander's sharp features and the angry strokes with which he petted Vihar's head when the wolf came to sit at his side. It was that fury, more powerful than the fear, that loosened Cistine's tongue and set her tears flowing as she recounted the events in the courtroom for Mira. Elsin brought tea and vanished again during the tale, Kendar and Hana already gone somewhere else, and finally Cistine wrapped shaking fingers around the cup and said through gritted teeth, "None of it worked. Darlaska, the anchor…"

"These things don't always." Sander stirred his tea. "It's an imprecise art, the mind, and Mira was one of the first to explore it in such depth. There are bound to be times when even her brilliance doesn't solve all."

Mira shot him a dry look, her hand still circling Cistine's back. That touch was as much an anchor as anything; between the clever-minded former Vassora and Kanslar's High Tribune, she finally relaxed, sinking deeper into the sofa. "What if one day, nothing helps anymore?"

"Then you find new things that do," Mira said. "It's the same with any illness. Certain methods help for a while, and then we grow too accustomed to them, or the pain waxes greater, so we adjust. Like a muscle that's been worked too often one way, we strengthen it another."

Sander's eyes lingered on Mira, softer than he looked at any of his other lovers. The softest Cistine saw him look at anyone. "Think of it like weapons training. You've done that, yes?" He fingered the ornate dagger on his hip. "To a child, the weight of a sword would be like lifting a mountain. But what is it to you, Princess?"

She smiled faintly. "It's nothing anymore."

Mira squeezed her hand. "It isn't the weight that changes. Our strength grows to carry it."

"It just feels so heavy right now."

"Then you need to do something else. Focus on something besides Darlaska and your anchor."

She mulled that in silence while she finished her tea. After a long moment, Sander clicked his tongue, and Vihar padded to the sofa and laid his shaggy head in her lap. She followed the frame of his ears with her thumb, smoothing her knuckles between his eyes.

"Thorne sent me with a message for you," Sander added. "When we're ready, he'd like all three of us to join him in the usual parlor."

If the summons surprised Mira, she showed no sign of it, merely nodded. Cistine strove to imitate that unflappable calm, rising and setting aside her cup. Vihar kept close to her side, all but steering her toward the door with his powerful shoulder against her thigh.

"Princess," Sander said. "Salvotor will not walk away from this. I assure you any one of us would sooner cut him down in the courtroom and face the consequences than see him lay a finger on you."

"Because I'm the Key," she sighed. "I know."

"Well, that. Also, you're a foreign emissary." Sander's eyes sparkled with mischief. "And worst of all, Mira would have my head if I allowed any harm to come to her friend."

"Ever the altruist." Mira took Sander's hand and pressed a kiss to a scar on his wrist, and he to one across the back of her knuckles as they slipped from the room.

They arrived at the usual parlor to find the cabal already assembled. Ariadne and Aden took up one sofa, matched for bleak faces and taut muscles. Quill and Tatiana perched on another, scowling, Faer swaying on Quill's shoulder. To Cistine's unease, Saychelle and Iri were absent.

Thorne rose from his chair when they entered and held out his hand to her, a silent question in his eyes. Cistine crossed the room on near-stumbling feet, and the moment her fingers twined with his, safety enveloped her.

He squeezed her hand four times. *Are you all right?*

She squeezed back once. *Yes.* "Saychelle?"

"Resting in her room. Iri is with her. The medicos gave her a sedative."

"*Please* tell me Salvotor is going to be punished."

"Unfortunately, that's rather the least of our worries at this moment." Sander tossed himself down on the sofa next to Tatiana, and Mira settled on his knees. "Legally speaking, Saychelle's outburst introduced enough doubt that we must have her rigorously examined before her testimony can be considered admissible. If even then."

Ariadne jerked her head up from her hands. "My sister is as much a victim of Salvotor's cruelty as I am. She should not be made to suffer more because of his actions today."

"Be that as it may, she publicly displayed what some might call questionable capacity in the face of pressure. Salvotor can and *will* twist that to suggest her memories of that day, and the ones following it, are skewed."

"Unfortunately, he's right," Thorne sighed. "I spoke to the Chancellors after they cleared the courtroom, and the prospects are grim. Although Iri and the Order can prove she and I never joined, if her mental competence can't be verified by an impartial party as well, the entire testimony is inadmissible."

"Which leaves us with Deja," Aden grunted. "Not our preferred witness."

Sander spread his hands. "There's nothing we can do about that."

"Mark my words, High Tribune," Ariadne hissed. "Saychelle deserves respect and leniency after what she's suffered, not to be paraded before the Courts as if *she* is the one standing trial."

"And you mark *my* words: this was decided by the Chancellors, not by me. Unless you prefer to live by the law of the wild again, I suggest you learn to abide by that."

"Don't tempt me. You'll be the first one I bring down on my way to Salvotor."

"Ariadne," Thorne and Cistine chorused. She glanced up at them, and Thorne pinched the bridge of his nose, his back heaving in a sigh. "I have no doubt Saychelle's competence will be proven and this trial proceed. But Sander is right, we're beholden to these laws now."

There was no fathoming what it cost him to say that, giving ground to his father's ruthless strategy. Cistine squeezed his hand, and to her relief, he returned the gesture without a moment's hesitation.

"I've requested Mira be in charge of Saychelle's assessment," he went on. "I assured Bravis there's no one better qualified after seeing to her wellbeing since she arrived in the city. And no one less likely to be bartered by one of Salvotor's spies."

Mira inclined on the arm of the sofa. "You know I'll show her the honor and respect she deserves."

The fight left Ariadne's rigid shoulders and tense jaw, her eyes softening with regret. "Of course you will. Forgive my temper, Mira, that was inexcusable. Today has not been easy."

"It's already forgiven. I'll look after Saychelle like she was my own sister."

"In the meantime, we need to put Deja in the seat," Sander said. "Any further delay is to Salvotor's advantage."

"Are you prepared for that, Aden?" Thorne asked.

He and Mira exchanged a look, heavy with secret meanings and knowledge shared outside courthouse walls. "I have to be."

That didn't inspire much confidence in Cistine at all.

Saychelle was awake at last, secluding herself in the bathing room when Cistine visited her that night. Laid out on her back on the tiled floor, feet plunged into the recessed pool, she stared at the ceiling and didn't even stir when Cistine entered—just blinked at her lazily.

"I brought tea," Cistine offered. "Do you mind if I sit?"

"As long as Salvotor is in chains, you're free to do whatever you want. So perhaps you'd best take advantage of that while it lasts. I doubt it will be for much longer."

Cistine set down the tray and dipped her toes in the water. It was still hot, soothing the tight muscles in her legs while she rested her weight on her hands. She hadn't come with anything particular to say, just knew Saychelle needed company from people who understood her pain and fear.

"It was the smell of him," the *visnpresta* said suddenly, "and the words he spoke. He said them before, when he caught me in the peristyle trying to tell the elites about what he did to my sister. It was like he plucked those things straight from one of my nightmares."

"He did the same to me in Kalt Hasa, with Thorne's voice," Cistine admitted.

Saychelle scoffed bitterly. "What sort of twisted, malicious man makes himself so excellent at breaking people?"

"One who's incapable of anything else." Cistine bent forward, gripping her ankles and resting her cheek on her knees. "He doesn't understand how to form bonds, so he has to control people instead. Baba Kallah said it was because of how his own father raised him, and how his father's father raised *him*, and so on."

"That's no excuse."

"No, it's not. But at least it ends with Thorne."

Saychelle sighed. "He was brilliant today. He commanded the situation like a Chancellor should."

Cistine's stomach churned at her soft, admiring tone. "Do you still love him?"

Saychelle tapped one finger steadily on her ribs. "Thorne is a reminder that I once dreamed different dreams...and, yes, he was part of them. But what's done is done, and we can't go back. Even if we could, he wouldn't want to. He's moved on and found his happiness, and as a *visnpresta*, unbelievably, I've found mine. Once we destroy his father, we'll part ways. I doubt we'll see each other again."

"It doesn't have to be that way. This cabal cares for you. You have a place here."

"Perhaps I did. But after today..." She dragged her hands down her face. "Stars, today was a disaster. I thought I'd healed enough to face him, but I'm just as wounded as I've always been."

"If it's any consolation, I know how it feels to be hurt that way. I'll have a long streak of good days, and then I'll have a terrible dream, or I'll catch the smell of roses, or something will happen like in that courtroom...and suddenly it seems like all the progress I made was just a way I tricked myself for a while."

"And what do you do then?"

"I cry. I let myself feel all that anger and wonder if it will ever end. And then I hold onto this," she tugged the compass pendant from the collar of her armor, "and I remind myself it's not going to last. I'm here, not in Kalt Hasa anymore. So I go train with Quill, or I keep Thorne company, or spend time with the others. Sometimes, like today, I visit Mira and just talk. I do normal things until *I* start to feel normal again."

Saychelle blinked owlishly and waited, as if she hoped Cistine would go on. So she did. "The truth is, I don't think wholeness is a place we're going. It's a lifelong journey. We'll never escape what happened to us because it's part of our story now, but we get to choose if we live on that page forever or move on and write the next one."

Saychelle's gaze darted back to the ceiling and lingered among the vaults. Then she dragged herself upright on her hands. "You know, I'd like that tea now."

Her shoulders relaxed slightly while they drank in silence, offering the simple comfort of company until a knock came at the door. Ariadne slipped inside, carrying a bouquet of flowers in a vase—lilies and lavender, petunias and daises, freesias, ferns, and dahlias. She lowered herself at the pool's edge and set it in her sister's lap.

"Oh, Ariadne, look at this," Saychelle whispered. "You haven't lost your touch. Mother and Father would be proud." A tense, wobbly smile floated across her face. "You know, I haven't spoken to them in ten years. Perhaps they blame me. Ever since the shop closed..."

"That wasn't your fault," Cistine said. "We all know Salvotor is behind that, regardless of what his reports say."

Saychelle's shoulders rose and fell. "I don't know how I'm going to face him again."

"You won't have to yet," Ariadne said. "Deja will testify first. You have time to recover."

"And pray to the gods he doesn't find another way to break me?"

"You aren't broken," Cistine argued. "None of us are. He's not strong enough to break us."

"She's right." Ariadne cupped her sister's cheeks in her hands. "I'm sorry I didn't reach you quicker today, but I won't be too late next time. For all my other flaws, my jealousy and pride, I will never abandon you again." She pressed her brow to Saychelle's. "I don't blame you for what happened that night. Do you hear me, *Malat?* I have never blamed you."

A tear slid down Saychelle's pale cheek. "I'm so sorry, Ari."

"So am I. But it's Salvotor who will be sorriest in the end." She drew back, freeing one side of Saychelle's face to clasp Cistine's hand on the marble floor. "Soon he will be encaged where he belongs, and we'll be free to walk these streets like elites. Like *queens*."

Cistine's heart rose on a current of determination and fresh strength at those words. Because Salvotor had kept aside a unique breed of abuse for all of them, but Ariadne was right—they were still free if they chose to be. And they would find their way down the path to healing together, like stubborn flowers blooming through the snow.

CHAPTER
TWENTY-SEVEN

DAYS OF DROWNING. Days of agony. Days of dragging herself down the tenuous tether of reason whenever Kashar fed her the strange water and tainted meat and demanded to know what was happening in Valgard now. What the Princess was doing there, what they had already done, what *she* had done...

She. Her. *Asheila Kovar.*

She fought to remember who that was. Some days, Kashar managed to take her name away, to convince her she was nothing but Shackle and Gag and Water. Rarely food. They kept her weak, famished. Sometimes she was dimly aware of the cuts on her face and hands pulsing hotly, oozing some purulent fluid.

Shackle and Gag and Water and Infection. A pleasant combination.

Yet even on the worst days, when she sweated out enough of the sweet water to feel the sickness raging under her skin, she remembered other things she was.

Rain-dancer. Beast-slayer. Someone she hated had called her that, long ago. *Fearless.*

Someone else called her that. The man who was Tether and Heart. The one she...

There were no words for it. They were all lost.

She gave them nothing when they changed from watering her to hitting her, to hanging her by the back of her neck over the cliffs, and back to the feeding and watering. Kindness and cruelty in waves, a vicious scale weighed in the palm of Kashar's hand. The leader, the man who decided her fate; the one with split knuckles from breaking her nose. The friend with the rations and kind touches. The stranger with the endless waterskins and glowing jars in his hand. The enemy who tried to make her forget who and what she was.

Rain-dancer. Beast-slayer. They soaked the gag, the only way to force water into her when she decided she'd rather die of dehydration than fight against her mind and heart, forever in conflict over what she should tell them. *Fearless.*

She was not a Warden, Kashar reminded her. Disgraced. Discarded. Her King didn't want her. No one was coming.

A week passed. Then more days after that.

No one came. Still she didn't yield.

They took it all away from her. Warden. Warrior. Asheila Kovar. Ashe.

Rain-dancer. Beast-slayer, she chanted in her mind while Kashar split her face open again. *Fearless.*

"Tell us about the Princess!" he roared.

Rain-dancer.

A blow to the gut. "Tell us what she's doing in Valgard!"

Beast-slayer.

"Kashar!" One of his men shouted. "Trouble!"

Kashar dropped her and snapped a kick into her temple.

Fearless.

The darkness claimed her again.

Her head was clearer when she woke—clear enough to know she wasn't where they'd held her for...days? Weeks? Gods knew how long.

Rounded walls. A cold echo of breath and murmuring voices.

Cave.

"What news from Camere?" Kashar's voice. Hated. Trusted. Enemy. Friend. Even now, she wasn't sure.

"It's done. The tunnels at the northern border were precisely where she claimed they'd be."

She. Had she told them—?

"It was too close," another man growled. "Had we not moved camp when we did—"

"My uncle would've had our heads," Kashar muttered. "I'm aware."

Keeping her eyes tightly shut, she wriggled slightly closer to their voices, the better to hear the next man's words: "Good that Reema made it to Valgard. She'll find the truth of this fallacious treaty soon enough."

Shock cracked through her, a whip of clarity so sharp she nearly opened her eyes and gave herself away.

She. Valgard.

A Mahasari in Valgard—where Cistine was fighting to solidify the treaty. If Jad's eyes were there, if someone made it through the siege tunnels Talheim dug below the borders, then none of this mattered. A few days, weeks perhaps in Valgard, and their spy would know the truth. And Jad would make good on his every threat against Talheim.

She flexed in vain against her bonds, struggling to dredge up strength and name and purpose through the absolute roaring in her head, the need to flee, to run. Nevermind that her King thought her a disgrace. Nevermind that the kingdom of her birth didn't want her. She would do this one last thing for them, crawl if she had to, to finish it. To warn them.

The next words from her captors stopped her cold. "Reema's all we need. This woman is no longer of use to us. It's time to be done with it."

Kashar sighed. "I know."

Those two words sealed her fate.

Ruthless fingers closed under her elbows, ripping her to her feet. She struggled to plant them, but there was no purchase on the slippery stone. A man on each arm—Kashar's familiar balsamic scent on her right—they dragged her from the cave, the whipping rain of a Talheimic windstorm lashing across their faces.

They'd climbed up one of the tallest mountains, the cave overlooking a sheer, dizzying drop to the tufted trees. The ledge was so gods-forsaken *narrow*, and Kashar and his man heaved her to the edge and dangled her over so she looked down into the void below. Into death itself.

It was different this time, the way they held her over it. She fought to marshal her wits, crying clarity back into her mind.

"This is your last chance," Kashar shouted above the pounding rain. "Tell us about the treaty!"

Mouth slicing in a wicked smile, she angled her head to look up at him. "Hoping to win favor with your uncle by breaking me before your spy comes back?"

Shock broke in his eyes, and she seized the chance, barreling her weight forward and ripping free of their arms. She swiveled, knees screaming against the rock, her ankles hooking Kashar's and her head slamming into his companion's belly, knocking the wind out of him.

But the impact dazed her, too. The wound on her temple opened back up; hot blood streaked her cheek as she shoved herself down the ledge a few inches—and stopped, panting. She had no weapon, not even her hands and feet to help her run. Just an addled head, a fever-hollowed body, and the necklace burning hot over her heart.

The necklace. The starstone. And the memory of Sigrid's voice, a storyteller's cadence on a dark, disastrous night.

Some call them the Eyes of the Gods. In the ancient epics, they were used to summon aid from all corners of Valgard.

With nothing to lose, nothing left at all but the perilous edge before her and Kashar climbing to his feet, bleeding from the mouth and swearing, she flipped onto her back, hauled the glittering stone from her collar in her teeth, and screamed with all her might, "Gods! Someone, *help me!*"

Kashar's boot slammed into her back, flipping her over the edge.

The descent was oddly silent. Oddly long, at least in her mind, seconds stretching out between every shocked, hopeless, raging thought. That it should end like this, after the war, after the Blood Hive, after *everything*—

Fitting. Fitting that when she'd fallen so far, a fall would kill her.

Some quiet part of her, mangled and raw, gave way.

Then a roar like thunder shattered in her ears. From the clouds embracing the mountaintops, a streak of pure gold ignited, a falling star spearing down from above, growing larger, closer, falling with her—

Another roar, burning the rain to steam, and fire erupted across the sky. That falling star barreled into Ashe, lighting her up, turning her to flame as well. Her head snapped back and shadows puddled across her vision as her body impacted.

She wasn't certain if it was unconsciousness or death that greeted her in the darkness this time. But she welcomed it either way.

CHAPTER
TWENTY-EIGHT

THREE VISITS TO Kadlin's grand house turned up no evidence of the thief, in the treasure room or anywhere else. Thwarted, Tatiana, Quill and Pippet attended a guild meeting together instead, searching for any trace of guilty faces or suspicious actions among them.

Though it was difficult to admit it, she wanted her *valenar* and his sister to meet these inventors. She wanted Pippet to enjoy herself somewhere that wasn't school, and erase the scowl Quill had worn ever since Saychelle's testimony. She wanted them to feel what she did: a sense of belonging in this safe place, so unlike anywhere from their past.

It was one of the better evenings in recent memory. Pippet sprang on Athlis and Vohrun like a beady-eyed raven the moment they were introduced, and that was the last they'd see of her for the evening. Morten brought them around to every face Tatiana had yet to meet, and some she already had, proudly introducing his *Dievka* and *Afiyam* with an arm around each of their shoulders. When Kadlin finally swooped in to rescue them, leading Morten off to see her latest designs, they snatched glasses of clean cider from a tray and reclined on one of the sofas by the hearth, watching the people mill around.

"There are a lot of them," Quill mused, rubbing Tatiana's bare feet propped in his leg. "Somehow I imagined a couple of people like Mort, scribbling on papers and not speaking to each other. But this..."

"They're like a cabal of their own," Tatiana finished.

"Right." Quill swigged his cider. "So, what are they helping you with?"

"Nothing. What makes you think they are?"

"You're getting out of bed earlier and earlier these days, creeping around behind my back, stashing tools in the armoire's false floor. And don't think I haven't noticed that look in your eye, Saddlebags. You only get that right-side dimple in your smile when you're fixing or making things."

She thumped him on the shoulder. "Maybe if you spent less time staring at *me* and more time searching for someone suspicious, we'd be through with this hunt sooner."

"I can't help it. You'll always be the most captivating scoundrel in any room." He planted a kiss on the corner of her mouth, then lounged back against the arm of the sofa. "Keep your secrets if you want, just remember I'm not a fool all the time. I know the real reason you wanted us all here tonight. You can't stop thinking about it ever since Kadlin showed us her gallery." He tapped his fingertip against his cider glass, forging gentle, tingling music. "You really love it here, don't you? With these people."

"All except the thief."

"I'm saying if there wasn't one, and if you didn't have Pippet and me to think about..."

"But I do. So it's pointless."

"Tati, just listen to me. If you didn't find the thief, if Kadlin wanted you to go along and keep searching in Blaykrone..."

"But she *won't,* because she knows my answer. So let's stop talking about it."

Quill's gaze locked on hers, all traces of humor gone. "Would you go?"

She was saved having to answer by Pippet and Athlis tumbling onto the sofa with them, laughing about delivery devices and wrestling for Vohrun's freshly-decapitated body. Quill intervened in their tussling, and Tatiana turned her attention to the people around them.

They all looked so happy. Certainly some were poor enough to profit from stealing plans from Kadlin, but if she didn't find that traitor before winter's end and Kadlin had no choice but to bring them along unaware of their identity, what would become of the guild? What if that thief needed mynts again, and another invention was within reach?

Despite what she told Quill, she wondered how different things might be if she were to carry on her investigation after they'd gone—carry it on from within *Heimli Nyfadengar*.

They left with empty hands and no leads long after the rest of the guild dispersed. Kadlin waved off Tatiana's apology with a tired, heavy smile. "I didn't really think you'd solve it tonight, but I'm glad you came anyway."

They departed in a storm of Pippet's chatter about Vohrun and Athlis and wondering aloud if *she* should start inventing things. Quill nudged Tatiana and grinned, but she barely bit back a curt reminder that all these people were leaving soon anyway; it would do Pippet's heart no good to take up inventing only to go after it alone when the guild left.

They traveled only a few blocks before Pippet cut herself off mid-word, yelping, "There's Inez and Solara!"

Tatiana squinted ahead through the ghostlit gloom to where a pair of girls Pippet's age stood on the curb, frantically waving. "What are they doing out so late?"

"Solara lives near here!" Pippet flagged an arm over her head.

"Pippet, come with us!" The smaller of the two girls yelled. "Solara's father just brought home a trained eagle from the Kroaken hatcheries!"

Pippet whirled toward Quill, eyes shining. "Can I go?"

"It's late," he said.

"I know, but there's no school tomorrow!"

"What about training?"

She perched her hands on her hips. "The *trial*, remember? Aden says no more training until after Deja's testimony, he's too busy with Mira. But I promise I'll be ready to train whenever he is, Quill! *Promise*."

Tatiana slid her hand into the crook of his elbow and squeezed hard. When he glanced down at her, she shook her head, and he deflated. "Be back by midnight, or it's the last time."

Pippet flung her arms around his middle and squeezed with all her might. "You're the greatest brother there's ever been in the Three Kingdoms! Thank you!" Before he could return the embrace, she scampered off to link arms with her friends and drag them off down the street.

"You don't have to like it," Tatiana reminded him, "but change is part of time marching on."

"I know." His eyes cut sharply to her, then gentled. He brushed a ringlet behind her ear. "I know, Tati."

She freed herself from his molten stare and tugged him the opposite way from Pippet. "So. No sign of anyone suspicious."

"Not a glance." Quill seamlessly matched his stride to hers. "I asked around the markets, and nothing that's being pawned off around the city sounds like the plans, either. I'll keep looking, though. I just have to wonder what Mort was working on that someone went to this much effort to steal."

Tatiana shrugged. "I don't know. Most of Papa's inventions are inspired, but I'm not certain they were worth this much effort to take."

"And Kadlin hasn't told you what it was, either?"

"Apparently, she never got the chance to look closely at them herself. Maybe we ought to just ask Papa."

"I wouldn't, not yet. Seeing him with her tonight, I can understand why she's keeping it from him. Saw the way he looks at her, too." Quill stuffed his hands in his pockets and looked away down the dark street. "I'm just not sure that man can take one more broken heart."

CHAPTER TWENTY-NINE

IT WAS FINALLY chilly again, those flirtations between summer, autumn, and winter sliding back toward the cold of the later months, and Cistine leaned gratefully against the grand room's outside wall to cool her sweating back. Unescorted and dressed in fighting armor, she stood apart from the assembly at the Tribune's feast—even Yager's true Tribunes, patterned in ombred red-orange gowns of different cuts and styles.

This was nothing like Talheim, which followed a set course of welcomes, mingling, a seated dinner, and dancing at its celebrations; Valgardans flowed from one activity to the next and back, mingling, dancing, plucking at the serving trays and tables, lounging on sofas, then back to dancing. It was nearly impossible to hold a conversation, though she'd tried to with Liv, Astrid, and Ingrid, the archer guards escorting Maltadova and Adeima tonight.

As for the Tribunes, few had time for her. They chatted among themselves, trading jokes and jabs, and most regarded her with something between curiosity and disdain.

Grimacing, she traded her weight on her sore feet, letting the pain dull her frustration. She'd been on the move since sunrise, training and then reading while she paced, preparing for this. She needed a way in with some of the Tribunes to make them see, as perhaps their Chancellors were beginning to, why Talheim's cause mattered.

With a rustle of fine threads, his dark jacket and pants glinting in the ghostlight strung from the rafters, Thorne sidled along the wall to recline beside her, offering a plate of roasted chard and feta. "Rallying for the next wave of the siege?"

"Was there a first one?" She nibbled a chard stem and watched the ever-changing pattern of Tribunes shift again through the sprawling room. "The only people I've managed to speak to are already allies. Tyve and Skyygan don't want anything to do with me, I can tell by how they look whenever I approach."

"Why do you think that is?"

"Well, if they know me, the cause I fight for becomes personal. It's harder to ignore a kingdom's plight when it's the people's plight instead."

Thorne nodded. "So, how to intimate yourself to people too wounded by Salvotor's schemes to trust again."

Cistine searched his strong jaw and intelligent eyes for a hint of the furious, cold leader she first saw when he brought her to Hellidom all those months ago. Then she grinned. "How, indeed?"

She plucked the plate from his hands, set it on the floor, and pulled him into a dance.

Valgardan waltzes were not so different from Talheimic ones, the tunes strange but the steps roughly the same. She'd watched the Tribunes and Chancellors ebb and flow to the music long enough to mark the patterns, and to her relief, Thorne hesitated in none of them. He followed along her scheme like it was his, guiding her in the dance while she paid attention to the Tribunes coming and going around them.

"Niklause and Kyost," she murmured as they twirled past the two men chatting at the edge of the dance. "High Tribunes of Tyve and Skyygan. How well do their fellow Tribunes like them?"

"Skyygan brims with infighting," Thorne said just as quietly. "There are rumors Noaam is searching for ways to unseat Kyost and become High Tribune in his stead."

Not a good first mark, then. "And Tyve?"

"They respect their hierarchy better. Almost too much." Thorne twirled her out, then brought her back into his chest. "They're insular and secretive. All the poison studies, all the trickery behind their backs...they trust no one like they trust each other."

"Beholden to their craft. It's the sinew that knits their Court together."

"One might say."

With a graceful half-step, she changed the direction of the waltz, turning them back toward the room's edge where she let go of Thorne, grazing the tips of her fingers with his in silent farewell. Then she latched onto Niklause and pulled him into the dance instead.

Whether out of surprise or dignity, the older man didn't break her grip, falling naturally into leading the steps as everyone on the floor followed suit, changing partners fluid as a stream.

"You're High Tribune Niklause, aren't you?" Cistine said. "Of Tyve Court?"

"That I am. And I know who you are, Princess Cistine." He glanced over his shoulder toward sanctuary at the edge of dance floor.

Cistine gently tightened her hold on him and raised her voice above the music. "I'm sorry about what Salvotor did with your Court. I've never met a man so conceited about what he's owed or so vicious in how he claims it."

Niklause's gaze revolved back to her, the faintest softening around his bright brown eyes. "I've heard rumors of what you suffered in that ancient temple. Very few escape unscathed when a cruel man swings his sword."

Cistine swallowed around the lump in her throat. "That's true. I hope things are better for you now with Salvotor in chains."

"They will be once Chancellor Thorne sniffs out what remains of his father's spies."

"Talheim is personally assisting in that effort. We're making some progress already."

New interest kindled in Niklause's eyes. "Are you, now?"

Cistine smiled wryly. "Yes, when we're not handling a thousand other crucial matters."

Chuckling, Niklause spun and dipped her. "Welcome to ruling. You will find there is always something else important nudging for your attention. The trick isn't to unbury yourself from the work, it's to prop up whichever part of the heap is about to come crashing down on your head while you deal with the next one."

The warmth in her chest was a reminder that she did this not just to win a kingdom's support, but to truly open her heart to Valgard's needs, its strength and wisdom—just as she had with the cabal. "Tribune, may I ask you a question about poison studies?"

The hard muscles in Niklause's brawny arm corded under her hand. "What use does Talheim have of Tyve secrets?"

"Not Talheim...me. I don't want you to tell me your Court's secrets, either, I'd never be so bold. It's just about poison."

Niklause halted mid-dance, shrewdly searching her face. "And what does a princess care for these things?"

Cistine bit the corner of her lip, holding his wary stare. "The threat we face from the South is led by a man sometimes called the Poisoner King. All our Wardens for the past twenty years have trained in poison studies because of his obsession with battle waged through herbs. As Talheim's princess, that battle is as much mine to fight as anyone's. I'd like to know more about those threats, and I thought Tyve would know best. Besides..." she blinked away a scattering of heat in her eyes. "I've already lost someone I loved to poison. I never want to see it happen again, if I can help."

Niklause's gaze darted left and right—searching again for escape, or ensuring no one saw what he was about to do. Then he led her off to a corner where a servant offered flutes of sweet wine, took one for himself, and handed another to her. "The power of life and death in herbs is never to be taken lightly. One misguided man in a Tribune's seat with vengeance in his heart and poison at his fingertips, and our very way of rulership comes crashing down."

"I understand," Cistine said. "And I would never try to subvert that."

"Be that as it may, if you hope I'll tell you how to poison someone, you're wasting your time. I'll tell you how to guard against a man who wields those gifts amiss, but I won't place a weapon in a foreign kingdom's hand."

"I don't ask you to. But I know the power your people wield. All I'm asking is that you tell me how to protect mine."

Niklause reclined against the wall, arms folded, clinking the wine flute against his chest. Then he said, "Tell me more about this Poisoner King."

Hours later, Cistine finally peeled herself away from the conversation with Niklause, haunches smarting from sitting so long at the table where they'd finally retired when they grew sick of standing, her mind whirling with all the information given and imbibed. The things Ashe taught her of poultices and tinctures in Hellidom was mere child's play compared to what Tyve knew. Horrific images of convulsions and foaming mouths and death played at the corners of counteragents and healing properties. She would be up half the night writing down what Niklause taught her.

But equally as important as what she learned was what she forged: an understanding deeper than mere talk of war, a kindred heart in Niklause, now confronted with the notion of a southerly King who used his Court's passion against children no older than his own grandbabes.

Cistine returned to her place at the wall with new respect for a Court she hardly knew before tonight, and with knowledge she was grateful to have regardless if that was all the aid Tyve ever offered.

Thorne found her again in minutes, this time with his jacket slung over one shoulder. The dark shirt beneath fit him unfairly well, making it difficult not to stare when he reclined on the stones beside her. "That looked like a scintillating conversation."

"I think my head is as stuffed as my stomach," Cistine moaned. "It's no wonder Salvotor wanted to control Tyve. If they were less honorable, they could poison Valgard and rule everyone with a cure held ransom."

Thorne nodded grimly. "Valdemar may have his flaws, but I'll never take for granted what he could do but chooses not to. There's more nobility in the Courts than it may seem when we're at one another's throats." He inclined his body slightly toward hers. "Did you tell him about Jad?"

"Yes. I never thought Jad would be the enemy I'd rather face, but thinking about him is easier than thinking of Salvotor. And the things Niklause taught me tonight make him less frightening, too. He feels beatable to me now. He hasn't always."

"Any enemy is beatable, *Logandir*. It's only a matter of having the right weapons to face them."

"I suppose that's true of anything, even forging alliances. You just have to find the common threads and weave them together."

"Do you think you made an ally tonight, then?"

"I hope so. I think...part of me forgot how to open my heart to Valgard after it was so trampled on, with Baba Kallah and Helga, and Julian, and Kristoff..." she trailed away, thumbing the compass pendant. "But this was how I befriended the cabal. I never would've found friendship if I wasn't willing to risk being hurt. That's what this treaty is about. It's not just telling the Chancellors what lies at stake, I have to lay my heart wide open so they can see what's inside and maybe find something in me they *want* to ally themselves with."

Thorne was quiet for some time. When he spoke, his voice was hoarse. "I'm proud of every risk you take and every battle you win."

Skin all but glowing with warmth, Cistine tapped her heel restlessly and folded her hands behind her back, watching Tribunes feast and laugh and dance together. She spotted Kyost among the crowd, and her stomach twisted. Another ally to make; another mountain to ascend. But already she was weary; a tired heart laid bare could only take so much, and she frayed more quickly now than she used to. "I think I'm through taking risks tonight. Kyost is a problem for a different day."

"Then we're done here?"

Cistine turned her head to the wall and looked up at Thorne. His face was near enough that their noses might've brushed if she rose up on the tips of her toes. His gaze drifted down to her lips, studying them in a way that made her heart absolutely pound.

"Between us," he murmured, "this isn't the best entertainment Valgard has to offer."

"Oh?" Cistine breathed.

Thorne's eyes flicked back up to hold hers, mischief sizzling in their depths. "Let's get out of here."

She blinked, leaning back. "Thorne, this is an official feast. As a Chancellor—"

"As a Chancellor, I would be remiss not to show Talheim's emissary that not all Valgardans are pompous, pampered elites wining and laughing in fine clothes." He tipped his head even nearer, his warm breath fanning her face. "It would be my honor to prove our kingdom is still capable of some real enjoyment."

She cast a last glance at the stuffy room, the bejeweled gowns and fine coats, all the conversations had and not had tonight, and her throat hitched. "I'm all yours."

Smirking, Thorne pushed up from the wall. "Meet me in the courtyard in twenty minutes. I'll show you the sort of fun Sillakove used to make in this city."

CHAPTER THIRTY

STORNHAZ SPARKLED UNDER waning moonlight, pale homes glinting with the thinnest sheen of ice. The frigid air reminded Cistine giddily of Darlaska, though here the gods themselves took pleasure in the decoration, adorning homes and shops with lacy patterns of frost whose subtle winking matched the smile on Thorne's face.

"Where in God's name are we going?" Cistine asked for the fourth time when they crossed from the elite districts and into the poorer ones.

"You'll see."

A quarter-mile later, he brought her inside a tavern.

After the disastrous night in Veran when she first met Quill, Cistine never expected to feel at ease in a place like this. Yet the rustic tenor of the wooden walls, antler sets, and beast hides on display, even the peal of a fiddle and drum were more welcoming than the gilded finery of the Tribune's feast. Here, she was not the only one in armor; hardly anyone looked at her twice. Everything felt like an echo of Hellidom or the Den, or even the place in Jovadalsa where she and Maleck journeyed on the hunt for Ashe.

Melancholy crested through her at the thought of him, scarred and strong and smiling. She missed that smile and the dark, looming shield of his presence guarding her back. She'd been apart from him and Ashe too much lately, and with time even the pain of her Warden's betrayal in Siralek was fading into sheer missing.

Thorne's hand brushed the small of her back and he bent his head to speak in her ear. "This was where I talked Quill, Maleck, and Aden into joining Sillakove. At that table in the corner."

He nodded at the place where so much began, a corner most would overlook. Blood running hot with glee, Cistine grinned at him. "Let's sit there!"

She snagged their seats while Thorne ordered meads, sliding one to her while he took up position across the table. She relaxed before her first sip, and Thorne wore a perpetual smile, sprawling in his chair, one hand braced on his thigh, eyes scouring the room with a blend of nostalgia and contentment.

"I like seeing you this way," Cistine blurted with boldness she couldn't blame on the drink. "Without the weight of a kingdom on your shoulders."

His gaze darted back to her, smile softening. "The feeling is mutual."

Flushing, Cistine buried her nose in her tankard again and surfaced with a question. "What's your favorite memory from before you left Stornhaz?"

"I'll tell you if you tell me yours in Talheim."

"Agreed."

He leaned forward to thumb a fleck of mead from her nose. "I was fifteen. Quill, Tatiana, Aden and I got into a tavern brawl, entirely *not* our fault..."

Cistine lost track of time after that; lost track of who came and went from the tavern, how many reels began and ended, when they traded mead for water. A plate of roasted pork and vegetables appeared between them, and they devoured it, still asking questions: their best and worst birthdays. Their favorite seasons. Places they would travel and things they would see if they could go anywhere.

"Now that I've been here, it's the Wild Islands." Cistine pointed at Thorne with an asparagus spear. "Did you know there's an entire *kingdom* of pirates out there? It's rumored to be one the most dangerous places in the world. Ships will add weeks to their travel just to give it a wide berth."

"So, naturally, the sole heir of the Middle Kingdom wants to go there." Thorne parried her asparagus with his so he could dip it in the bowl of horseradish sauce between them. "Knowing you, you'd soon have them eating from the palm of your hand."

"It's possible! If I can manage one treaty, maybe I can manage more," Cistine laughed. "And what about you? If you could go anywhere in all the kingdoms of the world, where—?"

"Talheim."

No hesitation. No teasing. Nothing but bare honesty in his face. Slowly, Cistine set down her asparagus. "Thorne."

"It sounds beautiful, the way you describe it. The Calaluns, the amber plains, the mineral lakes and gold deserts to the south. I want to see it all like you see it." His voice quieted. "I hope to see it *with* you someday."

Cistine swallowed the heat from her throat. "I'd like that. To show you my kingdom." An impossible, reckless hope winnowed into her heart; that perhaps he wouldn't only visit it, but perhaps, someday, beside her—

A man staggered out of the dance and bashed into their table, jolting it against the wall and ramming their chairs off-kilter. They righted themselves, and Thorne reached up to catch the man before he collapsed in a drunken, chortling heap on the floor.

"Well, that's that!" His partner laughed, pushing her short-cropped dark hair from her eyes. Fists perched on her hips, she nodded along to the changing tempo of the music, studying Thorne. "How's about a dance?"

He shot a glance at Cistine, equal parts hope and concern, and she flapped her hands. She needed a moment to quiet her raging heart and lock away that rash and errant thought seeding in her head before it could fully take root. "Go have fun! I'm not finished eating. Besides..." she reached into her breastpocket and tugged out the small bestiary he gave her in the library. "I have work to do."

"A bestiary, eh?" The woman arched a brow. "I'm a hunter myself. Don't let the look of all these men fool you, though. I doubt you'll have any need of that thing here."

"She's always prepared for the occasion." Thorne winked, following the woman to the dance floor.

Chair wedged against the wall, legs crossed on the seat, Cistine sipped and ate and read the bestiary, watching the room throb with glee and abandon between pages. It didn't matter which Court these taverngoers were sworn to tonight, who'd Named them if they were Named at all. As one people, they danced and drank and celebrated, none belonging to one partner; they were their own and each other's, a twisting ribbon of linking arms and pounding feet circling the floor, forever trading, forever changing. And there was her *selvenar*, dancing and drinking with friendly ease among them, then letting them drag him to a gambling table where his roaring laughter over a game of cards carried better and brighter than the music.

Cistine watched him in the ghostlight, his shirt collar undone and sweat streaking his hair and cheeks, looking far happier among the poor and luckless than he ever did among the elites. He came alive here in ways she hadn't seen since Hellidom and Geitlan, reviving a smile all but lost after Baba Kallah's death. She didn't realize how much she missed that until she saw it again; her own grin stole across her face until her cheeks ached.

Thorne had begun here. For all his lofty heritage, the plight of people like these first woke the leader within him; not his glorious destiny as Kanslar's Chancellor, a path set before him by his father, but the road paved with stars all the way to Sillakove Court. That dream had begun among the destitute rabble where Thorne spied needs unmet in bent heads and bowed backs—and resolved to do something more than what came about from fine feasts like the one they abandoned tonight.

In all those ways and so many more, he was her equal: born rulers both, but leaders by choice. She'd never met someone so like her, had never felt so seen as when his eyes found hers across the tavern, understanding searing between them so hot and bright it made flipped her stomach.

The fiddle picked up tempo, and Thorne excused himself from the gambling table, conveniently forgetting his hard-won mynts. He slid through the crowded room toward her, lifting his arms and twisting a few times to avoid barmaids and drunkards until he reached her chair. That mischievous glint was back in his gaze, both hands sliding back through his hair. "I have no doubt the Princess of Talheim can waltz, but can she dance a jig?"

Cistine's cheeks warmed. "It's entirely possible she's never tried."

Thorne offered his hands, palms upturned. "If you'll have me."

She slid her fingers over his, calluses to calluses. "I'll always have you."

He tugged her into the dancing circle, smooth and practiced as if they'd already done this a hundred times. And, by the gods, they danced.

Cistine's bare feet were rubbed raw and her calves ached worse than after any training session when she and Thorne finally fell in their chairs again, spent and sweating and laughing. The trace of his fingers still branded her hips, his hair a ruffled mess where she'd looped her fingers into it while they spun. Gulping mouthfuls of warm water until she was sated, Cistine wiped her mouth on her wrist and gasped, "I never want this night to end!"

Thorne draped his head over his seatback, eyes tumbling shut. "I'm not sure it's even night anymore, *Logandir*."

That was entirely possible. The windows were so gritty with dust from the streets and layered in frost, it was impossible to tell what time of day or night it was.

Cistine boosted herself from her seat and plopped sideways on Thorne's knees, and his head swung up. Surprise lit in his eyes, then cautious curiosity. And perhaps it was the mead, or the dancing, or that thought she couldn't quite bury even when reading and jigging; perhaps it was simply because she'd had a full night without a single dip into panic or one crippling sense of doom. Whatever the cause, Cistine felt bolder than usual as she laid her hands on Thorne's chest. "Say my Name."

"Cistine?"

"Not that one. And not *Logandir*, either."

His throat bobbed in a sharp swallow. Gripping the seatback in one hand and her waist with the other, he shoved himself upright, shifting her deeper into his lap, their faces inches apart. His nose brushed hers, his breath on her lips; his eyes fell to half-mast, then lower. "Wild—"

Palms slammed into a table and a shrill voice cried, "*That's not fair!*"

Cistine stiffened and rocked back from Thorne, catching his wide-eyed horror rising to match hers at that familiar voice. She spun out of his lap, and he shot to his feet beside her, turning toward the gambling table where the commotion emanated.

On the other side of the tavern, Pippet gambled at a table full of men twice her age. One of them rose slowly to his feet, towering above her, and in that instant Cistine saw an echo of herself—the girl who rarely argued with anyone who didn't love her, choosing the wrong fight.

Thorne started toward the table, and Cistine grabbed him under the arm. "No! Dancing in a tavern is one thing. If a Chancellor starts brawling in the streets..." She met his burning, frustrated gaze. If word of such an act reached Salvotor, he'd try to twist it; the tenuous trust of the other Chancellors might waver even more. "I'll handle this. Slip outside and meet us in the alley back the way we came."

Thorne touched her jaw. "Careful, *Logandir*."

He snatched up his jacket, and they parted ways: him toward the door, her toward the gambling table. She only made it two strides before the situation escalated from terrible to worse: Pippet spat something Cistine was too far away to hear, but the ringleader at the table, a brawny blond man, snatched her by the collar and yanked her close. "What did you say, girl?"

Cistine reached them and laid a hand on the man's wrist, letting him feel the power of a well-trained sparrer in her touch. "Thank you for finding my sister. I've been looking everywhere for her."

The man glanced down at her flexing fingers, then at Pippet. "This little cheat belongs to you?"

Cistine forced a cold smile, though anger tightened her mouth. "I'm responsible for her, yes."

"Good! Then I expect you'll pay back every mynt she just stole from us with those quick hands."

Cistine tightened her hold, pressing beneath the hinge of his wrist. "Pippet doesn't cheat. Now let go of her."

Scowling, the man obliged. Pippet snapped back on her heels, straightening her collar—and three cards tumbled from her sleeve.

Cistine gaped at her. Pippet peered up through her lashes, teeth bared in a sheepish smile.

The man roared, first in rage, then louder in pain, because someone flung a wine jug hard from his left, cracking him in the temple and sending him sprawling into his friends. The woman who'd beckoned Thorne to the dance floor now beckoned Cistine and Pippet the same way. "*Run!*"

Cistine grabbed Pippet by the hood and dragged her from the tavern on the woman's heels, three furious cardplayers in pursuit and the ringleader bawling at them to teach Pippet a lesson she'd never forget.

They burst outdoors and banked left, shooting down the street. No sign of Thorne anywhere between the dark buildings, and fear stabbed into Cistine's chest. What if this was some sort of trap? What if someone else had been lying in wait for him?

Pippet yelped, digging her heels into the colored cobblestones as two of the three gamblers appeared at the end of the alley. Cistine slammed to a halt as well, letting go of her hood and spinning to face the other man prowling up at their backs.

"Flee or fight?" the woman panted beside them.

Cistine glanced at Pippet. "Fight."

It was a quick but violent tussle; as large and brutish as the men were, Cistine, Pippet, and their savior had sobriety on their side, and one was trained by the former Lord of the Blood Hive, one by the entire cabal, and the third by someone clearly just as capable. In a matter of seconds, Cistine had one man down with a sprained ankle and a broken nose. Pippet tripped another and rammed into his back elbow-first, flinging him against the alley wall in a choking daze. With the battle-blood inherent in the Valgardan people, the woman landed two swift punches on the man enclosing them from the rear, snapped his wrist, wedged his arm behind his back and knocked him to his knees. Then she grabbed his head in both hands and twisted sharply.

"*Stop!*" Cistine's shout overlapped Pippet's horrified scream. "You don't need to kill him!"

She froze, then slowly released the gambler. "I wasn't going to. Only scare him off from chasing small girls." She chopped his throat, and he folded down in a retching heap.

A shadow annealed at the alley mouth, and Cistine's bark of warning turned to a cry of relief when Thorne stepped into view, breathing hard as if from running, blood on his knuckles. "That was the fourth. It won't be the last."

"Go," the woman said. "Talheim's Princess and Kanslar's Chancellor can't be found at a scene like this. What it will do to your reputation and your treaty..."

"She's right," Thorne said. "We need to leave."

Cistine backed away, keeping her eyes on their unexpected savior. "Who are you?"

"Daria." She glared toward a swell of shouting from the tavern. "Now go, will you?"

Pippet grabbed Cistine's hand, and with Thorne at their backs, they fled deep into the grayness that was nearly dawn.

"Shouldn't you be in bed at this hour?"

The mild, cool words were the first Thorne spoke since they left the alley, and now they were nearly to the courthouse. Even Cistine winced at the quiet edge in his voice.

Pippet scuffed every step heavily, shrugging. "Quill said I didn't have to be back until midnight."

"It's almost dawn," Cistine pointed out dryly, and Pippet groaned, burying her face in her hands.

"And I suspect Quill would've taken a different stance entirely if he knew what you were doing with that time." Thorne took Pippet's shoulder, steering her around a chink in the cobblestones she couldn't see. "Why were you in a tavern?"

Another shrug, sliding his hand from her arm. "Schooling isn't for free.

I know they're only letting me stay because you're a Chancellor and Quill's your friend. I've been trying to help earn the mynts back, that's all."

"*Been* trying?"

Pippet dropped her hands, worrying her lower lip between her teeth. "Since school started. Evian's uncle owns that tavern, we go there after classes sometimes. And sometimes I go at night, too. The betting is better after dark."

Thorne rasped both palms down his stubbled cheeks. "Who taught you to play cards like that?"

"The cabal did. Julian did. *You* did."

"I'm fairly sure I didn't teach you to cheat."

Pippet sighed. "Well, no. Inez and Solara taught me that."

"Friends from school?"

She nodded. "But they didn't want to stay as late tonight."

Thorne slowed, then halted as they reached the top of the bridge stretching across the Ismalete Channel to the courthouse. He squinted at Pippet, not in anger, but like he was trying to sort her out. "I'm grateful that you want to do your part, but mynts won by cheating do more harm than good. If you want to earn a portion in this city, I can find you a trade."

Pippet raised her gaze to the height of his navel. "At the library, maybe?"

"The public outhouses, to start. But once you've proven you can earn an honest wage, I'll see what I can do."

She slumped in resignation. "Fine."

"And no more sneaking out. No more gambling. If you're caught in another tavern, you'll face the law's judgement. And it will not be as pleasant as mine." She gave a sullen nod. "Can I trust you to heed my word?"

A beat. Then another nod—firmer. Still, she was the picture of dejection, wiping her nose on her wrist and examining the bridge between her boots. "You're not going to tell Quill, are you?"

Cistine glanced at Thorne. He held her stare a moment, then looked at Pippet. "Do you not want me to tell him because he'll be unreasonable, or because you did something wrong and you know he won't like it?"

Pippet scuffed her toe on the ground and shrugged.

Thorne dropped on his heels before her, taking her shoulders in his hands. "In this cabal, we don't run from our mistakes. We confess them and make amends. That's what keeps us strong, keeps us together. So, no, I'm not going to tell Quill. Because—?"

"Because *I'm* going to." Pippet sulked a few seconds longer, then finally raised damp eyes to his. "Will you come with me?"

Thorne pressed a kiss to her brow. "Of course I will."

"And I'll leave you to it." Cistine stifled a yawn with her hand. "I'm going to bed." And privately, perhaps cowardly, she didn't want to witness Quill's heartbreak at this fresh reminder his sister was growing up, as capable of being crafty as the rest of them.

Thorne straightened to his feet, guiding Pippet with an arm around her shoulders. "I'll see you tomorrow, *Logandir*."

A promise. And in his eyes, warmth and softness lingered from a night of casual intimacy like they'd never had before.

"Oh, Thorne. I think you were right," Cistine said. "It's already a new day."

CHAPTER
THIRTY-ONE

DEATH WAS DARKNESS. Peace. Dreaming. Cradled in wind and wreathed in fire, she drifted, unmoored from every sense of self. Identity. Purpose.

Whatever came next, she was ready. Fearless. Resigned.

Death was dark walls and iron bars, a litany of prayers raised in solitude and captivity. Death raised its head and looked at her with eyes of bright hazel shining in a gaunt face—an anchor to her spirit.

You do not die. Stay awake. I will find you.

Bitter irony. Not even Death wanted her.

She woke suddenly, thrust out by Death's vicious hands, pain arcing across the wounds on her face. A strange sound broke the world, broke her chest, her throat, and she realized it was her, sobbing with all her might, the words tearing out of her.

Just let me die, I'm done, I don't want to do this anymore.

The heat banked, steadied, wrapped around her.

Sleep, Life whispered back. *Sleep, and all will be well.*

She didn't open her eyes—didn't want to cling any tighter to living.

Tell me who you are, Life crooned.

Beast-slayer. Rain-dancer. Fearless.

She was not afraid of Death when the darkness reached for her,

230

wrapping her in its smothering arms. She was afraid she would have to wake again.

The pain had dulled when she surfaced next, yet the heaviness in her chest was greater now that the fever burned away, the addling of her mind settled. She knew what she wanted—that she'd begged for death and feared to live.

This was the bottom. This was breaking.

It was waking on a narrow cliff, curled on a bed of moss and leaf to the low throb of a face broken by Mahasari bastards, of cracked ribs and infection still hot in her wounds. It was knowing she was rescued and realizing it might be worse than what awaited at the end of that mortal plunge from the mountain. And it was shock blunted to nothing but a whisper when the soft thrum of a great wind moved behind her, and she rolled onto her other side to find herself staring at her savior: a great, golden dragon.

They stared at each other for a moment; then his maw tumbled open, spilling saliva-damp leaves and herbs on the rock ledge barely large enough for both of them. Morning dew sparkled like opal tips on his hide, and his massive head cocked as he watched her with eyes the exact color of a flame.

She ought to feel *something* more than this emptiness in her chest, this hole where most would carry wonder or terror or surprise at beholding a Great Dragon. She barely had the strength to wonder why he was carrying leaves, of all things. She'd been rescued from death by a gods-damned *dragon*, and it sparked no feeling in her.

Finally, the dragon sighed. "This is typically the moment where humans scream and beg for their lives." She couldn't even muster a shrug, and those glittering gemstone eyes narrowed. "I know you can speak. You told me your names while you thrashed with fever."

Beast-slayer. Rain-Dancer. Fearless.

She was worthy of none of them. That fever had burned away whatever remained of the Hive fighter, the Warden she'd once been; all that was left was the fearlessness, unafraid of death and this beast who could and likely should swallow her whole.

"I thought Talheim hunted dragons to extinction four kings ago." The first words out of her—begging for a reaction.

"And I thought it trained its damsels to put daggers in our eyes."

Damsel. The word sparked a low burning she quickly smothered, refusing its warmth. "I know you. You're that dragon Cistine told me about. The one who carried her and the others from Kalt Hasa."

"Astute. I believe I know you, as well."

A mirthless laugh rashed her throat. "That would make one of us."

He settled into a crouch, wings tucked close around his body. "You are the one they tell tales of in the North. Beast-slayer. Rain-Dancer." A pause while he considered her. "I've been searching for you."

"Kill me, then. Get it over with."

"If I wished you dead, I wouldn't have plucked you from your fall, would I? Nor would I have subjected myself to chewing herbal packs day and night for your face. It's going to scar, you know. But you'll live."

She waited for those words to matter, to inspire some sense of purpose or hope. But there was nothing.

The dragon heaved a steaming sigh. "Not since our kind first taught man the Old Language has there been one so *inept* at common speech. Now is where you *thank me.*"

"I'm not thankful. I don't..."

I don't want to be alive.

Exhausted, aching to her very core, she stared at the dragon. He stared back, his mocking expression folding into something quieter. "Then why did you call for aid?"

Her hand fell to the starstone dangling against her throat. Why *had* she called out? A desperate instinct for survival surpassing her own wishes? Was self-sabotage all she had left—an endless life of stealing the things she wanted from herself? "Why did *you* answer?" she deflected.

The dragon gazed at her fingers on the stone, and there was no question now—something did soften in his gaze. "It has been many, many moons since someone called to me through a starstone, since I was deemed worthy to be anyone's help. Nearly two decades by your mortal reckoning. When that call sang to me through a world that fell quiet twenty years ago, how could I not come?"

She let her fingers fall to her side, holding her up on the rock. "Well, I'm sorry to tell you this, but you wasted your time."

"The Great Father does not make mistakes. Of all the creatures in all the lands in all the world, that call came to *me*...the one already searching for rumors of the beast-slayer, the rain-dancer of the Blood Hive. And here I find you, a kingdom away, and your call came to *me*. What is that, if not fate? If not destinies entwined?"

"A cruel joke." Exhausted, she settled back on the leaf bed. "I'm not those things anymore. I'm just Asheila Kovar." Hollow, dull words with nothing to give them meaning anymore. She no more knew who Asheila Kovar was than a stranger on Astoria's streets.

The silence lived and breathed, full of thought while she shivered, stroked by the brisk autumn wind swirling through the mountains. Then bright, golden warmth enveloped her as the dragon settled at her back, curling his massive bulk around her body. "And I am just Bresnyar. But perhaps together, we could be something more."

She snorted and offered no reply. It wouldn't take long for that cruel optimism to fade. He'd dragged her back from death's threshold; now she'd show him every honest inch of the thing he saved.

Then he'd be gone like the rest of them. And she could finally fade away in peace.

CHAPTER THIRTY-TWO

IT WAS HAPPENING again.

Kalt Hasa's dark walls around him, shadows locked like fetters over his wrists and ankles. But it was not Cistine his father attacked this time, it was Ariadne, her heartbroken face turned to him, eyes full of betrayal that he didn't help her, that he couldn't break free even to save her.

He hadn't stopped any of it. Hadn't spared her this trial or protected her sister or kept his cabal safe like he swore.

His cabal—

Kalt Hasa's walls became catacomb tunnels, a prison of rock and steel grates with Aden trapped on the other side, reaching out to him, a plea for salvation on his lips. But though Thorne's heart ached, his feet turned and he walked away from the man who'd been like his brother, who raised him like a father and loved him like the other half of his own heart.

Shadowed arms twined around Aden from behind and dragged him screaming into the pits of the Blood Hive, and Thorne just walked away.

He jerked awake from that, retching, flinging off the sheets and shifting to rise from the bed—but he couldn't. His legs wouldn't move.

Gripping the sheets in a trembling fist, he stared at his lower half, willing his toes to wiggle, his feet to press into the bed. Nothing. Only spectral sizzles of pain along his nerves—then gone.

Breathing hard, tears slipping unbidden down his cheeks, Thorne watched his body fail him. And he could do nothing about it, couldn't help himself—just like he hadn't helped his family.

It seemed like hours before Cistine said his name from behind the door, though he couldn't muster a response. It cracked open, and he felt more than saw her relieved smile when she spied him sitting up, awake. "There you are! Didn't you hear me call you? You missed breakfast, I waited forever for—"

"I can't move."

The voice didn't sound like his. The words *couldn't* be his.

Cistine halted on the periphery of his sight. "What?"

"My legs. I can't feel my legs." He raised his eyes to her, desperate, barely swallowing his panic.

Cistine came to the side of the bed and sat, running her hand up his bare leg. He might've felt immodest any other day, wearing only a pair of flannel half-trousers ending midway down the thigh and having her fingers on his calves and knees and feet, but he was too terrified to be embarrassed. "You can't feel that?"

"Nothing." His fingers twisted the sheet into sweat-soaked knots. "I don't know what's wrong with me."

"Were you having a nightmare?"

His vision danced with the imprint of her face, Ariadne's face, *Aden's* face. Haltingly, he nodded.

Crossing her own legs, Cistine lifted his foot into her lap and kneaded the sole. "Look at me, Thorne. *Breathe.* You aren't paralyzed, you're just tense."

He wanted to believe that, but nothing like this had ever happened to him before, and he couldn't *move his stars-damned legs.* "What if I'm not? If the feeling doesn't come back..." If he couldn't train, couldn't fight, couldn't walk into meetings or stand before his father—

Cistine held his gaze unflinchingly. "If you never walk again, then I'll crawl with you. But I promise you, it's going to pass. You have to let it go. As long as that fear stays in you, you're not getting up from this bed."

He forced himself not to look at his traitorous legs, her hands on his foot that he still couldn't feel. He focused only on her eyes: brown-flecked green pools full of conviction. "We'd make quite a pair," he conceded at last. "Crawling into the next treaty meeting together."

"We'd call it a show of good faith. Or a bold statement." The corner of her mouth quirked up. "Imagine Bravis's face. He's fed up with our nonsense already."

"A bit more wouldn't hurt him, uptight as he is."

She pursed her lips and squinted. "I'm trying to imagine what my *father* would say if I came into his throne room that way."

Thorne let go of the sheets, rocked his shoulders back, and adopted his most imperious tone. "No woman of the Talheimic royal family has crawled before a man in our history, Cistine. I know you are fully capable of putting your foot up my backside. Now, rise."

She burst into laughter. "That's him, that's my father *precisely*. How did you know?"

"I simply imagined you with a beard and mustache." She swatted his foot, and he winced, muscles clenching. "I felt that."

She flicked his toe. "And that?"

"No. But the first time..."

Waving a hand, she went back to massaging his foot. "Well, if you want to continue that imitation of my father..."

But this wasn't about Cyril Novacek, however poorly Thorne mimicked the man. It was his daughter, an island within her own hurt and healing—and his. If panic and pain were a dark sea, she was the shore he swam toward, a shelter of safety from black waters begging to drown him.

She didn't raise her head while he stared at her, her fingers still coaxing feeling back into his toes. "What was it this time?"

Thorne gritted his teeth. "Deja's testimony today, I think."

Cistine frowned. "Aden?"

He nodded. "Something happened between them in Siralek...though Aden won't tell me what, I have my suspicions, and it will all come out in the testimony. Everything that happened to him in that Nimmus-pit, everything we learn today, will be on my shoulders. Because I sent him there."

"He chose to go, to redeem himself." Cistine lifted her eyes to his again. "Mira says healing's greatest hindrance is when we carry burdens that aren't ours to hold. We can't mend those ones...we have to let them go."

"And how do you know which burdens belong to you?"

"Honesty with yourself, I suppose. I know I shouldn't have gone after you in Jovadalsa without armor. I shouldn't have let Julian come without it, either, but I was desperate. That's my burden to own." Her hold on his foot tightened, singing a faint note of pain down his muscles. "But his decision to come back for me when I told him to go...I can't pick up that weight. It was his choice and I have to let it be. I won't carry the burden of guilt for being with you so soon after Julian died, either. That's a weight Salvotor tried to bury me under, to make me feel like I owed it to Julian's memory to be alone and not have the things I wanted. But I ended things with Julian because he tried too hard to control me, and I wouldn't let him have that power over me in life. I can't hand it to him in death."

Thorne cupped her cheek. The brutal cut of the bone was fading now that she ate and slept—and healed. "You take the power back, one moment at a time."

She covered his hand with hers, tilting her head into his touch. "Wiggle your toes for me, Starchaser."

With his Name singing down every path to his heart, he obeyed.

An hour later, Thorne and Cistine entered the courtroom to join the rest of the cabal, clustered against one wall with varying looks of unease, unhappiness, and well-hidden curiosity. Aden reclined into the window, the picture of composure, one foot braced back on the glass and arms crossed. But a familiar challenge brewed in his eyes.

"How is Saychelle?" Cistine asked in greeting.

Ariadne cast an arm around her shoulders and squeezed her. "With Mira this morning. She's glad it isn't her facing him today."

"I don't blame her." Arms cinched, Quill tongued a cinnamon stick across his teeth. "Salvotor looks like he's in rare form today."

It was difficult to know what to hope for when the Vassora escorted Deja into the room. She was little more than a name linked loosely to Nordbran in Thorne's memory, but she could be the one to seal his father's fate. He ought to be cheering silently for her; yet the *look* on Aden's face when he saw her—the collision between revulsion, rage, and something almost like *shame*—mattered far more than victory today. While Bravis called the room to order and Deja stated her name and ranking as a profitable elite from the northern territories, Thorne watched his cousin fidget, lurch up from the window and sink back against it again, scowl, then rub his face and clench his jaw so tightly it visibly ticked.

"What are your interests in Nordbran?" Tribune Eskil's question dragged Thorne's attention back to the room.

Poised and unsmiling, Deja said, "I help ferry criminals from overfull prisons to the Blood Hive."

"Purely legal, yes?"

"I do not deal in flesh markets."

Quill tensed, a low growl sliding through his teeth, and Tatiana pressed a fleeting kiss to the back of his shoulder.

"It was reported by the Nordbran Tribunes, including High Tribune Sander seated on this Tribunal, that you are also a patroness of Siralek who sponsored Blood Hive fighters in the past."

Aden rocked forward, shaking hands braced on the fencing, forearms locked at the elbows.

"I have, yes."

"That isn't a privilege allowed to most elites. How did you come by it?"

Deja didn't show a single flicker of emotion—no remorse, no fear. "Chancellor Salvotor used his considerable resources to secure me a place of influence among the Blood Hive's most powerful."

"And what precipitated his generosity?"

"My silence." There was something admirable, however corrupt, in the unwavering calm with which Deja beheld the man she bore witness against.

"I saw him nail the *visnpresta* acolyte Ariadne to the door of a house here in Stornhaz."

A storm of murmurs went up at this, and fury knotted Thorne's stomach. He wished with all his heart the last session had evoked so much intrigued scrutiny. Saychelle's testimony would be remembered, not for her words, but for her screams; Deja, delivering such damning accusations without a flicker of emotion, would be remembered differently.

"Describe the events of that night for us, if you would," Eskil said.

Deja did, a testimony as mirrored to Ariadne's as a dance. For the first time, some part of Thorne was glad of the whipping post he'd been tied to the day Sillakove was driven out, glad he only had the strength to break his chains, free Baba Kallah, and run. If he'd had his mind about him, had *he* seen Ariadne on that door, he would've gone straight back to the courthouse and died with his blade at his father's stars-damned throat.

Any flicker of satisfaction from Deja's precise testimony cracked at its subtlest seams when Eskil finished his examination and Salvotor rose, his quiet a herald to the breaking storm. Thorne knew it so well, like a scarlet door and tines of pain raging through his scalp.

Down the fence, Cistine took Aden's hand, ignoring his sharp flinch, and pressed something into it. In the look that passed between them, they might've known each other a lifetime, sharing a grief that sang across every space that made them strangers, forging a silent understanding.

With a quick nod, she squeezed his hand and let go.

"You are aware of what *perjury* is, I presume," Salvotor began.

Deja sniffed. "Yes, I've had my schooling, the same as any elite."

He didn't join in the smattering of chuckles throughout the room, though his eyes brightened slightly. "Then you would have the Tribunal believe not a word of your statement was falsified or embellished in any way?"

"Correct. I stand by my testimony."

"And you would have no reason whatsoever to fabricate such a testimony? No bias whatsoever toward Chancellor Thorne's personal retinue that would make you inclined to prop up their stated accusations?"

Aden stiffened. So did Deja. "I'm not certain I take your meaning."

"Allow me to clarify." Salvotor let the pause build. "Certain reports are afoot that in recent years, you developed a relationship with my own nephew which was...intimate in nature."

Deja's eyes flickered. "My *relationship* with Aden began years after the incident in question."

Relationship. There was hesitation in that word...delicacy. The same way Thorne's mother spoke of her bruises and cuts to her friends in the teahouse; a matter for closed doors and private conversation.

"Curious, nonetheless," Salvotor said, "that you had no inclination to come forward with these accusations until after that association began."

"The two are unrelated."

Salvotor smiled coldly. "The Courts will decide that. Would you tell me why you were at the house where you claimed to be the night you witnessed these so-called atrocities?"

Deja's throat bobbed. "I was...waiting for someone."

"Indeed. And who might you have been lying in wait for at the house in question, belonging to my nephew?"

Silence and bile built together, one harsh in Thorne's ears, the other in his throat. Deja didn't answer, her gaze narrowing.

"If you would," Salvotor enunciated slowly, "elaborate on the nature of your relationship with my nephew."

"Objection!" Eskil barked. "What relevance is that?"

"He was one of the many who insisted on my arrest, was he not?" Salvotor shot back. "Not to mention he and my accuser both share a personal connection to the Chancellor who succeeded me. I would think the Tribunal should be *very* interested to know of any connection between this man and the witness...particularly if she is the *only* witness remaining."

Eskil gave no further protest; there was none to give.

So the horror began to unfold.

In lieu of perjury, it seemed, Deja gave far more than the Courts needed to hear—about her interest in Aden as a boy training to become a Tribune, then as a virile young man; how she'd wondered after him for five years when he vanished, only to encounter him purely by chance when he arrived in Siralek. She told them of the first time she bought Thorne's cousin and did things to him that made Thorne's heart stumble and nausea soak his mouth. He couldn't bear to look at Aden, his greatest pain laid out before the very ranks Thorne wanted him to join.

Deja gave them everything: the truce she made with Aden, how she asserted her own influence over the Hive to ensure no other fighters could be bought and made use of, and in exchange he came to her willingly.

Here Salvotor paused. "You agreed to that truce, though you already had him?"

Had him. As if Aden, like Cistine, was a prize he saw to be claimed.

"It was my penance for what I kept secret," Deja said. "For not reporting your heinous crime."

"Objection," Salvotor said softly. "Leading."

"You are the one who led us down this topic."

The silence swelled again. All Thorne could hear was the cabal's rattling breaths around him; all he could see were the clenched fists that fought not to cover their mouths, the tense bodies that wanted to pour out rage and grief into Deja, into Salvotor, into each other's compassion. Cistine silently wept; and to his shock, so did Ariadne.

"So, then," Salvotor said at length, "we have a woman unashamed to confess that her silence was bought for an unproven act in exchange for my alleged influence within the Blood Hive. Can we truly believe she couldn't also be bought and coached to testify against me by the man whose intimacy she craved since he was a youth? By the man with whom she's already joined *countless* times?"

All the Tribunes muttered among themselves—except Sander. His gaze was fixed on Aden, blank with horror.

"Are you finished?" Bravis growled.

Salvotor shuffled his papers. "Nearly, Chancellor."

The courtroom door burst open, a gust of fresh air battering Thorne's aching legs as he whirled to face it. In all his years of schooling and the few he'd spent as High Tribune seated on Kanslar's Tribunal, he'd neither heard of nor witnessed a common Vassoran guard storming into an active session before. Yet here one was.

Bravis slowly rose, face like thunder. "This had better be the end of the stars-damned *world*."

The guard snapped his heels together. "Chancellor, word has just come from the north. The Blood Hive is destroyed."

Thorne whipped his head around and found Salvotor watching him. For a moment, the world shrank; it was only them, Deja's horrific tale, and this report bringing Siralek so close the air tasted of hot sand—this revelation, the struck match setting the world aflame.

Salvotor had done this. Even inside these walls, he made it possible.

His feral grin, just for Thorne, was proof enough as the courtroom erupted into chaos.

CHAPTER
THIRTY-THREE

STUNNED SILENCE SUFFOCATED the Chancellor's sanctum for one long, breathless minute after the Vassoran guard gave his full report.

"How?" Maltadova growled at last. "*How* did this happen, Branko?"

"We're still compiling the reports," the guard replied. "Not all of them comprehensive, but we gather it was outright bedlam. Not a single prisoner remains in the Blood Hive."

"The animals?" Benedikt asked. "I'm told they're kept hungry. Could they have broken down the gates to reach the prisoners?"

Branko scratched his chin. "Possibly. But to break down two gates, reach the catacombs, and then devour every last prisoner and leave hardly any blood or bodies before they themselves escaped into the sands without a trace..."

"Wait a moment," Bravis interrupted. "Without a *trace*?"

Branko spread his hands in a helpless shrug. "The perpetrator vanished while Siralek burned."

Thorne and Maltadova exchanged a disbelieving glance.

"Thousands of mynts squandered, just like that," Valdemar said bleakly. "Nordbran will be devastated, as will its coffers."

Thorne plunked his hindquarters on the tabletop and rubbed his face with both hands. He didn't regret the loss of Siralek; he would have torn it down himself if given the chance. But this rang a blow against Valgard's bones, setting them all out of joint. Welcomed target or not, an attack was still an attack—and he knew where this one came from. "First Detlyse Halet, now this. Someone is trying very hard to distract us."

"Get off my table, Thorne," Bravis sighed, and Thorne dropped back to his feet. "You think you know what's happening?"

"The timing can't be coincidence, not when you consider the fallout." His father's face in the courtroom flashed across his mind, that cunning satisfaction a revolting echo of the night he dragged Thorne and Baba Kallah out to be whipped and broken. "Siralek falls the day one of its patronesses testifies. And because Nordbran is Sander's territory, I have no choice but to send him to investigate."

"The trial," Benedikt groaned. "We'll have to postpone it."

"A welcome reprieve, perhaps, for our other witness," Bravis mused, "but also for Salvotor. I agree, this reeks of his involvement."

"And of Devitrius and Rakel doing his filthy work for him," Valdemar added.

"To what end?" Maltadova asked. "Why these targets?"

"Perhaps they're trying to prove that no prison is above their reach, and no prisoner beyond their freeing," Thorne said. Benedikt swore, and Maltadova reclined, scowling.

"Send out more Vassora to search for the prisoners. As many as you can spare, whether it's ten or twenty or two hundred," Bravis said to Branko, and with a clip of his heels, he hurried out. "Maltadova, I beg for any Tribune you can spare. We need to find Devitrius and Rakel and stop them by any means necessary."

"No need to beg. They will go at once."

Bravis turned to Thorne. "Muster the Tribunes over Nordbran and tell Sander he's over them all. I want every inch of Siralek searched."

"Consider it done. I'd like to send two of my best with him as well."

"The more the better. We need to find out what they're planning and how they're managing these sieges. One man and woman alone should not be able to break down the most fortified prisons in our kingdom."

Thorne didn't bother voicing what balance-tipping truth that shone in every pair of eyes: they were not one man and woman alone. Somehow, despite the locked doors and guards between them, they had Salvotor.

The cabal waited in the usual parlor, Sander with them, snapping to attention the moment Thorne stepped inside with Mira behind him—all except Aden, still slumped over on a sofa, head in his hands. That sight made him more confident than ever of the plan he'd detoured into Mira's room to set in motion.

"So, it's true?" Sander asked.

Thorne nodded. "The Blood Hive has burned. The prisoners are gone."

Cistine cupped her mouth. "Gods have *mercy*. All those fighters..."

Aden yanked his hands through his hair, lifting his head at last. "*How?*"

"That remains to be seen," Thorne said. "Sander?"

The High Tribune climbed to his feet. "Right, then. Off I go."

"Tati," Thorne added, and both she and Quill stiffened, "and Aden. You're with him."

His cousin's eyes flashed. "You aren't serious."

"You're my best tracker, and you taught Tatiana a good deal of what she knows. Sander and the other Tribunes will find out how this happened. You two will find out why and what happens next."

Tatiana nodded, and Quill squeezed her hand.

"Three times," Thorne added. "This is three times Salvotor has landed a blow when we weren't looking. Let's not make it four."

"I'll continue working with Saychelle in the meantime," Mira said. "We'll use this diversion to our advantage. She'll be ready to take the witness chair again when you return, Sander. I give you my word."

"I trust that word more than any sword at my side." He brushed a kiss to her forehead in passing and took her hand, tugging her out the door with him. Cistine frowned after them, shaking her head slowly.

"What do you want the rest of us to do, *Allet?*" Quill asked.

"Actually, *I* could use your help, Quill," Cistine said quickly, breaking her pensive stare after Sander and Mira. "There's something I want to do before Salvotor rallies enough to swing another blow. It might help us defend against him."

Thorne tipped his head. "You have our attention."

She fidgeted with the betrothal ring hanging around her neck; for the first time in weeks, she wasn't wearing Kristoff's compass pendant beside it. "I've been reading about Atrasat blood. I think we can use it as ink, like Morten did on his ankle."

"You want to ink Atrasat blood into us?" Tatiana frowned. "Why?"

"Because it's an element of the world. It conducts augments like Salvotor's scales." She let go of the betrothal ring, jaw firming. "That way, with or without armor, we'll never be vulnerable. One less way for him to hurt us."

Ariadne sat forward beside Aden, fingers tapping her elbows. "There's no reason it shouldn't work, given the properties of Atrasat blood. And it's true, the advantage. Salvotor went to such lengths to reinforce his skin because the danger from augments is ever-present. If we could forego that danger..."

"It could turn the tide of a battle," Tatiana finished.

Quill shrugged. "Augmented inkings sound impressive, and I could do with a new way to strike terror into my enemies. Clever thinking, Stranger."

Cistine shrugged modestly. "It was going to be my gift to all of you for Darlaska, but I don't know if we should wait that long."

"When do we go hunting?" Quill asked.

"Give me one day. I think I found someone who can help us track the Atrasat."

"Go prepared," Thorne warned. "All of you."

As one, everyone departed except Aden and Ariadne, lingering on the sofa, and Thorne, holding the door. Shadows haunted his cousin's eyes when he stood. "So. Now you know. I understand if you don't want me on your Tribunal, in your council. That weakness..."

"It is not weakness," Ariadne cut in. "It was not weakness when it happened to me, it was not weakness when it happened to you."

Aden's eyes cut to her, not quite meeting. "It isn't the same. You were untrained, unable to fight him. I was...I *am*—"

"A victim. You were as much a victim as I was. No sword can cleave the power of herbs, and anyone, man or woman, can be taken advantage of if the circumstances are right." Ariadne surged to her feet, pulling him around by the arm to face her. "Look at me." Slowly, his gaze dragged to hers. "I forgive you. For that night, for that choice, for everything that came of it. You have done enough, Aden. You never owed me penance, but even then, you've done enough." She laid her hand on his cheek. "*I forgive you.*"

He bowed his head, but in the stiffness with which he withdrew from her grip, it was clear he had not forgiven himself. He had far to go still before he could release what happened in Siralek.

So Thorne said a silent prayer that his plan would succeed. Then he said to his cousin, "Go. The Blood Hive needs you one last time."

CHAPTER THIRTY-FOUR

IN MOROSE QUIET, Tatiana and Quill packed their satchels—admittedly with finer threads and more augments and weapons than they ever took from the Den. But Tatiana's heart still ached, missing him already. Missing Pippet, too, who perched on the edge of their bed, heels stirring the air, weight braced back on her hands. "*Please* can I go with? I hate being left behind."

Quill shut his satchel with a sharp yank. "That's not happening."

"But Cistine's even hiring that hunter we met in the tavern...Daria! She gets to go, why can't I? I'm trained, ask Aden! He trusts me!"

"Aden wouldn't take you to Siralek any more than I'm going to take you beast-hunting." Quill pulled out his custom-made dagger, then slammed the chest-of-drawers shut. "That's the end of the discussion."

Pippet pouted. "This is just like Starhollow."

Tatiana stepped from the closet and shot her *valenar* a look. He held it for a moment, then turned to the bed, his face softer toward his sister than ever since Thorne marched her into their room from a night out *gambling*, of all the stars-forsaken things. He walked over to the bed and planted his fists on either side of her, bending on her level. "You know what? I might've let you come if this happened a few days ago. Do you know why I won't?"

She looked down at her lap. "Because I *gambled*."

"Listen to me. Because you kept secrets." Quill took her chin, lifting her head. "If I'm going to take you along on missions, I have to know I can trust you. Maybe Aden already can, but I can't, and until you prove that to me, you're not flying this nest, Hatchling. Understood?"

Her jaw bobbed against his hand.

"Besides," he added, "you're still stuck here for another month. *That's* for gambling."

"Fine. Then while I'm here I'm going to be the best, honest, most trustworthy warrior who's ever been."

"Believe me, I'd sleep a lot better at night if you were."

"I could pay Daria!" she added. "I still have mynts!"

Tatiana bit back a laugh at Quill's wild stare. "You don't have to—"

"I'll do it! I want to." She dove off the bed, wrapping her arms around his chest, then slithering past him to do the same to Tatiana. "And then I'll stay right here the whole time you're gone! Ariadne will help me with my schooling. You'll see...I'm going to be *so* well-behaved!"

"Only while we're gone," Quill muttered when she dashed from their room and slammed the door to hers. "Stars damn it...*gambling?*"

Laughter scraped Tatiana's throat. "She's truly her brother's sister."

"Don't remind me. If I come back and she's down to three fingers..."

Tatiana banded her arms around his waist, inhaling the smell of cinnamon and steel-polish from his clothes. "I wish I was going with you."

"I don't blame you." Quill twisted in her embrace to splay his hands on her hips. "Beast-hunting, or searching some stars-forsaken catacombs? I actually feel bad for you this time, Saddlebags. We're going to have all the fun without you."

"Doubtful. I *am* the fun."

"Don't I know it." Even in his quick kiss, she found a flirt of eagerness. Quill was like her—he wasn't built for a life inside courthouse walls. The wilds beckoned and sang to them both.

She drew away first, eyeing him shrewdly. "Remember. First one back—"

"Starts questioning the inventors." He kissed the tip of her nose. "I know. I'll check the markets for the schematics again, too."

"You really *are* going to have all the fun without me!" Swatting his haunch, she grabbed her satchel and slung it across her body, went to the door, then looked back. Melancholy pulled at her nerves; it was her first time going on a mission without Quill since the one that brought her home to the Den with a poisoned arrow in her shoulder. Back then, just like now, the thought in her head was singular and screaming: just get home. Just get back to him.

"Quill." He turned at the crack in her voice. "You know I love you, right, Featherbrain?"

A brash smirk cut across his face. "What's not to love?"

She gestured rudely, then slammed the door on his laughter, carrying that sound with her all the way from the courthouse.

She'd never been so grateful for augments. Any other journey from Stornhaz in Sander and Aden's company would've proved uncomfortable beyond words; instead, it was a matter of moments before they traded the unseasonable heat at the heart of their kingdom for Nordbran's dry red sands. The northern territory opened its arms to them, an embrace of vicious beauty from a place Tatiana had hoped never to see again after she and Quill departed one of its many bazaars and traveled into the wild lands beyond the Isetfells. But this time, rather than a view of endless dunes and distant steppes leading up to the mountains, something dark and terrible rose on the horizon.

Siralek. Or what remained of it.

It must've been impressive once, but the many-tiered elliptic structure lay cracked in half now, halberd-bearing statues toppled, the gates ripped from their hinges and speared into the sand like a parting challenge from the prisoners they once contained. Tatiana, Aden, and Sander passed under the ruined archways and climbed stone slabs ripped from seats and walls to meet a contingent of Vassora—too few, in Tatiana's opinion, but they were stretched thin between here and Detlyse Halet these days—and took an official report.

It wasn't only the prisoners gone; the fighting animals were as well. The nomad camps and the white stone homes sat empty now, not one person left. And no trace of a struggle, either. Nothing but the Hive itself remained, broken wide open.

"Sand hides a multitude of evils," Sander said with a sharp glance at Aden. "Let's rest the night. Come morning when the other Tribunes arrive, we begin the hunt afresh. Make no assumptions, base nothing off what we've seen thus far. We scour this place and the city to the last inch. And we will not stop until we learn something about Rakel and Devitrius...and what they're doing with all those fighters."

When Dusan, Noaam, Ambrose, and Jesper—with his *valenar* Sabra, true Yager Tribune over Nordbran—arrived the following dawn, they declared the catacombs too unstable to be searched. Aden scattered half the Vassora and Yager's hunters into the city to turn over every stone; the other half, Sander dispatched with earth augments to begin propping up the catacombs.

"Dangerous, but necessary," he said with an unexpected clap on Tatiana's shoulder while they watched the guards depart. "If they made these places unnavigable, then perhaps the clues we're searching for lie there."

Tatiana certainly hoped so, because the city gave up little of worth. After two days, they discovered no patterns. Some people had vanished and left all their belongings behind; some took everything with them, stripping walls bald to the last stained patch where mirrors once hung to help light the dark stone abodes.

Never a trace of blood. Never a sign of struggle. Never a hint of a clue.

"I give up!" Tatiana barked halfway through the third day. Standing in yet another unscathed dwelling, hands on her hips, she scowled at the unruffled cushions and dead hearth. "You're the one who taught me that even the effort to *not* leave a trail leaves a trail, but look at this place! There's nothing! Who attacked it, the stars-damned *Undertaker*?

Halfway up the steps to the upper level, Aden halted, smoothing his palm on the broad, flat stone railing. He frowned at his empty palm, then met her eyes.

Tatiana tossed up her hands. "Fine. Don't tell me what you're thinking, don't tell me you're as confused as I am. I can see it in your pretty *face*."

His brow tweaked, but that was all the emotion he showed. Then he went back to staring at his palm.

They turned over two more homes with no luck before the sun began to sink and the bitter cold of another desert night set in; it was time to build a fire and surrender for the day. They chose the same place they had the last few nights: an oasis at Siralek's heart. While other fires kindled—Vassoran fires and hunter fires, and somewhere out there, one where Nordbran's Tribunes gathered together—there was little talk and less laughter. Eeriness stamped the world, and the feeling that whatever had vacated this place could return at any moment and vacate them as well.

To distract herself, Tatiana built the fire high enough to work by, then spread out the only items she stuffed in her satchel besides battle armor and rations: a cloth wrap, a set of tinker's tools, and her newest invention.

It was a ridiculous form of absolution: since she couldn't search for Kadlin's thief right now, she would at least make use of the woman's schematics. So by firelight where she didn't risk anyone spoiling the surprise, Tatiana tinkered and built, pouring effort into her invention. Hair tied back, tongue poking between her teeth, she sat cross-legged with the tools before her and her handiwork in her lap, passing the hours that way.

Better than thinking about what lay around them. Better than wondering where these people went. Tinkering was pure logic. Things either fit together or they didn't, and the latter could be amended with the right tools. Nothing at all like entire cities vanishing or catacombs being broken into, leaving no trace of people or beasts behind.

She was so absorbed in her work, she didn't hear Aden approach until the flames guttered as he sat across from her. He offered a gourd of water, then two fruits from the oasis. Tatiana took the drink but not the fruit, rolling the bottle neck between her palms while she watched him.

She'd spent five years wondering where Aden was, alternately hating him and missing him—unsure if the boy who helped raised them, growing into the man who betrayed them, had died believing they never wanted to see him again and were better off with him gone. And not knowing herself whether that was true.

Hearing what came out in that courtroom made her regret every terrible thought she had about him for all those years. Clear as the moonlight in this empty, endless desert, he was just like her: riddled with mistakes, hung on hope, desperate to make amends. Her weakness had been a love of numbness found in strong spirits; his was the promise of seeing his father again. Both of them were saboteurs seeking redemption. He put himself in this place to save members of Sillakove imprisoned by Salvotor, and she threw the doors of her heart wide open, let in Cistine, Quill, the rest of the cabal, even strangers like Kadlin, and tried every day to make up for years of resenting and shutting out and hating anyone who hurt her.

Maybe Thorne saw all that. Maybe that was why he really sent her along on this mission.

Tossing up a silent prayer, she offered the gourd back to Aden. "It must be a nightmare for you. Being back here."

His eyes flicked up to her face, then back toward the cracked-open elliptical that was his prison for five years.

"You don't have to say anything," she added. "Stars know I wouldn't want to if I were you. But don't forget who made tea and sat on your sofa listening to you talk about schooling and training to become a Tribune for *hours* after the others left those Sillakove gatherings. I'm not like Mira, and it's been years, but I'll still listen if there *is* anything you want to say."

Aden accepted the gourd, swigged from it, and went on staring at the ravaged arena. Tatiana went back to tinkering.

"I swore an oath to myself that I would take my own life before I ever came back to this place." A quiet admission. He still didn't look away from the arena, crouched on the horizon with its spine split open. "Mira tells me such oaths are beneath people like us, that there's no world where my death is an acceptable trade for Siralek's clutches. And that having escaped once, I could do it again."

Tatiana set her tools aside. "So, do you feel better, knowing it's destroyed and no one can lock you away in here anymore?"

"Yes." A beat, and Aden towed his hand back through his long hair. "But also, no. No, I don't. It isn't Siralek that remains a fortress, it's the pieces of it in me. I haven't escaped that. If I ever will."

She wondered what shackles kept him bound to this place; if it was Deja, or Nimea and the Tumult, or even Ashe. If it was the fighters he didn't save. "I think you can walk out of here if you want to. When Quill and I used to talk about where you went after you left Hellidom, I always thought you stayed away because you didn't *want* to come back, not because you couldn't. If you really wanted to leave, you would've found a way. And I still think you will."

Aden was quiet as she took up her tools again, hiding the shakiness of honesty in busy hands and downcast eyes. When he spoke at last, gratitude quieted his voice. "I won't say I'm not surprised, but I'm glad you never stopped believing in me. Thank you."

Heat needled her throat and sinuses, and she could no longer see her invention through blurry eyes. "I've given the cabal plenty of opportunities to stop believing in me, too, but they always hope. That's what we do for each other. And you're still part of that, Aden." This time his answer was wordless, a hand extended around the fire, that fruit offered again like a truce. So Tatiana took it and toasted to him. "To always believing."

"To believing," Aden echoed, and they bit into the succulent flesh.

The first taste was achingly sweet—then sickeningly so, writhing with complexity like the first notes of a harsh beer. Tatiana gagged and spat out the fruit, flipping it over in her hand. At its very core, past her teethmarks, it was rotten and syrupy. Maggots plopped onto the sand.

Tatiana hurled the fruit away, cursing and retching, and Aden did the same, gaze racing up to meet hers again.

"What in the stars is happening in this place?" Tatiana gagged.

Aden, for once, offered no consoling explanation, merely sat narrow-eyed, staring at the rotten fruit while the wind stirred the trees in the oasis.

Somehow, its beauty wasn't as comforting as before. Not knowing the blight that lurked inside.

CHAPTER THIRTY-FIVE

NOTHING ASHE HAD endured was a dream.

Every day, she remembered this when she woke on the clifftop, pain and residual fever abating, to the sight of a dragon sitting across the rock from her. Sometimes it stopped her heart like a nightmare still fading; sometimes it coaxed up a sense akin to wonder; of all the help the gods could've sent, they chose a *dragon*.

By the fifth day, she just wished he would *leave*.

He watched her every movement intently, whether she struggled to her feet to relieve herself or ate the fish he caught from gods-knew-where, or tossed and turned at the threshold of sleep, uncomfortable and hopeless. He fed her herbs to help drive the infection from her body and mixed tinctures with shockingly-nimble claws for her wounded face. And he was far more eager to talk than she was, to tell her of the rumors he hunted for weeks in northern Valgard, tracing out from Siralek and beyond. The rain-dancer, the beast-slayer, supposedly killed in the catacomb riots, but he never believed it. Far too many rumored to be dead in that incident had turned up alive, including the Hive Lord himself.

Strange, to have that reputation and not know what to do with it stacked atop the terrible weight already in her chest. She didn't want to talk, to mix tinctures and poultices herself. She wanted to sit and think long and hard about everything that had happened, to sort out what she wanted, to reach into the blackness at the bottom of her descent and see what lay around her, if there was anything there at all. But Bresnyar, as he called himself, never left her alone or stayed silent long enough for her to observe, consider, or reflect. And by the end of that long week, her apathy gave way to rage.

"Will you stop *talking?*" she snapped.

Bresnyar paused while mixing yet another tincture and telling yet another story, gazing at her for a moment. "You know, it's considered not only terrible manners, but also poor for one's mortality in general, to scream at a dragon."

"I don't care. I don't *care* if you eat me," she snapped, staggering up from her bed of moss and leaves. "I'm sick of you talking. I don't want to hear about my feats in Siralek...I was *there*. And I don't need to know about the places you've traveled since you left Kalt Hasa. I'm happy you've found your freedom, but *I* haven't, and you're making me want to throw *myself* off the next cliff. So if you're really as invested in me as you're pretending to be, will you please, for the love of the *gods*, shut your giant maw for *one hour!*"

Bresnyar's eyes narrowed. "I'm only trying to help, you know. You always look as if you're suffering from indigestion when we're silent."

"I don't *need* your help! I didn't ask for your help, and I don't *want* it!"

"Ah, but ask you did. Through the stone."

"If I'd known what I was getting myself into, I wouldn't have!"

"Yet still you carry it."

Roaring in wordless rage, Ashe stripped off the starstone and flung it with all her might.

A beat of silence so absolute, she heard the thing knock into faraway tree limbs as it fell. Then a gust of wind shoved at her as Bresnyar swept out his wings and plunged into the valley. He returned in seconds, starstone in his clawed grip, and dropped it at her feet. "Don't do that again."

Ashe gritted her teeth, snatched up the necklace, and pitched it in a different direction. Again Bresnyar lunged, flew, retrieved it, and flung it at her feet. "I said—"

She dropped it straight off the cliff this time. He tucked his wings and fell backward off the ledge; when he clawed his way back up to her, annoyance flattened his brows. Ashe yanked at the necklace dangling from his tooth, and he swung it out of reach. "Stop. This is infantile."

"I told you, I *don't want your help.*" His, or Maleck's, or *anyone's.*

"Why not?"

"Because I'm in this...this *Nimmus* where everything I ever was is breaking apart, and I'm trying to rebuild myself, if I even *can.* I can't afford anyone's charity!"

"It is not charity. If you are being remade, why not into someone who needs others?"

"Because that's not who I am. It's not who I've ever been."

"Everyone needs help from time to time. Even dragons locked under mountains need mortal girls to help set them free." Bresnyar cocked his head. "It is not, I think, that you've never needed anyone's aid. It's that it was never offered when you did need it. You are not frightened of needing help...you're frightened because you *know* you need it, and you fear you'll be dead before anyone sees you're drowning."

Ashe stared at him. The dragon gazed back, unblinking.

"What in God's name gives you the right," she hissed, "to think you know *anything* about me?"

Bresnyar slung the starstone down on the rock ledge. "Because I know what it is for your whole world to turn its back on you for one mistake! I know what it is to have your life crumble so utterly that death seems preferable. I left my homeland seeking a glorious end, Asheila Kovar, and instead I was held by a madman who stripped me of my hide, piece by piece, for *years.*" He bared his teeth, breaths rasping between their jagged tips. "I was kept alive against my will so long I began to dream of what purpose might feel like again, until a princess stumbled into the darkness and offered me help I didn't think I wanted—or needed." He towered above her, the steam of his breath stirring her hair. "I know you because I *was* you. I *am* you. I have danced long enough with my failures that we've reached an understanding. I would like to teach you that dance if you'll let me."

"*Why?*" Ashe spat. "Cistine told us how you barely agreed to leave that mountain with them. Nothing in these kingdoms comes for free! But you started this when you pulled me out of that fall near the cave, now tell me *why!*"

"Because you remind me of Ileria!" His roar thundered off the spines of the mountains. Below their feet, flocks of birds took flight in terror.

Ashe bit back a sigh. "And who is that?"

"My Wingmaiden," Bresnyar's voice broke. "Fierce. Untamable. We were raised together in Oadmark from hatchery to hearth. She too fought to her last breath, as you would've done against those men. She died screaming my name. And when I saw you fall, when I heard *your* scream..." Smoke puffed from his nostrils. He shook it viciously away. "You are not the only one who has lost things, not the only one who has been too late to save what was precious. A dragon without a sworn Wingmaiden will go mad over time. I've felt it begin to creep over my edges. I know I have lost much and have more still to lose, but I am *here*, and I am trying to help you. You do not have sole claim to self-pity, and loss does not give you the right to be cruel."

He bent his head and nudged the starstone closer to her.

"Your voice through this stone helped clear my mind. So forgive me if I linger with you for whatever time I can. I choose to believe the Great Father gave you this stone for a reason, brought us near each other for a *reason*. Believing it is all that keeps my thinking sharp. Having enough pity not to cast aside someone else's last hope is the least you could offer after I did the noble thing for you."

With that, he took to the sky and shot off to the east, leaving Ashe stunned, shame unravelling in her middle, watching him go. When he didn't return after several long, painful minutes, she crouched and picked up the starstone, cocked her arm to throw it again—then hesitated.

Patchy memories of that rain-veiled night slithered back into focus. How desperate she'd been to escape. How she tried to crawl, to save her own life. And why.

For a long time, she didn't move. Simply stared across the mountains to the west, toward Middleton.

It was long after dark when Bresnyar returned, and Ashe had sharpened skewers and built a fire. She fed most of her leaf bed to it, keeping it alive since sunset; a storm rolled far away over the flatlands, and every boom of thunder tolling through the world she hoped against her own will was the echo of the dragon's wings. After half a day alone, she wondered if he would come back at all, or if she'd have to make use of the skewers and actually hunt. The mere notion made her legs quiver.

And then there he was, alighting on the ledge and heaving up a mouthful of fish. Ashe wrinkled her nose as their slick bodies slid down the slimy track of his saliva. "Appetizing." And then, with a pinch of remorse at the memory of their argument, she added, "Thank you."

Bresnyar looked between her and the fire. "You have never made this effort."

She shrugged. "I wasn't sure you'd come back. And I got cold."

Too late, she realized her attempt to save face had laid her soul wide-open; knew by Bresnyar's satisfied hum that he'd expected her to simply lie down and wait for death if he didn't come back.

Instead, she'd built a fire.

"I'm not saying I'm ready to walk down from this mountain," Ashe warned, spearing a fish and holding it over the flames.

"No, of course not." Bresnyar settled on the rock, forelegs crossed.

"I'm not saying I trust you yet, either. Or that I'm grateful for how you stuck your oversized snout into my life." She paused at the dragon's sardonic snort. "What I *am* saying is that you're right about one thing: I'm the one who called into the stone. I asked the gods for help, and they sent me you." She stroked the pendant hanging loose over her heart. "It's easy to think you want something until you have it...even death. So maybe I'm not ready to give up just yet, no matter how tired I am. Maybe we both still have a purpose to fulfill. I'm not certain what that is yet, but I'm at least willing to help you stay sane while I think it through." She offered the fish to him—

a truce. "So, you tell me more about Ileria. I'll tell you about the people I lost. Kallah and Julian and Helga. And I'll tell you how I got this stone."

Bresnyar considered the offer, the fish, and everything she refused to say yet—but at least she was willing to listen.

Then, gentle as a warm breeze, he plucked the skewer from her hand.

CHAPTER
THIRTY-SIX

THE SOTEFOLD FOREST was unseasonably warm and uncommonly green, distant clouds threatening a storm that would likely veil northern Valgard in a fresh burst of rain, then more snow, as was the pattern this year. But for now, Cistine sweated profusely, moaning with relief when she and Quill rode into the shade of one of the thickest groves following Daria's tracking.

The moment Cistine had found her in one of taverns near where they first met and offered her the hunt, the grinning Valgardan hunter took it with a grin and a last gulp of ale. Now they were days from the city, riding through splashes of heat and shadows, and with her cloak lashed around her waist and her bow and quiver strapped across her body, Cistine turned her face up toward the sun. She didn't really mind the lack of wind augments for the journey; the Chancellors had spent a fair amount moving Aden, Sander, Tatiana, and their Vassoran contingent north. According to Thorne, the use of so many flagons at once always made the Courts restless, a solemn reminder of their depleting stores however many remained.

With the treaty still in the balance, it wasn't the time to argue for the casual expediency of travel; so they had their horses, and these glorious days of heat and sunlight as distant from cold Kalt Hasa as possible. Really, she was enjoying herself.

"You couldn't have picked a better time for this little mission of yours, Stranger," Quill remarked. "It's almost like springtime out here."

Cistine grinned at him over her shoulder. "I noticed. Are Valgardan winters always this fickle?"

"Never. But I'll take it. I'm not very fond of snow anymore." Quill squinted ahead. "So, Daria, you said Atrasat are usually found around Nygaten Temple?"

She nodded. "It's the most secluded, and they prefer to be left alone."

"Like the *visnprests*," Cistine laughed. "Ariadne suggested we give the temple complex a wide berth."

"You don't say," Quill drawled. "And here I was thinking a healthy dose of our charming company would be just what they needed." Cistine jutted her tongue, Daria rolled her eyes, and Quill laughed. "So, we should reach the temple today, right? Battle strategy?"

"Atrasat are peaceful creatures by nature, so we shouldn't have much trouble," Daria said. "All we need is to subdue it by one of its legs, slit its skin, and collect the blood in Cistine's jar."

"And then we let it go," Cistine added. "We shouldn't need *all* its blood for the inkings."

Quill slowed his mount. "We're about to find out if that's true."

They'd reached Nygaten Temple.

They dismounted and lashed their horses to a tree, then approached the overgrown outer wall. A thick brook branched before it, hooping the temple grounds in an iridescent skirt. The wall's arched entryway was accessible only by a land bridge; beyond that, broad stone stairs climbed up toward the temple body itself, a complex comprised of scattered outlying buildings and one high central tower, all furred in creeping ivy. The steps sunken into the hillside and leading up to the temple were overgrown with lichen, and grass sprouted in the rock seams, muffling the tread of Cistine's boots when she mounted them.

Nygaten's focus was on the integration of augmentation with cultural advancements, Ariadne had told her—on crafting things like augwains and harvesters once powered by the very augments they dug up from the wells.

It was eerily quiet, for a temple dedicated to such things.

The pit of Cistine's stomach churned, her fingers curling into fists at her sides. It was coming back to her now that she climbed the steps: the strange, uneasy sensation she'd forced aside ever since Detlyse Halet. The unsettled tilt of a world out of balance.

Nazvaldolya.

Steel sang as Quill fingered his sabers. "It shouldn't be this quiet. Cistine, get back here."

She kept walking, some dark thread tugging at her middle, drawing her up the steps.

"Cistine!" There was an edge to Quill's voice now. "I hate to raise concerns about entering a temple *Ariadne* told us to stay out of—"

"No, you don't," she said absently. "I'll just be a moment."

She pushed open the thick front door with her shoulder and ducked into the temple, then halted just over the threshold.

It was abandoned. Not a whisper of presence, not a lick of sound but the wind moving down the halls. Through gaps in the roof, sunlight washed the floor and inlaid bookshelves in glorious butter-yellow patches. When Cistine walked into the entry nave, that blistering sense of wrongness stirred and rose, clotting her throat with dread.

She swallowed and glanced over her shoulder. Quill and Daria had not followed her, and she couldn't blame them. Two steps inside, her curiosity evaporated, and she wanted nothing more than to run from the temple.

Except when she faced forward again, she was no longer alone.

Cloaked, hooded, and utterly ignorant of her presence, a man stooped over a pile of broken rock halfway down the nave, bathed in sunlight. He brushed his long, bone-thin fingers over the stone bookshelves and chose one, flipped to the middle, scanned its contents, then tucked it into the front of his robe.

Cistine took a step toward him. "Excuse me, are you a *visnprest?*"

He didn't turn, didn't acknowledge that he heard her at all. With a brush of the wind kicking leaves across the floor, he disappeared.

That shadowy thread in Cistine's middle jerked, and she ran to where he vanished at the mouth of the inner sanctum. There she slammed to a halt again, a scream ramming against her teeth.

She'd found the *visnprests* and *prestas*. What was left of them.

Quill's wordless shout from outside barely penetrated the roar in her head as she stared at the ravaged bodies heaped in the middle of the sunken atrium. The bookshelves on the walls were stripped of their contents, too, leaving nothing but heaps of loose-leaf paper behind.

"Cistine!" Quill bellowed. "Get out here, *now!*"

She hadn't realized she stopped breathing until air shuddered into her straining lungs again. Whirling, she dashed from the temple, lunging down the steps until she collided with Daria's back, the hunter flashing out a hand to steady her. "*Quill!* Quill, they're dead, they're *all* dead—all the *visnprests* and *prestas*."

"I figured as much." His voice was too calm as he unsheathed his sabers. "And I think I know what killed them."

The Atrasat was a vision plucked straight from the bestiary, its form like the octopi sold for exorbitant cost at Talheim's coastal markets. But this one was dry and land-loving, its skin the texture of a crinkled raisin. It crossed the grounds with controlled flails of its tentacles, each one ending in a massive, pronged barb that sank into the soil, heaving the rest of its body along. Cistine cringed at its six white eyes and needle-studded open beak.

"Does that thing look friendly to you?" Quill muttered. "Or are those our horses' bridles dangling from its mouth?"

Not just that, but bits of robe and banners of human flesh.

The Atrasat dragged itself around to face them with a wet, gargling moan. From a body of that stature, it was nearly a battle cry.

"I thought so." Quill shoved Daria out of the way, grabbed the back of Cistine's armor, and heaved her to one side as the Atrasat's rubbery limb descended, smashing the steps to gravel.

Cistine's heart slammed into her throat. She forced aside all thought of the dead Order, the book thief in the temple, everything but the imminence of danger while they lunged behind a broken chunk of the wall and took cover. She slung her bow from across her chest, and Daria nodded. "You shoot for the eyes and maw. We'll cleave through those limbs."

Quill spun his sabers in a deft twist, loosening his wrists. "On my count."

He numbered back from three, then they broke cover: Cistine shooting upward, Quill and Daria darting around the stone. The Atrasat was far closer than she expected, moving more swiftly than seemed natural, and she had to adjust her aim. The seconds that cost her were few, but irredeemable. The arrow skirted wide, smashing off the creature's hide rather than through its eye. But Quill and Daria were there, dodging its limbs and ducking low, sweeping their weapons with cold precision into the Atrasat's nearest tentacle.

The blades bounced off.

Cistine's yelp of shock morphed into a scream when the Atrasat caught Daria across the stomach and hurled her against the hillside. She cracked headfirst against the steps and faltered with a groan, digging her blade into the soil as she struggled to rise. Then she fell back, eyes rolling to the whites.

Molten terror poured down Cistine's chest and back. She fitted another arrow and fired, drawing the Atrasat's focus from the unconscious hunter. This time, the beast knocked the projectile away when it wheeled to face her. For a moment, Cistine was consumed in the breeze of its turning and trapped in the shadow of its body. Those unblinking, opaque eyes branded her as the creature churned closer, and a cold certainty rooted her in place, arrow dipping, tongue cleaving to the roof of her mouth.

This shouldn't be happening. The temple this creature attacked, the dead within, or this battle. None of it was right, none of it natural. This was what Saychelle and Iri had warned her about, what Thorne believed she was sensing—that their world was imbalanced. Gentle creatures becoming savage. Men melting into the wind. Temples, ransacked.

Nazvaldolya.

Cistine flung herself sideways just as the tentacles slammed down, rutting the soil into clots. She heaved back the bowstring and fired, and this time the arrow landed true, sinking into one of those milky eyes. The Atrasat swiveled, another thick, moist gag coming from its throat, the arrow-riddled eye jumping wildly and waving the shaft like a flag of surrender. But it still had five eyes to spare.

The creature plowed toward her again, and she rolled to escape, but the barb of a tentacle caught her leg in mid-twist; though it didn't pierce her battle armor, it encaged her ankle, pinning her in place. Cursing at the top of her voice, she yanked out her dagger and struck at the beast's hide, but that, too, rebounded.

They needed *Svarkyst* steel—or an augment.

Cistine's free hand leaped toward the pouch on her hip.

With a bellow of fury, Quill plowed into the Atrasat's face, hacking deftly. Fluid burst from two of the eyes, and the beast moaned, reeling backward. Its barbs retracted and Cistine stumbled to her feet, testing her ankle. Though it pulsed with pain, she could still put weight on it.

The Atrasat wrapped Quill around the waist, plucked him from its face, and hurled him against the stone wall. His pained shout launched Cistine into motion; she scrambled to retrieve her bow, then watched it shatter into splinters when the Atrasat clambered over it. Reeling backward, she sprinted to Quill, sliding onto her knees beside him and heaving at his arm. "Quill, get up!"

"I'm trying," he gasped, face drained of color, struggling to catch his wind. The Atrasat's tentacles pounded the dirt as it hauled itself toward them; Cistine dragged Quill's arm across her shoulders and heaved him up, his feet fighting to anchor into the soil while they staggered backward toward Daria.

That bubbling, scalding *wrongness* choked Cistine; it should've been easy to retrieve the ink, to return to Stornhaz safely. Instead, Quill was bleeding, Daria unconscious, and Cistine's ankle buckling underneath her as the Atrasat bore down on them. Its tentacles sailed out, and she ducked, yanking Quill aside as the temple archway exploded into lethal chunks of stone raining down behind them.

"Augments, Cistine!" Quill shouted in her ear. "Use your stars-damned augments!"

She fumbled the pouch open with her free hand and drew the first flagon. But then she hesitated.

It was lightning. She could feel it without even breaking it open.

Just for a moment, she froze—but that was a moment too long.

The Atrasat's tentacle snapped out, snatching Quill from her grip, and as it tore him away, the stillness in Cistine's mind fractured. She reached back into her pouch and *roared*, a sound so brutal the Atrasat itself hesitated.

The whip of augmented fire cracked out in less than the heartbeat it took her fingers to choose, to break, to answer the call forever ringing at her side. It severed the Atrasat's limb, spraying inky blood. Quill reached out as he fell, bringing the loose flames into his middle as he tucked and rolled across the saturated grass. He came up sliding on both knees with sabers in hand, swiping them on the bloody leaves, coating the silver steel black. Then he pushed the fire out from his armor's threads and down the metal, flames dancing against the Atrasat's blood as the creature retreated and rallied.

Cistine lunged to Quill's side, power coursing over and in and *through* her, and whirled to place her back to his as the Atrasat coiled to strike.

"Don't stop," he growled. "Whatever you do, don't stop moving."

The tentacles speared at them from left and right. Cords of fire met it on one side, flame-licked steel on the other. Cistine and Quill held their ground and guarded each other's backs, twisting together, the perfect steps they'd practiced in training session after training session. No strike could force them apart now; no blow winnowed past their joint guard. Gouts of fire plumed from Cistine's armor with every kick and swipe and jab. Quill's sabers left shimmering embers and glinting stripes sizzling on the air whenever he struck. Back-to-back, they whirled and pivoted, ducking blows, dismantling the Atrasat a piece at a time until it was the one retreating, its shrieks and moans rending the air.

But they couldn't leave it alive in this state.

"Push in!" Quill bellowed, and they drove after the Atrasat like a blade, a storm of steel and fire unrelenting until the creature broke down against the edge of the temple. Cistine shouted for a sword and Quill tossed it to her, then dropped to one knee. Spilling the last of her fire into the blood-coated blade, she stepped up on his broad shoulders, pushed off with all her might, and soared, steel leading in an arch above her. The fiery sword sank to the hilt in the Atrasat's forehead and slid through its skin like butter, spraying ichor as Cistine descended gracefully into the tangle of its hacked-apart limbs, feet touching down on the grass soft as the last steps of a waltz.

Absolute, ringing silence as she jerked the empty bottle from her pouch and let the blood run into it, then corked it, tucked it away, and turned to face Quill. He looked as filthy as she felt, blood dripping from the tips of his hair, his jaw and fingertips. Battlelight burned in his eyes, crying out to her adrenaline-laced ecstasy.

"Are you all right?" she panted.

"Sore, but I'll survive." He put out his hand, and she passed his saber back to him. "You?"

"Tired. But not..." she gestured vaguely, words burned up in the wildness of the aftermath.

"Like you're going to collapse. Like the rest of us after we use that much of an augment." He shook his head and sheathed his blades. "You're a wonder, Cistine. Sometimes I think *you* should be teaching *us*."

"Power or not, that, what we did just now..." she staggered toward him and gripped his shoulder. "That was all you. Everything I learned from *you*."

Eyes brighter now, almost like tears, Quill covered her hand with his and squeezed. "Proud to be part of it, Stranger."

They lingered a moment, the wind wheezing through the temple cracks, the Atrasat's blood plopping on the grass behind them. Cistine shivered, the memory of dead *visnprests* and wrecked bookshelves slithering through her mind. "We should check on Daria."

"Let's hope she's all right." Quill grimaced, looking over the fallen Atrasat. "It's going to be a long walk to anywhere we can find new horses."

CHAPTER THIRTY-SEVEN

OF ALL THE things he faced in his short time as Chancellor, this would be the most complicated to maneuver...and the most necessary. To prove himself a man of his word, unlike his lying, ruthless predecessor—few things could be more vital. And with Cistine and Quill in the Sotefold, Tatiana and Aden in Nordbran, and the trial at a halt, Thorne needed something to occupy his mind. Still, his palms gathered sweat like tavern rags when he knocked on the door of Chancellor's sanctum.

"Come in," Bravis called from inside.

The room was cozier without all five Chancellors there. A deep blue ghostlamp burned on the table where Bravis hunched over a heap of papers. Thorne brushed the door shut, descended the steps, and leaned back against the banister with his arms folded. "Ration requests?"

Bravis scowled. "I swear by the stars, it's always during our season. Every winter, some of the villages beg Stornhaz to meet their needs."

Thorne grunted sympathetically. "If Tyve and Yager supply more seeds in the spring, it might help lessen Traisende's burden."

"Are you a farmer now as well as a Chancellor?"

"I had to be many things in the wilds."

Bravis looked up from the papers, his scowl lessening. "And did you come here to hover and watch me work? Eager to see how it's done?"

Thorne chose to ignore that subtle jab. "Actually, I came to propose a law."

"I thought that was what Kanslar's season was for. To pass the laws *Kanslar* champions."

"As it happens, this law would directly affect my ability to govern my Court as I see fit. My hope is that if it could be passed before Kanslar's season, I could position my people preemptively and give my Court the best chance for a smooth transition."

Bravis sat forward, clasping his hands loosely on the endless mound of papers populating the desk. "And what is this law you find so advantageous?"

Thorne straightened up from the banister and approached him. "You know I'm having some issues with my Tribunes still showing loyalty to my father. I've been considering the best way to attack the issue." He balanced his fingertips on the table and leaned his weight into them. "I propose an alteration to the laws of leadership. I would like the freedom to place women on my Tribunal."

Bravis tipped his head, eyes hooding with contempt. "Sometimes, with all your posturing, a man could forget how long you've been away from the Judgement Seat. You don't remember how things are done in the Courts."

Thorne counted through five breaths, praying for patience. "I recognize the struggle you and the other Chancellors faced holding my father at bay. But don't *you* forget that I was fighting him just as fiercely from the wilds, where I had three women in council among my cabal. Their advisement and wisdom were among my greatest assets."

"It would be different if we were at war. Women are more than fit for battle, but for matters of law, they're too emotional."

"Let's discuss emotion, then," Thorne said. "When my grandmother died, I let *my* emotions rule. I hunted down my father, and if not for a woman's intervention, I would be dead today. Don't insult me by suggesting either that when you and Maltadova considered surrendering to Salvotor the night Kanslar set, that decision was bereft of emotion."

Bravis's eyes narrowed. "But a woman's emotions can make her petty. That's dangerous to the rule of law."

"Men are just as vindictive. That's what I'm facing now with my Tribunes. And with Benedikt and Valdemar, if that's escaped your notice."

Bravis changed tack. "The Tribunals are already in place. It would create chaos to introduce women into them now."

"You don't have to change yours. Nothing in the law would make it mandatory to select a woman as Tribune—though I highly recommend it. It would be at the Chancellor's discretion."

"Until the women all get it into their heads that they're *owed* the position, and what then? This is pointless talk, it would never pass."

Thorne shifted his weight as a twinge of pain charred the back of his right calf. "If you write this law, both Yager and Kanslar will support it. It will succeed."

"Then ask Yager to propose it, and I'll consider supporting it in *their* season."

"Then Kanslar would lose two seasons—crucial time to consider women for our Tribunal. And if you truly intend to support this law, then it doesn't matter who passes it, you or Yager. Your support would be behind it just the same."

Bravis scoffed, returning to his papers. "Except if *I* propose it, then it's Traisende that becomes the laughingstock of the Courts."

"Yes. Traisende, the Court under the constellation of the Wayfinders. Four powerful *women* who helped set Valgard free."

Bravis slowly raised his eyes. "Pressing me to pass the laws you want. Just like your father."

A personal stroke this time—Thorne had him. "If I was like Salvotor, I wouldn't ask. But I *am* asking, Chancellor to Chancellor. Pass this law so I can conduct my Court how *I* see fit. There's no reason the Courts should hold one another at arm's length, dangling favors."

"I hope you would take the same position if Traisende came to *you* for a favor in your season."

"I would. I consider the other Courts my allies, not my rivals. My hope is for unity in self-governance...something my father never believed in."

"Good luck with that. Short of war, I doubt anything would blend the hearts of our Courts that way." Bravis reclined, arms folded, looking him up and down. "If I press this law through, I'd like something in return: Kanslar's aid with all of this nonsense." He waved an arm at the ration requests. "Your Court is in session before mine. If you'll agree to double the labor in the territories during the harvest and require more stock for the stores in the city, I'll write up your law."

Thorne frowned. It was much to ask of the territories at the advent of winter, but if he shifted the demand onto the backs of the larger, more prosperous cities and towns, and worked with Tyve and Yager to increase the prosperity of the planting season... "I'll adjust the requirement for the stores *if* the law passes."

"Now you're thinking like a Chancellor!" Bravis chortled. "There may be hope for you yet."

Thorne hoped that the jumping muscle in his jaw wasn't visible as Bravis bent back over the stack of papers. "I'll look forward to seeing that law drafted soon, Chancellor."

Bravis waved his hand. "I'll consult with my Tribunes and write the proposal tomorrow."

Thorne accepted the clear dismissal and climbed the steps to the door.

"Thorne," Bravis called up to him as he opened it, "a word of caution: tread lightly. I have less reason to hold you in contempt than Valdemar or Benedikt, but I'm still not fond of you coming to the Sanctum with propositions of laws that benefit one Court only: yours. If you make demands like these of Tyve and Skyygan, you may find enemies hiding in all the same shadows your father did."

A chill riding down his spine, Thorne stepped out and shut the door. In the silent, empty hall, he glanced aside at the mirror next to the door. For an instant, he could see what others often found in his face: the contours and flecks of darkness like Salvotor's.

"Will I ever be rid of you?" he muttered.

A lurch of cold wind whispered against him, trying to sound like distant, cruel laughter. Shaking it off, Thorne flexed his fingers and strode down the hall. It was time to return to his other solace—his best distraction.

CHAPTER THIRTY-EIGHT

NO ONE REMARKED when Cistine, Daria, and Quill returned to Stornhaz astride different mounts than when they left, nor on the black stains in their hair and armor which not even vigorous washing in every stream between the Sotefold and the city could wash away.

Cistine almost didn't mind the reminder of what they'd faced. There was some thrill to reliving the battle with Quill and teasing Daria about missing all of it around their campfires on the journey back, and even a trace of melancholy when they parted ways with her at the courthouse gate.

"This hardly seems worth all the trouble you went through," Cistine said ruefully as she poured the last of the payment into Daria's coinpurse. "That concussion was terrible, I'm so sorry."

Daria chuckled, weighing the purse in her palm. "Please. It's what I do for a living. I knew the risks when I went along."

"You could've fooled me with how easily that Atrasat brought you down." Quill reclined against the gate with arms folded, smirking. "If it wasn't for us, you would've been minced on those steps."

"If it wasn't for you, I wouldn't have been there in the first place. So I'd say it all sorts itself out in the end."

"Really, Daria, thank you." Cistine squeezed her shoulder. "If there's ever anything we can do..."

"Just keep me in mind the next time you have a creature to hunt." She winked, tossed Quill a smile, and sauntered back down the bridge.

"I like her." Quill pushed up from the gate. "Tati would, too. But stars help me if they ever meet, that's more trouble than one man should have to handle in a lifetime."

Cistine's laughter sobered quickly as they ducked through the gate into the peristyle. It was her first time alone with Quill since they roused Daria after the battle; days' worth of unspoken apologies all gathered at once on her tongue. "I'm sorry about the lightning augment. If I hadn't hesitated..."

"Don't worry, all of us have bridges we're afraid to cross," he said easily. "When the time's right, when it means enough, you'll manage it. Until then, we'll make you the best flame-wielding augur in the north."

She punched his shoulder. "Not better than you!"

"If you don't succeed me someday, I've failed as a teacher." His hand dove into her satchel and he flashed the jar of Atrasat ink to the sun. "I'll take this to Mort and head to the markets...got to look for Tati's thief. You go and tell Thorne we're back. I'm sure he missed you more than me."

"You're just avoiding having to visit a bedroom without Tatiana in it."

He kicked her haunch. "Get moving, will you?"

Laughing, Cistine burst into a run for the courthouse.

It seemed someone sent word of her return ahead of her. Thorne was already waiting when she reached the bedchamber hall, leaning against her door with arms folded, a book open in one hand. He glanced up when she dashed toward him, clapped the book shut, and shrugged up from the door. She met him with an embrace and a kiss straight on his mouth; with a delighted sigh, he brought her flush against him, and it was more than a full minute before they broke apart to breathe.

"Hello to you, too." His husky voice chased a shiver down her spine. "I was going to ask if you missed me, but I think the answer is obvious."

Arms looped around his neck, she leaned back with a smirk. "But did you miss *me*?"

He arched a brow. "Difficult though it may be to believe, I wasn't lurking outside your door for the pleasure of it. Ariadne spotted you in the courtyard." He stepped back and laid a hand on her doorknob. "Which is good. I wanted to be here the first time you saw this."

"Saw what?"

"Your gift."

She peered up at him. "You do know it's not Darlaska yet."

"It doesn't have to be. This couldn't wait."

He flung the door wide with a flourish, bowing out of her way. The smell of wet loam, lavender, and rosemary filled her head with a brief but vivid memory of her garden in Astoria. Green sweeps and golden fronds opened before her like welcoming arms as she brushed past Thorne and stepped into her room, which had transformed into a greenhouse. Creeping ivy fastened to brackets on the walls, hanging pots overflowed with ferns and laceleaf, tendril vines draped from the rafters, and her bed canopy dangled with bunches of plumeria and larkspur. She cupped her hands to her mouth as she turned, finding peeps of begonia and foxglove, sweet pea and pansy, and a square box below her window where that dry smell of rosemary wafted from—and mint, she realized as she approached, and basil and thyme. Sweetsap and redroot and poultice herbs, too, and small clay jars lined up along the box's left side.

She knelt and rested her palm on the damp soil. "Is...is this a garden?"

"Yes. With seeds in those jars for you to plant," Thorne said. "Seeing as the garden outside is rote until winter ends, I thought I could bring one into your rooms instead."

Cistine's throat tightened. "You did all of this while I was gone?"

"Mira helped. And Mort built the box." He shrugged modestly. "According to my research, lavender is calming, but I know you don't like the color, so I tucked them behind the hydrangeas. If the smell is overwhelming, I'll send Faer up to thin the blooms."

His research. The botany books he snuck in between reading ledgers and lawbooks. She could feel every fiber of his care and concern when she buried her fingers in the loam, anchoring herself to its familiar, damp density.

"Morten built it deep enough for the roots to grow," Thorne added.

"We may have to transplant in spring, but for now, stars willing, it will suffice."

"*Suffice?*" Shrill with shock, she spun to her feet to face him. "Thorne, look at this place! You turned my room into a *garden*. It better than suffices!"

He laughed, dropping his weight back against the closed door. "I'm glad to hear it. If the state of our garden in Hellidom was any indication, horticulture's never been my greatest strength."

She laughed too, flinging her arms around his neck again, and he lifted her off her feet. He smelled like the room around them, rich dirt and the perfume of flowers, like he just finished putting the last touches on this surprise before she came home. She buried her face in his neck and inhaled the earthy scent of him. "*Thank you.*"

"My pleasure, *Logandir.*" He settled her onto her feet again and rested his hands on her shoulders. "So, tell me about your journey. How was traveling with Daria?"

"It was..." she trailed off, the memory of corpses and shadows stealing her joy. "I need to tell you something first."

He frowned. "What's wrong?"

Swallowing the tangible taste of darkness lingering on the back of her tongue, she told him of Nygaten Temple. He moved to sit at her table while he listened, his focus trained on her face, and didn't interrupt except to audibly catch his breath when she spoke of the decimated atrium and the dead *visnprests*.

"Daria thought the Atrasat might be sick, hungering for human flesh, but that isn't enough for me," Cistine admitted. "Even if it killed the *visnprests*, who took the books?"

"That man you saw," Thorne said, "could it have been Devitrius?"

She fought to remember that illusion of wind and shadow, a mirage at midmorning. "Maybe. I never saw him from the front, but...it could've been him."

"If so, then he and my mother are hard at work. First Detlyse Halet, then Siralek, now this." Thorne rubbed his face with both hands. "Their first two targets, I understand. There could've been any number of prisoners who would trade information for their own freedom. But why a temple? What do they need with those books?"

"I don't know." She raked the gooseflesh from her arms. "Whatever happened out there, Thorne, it felt strange. It felt like..."

Nazvaldolya.

Thorne offered his hands to her. She took them, and he tugged her forward to stand between his knees. When he tilted his head back, she laid her forehead against his. "Whatever this was, we will solve it together." His vow warmed her face, her lips, her heart. "Us and the Courts. Like we're solving the spies, the trial, the treaty...all of this."

His promise pushed against the shadows, held them at bay. But still that vicious darkness churned in her core.

That sour, snarling call.

CHAPTER THIRTY-NINE

GRITTY SAND, HOT days, and cold nights consumed Tatiana's world. Spies and thieves, trials, and thoughts of Stornhaz dimmed; even missing Quill was an ache blunted by the maddening mystery of the Blood Hive's absent population and the blight lurking within its heart.

"I hate this," she growled, standing behind Aden beyond the edge of the oasis. "That's *every* home turned over *three times* now, every nomad tent ransacked, and for what? We've wasted more than a week here!"

He crouched, picking up a handful of sand and watching it sift down again. Then he turned his gaze back to the horizon shimmering in noonday heat. "How long do you suppose it takes word to travel from Siralek to Stornhaz?"

Hands planted on her hips, Tatiana shrugged. "By horseback? Days. By a wind augment, just long enough for a guard to make it to the wall and cross the city. Why?"

"Because the Vassora who found the arena like this were not here when it happened, they traveled down from Spoek to trade shifts. To have timed the attack so perfectly that news arrived on the day, even at the hour of Deja's testimony..." Aden trailed off as the last grains of sand poured from his fist. "Assuming Salvotor was responsible, he would have had to know the day of the shift trade and how long it would take news to reach the courthouse from here. With knowledge so precise, do you know what else he could've planned for? What his accomplices could've replicated, given enough time to act before the shifts traded?"

Tatiana stared at the heap of red grains piled before him, her hands sliding off her hips. "A sandstorm."

"A sandstorm." Aden straightened, dusting off his palms. "A swift attack, an augment-crafted storm, and all trace of movement erased. Every moment, every detail of this was laid precisely."

"But that still doesn't explain why *everyone* is gone. What did they want with the elites, the nomads? What about the *Vassora*, did they *all* just defect? Run away? Not even fight back?"

Aden cast her a rueful look. "Do you know what we did to hide bones too shattered to be picked up from the arena?" When she shrugged, he turned and strode past her, squeezing her shoulder on his way. "We raked sand over them."

Gut plunging, she cast one last look at the empty horizon, then pivoted to follow him. "Then we have nothing. No way to be certain of that, nothing to report, and no idea where Rakel and Devitrius are going."

"On the contrary. Sand can hide everything but itself." Aden jerked his chin. "Look at the dunes."

It only took one glance, now that she knew what to search for; and Tatiana realized what they'd been standing on the edge of the oasis looking for all morning.

Sander's private encampment lay in the shadow of the broken arena, where presumably far less of his own bad memories crouched. It was the first time Tatiana had seen him in days, and perhaps that was on purpose. He certainly didn't look happy to see them when they dropped down in the shade beside his bedroll and dead fire, passing a water gourd between them.

"The attackers went southwest," Aden announced. "They buried all evidence of their presence in a sandstorm, but there's no hiding the shape of dunes changed by a wind augment."

"Or the direction of sand thrown against the houses," Tatiana added, slinging off her satchel and pulling out her invention.

Sander eyed it, head slowly bobbing. "That's something more than we had, anyway. Can you confirm it was Devitrius and Rakel?"

"No, but I can confirm Salvotor is communicating with someone outside his apartment walls," Aden said. "Every step of this was plotted. They knew the timing of Siralek's guard change and the exact moment to strike in relation to Deja's testimony."

"A stream of thought flowing from Salvotor to his sympathizers." Sander raked his palms along his stubbled cheeks. "Damn. I'll send word to Thorne at once. Perhaps he and Cistine will find a name that's worth something in those ledgers they're deciphering."

Tatiana sent up a silent prayer they would, then concentrated on tinkering again to calm the buzz of nerves storming up whenever she thought of what bones might lie under this sand now.

"About the trial," Sander said after a beat.

Aden started up. "We have things to attend to. This discovery ought to be reported to the guards."

"It can wait, Aden."

Tatiana paused, glancing up. It was the first time she'd ever heard Sander employ the tone of a High Tribune, like Thorne did for ten years in Hellidom, commanding attention and demanding respect.

Scowling, Aden sank back down, every muscle taut. "Say it."

Sander unwound the wrap from his tight, dark curls, letting them spill across his shoulders, and sat up from his bedroll with wrists hanging from his knees, staring at the dead firepit before him. "I'm sorry. For every cruel, crass word I spoke to you over the years, every taunt about how the Hive owned you, every allusion to what you were, what they did to you." His fingers slowly clenched and unclenched. "Had I known...had I realized what was *truly* done to you, what you sacrificed—"

"You would have still behaved as you are," Aden said flatly. "A ruthless, ambitious *bandayo*."

"Well, all right, yes. But one who would've curbed his tongue about certain things." His gaze met Aden's, hollow and pained. "I didn't think such atrocities were happening, least of all to you."

"According to Mira, men rarely do."

Sander's fingers splayed on his knees, flexing. "She is...helping you, then? With...that?"

"We've rarely spoken of it. You can understand why."

"I can. Perhaps better than you realize." He grazed his thumb over his knuckles as if feeling out some old wound beneath the scar there. "More than half the women in my household came from flesh markets bound for Siralek." Tatiana cursed quietly; Aden made no reply. "Some were criminals. Some captives. I offered them all a clean slate, paid their debts, erased their pasts. I've seen from far too close what the cruelty of men and women like Deja can do. And I do not make light of that pain. Forgive me for any time I've made light of yours."

Aden was silent for some time. At last, he shrugged. "You didn't know. I made certain no one did."

"Regardless. You were...well, not a friend in Stornhaz, but I knew we wanted the same things before Salvotor drove you out: a better Chancellor. A better future. And I still ground you into the sand with my heel when you came here." Sander peered up the vast height of the broken elliptical. "Seeing this place like this, seeing the state of my fellow Nordbran Tribunes when they behold it...stars, it was all pointless, wasn't it? Our scrabbling for power over something so easily ripped away. Siralek was never Noaam's, never anyone's, really. And the things we did here, how we profiteered from the pain of people like you and Ashe..." Sander trailed off, shaking his head. "I was no better than Salvotor."

At a loss for what else to do, Tatiana offered him the water gourd. He sipped from it, still craning his head back to gaze at the dark glory ripped to ruins around them.

"I did what I did to protect what was most precious to me," Sander went on. "But that is no excuse for the agony it caused...the ones we knew about, and ones we didn't. I'm sorry, Aden."

This time, Aden was quicker to answer, his voice rough but steady.

"We were both lost in this place on the path to proving ourselves. But you've more than proven your loyalty. You risked not only your title, but your life when you voted to help Thorne retain his." He bent forward and offered his hand. "We put the rest of it behind us and move forward. For the sake of that better Chancellor. And the better future."

Grinning, Sander inclined and clasped Aden's forearm. "To being better."

They sat back, the strain easing out of the air, and Tatiana returned to her invention with a smile.

After a comfortably-long pause, Sander deemed fit to change the subject to less personal waters. "We've made progress in the catacombs. The augurs requested a few more days to make the tunnels navigable. As High Tribune, it was my...*privilege* to be the one selected to investigate when the time comes." His face twisted with disgust. "I'd like the pair of you to accompany me down."

Tatiana shot a sharp glance at Aden. His bearing didn't change but for the slight tilt of his head. "Why us?"

"Because I know that despite the failures of this place, one thing is certain: there was never a better fighter in Siralek than the Lord of the Hive. So there is no one else I'd rather have at my back when I descend into that fetid corner of Nimmus."

Aden assessed Sander with cool, calculating eyes, then glanced at Tatiana. She shrugged, and at her consent, the former Hive Lord dipped his head. "We're with you. Whatever comes."

CHAPTER FORTY

I T WAS A moment of triumph when Ashe was finally strong enough to bathe. After days of talking with Bresnyar, stretching her aching, tired muscles, and eating her weight in fish and nuts, it was finally time to make her way down from the cliff. To her relief, the dragon knew the way to a small pool within the valley, and followed her down the switchback trail to it, grumbling the whole way that she ought to let him carry her.

But she wasn't ready for that. Not when it still felt strange to even stand on her own feet.

She washed in privacy behind a tumble of rocks while Bresnyar's breath heated the water. Rinsing weeks of grime from her skin, she watched the dregs of Kashar's torture eddy away with the flickers of fish below the pond's surface. She hadn't let herself dwell much on him since she woke; the surreal companionship of a dragon made the days before it seem insignificant at best.

But it was Kashar she thought about now while she scraped her scalp and dunked under the water three times—him and his strange drugs, his tides of kindness and cruelty.

Eventually she rejoined Bresnyar on the shore, a collection of smooth, flat stones in her hand. She skipped them, watching the sun sink lower into the shroud of the Calaluns, its last rays flung long between the trees. The repetitive motion, like training, opened the clogged channels of her mind. "Those men who threw me off the cliff. Did you kill them?"

"Regrettably, no. They were swift to dodge my flames...I suspect they've danced with dragons before." Bresnyar laid his chin on his folded knuckles. "Why do you ask?"

"They mentioned a spy." Ashe waded in, finding and flinging another stone, counting ten skips. "Someone went to Valgard to find out the truth about the treaty I mentioned...if it was real or not."

"I see." Bresnyar's breath warmed the water around her calves. "That could be problematic for Talheim, yes?"

"Potentially."

"Will you go back, then? Tell them of the spy and help find them?"

Ashe shrugged. Her way had never been so unsure before. Ever since Cistine's birth, she had a role to play that would last a lifetime, because a princess would never stop needing a guard—or so she thought. Now she had a princess who didn't need her and a kingdom that didn't want her, that didn't even search for her when she went missing. She had friends whose backs she'd stabbed and hearts she broke, with whom reconciliation was daunting if not utterly impossible.

For the first time in her life, the path split. Down one side was darkness, discomfort, misery, and despair, much of it her own making. Down the other, there was Ashe, alone—except perhaps for the dragon at her side.

"I'll worry about the spy later," she decided. "For now, I have business to finish."

Bresnyar tipped his head. "And what is that?"

She traced her thumb over the new scars running parallel down her cheek. "I want to go back where you found me and give Kashar az-Kyrian the death he deserves."

"I would gladly eat him on your behalf."

"No. This is my kill. We'll go when I'm ready." She trudged up the shore and sank down at Bresnyar's side, the heat of his scales quickly drying her armor. "Then I'll decide about the spy."

"And after that?"

She dug her elbow into his hide. "Don't press your luck, Scales. Let's head back to the cliff."

Bresnyar stretched and yawned, settling his chin on the ground and shutting his eyes. "It's pleasant here. I think I'd like to stay."

"Oh, *now* you don't want to move around? How convenient, you overgrown lizard."

One fiery eye flicked open, revolving to stare at her. Then the wind plunged out of her as she went soaring through the air toward the water. By the time she realized Bresnyar had flicked her off the shore with the tip of his tail, the water crashed over her, the cold stealing whatever was left of the air in her lungs.

She surged wildly up, breaking the surface with a gasp and plowing toward the shore. "*Bresnyar!* You can't just toss people because you don't want to move! What's the matter with you?"

"Ah, but I just did." She picked up a handful of mud and flung it at his muzzle, and he twisted lazily away, chortling. "You're quite immature when you're angry." He heaved himself to his feet and stretched. "Fortunately for you, *I* am quite *hungry*, so I suppose we'll go back up."

Ashe raised a brow. "No."

Bresnyar stretched his long neck and shook out his wings. "I beg your pardon?"

She perched her hands on her hips and flashed him the savage grin that sent the deadliest Blood Hive fighters cringing. "No, I just decided I like it here! Let's stay for a few more hours. Your stomach can wait."

Bresnyar narrowed his eyes. "I wouldn't suggest that if I were you."

"What are you going to do...*finally* eat me?"

With a tree-quaking roar, he sprang forward and grabbed her in the cage of his fist, lifting her from the shore. With a surge of his wings, they flew.

The nearest sensation was a journey by augwain—but even that couldn't compare to this, nothing in her whole life did: the exhilaration of the treetops spiraling away below, the wind tearing her hair, her stomach plunging away and her heart surging into her throat. She nearly wept at the terrifying ecstasy, Bresnyar's claws bearing her up above the Calaluns themselves; then they shot back down onto their ledge, landing softy and safely on the stone. The dragon opened his fist and Ashe rolled from it, coming up to her feet panting, staring at him. "That was..." she broke off with wild laughter. "Holy *gods.*"

Bresnyar blinked, brows tweaking. "That didn't frighten you?"

"Was it meant to?" She tore her hands back through her hair, hunger and exhaustion forgotten. "Again."

He flashed a draconian grin. "If you wish."

"Oh, I wish. What's the best way? In your hand again?"

"Wingmaidens tend to ride our backs, but they have saddles."

"I've always preferred bareback myself." She grabbed his wing joint and swung onto his spine, pressing her knees into the hinge where his long neck began. "Like this?"

"Yes. I'll go slowly for you...a lovely airborne trot."

"No." Recklessness spiked through Ashe, bending her low on the dragon's neck. "Show me how fast you are."

His ribs rumbled against the insides of her thighs—a chuckle at the challenge. "As you wish, *Ilyanak.*"

Golden wings spread out, pushed down, and caught the frigid air; then they shot upward into the sky.

The wind screamed by, raking Ashe's ears and thudding down every inch of her armor. Her stomach vacated her body to wait for her return on the ledge, and she choked back an exhilarated scream as Bresnyar rose above the low cloudbank wrapping the Calaluns, the frozen droplets clinging to Ashe's skin. With one powerful thrust, he launched forward, and this time she did shout in disbelief that she was riding the wind astride a *dragon.*

The clouds whipped into a gale as Bresnyar tore like a specter across their faces, every stroke of his wings sending him forward swifter than an arrow's flight. Ashe could do nothing but cling to him and toss up wild prayers that she wouldn't slip off as they hurtled deeper into the Calaluns, the clouds peeling back to reveal taller peaks straight in the dragon's path.

"Bresnyar!" Ashe shouted in warning. "*Bres*—!"

He slammed into the first mountain and pushed off, laughter booming like thunder when he latched onto the next cliff and shoved away to the one past it, then the next. Every lurch sent Ashe's insides somersaulting, and her shouts dissolved into laughter like his. When they reached the last mountaintop, Bresnyar leaped and spread his wings, catching the wind howling through the crags. It punched them forward again, faster than ever, and Ashe dug her boots into his wing-hinges and whooped with sheer joy. The dragon cut forward like a gleaming golden dagger, the breeze shifting around them while they traveled. Salination impregnated the clouds; the atmosphere thickened.

Bresnyar vaulted upward without warning, sides pumping, neck stretching as he rose up through the clouds, bursting above them into the glorious light of sunset. The thin air pricked Ashe's lungs and light burned across her face, the same gold as the dragonhide between her knees. Tufts of condensation lay below them, an endless, fleecy mountain range hiding the world. Bresnyar stopped flying, hanging suspended like a dark decoration against the shimmering sun.

Ashe knew what was coming. So when the dragon spread his wings, she spread her arms—let go of everything.

Together, they *plunged*.

Down through the clouds, the wind erasing Ashe's tears of joy the moment they left her eyes, she and the dragon fell for endless seconds— then twisted and leveled out, bursting from the cloudbank and shooting over the Agerios Sea. Fathoms of blue water, dappled by the setting sun, spanned out on every side. Bresnyar dipped his talons in the waves, tossing up a whitecap surf and soaking Ashe's hair. She laughed when he tucked his limbs and spun, letting her do as he did, trailing her fingertips through the water and feeling the world around her as she never had before.

When he righted them both, Ashe opened her arms again, breathing in the world, the sea, and the warmth of the dragon's body that kept her from freezing to his back. There were no pike walls or prison catacombs here. No Wardens, no royalty, no enemies. Guilt, grief, and worry peeled away, falling into the sea as the wind turned her hair to a storm and the exhilaration of flight reduced her anger, hurt, and shame to cinders.

This was what it was to be truly *free*.

They flew for nearly half an hour into the ranges of the ocean before Bresnyar slowed and descended toward a dark mound climbing from the equally-dark horizon: a ripple of palm trees, the newly-minted moonlight reflecting on undisturbed sandbanks and finger shoals.

Bresnyar banked and made several small, tight turns to angle his descent, then touched down on the remote island and swiveled his head to peer at Ashe. "Not that you're tremendously heavy, but *I'm* tremendously tired, and we never did eat. So if you wouldn't mind..."

She slid down, peeled off her boots, and picked her way down the shore past washed-up starfish and sand dollars and shells sparkling like precious gems. Bresnyar reclined near the trees, resting his wings; when Ashe looked back, she could see their varicose veins pulsing steadily. "How long can you fly before you have to rest?"

"I've only ever broken down in flight once, the night Ileria died, when I tried to rush her to our Legion's healers. It's less a matter of distance, and more how we pace ourselves. A dragon has two hearts, did you know that? But if he flies too hard, both may stop."

Ashe reached the very tip of the surfline and wiggled her toes into the wet sand. "You must've really loved Ileria, to almost kill yourself trying to save her."

"The bond between Wingmaiden and dragon is different on the human side of things, or so I'm told. I doubt you could ever feel any equivalent. But imagine if your life and another's were so tightly woven together that without their breath, your lungs would fail. If their heart no longer beat, neither would yours. If you wondered every moment where they were, and what they were doing...not always consciously, but in the back of your mind—"

"And you couldn't help hoping even if you did something that put them in danger, they'd somehow be all right. That maybe you could mend things no matter how badly you broke them...no matter how far you pushed them away."

Bresnyar was quiet for a moment. "So. Perhaps you do know the bond."

She tried so hard not to think of any bonds lately; not to wonder if Maleck would've searched for her had she not used such calculated blows to destroy that unfathomable *selvenar* bond between.

But what was done was done. He was home, and now she would do what needed doing with Kashar, decide how to handle the Mahasari spy, then find a home for herself.

Leaving the surf, she went up the shore to Bresnyar and crouched to look into his eyes. "Thank you for bringing me here."

He studied her in turn. "Your scent has changed. I smell no sorrow in it tonight. No despair."

She laid her hand on his snout, his breath warming her all the way through. "Tonight, I don't feel like giving up."

And in this place, with the world so open around them, promising a new beginning...tonight was enough.

CHAPTER
FORTY-ONE

THE BAD DAYS returned with the onset of another cold snap. Cistine woke most mornings with wrists and knees sore from the cold despite her heap of blankets, stirring up memories of Kalt Hasa. Though these things didn't make her quite as unsteady as they used to, she retreated to Darlaska in her mind more often and fell asleep slowly, nipped with urgency that time crawled by without the treaty and Salvotor was not yet convicted.

But there was no helping either one. According to Thorne, the Chancellors still deliberated over Talheim's proposal, but their attention was mostly on reports from Siralek, and now cleaning up the mess of Nygaten; and she couldn't blame them or rush their work.

Busyness kept her sane despite poor sleep, bad dreams, and the low gnaw of dread in her stomach since the incident with the Atrasat. She spent every spare moment training, cracking the cipher and amassing a list of spies with Thorne, meeting with Mira and Ariadne, and pushing the others to visit Morten for their inkings—or visiting him herself.

"Honestly, I wish we had these years ago." Quill flexed shamelessly, sitting cross-legged on Cistine's feet, pinning her boots to the training hall floor while she counted aloud through her core-strengthening exercises. "Think of all the terror I could've struck into Vassoran hearts."

Cistine grinned as she hefted up, wrapped her arms around her bent knees, and studied his fresh inkings: broad raven wings like spirals of shadow spread cross his arms, chest, and torso. "I don't think it would've been worth going into battle shirtless just to show off."

"You're painfully underestimating the lengths I'll go to for a good hair-raising swagger, Stranger." Quill thrust her back down to the floor, then flashed his palms. "Again."

Groaning, she swung herself up and landed two punches into Quill's hands, fell back, sat up, and punched, again and again.

"What's bothering you?" he asked after several repetitions. "Usually you're ready to stop after fifty of these."

"What *isn't*?" she panted. "Salvotor, the suspended trial, the treaty, my bad feelings. And now all these attacks, and however they're connected to the rest of it."

"Fair." Quill scratched below the fringe of his hair, then offered his palms again. "I don't envy you and Thorne, especially about the treaty. I'd take battle over politicking any day. But I can't think of two people better for negotiating the peace between kingdoms. You've already done it between yourselves, so what's a few more minds to change?"

Cistine smiled, resting a moment against the floor. "I appreciate that."

"Anytime." He curled his fingers twice, and she moaned, hauling herself up to land two more cross-hooks.

When she lowered herself back to the floor this time, footsteps scuffed on stone, announcing Ariadne's arrival.

Cistine sat up slowly this time, arms curled under her knees, a greeting dead on her lips; Ariadne's hands were wrapped, hair bound sternly at the back of her head, eyes flashing for battle. Mira descended behind her, face impassive but a strange melancholy in her eyes, and followed Ariadne to the side of the room lined with grainsack mannequins for swordplay.

"Ari?" Cistine called after her.

Mira held up her hand. "She needs time right now."

Ariadne took up a fighting stance halfway down the dim room, saber braced just above shoulder height, elbow cocked and level, gaze fixed straight ahead. Then she lunged with a perfect right-guided swing, ripping into the first grainsack just below its left arm.

"Again." Mira's voice belonged to the Vassoran guard she'd once been, rising through the practiced calm of the counselor she'd become. Ariadne danced back and plowed in again, bringing down uppercuts from the right and left, spinning behind the mannequin to deliver a deft slice at kidney-height, then a backhanded stroke plunged straight into the ribs. The frenzy in her movements was not bloodlust; it was the same hectic anger and fear that drove Cistine into augment training with Quill after her worst dreams, into sparring with Thorne when she couldn't sleep.

Whatever Ariadne and Mira had unburied in their session today, it rocked her foundation.

She landed two more blows against the mannequin, and Mira asked, "Who are you striking?"

"That gods-forsaken *kurak*," Ariadne spat.

"What does that mean?" Cistine whispered.

Quill rested his chin on her knee, frowning. "Nothing good. I don't know how to say it on the common tongue exactly, but Helga would've washed our mouths out for it."

Mira cut a hand toward the mannequin. "Hit it again."

Ariadne's sword severed the left arm, then the right.

"Again!"

The next strike walloped the target so hard, it rocked on its fastenings and nearly crashed to the floor.

"*Again, Ariadne!*"

She bellowed in rage, arms pulling and sailing in a succession of swings too quick to track; then, with one last deft swing, she severed the mannequin's head.

For a moment, there was no sound but the grain pouring out onto the floor.

"I'm afraid the trial won't be enough, Mira." Ariadne gazed at the devastated mannequin, the words a close to whatever conversation brought them here today. "It terrifies me how badly I want to kill him even though it doesn't bring me a future. I fear his darkness is *in* me. That I'll never be rid of it."

"Don't mistake feelings for actions," Mira said swiftly, "and don't think that wanting to do something is the same cruelty as doing it. Wasn't it you who told me during our first session that the True God can change our hearts if we ask? But he cannot undo our actions. It's in the stepping over that we create wounds which never heal."

Ariadne sucked in a damp breath through her nostrils and slowly nodded.

Mira walked to her, took her shoulders, and turned her in a sharp pivot. "There is a gift in you, Ariadne Lightfall." At the sound of her Name, all three warriors stiffened. "You understand that, don't you? You have a gift of love. Your task was not to become a *visnpresta* or to serve in a temple, it was simply to use your gift. Salvotor has not taken that power from you, you withhold yourself from using it as long as you dance with him in the past, in that apartment." She released Ariadne, gripped her sword-wielding fist, and pressed it to her heart. "Use your gift, and you can still change the world. But you keep it hidden as long as you keep dancing with him."

Ariadne stared at the saber's hilt, then raised her eyes to Mira. "If there is some way to do that, why has the True God not shown me?"

Mira tilted her head. "And what if he already has? Are you listening?"

Cistine tapped Quill, and he let her up. They slipped out in silent accord; Ariadne's pain was not theirs to witness today.

But it was all Cistine could think about on her way to and from Morten's house that afternoon, where he worked over her inkings in silence, bereft of his usual jovial smiles. The cold hadn't changed things just for her; melancholy gripped the courthouse, the whole city, and her friends—a sense like this trial and this strange season might never end. Perhaps there would never be a treaty, or a verdict, a thief caught or justice brought for Detlyse Halet, Siralek, and Nygaten. She didn't like thinking that way, but today, everything seemed so hopeless.

She had to do something about it.

The idea came when she left Morten's, passing the solid, frozen fountain in the desolate square outside. She stared at it for several minutes, a hopeful notion forming in melancholy's cracks; then she took off at a run all the way back to the courthouse.

The cold stung her nose when she hurried into the peristyle at last, mostly deserted at this hour but for a lone figure hurrying away from the main courtyard toward the visitors' apartments. Excitement pierced Cistine's wandering thoughts when the wind tugged the woman's hood back, revealing short-cropped dark hair and russet skin. "Daria?"

She halted, eyes wide. "Princess?"

Cistine jogged to join her. "What are you doing in the courthouse? Were you looking for me?"

"Not tonight, no." Daria glanced back the way she came, stuffing bloodied knuckles and bruised fingers into her pockets like she'd been hitting walls. "I didn't say before...it would be poor manners to seem like I'm procuring favors, knowing you were with Chancellor Thorne that night we met, and his affinity for Blaykrone..."

Cistine's pulse sped at the mention. "What about Blaykrone?"

Daria's shoulders slumped. "It's my home. I left it seeking a place in Yager Court."

"What kind of place? As a hunter? Vassora?"

"Anything, to start." Her mouth slid up in a half-smile. "However they'll take me is how I'd like to serve."

"Well, I'm glad you came when you did. With everything so out of balance, like with the Atrasat, Yager could use someone of your talents."

Daria's smile widened. "Do you really think?"

"I absolutely do." Cistine squeezed her hand. "I have friends in Yager Court, I'd be happy to put in a word for you."

Eyes fixed on their joined hands, Daria sighed. "Kind as that is of you to offer, you have too much to concern yourself with already. The trial, the attacks, the treaty..."

Each word slid over Cistine like another weight, one heavy shawl after another until she nearly stooped. But she forced her shoulders back, swallowed that faint trill of panic, and took Daria's other hand. "It would be my honor to help a woman of Blaykrone find a place in the Courts. Just let me speak to Chancellor Maltadova's personal archers. I won't interfere any more than that."

Regret crinkled Daria's mouth, then resignation. "You're a good woman. Valgard does not deserve the kindness you've shown us."

Flushing, Cistine studied Daria's withdrawn face, her gaze turned toward the heart of the courthouse. Then she gave her a tug. "I want to show you something."

She led the heel-dragging, protesting hunter all the way to Kanslar's wing and straight to Ariadne's door, finding her precisely where she expected: playing cards with Saychelle, Iri, and Pippet. Cistine beckoned the girl away from the game first, whispered in her ear, and sent her running. Then she threw the women their coats. "Come with me."

Ariadne raised a brow, her countenance far calmer than when Cistine saw her in the training hall that morning. "Where?"

"We're meant to be under guard, you know," Saychelle added.

"They can come, too!" Cistine flashed a grin at the bemused Vassora lining the walls. "Where's Quill? Isn't he on duty tonight?"

"Here." He jutted his head into the room. "Why did my sister just go tearing past me like Nimmus itself was on her heels?"

"An assignment from me."

"Ah." Quill inclined his head to Daria. "We meet again."

"Stars help us," she deadpanned through a crooked smile. "Do you have the slightest idea what our friend here is plotting?"

"Knowing her, something intriguing. I'm game if the rest of you are."

Around the room, nothing but nods. Cistine suspected any excuse to escape, particularly for Iri and Saychelle, was a welcomed one.

She led the odd procession of *visnprestas*, warriors, and guards outside to Kanslar's garden. At this hour, most ghostlamps had dimmed; only moonlight showed the way through frost-laced hedges and snowbanks that hinted this time, the cold intended to stay. They found Pippet sitting on the rim of the fountain at the heart of the garden, lacing on her boots. Lined up beside her were five other pairs, all with blades glinting at the soles.

Saychelle slowed, face scrunching. "What is this?"

"Ice skating," Iri laughed. "You remember this, don't you?"

Daria balked. "I'm sorry, I—I can't."

"You mean you've never *tried*. All it takes is one night of learning! Surely that's better than staying in your apartment alone?" When Daria scowled at the ice and the boots but didn't leave, Cistine took that as grudging acceptance and hauled her to the fountain's edge. "I'll teach you myself!"

Ariadne was the first on the ice, turning back to offer both hands to Pippet, then Saychelle, then Iri. By the time Cistine had her boots on, they were all skating a trained series of frontward and backward loops and twists, occasionally with hands locked, often spinning on their own. Pippet's balance and movements were masterful, a testament to long winters practicing on the pond behind the cottage in Starhollow. Ariadne was nearly her equal, as steady on the ice as in battle. Saychelle and Iri fumbled and clung to each other, laughter pluming the frigid air, and Daria watched them with equal parts longing and reservation in her eyes.

Swinging her feet onto the ice, Cistine bumped shoulders with her. "This is the future you'll have in Yager."

Daria nudged her right back. "And you? What future will you have, Princess Cistine Novacek of Talheim?"

She cast up a hand to catch Ariadne's in passing, letting her friend haul her up in one lithe pull. Centering her balance, she offered an arm to Daria. "I'm still finding that out myself. Care to join me?"

With a bark of laughter, she let Cistine drag her onto the ice.

Time lost itself in the deepening night while they skated, powdering the ice and whirling around the stone monolith at the fountain's center. Quill and the Vassora were a boisterous vigil seated on benches around the fountain's rim, bantering about card games and comparing scars. Iri and Pippet took over tutoring Daria when it became clear Cistine was out of practice herself; she relied on Ariadne's arms as much as her own feet to keep her from falling.

"You've been plotting this all day, haven't you?" Ariadne asked, helping Cistine skim backward across the fountain.

"To distract you by watching me make a fool of myself?" she laughed, breathless from another near-fall. "You know me so well!"

"Well enough to know you remembered what I told Mira, about how I used to love skating before we left the city. Before...everything." Ariadne's eyes, gentle and bright, held hers. "Thank you, *Logandir*."

Then they were off again, twirling across the silvery surface. With every revolution, Cistine imagined this moment complete; imagined Ashe and Maleck walking among the hedges, discussing weapons or music or whatever it was they argued about these days while pretending not to look too deeply into each other's eyes. She imagined Tatiana on the ice, pelting Pippet with handfuls of snow, her laughter filling up every gap of silence. Aden, with Quill and the Vassora, his laughter like his father's, rumbling through the air. And Thorne—

Thorne was here.

Cistine's skates dug into the ice and she slid to a halt, staring at him.

He didn't leave the shelter of trees where he watched them, shoulder propped against an evergreen, eyes heavy with exhaustion from yet another Blood Hive report or whatever sort of meeting took him away all day. Temple and fist to the tree, he watched her, knocking absently on the bark.

Tap, tap, tap.

Stillness.

Tap, tap, tap.

Tears burned Cistine's eyes. Thorne's smile softened. He knocked his fist gently on the tree again, slow and deliberate, unmistakable as if he called the words to her across the space between them.

I love you.

Three taps.

Three times more.

CHAPTER FORTY-TWO

 OR THE FIRST time since Tatiana, Aden, and Sander arrived in Nordbran, they woke to overcast skies and strong winds, the promise of a natural sandstorm brewing on the horizon. The perfect weather to escape into the catacombs.

Aden's tension was palpable when they reached the steps leading down from the ruins into the dark maw of stone; the gate fastenings were intact but the bars themselves gone, and in the room beyond, old stone pillars crumbled in heaps. Pressure girdled the air, a faint hum of lingering power where earth augments propped up Siralek's weakened bones. Still, it reeked of death.

"Something feels strange about this place." Sander echoed her thoughts, lifting his ghostlamp high. "Something waits for us."

Tatiana glanced at Aden. "Are you ready to do this?" she asked— wondering what in the stars she would do if he wasn't. She wasn't ready to strike off with Sander alone into this Nimmus-pit, and he was right; something was lurking down those twisted halls.

After a moment, Aden stepped forward. "I *will* do this."

They passed through half-collapsed halls in a single line, Aden at the lead, Sander at the rear, which suited Tatiana fine; from between them she could watch the walls more closely, read the history out of this place.

It was a brutal one. Walls dark and fetid, sand spotted with old blood, branching corridors lined with flattened ledges as long as a man but only a few feet tall. Aden caught her gazing down that corridor, and a sigh dragged from him. "Ashe slept here with the other fighters."

Tatiana wrinkled her nose. "I would've rather died."

"Many of them did."

They continued past broad, sandy training rooms with heaps of stone fallen across them, past a chamber with twin, gnarled gates hanging from their hinges, so warped they may well have been melted by a fire augment. Here again Aden slowed and stared. "Who lived here after the riots?"

"The new Lord of the Hive, I presume," Sander said. "None of the other Tribunes know who it was, only that it was a woman."

"I pity her." Aden's gaze traced the skull-stocked walls.

On and on they walked. Tatiana didn't know precisely what she was waiting to see, but the hairs on the back of her neck prickled when they took the tunnels deeper. Aden and Sander bristled with tension as well, a pack of wolves all scenting the same danger without a name to put to it.

At long last—far longer than Tatiana liked—Aden slowed again. "This corridor dead-ends."

Sander swore, tossing up his hands. "We've been down here for hours, and nothing! What were they burying if not evidence of their plans?"

"Maybe the prisoners were the ones who brought down the roof," Tatiana offered. "Some last stroke of defiance against the Hive?"

Sander grunted, but said nothing.

"We should go back," Aden sighed. "There's nothing more to see here."

Relieved to be out of the stale, murky air, Tatiana swung her ghostlamp wide and turned to follow them up the hall again—then froze, her heart sinking. "Aden. Yes, there is."

Far in the distance, barely gleaming in the teal ghostlight, a swath of stone sprayed down the tunnel like someone had used an earth augment to blast it open. Aden was at her side in two steps, frowning. "That was the end of this corridor. I know it, I walked these halls a thousand times."

"It *was* the end," Sander said grimly. "But it seems someone knew of a path beyond it."

Not a way out, but deeper into the catacombs.

They took it without another word.

In time, Tatiana began to doubt it was a catacomb they walked through at all; it was too long, too grand. The smooth black rock gave way to ancient deep-relief renderings of pillars set into the stone itself, arches and columns with men and creatures carved between them. She'd never seen anything like them before. Eventually, corridors changed to steps, leading them so far down the desert heat was a memory replaced by a deep, armor-biting chill. Their breath made soft puffs on the air.

The way leveled out again at last, opening into a vast stone atrium. Tatiana could only guess its size by the echo of their footfalls. Aden cast out an arm, and they all came to a halt. Scooping up a rock from the floor, he hurled it into the pitch-blackness with all his might; when it clattered against solid ground, Tatiana stepped forward, ghostlamp aloft, measuring the room with her eyes: a quarter-mile from wall to wall, and deeper than that, beneath a roof so high nothing touched their shadows. "What in the stars is this place?"

Sander's voice was strangely soft. "I believe it was a temple."

Frowning, she turned back to him. "What makes you say that?"

He gestured to the wall he faced, and she hurried to join him, ghostlight shedding across ancient Valgardan glyphs and drawings chiseled into the stone—hundreds of years old at least, detailed in sharp angles and misshapen bodies with knots and symbols woven throughout. The language of long-lost tribes and epic tales.

"Stars," she breathed. "These are at least as old as the wells."

Sander moved up behind her, his warmth a welcome buffer against the cavernous cold. "You can read them?"

"Not really read so much as recognize. But let me get a closer look." She raised her ghostlamp higher, and Sander joined his light to hers. It was true she didn't know what she was reading, but when she followed the drawings, then the carvings, her heart started to pound.

Seven craters drawn into the world, an eternal knot at the center of each. Around the hollows, men hooded and robed knelt with hands upraised in supplication. Above them, Old Valgardan runes, repeating over and over.

Stoj. Haval. Sinn. Faravost. The only four Tatiana could read. Life. Death. Time. Perception.

"What in the *stars...*" she hissed.

A clap of footfalls, and she cursed, whirling, her swinging ghostlight painting the ashen, sickly planes of Aden's face. "This isn't a temple anymore. It's a burial ground."

The reek of death clung to him, and Tatiana covered her nose with her sleeve, looking back where he came—deeper into the atrium, toward a heap of darkness fringed by Aden's ghostlight.

"The missing guards," he said, "and the elites."

Everyone who'd fought back. The secret buried under the sand.

"We need to leave," Sander said. "*Now.*"

Tatiana didn't dare draw enough breath to agree. She let Aden and Sander brush past her, jogging toward the winding steps back up into the catacombs; but she paused, looking back to that wall.

Stoj. Haval. Sinn. Faravost. And the three symbols she didn't know.

Those craters. The men worshipping before them.

When she blinked, a memory darted across her mind: fire and wind, snow and terror, a cliff at the edge of the mountains. A place she still had nightmares about.

"Tatiana!" Aden barked, jolting her from her reverie. She stepped back, lowering her lamp, and a dark wind licked the nape of her neck.

Wind. Here. In a place no natural breeze could reach.

Tatiana dropped her ghostlamp and fled.

CHAPTER
FORTY-THREE

ASHE'S SECOND RIDE with Bresnyar was not as exhilarating as the first. Adrenaline pooled sweat on her palms while they ascended, using the cold morning fog as a veil. Bresnyar climbed this time, scuttling up the dark crags, and she laid low on his spine, one hand braced on his back, the other laid to her crude weapon: a stick whittled to a dagger's point on one of Bresnyar's fangs. It was rustic and brutal, precisely what she wanted to jam into Kashar's gods-forsaken chest.

Up and up they climbed, Ashe trusting Bresnyar to find the right cliff; her own recollection of that night was a rain-battered, fever-stricken blur. She really did owe the dragon her life—and day by day, that was starting to mean something more than just prolonged suffering. It was beginning to be a reason for hope.

Bresnyar halted, claws gouging deep into the rock. His neck arched back, and he squinted up through the fog, haunches rocking in a silent signal.

They'd arrived.

Ashe bucked onto her feet, bending double on the dragon's back, and raced up his opalescent scales. When she stepped onto the bone plate between his brows, he surged up, and with a heave and a flip Ashe landed on the rocky ledge that had nearly marked her doom.

"*Kashar!*" She hurtled toward the cave—and skidded to a halt, staring.

There was no fire, no bedding, not even the heap of dirt and leaves where they left her sweating and sick while they discussed the spy. Ashe scoured every inch of the cave, searching for something, *anything*—a muddy bootprint, a stray hair, a fleck of ash or kindling—but the Mahasaris had vanished like specters into the rock. There was no sign that anyone was ever here, that *she* nearly died in this place.

Kashar had fled. And taken her vengeance with him.

"No." Ashe stabbed the butt of her pike into the rock. "No, gods *damn* him, no!"

She backed from the cave and bellowed profanity at the mist-heavy sky—not the signal she and Bresnyar agreed on, but she was too furious to do anything but seethe into the cave's empty blackness. Rocks clattered as the dragon clawed up to join her. His heat swept her back, comforting, calming—

A war-cry echoed from their left, and Bresnyar's pained roar in answer was like a blade cleaving straight through Ashe's chest. She whipped around as he staggered and crashed to his shoulder, an arrow wobbling in the part of his tail where Salvotor chipped away his scales.

Someone had shot him; someone who now flipped one-handed onto the ledge, her scream of rage still echoing, and dashed down the verge of rock with sword upraised, aiming for that same spot on his tail.

Ashe was between them in a heartbeat, catching the blade on her pike, and though steel bit deep into the wood, it held. Ashe slammed her foot into their attacker's gut, separating her hands from the sword's hilt, and with a deft twist she freed the blade and lunged, diving in for the kill.

But her enemy didn't fight back. She flung up her hands and cried, "*Ashe, stop!*"

Ashe did, the tip of the sword grazing the woman's neck.

Hands trembling, Rozalie Dohnal ripped back her hood and tore down the cloth covering her nose and mouth. Wide eyes glistening, damp, golden hair swirling against her neck, she stared at Ashe like she was an illusion glimmering in the chilly air—and Ashe did the same. Because Rozalie was here, so far from Middleton, armed to the teeth, hand itching back toward her bow again.

"You *shot* my *dragon?*" Ashe shouted.

Rozalie blinked, a flicker of temper heating her eyes. "*Your* dragon? He was creeping up behind you to *eat* you, he had his gaping *maw* open—"

"To offer words of comfort, thank you!" Bresnyar twisted to rip the arrow from his tail with his teeth.

Rozalie stared at him. "It can *speak?*"

"*He* knows many tongues, and would feel justified calling you something foul in each of them." Bresnyar lashed his tail, raining blood on the trees below. "I'd forgotten how much your piddly human projectiles *sting.*"

Rozalie's mouth opened and shut in helpless gasps. Ashe cast aside her blade and gripped her by the shoulders. "Roz, what in God's name are you *doing* out here?"

"Wh-why do you have a *dragon?*"

"Focus!" Ashe snapped her fingers, bringing Rozalie's stunned gaze back to her face. "Where's the rest of your patrol?"

She shook her head. "Back in Middleton by now."

"What were any of you doing in the Calaluns in the first place?"

"What do you *mean?* We were looking for you!"

Ashe fell back on her heels. "That...that can't be. There was no patrol. No one came." Kashar had told her—he'd been *adamant*—

But why did she believe him? Why had she been so *certain* that was true? She couldn't remember anything except the sweetish taste of some herb on her tongue, braided into the conviction that her kingdom abandoned her. That they never looked for her at all.

"We found one camp, but it was deserted," Rozalie said. "I was sure it was recent...they knew we were coming and took you away. Viktor disagreed, he said we were needed in Middleton and couldn't chase rumors through the mountains forever."

"You argued?"

"I broke his smug, disgusting face and went on my own."

"Roz. That was *weeks* ago. You've been out here alone that long?"

"What else was I supposed to do? Leave you to die?"

That was precisely what she assumed they did. But here was Rozalie, haggard, unwashed, sticks and leaves woven into her hair, weapons and eyes sharp, who stayed behind when everyone else left.

"I tracked movement from the deserted camp to this place, but then the trail went cold," she added. "So I've been watching this cleft, waiting to see if whoever took you would come back. If *you* would come back. And here you are. What *happened?*"

"Mahasaris took me, interrogated me about the treaty, then threw me off this cliff." She jerked her chin at the trees far below. "That's how I met Bresnyar. He saved my life."

Rozalie's brows leaped. "Only you, Ashe. Only you." Her smile broke out then, so sunshine-bright it could've melted the mist. "Wait until the King sees you, he'll have a fit! Not to mention Viktor and *Rion*. This will change everything!"

Cold fear snuffed the warmth that crept into Ashe's chest. To face her King, who had searched for her, but was still so disappointed; and Rion, who would think her even weaker now than ever before; and Viktor, who proved his indifference by searching as little as possible and turning Rozalie out alone in the wilds to continue the hunt while he went home...

But it wasn't about them. Not really.

She glanced over her shoulder at Bresnyar. He was uncharacteristically silent, grooming the blood from his tail with his forked tongue, hot saliva cauterizing the arrow wound. His eyes met hers, and she recognized that look from watching him speak of Ileria: anguish—and concern that she would leave him now and journey back with Rozalie.

Wouldn't she?

Ashe reached deep, feeling around in the darkness at the bottom of herself, that place where she hovered on the edge of hopelessness for so many days. But now her fingers met textured gold in the darkness. Sleek scales.

She let go of Rozalie's shoulders. "I'm sorry, Roz. I can't."

She blinked. "What?"

"I can't go back. I still need to find that bastard Kashar, wherever he's squatting in these mountains. You can tell Cyril what the Mahasaris did...warn him not to trust them, whatever they offer. But I'm not going to bend the knee to a kingdom that doesn't want me anymore."

"Ashe, you don't understand—"

"I understand better than you think." She forced a tired smile. "I'm grateful you came for me. You proved that some of Talheim is still good. But that's not enough for me to come back and serve with you." She strode toward Bresnyar. "We'll fly you back to the valley, close to Middleton. It's the least we can—"

"Ashe, they have Maleck!"

Her boots snared the stone, slamming to a halt so hard her hair whipped across her cheeks, stinging her eyes. Bresnyar's head lifted, nostrils flaring.

Slowly, Ashe pivoted. "What do you mean, they *have* him?"

"How do you think we knew where to look for you? Maleck told us about the signal fires in the mountains. He said there were spies out here, that they took you—"

"*Stop.* They *have* him? He came back?"

"He was the one who found your room torn apart! He accused Jad, but Rion accused *him.* A servant heard you two arguing after the last meeting before you vanished. She said you told Maleck not to put his hands on you. That there were sounds of fighting, and then in your room, there was so much blood..."

Ashe's fingers flexed at her sides, limp, weak, the world slipping out of her reach. This wasn't happening. It couldn't be.

"They have him imprisoned under the estate now, facing charges of murder." Every word from Rozalie's lips was worse than the last. "*Your* murder, Ashe. They found him in your room with your blood on his hands, no sign of you anywhere. He struck some sort of bargain with the King, I don't know how, but that was why he sent us. He said if we found proof you were abducted by Mahasar within three weeks, he'd release Maleck. If not..."

A dim hum slithered into Ashe's head. "If not, *what*, Roz?"

"What do you *think*? Rion's wanted his head ever since that night outside Stornhaz! And not just him...Jad was *furious* Maleck accused him in front of everyone. I've been looking for proof all this time because even if you were dead, if I could prove Maleck didn't do it, that would be my last gift to you."

But there was no proof; none but that Ashe still breathed.

She laid a hand to her chest, reaching into her heart blended with his. He wasn't dead yet—she would've felt if he was. But at any moment, that could change. "How long does he have left?"

Rozalie stared at her, and that look was all she needed to guess.

Three weeks *today*.

Ashe strode to Bresnyar, but Rozalie balked, shaking her head. "I'm not sure this is precisely *natural*..."

"Roz, we don't have time to walk back. We need to go *now*."

Rozalie cursed and raced after her.

The moment she was astride Bresnyar's back with her friend behind her, arms locked around her waist, Ashe leaned low and hissed to the dragon, "I need you to fly faster than you ever have. Fly like you would for Ileria."

With a roar, Bresnyar launched into the sky.

Rozalie's petrified scream barely broke through the bellowing in Ashe's ears. The trees blurred into a dark continuum below, and they moved so quickly she would've felt sick even if she weren't nauseous already.

Maleck had come back, had sent every scrap of help he could for her, and Rozalie had gone far beyond duty's merits to follow that trail. And by staying away, keeping to herself and then pursuing vengeance, not justice, Ashe might've damned the last hope for peace. And damned her *selvenar*.

Was that fraying in her chest just her fear? Or was something happening even now, shattering that bond between them?

Trenches and mountains floated away beneath them, swift as a river, and in minutes they broke out over the plain. Bresnyar banked almost at once, losing height and speed, and Rozalie and Ashe shouted as he crossed Middleton's pike wall and plowed into the cold, hard soil at the edge of the inner grounds. With a great shudder, he collapsed on his side, ribs heaving; Ashe and Rozalie leaped clear at the last moment, Ashe spinning back toward him. The dragon raised his head and jerked his muzzle. "*Go. Save him.*"

Ashe pressed her hand to his snout. "I'll be back for you."

Exhaustion dimmed the red of his eyes to pulsing embers. "I will be waiting, *Ilyanak.*"

Heart tearing in two, Ashe broke into a sprint toward Dorminger's estate, Rozalie at her side. Every breath was a dagger plunged into her lungs and torn up to her jaw; her heart jabbed brutally into her ribs as they passed the ivy-mortared walls, then the slope down to the garden, the hoop of the path bobbing into view.

A cluster of men and women gathered out front: Jad and his Enforcers, unmistakable in their jagged armor; Cyril and Rion in Talheimic regalia, an equal count of Wardens at their flanks; a man of Dorminger's household, carrying an axe.

And Maleck standing in their midst, head erect but shoulders slumped.

Cyril ordered him to kneel, voice carrying clear and cool on the wind.

Ashe poured every scrap of strength into her legs, skidding along the dew-damp grass, and with the last heave of free breath she had left to give, she screamed Maleck's name.

She didn't care who heard or how they looked at her; let them all hear her scream for him like her heart was breaking—because it was. Let them hear her scream with fear—because she *was* afraid, terrified of losing him to that upraised axe catching the first glints of sun spearing through the clouds.

Let them hear a woman of Talheim scream for a man of Valgard, laying claim to him with everything she was. They'd never doubt the treaty was true after this.

Cyril whirled first, then Rion, the turn of their bodies cleaving a path. Ashe hurtled past them straight into the circle of bodies, slid on her knees into the too-small gap between Maleck and the executioner's axe, and faced that brutal edge with her arms outspread.

"*Stop!*" Cyril shouted. "Back away. All of you, *back away now!*"

The axehead thunked into the soil, the circle fanned out, and the King stepped forward. Ashe flinched when his hands caught under her elbows, dragging her back up to face him. "Are you hurt? Asheila, are you all right?"

"I'm fine!" she snapped, cutting her gaze to Jad. There was no mistaking the fury in his despicable face. "Maleck didn't do this. Jad's *nephew* took me."

"Outrageous!" the Mad King cried. "Accusations on top of accusations! Execute them *both*, they're clearly in collusion—"

"Enough." Cyril's voice was so deadly in its quiet, even Jad fell silent. "These are steep accusations, Ashe. Let's hope there's no truth to them. Because an attack on Asheila Kovar is as good as an attack on the royal family itself." Shock sliced through her fury as Cyril released her and beckoned the Wardens. "Escort King Jad to the pike wall and return the prisoner to his cell."

Ashe whirled as Viktor and another Warden pounced on Maleck, hauling him up with arms twisted behind his back. He wrenched one free with a bark of pain, hand extended, desperately reaching. Ashe reached back, catching the tips of his fingers before the Wardens dragged him inside the estate, the door clattering shut behind them.

Seething, she whirled on her King again. "Release him."

"We need to talk."

"I'll tell you anything you want to hear, just let him go."

"This is a complicated matter, Asheila, a *royal* one. I need you to recognize that. Meet with me, then he's yours."

He wanted her to play the Warden, guardian to the princess, confidant of the royal family again. Fine. She could do it one last time.

She fanned an arm to the estate. "Lead the way, Your Majesty."

Seated on opposite sides of the King's desk, they shared a decanter of mulled wine. Ashe managed no more than a few sips to steady her nerves between bouts of storytelling.

It was more difficult to relive than she'd expected; not because of the painful ordeal itself, but because of the hopelessness that dragged her so close to embracing death or walking away from her kingdom forever, and the shame of how readily she'd believed that no one—not Cyril, not Rozalie, not even Maleck—would come for her.

The King listened intently, interrupting only to ask clarifying questions. When everything was laid bare, he swirled his wine goblet and stared thoughtfully into it. "A dragon saved you."

Ashe fought not to roll her eyes. Trust him, like his daughter, to focus on the fantastic details over the practical ones. "Yes, and he's sulking around somewhere on Dorminger's property right now. I'm sure you'll hear all about him from the Wardens who saw us fly over."

"Undoubtedly." Cyril set down his cup, shaking his head. "Jad's treachery knows no bounds."

"I know. Jad plotted every step of this from the moment his people saw Maleck and me crossing the mountains."

"I believe it. He may be a few arrows short of a full quiver, but he's conniving, that bastard. And now he's trying to provoke two fronts. By your death, particularly with Maleck accused, he would've broken any truth or illusion of a treaty between us and Valgard. But by your survival and the accusation you made without proof, he may have all the leverage he needs to convince his kingdom we're spoiling for war."

Ashe swore, banging down her cup and rubbing her brow. "I shouldn't have done that."

"Something you and Maleck have in common. But what's done is done, and we haven't lost yet. There's still one place we can strike." Cyril leaned forward, hands folded on the desk. "Find that spy you mentioned, and we'll have proof he tried to provoke war by playing Valgard and Talheim against each other. We could even send it to his Magnates to show he's trying to manipulate their support by subterfuge...a blow he'd never recover from."

"I'll start the hunt," Ashe said, "but you need to release Maleck. Send him with me."

Cyril shook his head. "Jad needs to believe I haven't taken your accusation seriously, or he may retreat behind his borders to stir up war. Bring back the spy, and Maleck walks free."

Ashe breathed through a brief spurt of rage. It was sensible, but leaving Maleck shackled under Middleton with an axe still braced above his head would haunt her every mile between here and there. "Rozalie, then. I need someone at my back I can trust."

"She's yours."

Ashe lurched up from the chair. "I'll leave as soon as I see him."

"And I'll see to it you're given privacy." Cyril's smile, though tired, was warm. "There are no words for how glad I am to see you alive. When Viktor returned empty-handed from those mountains..."

He broke off, rubbing a hand over his mouth, and a deep, aching love rose in Ashe's chest. "I'm grateful you even tried."

He rose and rounded the desk, taking her shoulders. "For you, I will always try."

"Even after I disgraced you in front of Jad?"

"Even then. You are not my blood, but you *are* family. There is nothing I wouldn't do for you, even when we're at each other's throats."

She breathed in, deep and trembling, staving off tears. With a swift dip of her head, she turned from under his hands and strode to the door—then stopped. "Did you really think Maleck did it?"

"There were times I wondered. How convinced he seemed of where you were. That day in the corridor, when he had his hands on your neck, with the bruises. I wish you'd told me then what Jad was doing."

"I wish I had, too, but I was lost. I'm still finding my way back." She shook her head. "Regardless of where I am, you have to know Maleck wouldn't do that. He's never been anything but good to me."

"You above all others know how difficult it can be to trust Valgardans." Cyril brushed his thumb along the ring he wore for Cistine, the emerald stone glinting dully in the firelight. "But I hoped it wasn't him. I never stopped hoping."

With a parting nod, Ashe slipped from the room and ran the length of the estate to the circular steps leading down to the dungeon cells from the south wing. True to his word, Cyril's command went ahead of her; one of the Wardens handed her a key and let her into the long, dark corridor, empty except for the cage at the very end.

Heart thundering, she unlocked Maleck's cell and stepped inside.

His head shot up when she shut the door, the dried tracks of tears still visible where the amber-and-red light scraped his cheeks. He gazed at her like a specter who might vanish at any moment.

Ashe leaned against the door, folding her arms. "Hello, augur."

A faint crease of his lips. "Hello, Warden."

He snapped to his feet and she shoved off from the door, closing that unbearable distance between them, and the dull clatter of the iron shackles on his wrists and feet nearly broke her heart in two. A curse slid from her throat as she gripped his face, and his fettered hands took hers in turn; then she kissed him with everything in her, shoving away the memory of how he'd fallen to his knees, ready to bear the accusation for her death to hold to what remained of the treaty.

"You're such a *fool*," she growled against his mouth. "You never should've come back."

He pulled away only enough to rest his brow against hers, hands still tangled in her hair. "I never made it past the lakeshore. I came back to throw myself at your mercy, to tell you I *see* you—"

She silenced him with another kiss. Then another. "I didn't mean it. Nothing I said to you that night was real, Mal."

"That night..." Sucking in a damp, rattling breath, he pushed back, studying her face, his thumb brushing the new scars from her temple down her jaw. Rage and regret hardened his eyes. "I would've torn this kingdom apart to find you. But they threw me in this pit where I couldn't reach you, even knowing who must've taken you, and where, and *why*. Forgive me, Asheila."

"There's nothing to forgive. You sent the Wardens. You did enough." She slid her fingers into the long tangles of hair hanging damp against his brow, and the way his gaze devoured her speared heat straight to her core. "I'm the one who was almost too late."

A deep laugh rumbled in his chest. "You mean to tell me you weren't waiting for that precise moment to make your grand return?"

She grabbed the back of his neck and brought his mouth down to hers again. Perhaps she would regret this in time, kissing him this much, shredding that last wall between them. But for now, she wouldn't waste a second of it—especially when she already had one foot over the threshold, knowing she would leave him again.

The thought jolted through her like a blow, and when her breath hitched, Maleck withdrew. "What's wrong?"

She let her hands slide from his neck to rest over his heart. "I have to go. There's a Mahasari spy in Valgard, and Cyril wants me to root them out. It's the only way to save the treaty...to save *you*."

His shoulders sagged. "They won't let me go with you."

"You're the surety we need to keep Jad here. As far as anyone but us knows, you still stand accused."

"And what do *we* know, Asheila?"

She raised a brow. "Do I need to show you again?"

His answering smile was exhausted, and his arms wrapped around her, bringing her into the shelter of his grip. When she held him back, she didn't think she'd ever clung to anyone or anything so tightly in her life.

"Go save your kingdom," Maleck murmured into the side of her neck. "I'll be waiting."

She backed away, drinking in the sight of him alive, his fate hanging in the balance. "I'll come back for you."

"Wait." At the edge of his shackles, Maleck caught her hand and pressed something into it: his small leather journal. "Just in case."

Halfway to the steps leading up into the estate, curiosity got the better of her. She undid the cord and laid open the pages he'd kept hidden during their entire stay in Middleton.

He'd been drawing again—drawing *her*. At breakfast, an apple in one hand, a book in the other; with Rozalie, leaning on the walkway ledge, their profiles sculpted in sharp relief; in the training room, twin daggers braced back along her arms, ready to strike.

He didn't just render her frame in flawless detail; he captured the battle raging within her, the conflict fleshed out in lead, in the slant of her brows, the tilt of her mouth, the unhappiness in her eyes. In every drawing except one he must've captured from pure memory: her in Astoria's music hall, legs dangling from the balcony, a smile on her face while she listened to the symphony below. The music moved through her in the sketch, drawn in gentle whorls and curlicues.

Ashe wiped her nose on her wrist, then balled her sleeve and hastily scrubbed a tear that plopped on the corner of the page. She shut the journal and tucked it in her breastpocket, close to her heart.

Then she dashed up the steps to find Rozalie and Bresnyar, to save her kingdom—and her *selvenar*.

THE

SPY

OF

STARS AND
DREAMS

CHAPTER
FORTY-FOUR

THE SOOTHING SMELL of fresh soil filled Cistine's nostrils, easing the ache of another bad dream and more uneasy feelings. She delicately shifted the sweetsap from pot to gardening box, cradling the roots gently in one hand and inhaling its pungent aroma.

Her bedroom door slammed open, startling her so badly she nearly dropped the plant. "Aden's back and he won't train with me!"

Heart pounding, Cistine glanced over her shoulder at Pippet. "Well, thank you for waking me up all the way! Why don't you take Vihar and Faer into the garden for another race, then?"

"Mira took Vihar to the courtroom today." Fuming, Pippet threw herself on the foot of Cistine's bed. "For Saychelle, she said."

Cistine stared at her, tired mind weaving these things together. Then she dropped the sweetsap into the soil, covered the roots, and dashed from the room, leaving Pippet moaning about being abandoned *twice.*

Though she ran the entire length of the courthouse, Cistine still wasn't quick enough; elites were dispersing and Mira and Vihar descending the steps from the upper mezzanine when she reached the courthouse market, the Door growling for attention far below her feet. She clamped down on its call and strode to meet Mira. "I missed it?"

Mira looped her hair off her neck with both hands. "Honestly, you're fortunate you did. Bravis was just short of savage. It's been more than a week since Sander and I saw each other, and our reunion was barely a *hello, you stink of the desert* before they rushed us into the courtroom."

"How did the assessment go? How was Saychelle? Did Marcel give his testimony for Salvotor today?"

"Yes, he did. It was precisely how you'd expect." Mira mimed a yawn. "Pure lies from one ambitious fool about another. But Saychelle was marvelous, precisely how I've observed her: no hint of hysteria, no mental instability. When Salvotor isn't given a loose enough leash to overpower her, all is...well."

She spoke the last word oddly soft, and Cistine frowned. "Is it?"

Mira didn't speak again until they emerged into the courtyard, the shadows of the statues cast long in the midday sun. "Salvotor was the picture of restraint today. He all but laid out the circumstances for Saychelle's testimony to go smoothly."

Though her nape prickled, Cistine grasped for optimism. "Maybe he's learned his lesson about what he can and can't get away with."

"Perhaps. Or else he's gotten away with something far worse than we know."

The thought haunted them through Kanslar's wing, moving in silent tandem toward another session. Finally, Cistine said, "You must be so glad Sander is back."

"I am, though I didn't like the look on his face one bit. I'm sure I'll hear all the good news about the *Blood Hive* soon enough."

Mira's sharp tone brought Cistine's gaze back to her. "Are you glad Siralek is gone?"

She was quiet for a time, one hand on Vihar's shoulder as if to steady herself. "Whenever we love people, no matter how wonderful they are, there are parts of them we won't like. Habits. Vices. Ambitions. I've never shared Sander's belief about the necessity of the Blood Hive, what it stood for, what it accomplished. But I love him enough to let him walk that path and decide for himself where it will lead him. I hope...I *pray* he's realized now how despicable that entire place was."

Cistine's mind drifted to Finally, of dark hair and midnight eyes, and she tweaked the twisted ring around her neck. "Do you think the parts of someone you don't like are reason enough to walk away from...from love?"

"Only you can answer that. You do have to love a person as they are, accepting they may never change. But there are boundary lines."

Cistine squeezed the betrothal ring again. "What if they—?"

Vihar froze, stiff-legged, a growl booming from his chest, bringing them both to a halt.

Ahead, the door to Sander's apartment swung on its hinges like a broken limb.

Mira ordered Cistine back and sent Vihar forward in the same breath, but she didn't heed the warning; hand on her augment pouch, she dashed into the room on the wolf's heels.

Furniture was overturned, dishes scattered, screens ripped down from their fastenings on the ceiling, clothes scattered along the floor and tiles pulled up and broken in half. Snarling, Vihar stalked through the room, sniffing at every corner. Mira shot past Cistine into Sander's bedchamber; a moment later, a stream of profanity issued through the kicked-open doors that would've made the most seasoned Warden blush. Cistine bolted inside.

She'd never seen Sander's bedroom before, but it matched the man: ornate, tiled in deep mauve and gold accents, ferns and garlands everywhere—but even those were cut down. Mira stood amidst the destruction, gripping the edges of an open armoire. "They're gone. All of them."

"All of *what*?" Cistine demanded.

"My client notes from every person I've ever helped." She pressed both hands, violently shaking, over her mouth. "And my...Sander's..."

Mira collapsed without warning, limbs jerking, body rigid.

Shock froze Cistine for a moment. Then, screaming for help, she dropped down beside Mira, trying to grip her thrashing head.

It took no more than a minute for the scent of spice to envelop her, broad hands shifting her out of the way, and in a whip of sand-crusted robes

Sander was on his knees beside his lover. The look on his face was not panic, but pain; he shouted at Vihar, gave a sharp whistle, then swooped his arms around Mira and lifted her carefully, trapping her limbs in such a way that she could hurt neither him nor herself. "Flip one of those sofas in the parlor."

Desperate to be useful, Cistine did as he said. He laid Mira down, turned on her side, his hand resting on her shoulder while she spasmed. Then he jerked his chin toward the hearth. "The lockbox there contains a tonic. Measure out half a cup."

Cistine hurried to obey, though her fingers rattled so badly it was difficult to pour the clear liquid into its tin cup. Behind her, Sander murmured in a low, soothing monotone.

"Is she going to be all right?" Cistine's voice trembled.

Sander motioned her to set the cup on the floor. "She will be. This isn't the first time this has happened."

"How did you find us so quickly?"

"I followed you from the courthouse proper—and it's a good thing I did." Sander raked the room with a glance. "This is what I come home to after serving my Court. Someone will pay in blood."

The door croaked on broken hinges, startling Cistine so badly she nearly yelped when first Hana, then a drove of Sander's other lovers poured inside. Her pale gaze leaped from the destruction to Mira, still jerking on the sofa, and she paled and cursed, rushing to kneel at Sander's side. Her hands clenched one of Mira's and she pressed a kiss to her knuckles. "What in the stars *happened*?"

"What does it look like, our rooms were raided! And where were you?"

"At the teahouse, answering your summons!"

"I just returned from the stars-damned desert and went straight to the trial, I sent no summons!"

The look that passed between them sent chills skittering up Cistine's spine. Hana half-rose from her crouch and laid a hand on Mira's brow. "You'll stay with her?"

"Of course." Sander nodded to the bedroom doors. "Take Kendar and

Vihar and search for a scent. I want this person found and *punished*. I don't properly care if it's done the legal way."

With a grim nod, Hana obeyed, while Eyva and two other women picked up swords and stepped into the hall. Sander remained at the couch, and Cistine hovered at his side, watching how gently he held onto Mira's shoulders, how he kissed her brow and whispered in her ear, his touch focused and controlled but anguish bright in his eyes.

There were things about these people she understood better the longer she was with them; the way Sander looked at Mira now was clearest of all. "Should I go?"

He shook his head. "When she returns, she'll ask for you."

Cistine lowered herself cross-legged onto the floor at his feet. "She said all her notes were gone, and something of hers and yours."

Sander's eyes widened. "The armoire?" At Cistine's nod, he shot to his feet. "Stay with her."

She shifted to take his place as he stormed from the room, mimicking his gentle grip on Mira's shoulder with alternating strokes to her back. It might not help, but she had to do something with her shaking hands.

At long last, the rigidity in Mira's limbs slackened. It was another few minutes before she rolled over, squinting up with a hand pressed to her brow. "Cistine?"

She brushed the hair from Mira's face. "Do you know where you are?"

"Our room, I think. What happened here?"

"You don't remember?"

A beat of silence. Then Mira rasped, "Tonic."

Cistine pressed the cup into her hands and helped her sit up so she could sip, propped against the arm of the sofa. After several minutes, Mira sighed, staring down into her cup. "The Vassoran guard has no place for a woman whose distress sends her into spasms."

Curling her legs under her body, Cistine said nothing.

"I was still a girl when it began," Mira went on. "My parents thought I was only absentminded at first, that it would pass in time and guard training would help...and for a time, it did. But during the war, Sander and I crept off to spy on the front lines. We were caught in a terrible storm, injured. I was his guard at the time, and on my watch his life nearly ended." She slowly tapped the cup, her gaze a different sort of remote. "That was the first time I...lost myself to the spasms. When I woke after that fit, I couldn't remember who Sander was. Who *I* was. It was the most terrifying moment of my life.

"It took us some time to journey home while I continued with these spasms. Weeks more for the medicos to deduce that our ordeal broke the dam, allowing what was a nuisance for the child to become debilitating for the woman. Distress is as much a cause of my fits as it is your panic, and once I discovered there were ways to limit them, I realized how many others needed that help. So I pursued it with my whole heart."

"And...Valgard allows that?" Cistine asked carefully.

Mira's smile was cool and frank. "They do, for Sander's sake. They still call it a senseless craft, indulgence of the weak. But indulging my weakness has given me back my life."

"How many people have you helped, really?"

Brows furrowing, Mira peered around the room. "Many. Even Chancellors and Tribunes who come to me in secret. I've kept every report in case they returned in need of further help, and now..." she trailed off. "Cistine, that armoire's seal was unbreakable. I've never known *anything* that could penetrate it without a key. Sander and I tested its sturdiness ourselves. Whoever did this was crafty and very, very prepared. They knew precisely what they searched for and how to find it."

"Do you know what it was?"

"Not with any certainty. But they chose their moment perfectly, with Sander and I both in the courtroom today. I would bet every mynt in my coffers that someone called away the other women on very important tasks."

Lips half-numb with dread, Cistine whispered, "Salvotor?"

Mira lowered her cup, her eyes returning to Cistine. "Stars willing, no. I shudder to think what he would do with the truths those pages contain."

Cistine and Mira talked long into the evening about pointless, calming things while the Vassora came in a thin but steady trickle, taking note of every displaced object and item in the room. They ate supper while a Vassoran guard named Branko questioned them about what they saw when they first arrived, whether anyone was leaving the corridor at that moment. Cistine could think of no one, and Mira artfully dodged the gaps in her memory from before her fit.

Hana and the other women rotated to and from the sofa, checking on Mira a dozen times; some Cistine hadn't met yet trailed in and out, and though Sander left to report to Thorne and didn't come back, his words came from their mouths—asking after Mira's condition, whether she was comfortable, if she needed anything.

"Listen to me," Mira said after the thirteenth new face came into the room, lips primed to question, "go and tell that hand-wringing peacock that if he's not convinced of my stable condition, he can come and check his stars-damned self. Tell him that exactly, Mona."

The woman grimaced. "I'd sooner wrangle an adder."

"Do it, or wrangle with *me*."

Cistine hid a faint smile in her cup of vanilla tea. She supposed it was a mark of how much Mira trusted her now that she behaved this openly in her presence. The day's alarms aside, it felt good to belong.

She didn't remember falling asleep after Mona left, only closing her eyes for a moment, but all at once it was dark and she wasn't on the couch anymore. Someone had carried her to a bed in the corner of the parlor. She lay awake for some time, wondering if she ought to return to her own room. But in these peach-scented sheets, cozy and warm, she felt safe. And if the thief returned, she wanted to be the first to confront them.

She burrowed her chin into the blanket and drifted nearly to the edge of slumber when the parlor door whispered open.

Her eyes flicked wide, heart drumming, and she strained to hear the thudding footfalls. A tall, bent-shouldered shadow passed along the curtain's fabric, and with a heavy sigh someone settled in one of the plush armchairs righted by the Vassora.

"Aden?" Mira's voice carried in a half-whisper seconds later, full of surprise. "Why are you here at this hour?"

"It's over."

Cistine could see little through the refastened screen, only the suggestion of Aden's profile slumped in the armchair and Mira's frame reclining against the hearth. "You and Sander and Tatiana finished your investigation, I know."

"No, it...the weight." Aden's tone gentled with wonder. "That specter you accused me of carrying—it's gone. Being there with Tatiana and your...with Sander, in Siralek. It set something free."

"I see."

"He apologized to me for what was and was never done. We reached an understanding. The moment we did, it felt like I shook the last of Nordbran's sand from my boots. Like I could breathe again."

"Because Siralek is gone?"

"No. Because *I* walked out of it, gates or none. I accepted it was over...everything that happened to me there. Everything I could and couldn't save in that place."

Mira pulled away from the mantle, settling on the usual sofa. "You saved what mattered. Ashe. And Sander. And yourself."

"True. It only lives on now if I let it. And I won't. For my own sake...for my family's legacy. For the family I still have, by the grace of the gods." A beat. "Tomorrow, I'll tell you about Deja. She's all that remains of that Nimmus-pit for me, and I want to be done with the claws she's sunk into my life."

Mira rested a hand lightly on his back. "If you're truly ready."

"I am." Aden scoffed. "You wicked, clever woman. It was you, wasn't it? You told Thorne I should go to Siralek. You arranged this."

"I might have. Your Chancellor trusts me, you know."

Cistine bit her fist to stifle a giggle at Aden's curse. "Did you destroy the Blood Hive yourself to force this healing between your lover and me?"

"Is that what it is, Aden? Healing?"

"I think it may be." Surprise lilted his tone.

"Well, then perhaps I did. Now that you and Sander are *such* good friends, you should be able to solve that mystery together." Her tone brimmed with mirth. "And where is my preening peacock?"

"Either lost admiring himself in a mirror somewhere, or still investigating what happened here tonight." He paused. "How are you?"

"Safe. And *furious*. Whoever did this, I want them found, Aden. I want them punished. More than just my peace was taken today."

"Whatever I can do to help, I will. I owe you that much."

A rustle of movement, and Hana's voice brushed through the dark. "*Mirassah*. You ought to be in bed."

"*Hana*. I walked five steps to get here. I'll survive."

"It's late for visitors."

"He's a friend, and we're going to drink until Sander decides to grace us with his presence again. Either join us or go watch over my empty bed. Something exciting might happen...a sheet may flicker."

"You're always so sassy after a bad day."

"Hence why I'm always so sassy."

To the tune of mead splashing into cups and a toast too quiet to make out, Cistine drifted back into slumber. When she woke next, bright morning light slid through the screen; and in her open palm, gently coiled, was Kristoff's compass pendant—still freckled lightly with red sand.

CHAPTER
FORTY-FIVE

B Y DAWN, WORD had spread through the courthouse of the attack on Sander's rooms. Thorne brought the cabal together first thing—Tatiana, Aden and Sander all with bloodshot eyes and deep yawns—and gave them the latest report over steaming mugs of spiced cinnamon milk: the Vassora had found no hints of the thief's whereabouts.

Quill scowled at Tatiana. "I'm starting to sense a pattern."

She nodded grimly. "It sounds like the thief who broke into Kadlin's house. But why? What do Mira and Kadlin have in common that would make them both targets?"

"Do you know why they took her journals?" Aden asked Sander.

The High Tribune kneaded his temples. "If you mean do I know who they sought information about, no. A single torn-out sheet would've made their intentions plain, but every last ledger she's ever written...that's nearly twenty years of information. Impossible to know which bits the thief was truly after."

"How is she?" Ariadne asked.

"Shaken. Today she doesn't wish to be in the room at all."

Tatiana squeezed the High Tribune's shoulder. "We'll find that thief."

"Maybe we already have." Quill shot a pointed look toward Thorne and Cistine.

"One of Salvotor's spies?" Cistine guessed.

Thorne nodded. "That was my thinking as well. We need to finish deciphering those ledgers. In the meantime, we double the watch on Saychelle and Iri, and add one for Mira. Salvotor is becoming desperate, and desperate men are the most dangerous."

"Siralek is proof of that," Sander muttered.

Cistine's skin crawled with shivers; Tatiana had told her over breakfast that morning of the dark stone atrium deep beneath the Blood Hive where they found the heap of bodies, its muraled walls telling tales undefined. Something about it resonated, not in the way of a story she heard before, but an echo of the call deep in her bones.

Thorne got to his feet. "I'll start on those ledgers. Join me when you're ready, Cistine."

"I'll be there soon, I promise." She grinned at Tatiana. "I just have to introduce Tati to someone first."

To Cistine's relief, Daria struck off with Tatiana like they'd known each other their whole lives, bantering over a pot of jasmine tea under the peristyle's humid glass dome. Daria asked nothing about the upheaval in Kanslar's wing or the trial; instead she told the tale of her pilgrimage from Blaykrone, her life as a hunter, and the adjustment to civility in Stornhaz.

"I'm almost jealous, seeing the pair of you together," she admitted. "That friendship doesn't come easily to most."

"You think it came easily to us?" Tatiana laughed, refilling her teacup. "I was a prickly, angry drunk when we met."

Cistine elbowed her. "And now you're just prickly and angry."

"And *you're* about to be soaked in tea and very *sad*."

Daria chuckled. "This is what I mean!"

Tatiana shrugged. "Cistine is just that kind of person. You can't help but like her, even against your best intentions."

"Yes, that's very true." Daria reclined in her seat and cast her head back to gaze through the glazed glass above. "You make it seem so effortless. Dancing in a tavern is the closest I can come to feeling like I belong anywhere, yet you walked into this kingdom of former enemies and made a treaty with them, just like that."

"Well, the treaty isn't fully established yet. They're still deliberating. But to have come this far, you have to lay your heart at the mercy of the people you want to befriend." Cistine smiled at Tatiana. "Risk the pain of being vulnerable and hope they reach back."

Daria slowly shook her head. "Well, false treaty or not, you're fortunate to have friends who would lie or fall on a blade for you."

"You'll find those sorts of friends, too," Cistine said. "In Yager, and in us. There's always room for one more in the cabal."

The teahouse door burst open without warning, scattering the steam like frightened birds and framing Pippet in the doorway. "*Ashe is back!*"

Cistine shot to her feet on a surge of disbelief, knocking over her chair. "*What?*"

"Ashe is back! She's at the courthouse gate, I saw her!"

Heart singing with disbelief, Cistine whirled to Daria, who waved a dismissive hand. "Go, I can finish this pitcher by myself."

Grinning so wide her cheeks ached, Cistine beckoned Tatiana, then dashed from the teahouse.

The distance to the gate was too far, stretching wider with every stride. Cistine hadn't realized how much she missed her Warden, all hurt and betrayal aside, until she spotted her locked and pacing outside the grounds.

"*Open the gate!*" Cistine shouted, and the Vassora scrambled to obey. Then there was nothing left to stop her from closing those last few yards and flinging herself into Ashe's arms. Warden and Princess crashed back into the bridge railing together, and Cistine laughed into Ashe's shoulder. "I missed you *so much*, I can't even believe it! I'm so sorry I had to send you away, I'm sorry I didn't say a better goodbye. We have to talk about *everything*."

"We will, Princess. I missed you, too." But though Ashe's arms were tight around her, stiffness girdled her words—the voice of the Warden at work, not the friend returning home.

Cistine withdrew to study her face, and Pippet wriggled in, flinging her arms around Ashe's waist and bursting into chatter about training and school. Dread splintering in her chest, Cistine took in the new scars on Ashe's face, the gauntness of her cheekbones, the raging fire in her eyes; then she glanced past her to the woman standing at attention halfway up the bridge. "Rozalie?"

She dipped her head. "Princess."

Pippet fell silent, withdrawing from Ashe to frown at the other Warden. "You're not supposed to be here."

"Where's Maleck?" Tatiana demanded, catching up behind them at last.

Ashe's hand trembled on Pippet's head. "Muster the cabal. We have a problem."

CHAPTER FORTY-SIX

CISTINE SNAPPED INTO action quicker than Ashe had ever seen, sending Pippet and Tatiana to summon the rest of their friends; then she led Ashe and Rozalie to a parlor in Kanslar's wing, dispatching guards to watch the gates along the way. It wasn't until they were alone that a glimpse of the anxious princess showed through—gnawing her lip and pacing without asking about Maleck. Ashe sat back-to-back with Rozalie on a plush footrest, cradling her head in her hands. Urgency sparked like lightning in her fingertips, but she didn't dare pace with Cistine; she had to conserve her energy for the hunt ahead.

At long last, the door burst open. Aden was the first to stride in, his eyes and then his feet carrying straight to Ashe. She pushed herself up to meet him, a sliver of the tension unraveling within her.

"Welcome home." He yanked her into an embrace, and she leaned into him, shamelessly soaking in his strength. She was almost sad when he withdrew, staring at Rozalie. "I didn't expect to see you again."

"Or maybe you *hoped* not to, after I slipped past your guard in Keltei," she quipped. "Still bruised, Valgardan?"

"If you wanted to leave your mark, you should've hit below the waist."

"Oh, I wasn't talking about the bruises on your *skin*."

"Where's Mal?" Quill interrupted, swaggering in last and kicking the door shut.

Ashe rubbed her brow. "You're going to want to sit down."

For Maleck's sake, she told them everything—even the parts where she was weakest: from Darlaska's ethereal glow to Astoria's grand music hall to the cliffs of the Calaluns; from Middleton to caves deep in the wilds and the brushes with death there.

"Wait! Bresnyar?" Cistine cut in, hand over her mouth. "*He* saved you?"

"And flew us here. It's a long story." Waving off Cistine's shock, Ashe told them the rest: her long recovery in the forest with only Bresnyar for companionship, the ultimatums she struggled with, the search for Kashar and how Rozalie found her instead. Then, at last, the circumstances of her return to Middleton, the man she had no choice but to leave behind—and why.

Quill shot to his feet at that, dislodging Faer from his shoulder. "I'm sorry, did I hear that right? Mal's in prison? You left him in *prison?*"

"A *Talheimic* prison?" Anger smoldered in Aden's eyes.

"He's safe for now," Rozalie interjected. "But Jad wants blood. Either we give him that blood from his own spy—"

"Or he takes Maleck's," Ashe finished.

Ariadne hissed a prayer. Thorne folded his palms together and pressed them to his lips, sitting forward in his chair. "A Mahasari spy in Valgard."

"*That's* going to be a hunt," Tatiana muttered. "There are thousands of people in this city alone."

"Ashe, you said Bresnyar brought you to the city wall," Cistine said. "Can he sniff them out for us?"

"He can't just track out of thin air, he'd need a scent."

"And we don't even know whose scent to give," Aden scowled. "It would be simpler to find one silver grain of sand in the Kroaken dunes than one Mahasari in all of Valgard."

Ashe shot him a dry look. "It's good to know I can still rely on you for a word of encouragement."

"What you can rely on is my sensibility, which you *clearly* still require."

"I don't think it's hopeless," Rozalie interceded. "The spy is after proof of the treaty Ashe and Maleck fabricated. The real treaty is being discussed in this city, among its Chancellors, so the spy is most likely here."

"She's right," Ariadne agreed. "And given what Ashe overheard between Kashar and his men, the spy must have arrived within the past several weeks."

Quill flipped his hair raggedly across his head. "So we're looking for someone who appeared in the city a month ago or less and started putting their nose into Talheim and Valgard's business."

"Did you two notice anyone odd at the Tribune's feast?" Tatiana asked of Cistine and Thorne. "Anyone who didn't belong there?"

"Only the usual faces," Thorne said.

But Cistine, swiftly and audibly, stopped breathing.

"After. At the tavern." She ground the heels of her hands against her eyes, the low groan in her throat building into a snarl. "A *false* treaty! No one knew about that but us. I should've known, *gods*, I should've *known*..."

"Known what?" Aden demanded.

"*Daria.*" Cistine dropped her hands, looking at Tatiana this time. "Daria was talking in the teahouse about the treaty, telling me how fortunate I was to have friends who would *lie* for me."

"Where is she now?" Aden demanded.

"I don't know for certain, but I can guess." Cistine wrenched to her feet. "She's leaving. And we have to stop her."

Thorne rose as well. "Cistine, the hunt is yours. The rest of you follow her word as if it were mine."

"Where are *you* going?" Ashe asked.

"To do my duty as a Chancellor and report a spy in our city."

With a deft nod, Cistine whirled on the others. "Ariadne, Tatiana, and Quill, you know what Daria looks like. Put as many Vassora on watch for her as you can. Aden, with them. Ashe and Roz, we're going to check the gate. And then we're going hunting."

Ashe nodded. Whatever she felt toward Talheim now, she would always follow her princess to the edge of the world. And to save Maleck, she would leap off that edge and face whatever lay at the bottom.

CHAPTER
FORTY-SEVEN

I T TOOK JUST minutes to reach the courthouse gates, but they were among the longest of Cistine's life. If Daria had left already, finding her might be impossible.

But no one had left the courthouse, the Vassora informed them; none had even tried.

With the order given, Cistine and her Wardens changed direction, shooting back toward the apartments.

"If she's not there, her things will be," Cistine panted.

"Something Bresnyar can use to track her, no matter how far she goes," Ashe nodded grimly. "Good thinking."

Daria's apartment was on the third level of the visitor's wing, not far from where Cistine, Ashe, and Julian stayed on their first visit to Stornhaz. But it was utterly empty, not a piece of clothing left behind. The sheets, braided into cords, hung from the open window and out over the peristyle.

"She must've run the moment she heard you were here," Cistine gasped, bending double with hands on her knees.

"She won't get far." Ashe stalked to the window, reeled in the sheets, and with Rozalie's help, cut a swath free. "These should be enough for Bres to track by."

Cistine went to the window as well, bracing her hands on the stone sill and peering across the peristyle. Daria hadn't gone to the courthouse—they would've crossed paths with her already. But there was no reason for her to go into the courtyard itself, unless—

A memory flashed across her mind: scuffed knuckles and bloodied palms the night she brought Daria ice skating.

She flexed her fingers around the memory of what those wounds felt like. She'd felt them herself the day Ashe was taken to the Blood Hive. "She's going through the *sewers*."

Ashe froze. Rozalie asked, "Do those lead out from the city?"

"Not directly. But if she catches a barge close to the wall where the Vassora don't know to stop her..."

With a low curse, Ashe balled the torn cloth in her fist. "I'll find Quill, send Faer to the wall, then get this to Bresnyar just in case. Roz, you go with Cistine and try to head her off."

Cistine swallowed a plea for Ashe to come with her instead. Rozalie on her heels, she sprinted from the room.

⌒◠〜

The memory of a Vassoran chase made Cistine's upper lip and the tip of her nose tingle when she dropped into the sewer. Ankle-deep in fetid water between the dark rock walls, she pressed on Kristoff's compass necklace and took a deep breath despite the putrid air.

"Are you ready, Princess?" The rush of runoff at the base of the slope nearly muted Rozalie's murmur.

"Of course I am." With one last whiff of fragrant air from above, she reached into her augment pouch, broke open a light flagon, and drew it quickly into her armor threads, casting a low golden glow along the walls.

Rozalie gaped at her. "You're shining like a star. Does it hurt?"

"No more than your swords do if you know how to use them." She motioned Rozalie with a jerk of her head. "Let's catch that spy."

They jogged down the slick ledges framing the water, moving south, their way illumined only by Cistine's glowing armor. Rozalie kept them to a course, finding markings within the grit and paste along the stone that

Cistine would never have noticed. She needed more tracking lessons; she'd have to ask Maleck for them as soon as this latest crisis was over.

Her heart pounded harder the deeper they went—not only at the cold, dank rock and the memory it invoked, but at the distance Daria had covered. How near they must be to the curtain wall.

"What will we do if the light fails before we find her?" Rozalie murmured.

"It won't. I know how to portion out an augment to make it last."

The Warden's gaze drifted to her. "You really aren't afraid of it."

"I'm not. This gift came from the gods. It should be used to help people just like this."

Rozalie shook her head. "I might've argued with you even a few months ago. But I think you may be right, Princess. And that terrifies me."

"Well, if life doesn't scare you a bit, are you really living?"

Rozalie laughed under her breath. "You have changed."

With a sudden, sharp bark of pain, she toppled toward the water—just as a second throwing stone sailed from the blackness ahead, barely missing Cistine's brow. She screamed, lunging to grab Rozalie's arm and haul her clear of the waste before her head submerged; the Warden collapsed where Cistine slung her on the ledge, moaning and clutching her bleeding brow. Ahead, footsteps raced on into the dark.

Cistine squeezed Rozalie's shoulder. "Stay here."

Daria wasn't far enough ahead to outpace Cistine and her augment. She balled it tightly and sent the light spearing ahead, revealing the spy's fleeing form, then the tunnel beyond her; then it boomed out like fire that day in the mountains, the sheer white energy blasting Daria to her seat. Cistine was on her in a leap, tackling her to the ledge; but her momentum barreled her forward too far, and with a deft flip Daria sent her skidding down the sludgy verge, scrabbling to brace herself.

They came to their feet at the same time, Cistine further down the ledge, blocking the way. Enough light remained in her pulsing armor to show the viciousness in Daria's face. The liar, the hunter, the woman of Blaykrone was gone, revealing a countenance as cold as every nightmare

Cistine ever had about King Jad.

The Mahasari spy was out to play.

"Out of my way, Cistine," she snarled. "I meant what I said back in that teahouse...against my better judgement, I'm beginning to like you. But you can't keep me here."

"We'll see about that."

Daria's hands flashed, one drawing a black *Svarkyst* knife, the other a flagon. For the first time, Cistine realized she was wearing battle armor.

Planting her feet, she let her own hand drift to her augment pouch.

Daria's eyes narrowed. "I suppose that's another way to ensure the treaty fails. What will your sentimental father think of Valgard when his sweet daughter dies in their kingdom?"

With a roar of fury, Cistine smashed the flagon in her fist. Daria did the same, her fire lighting up the tunnel's curve. Cistine stepped into its might, giving it permission to course over her like the hottest river, grinning at Daria's stunned face. Whatever training she'd stolen about augments these past few weeks, she didn't know everything.

For once, Cistine was the better augur in the room.

With a shout, she rallied the fire and sent it out. Daria handsprang away, careening closer, slashing with her knife. A deft backward dodge on the slick ledge, a pause to lock her footing, and Cistine unleashed her power.

Wind roared through the tunnel, knocking Daria close to the water's edge, the knife clattering from her hand; but she was quick to retaliate, breaking open a second augment and dispatching a slash of her own wind. The two gales collided, blasting through the sewer and pushing the women farther away from each other—too far. If Daria turned and ran back the way they came, Cistine would have to give chase again.

The next augment was already singing to her, a plan laid out between breaths. She grabbed the flagon, shattered it, and scooped up Daria's fallen blade; cocking her arm and sighting, she threw.

The *Svarkyst* dagger flipped end over end, and Daria whipped out of its way, hair snapping against her cheeks. The blade clattered somewhere in the dark, and she pivoted back, teeth bared in a savage grin. "Poor aim."

"Was it?"

Daria's gaze dropped to the gash in her shoulder, the threads split wide, blood leaking out. With a snap of her fingers, Cistine sent out the fire, roaring past Daria up the tunnel. The putrid walls and washed-up refuse on the ledge caught like kindling, trapping the Mahasari spy between a barrier of flames and Cistine.

"You can try to leap through them," Cistine said, "but with your armor torn, I wouldn't. Augmented fire burns quickly."

Spitting curses, Daria wheeled and rushed back, armor glinting, skin licked in firelight, and Cistine put up her fists. A fluster of blows followed, double-kicks, elbows gouging into ribs, punches aimed at one another's faces. Cistine didn't have time to wonder who'd trained Daria; she only knew they did it well. When a blow smashed into Cistine's ribs, her eyes watered.

Brace! Quill's voice roared in her memory.

She planted her feet and dropped her breath, letting the next punch land harder against her middle; then she seized Daria's wrist, whirled, and smashed a heel into her ribs, flinging her against the wall and dropping her like a stone. But she was up again in seconds, hate in her face, determination in every movement.

Well-trained, indeed, and likely for far longer than Cistine. She had to end this before her will gave way to her lesser stamina.

She freed the last augment with shaking hands, the signature of its power kissing her fingertips as it rolled across her palm. In that moment, it was Maleck's voice that whispered to her, a feeling like his hand closing hers around the hilt of a sword so many times.

Instinct, Logandir. *Your body knows what to do.*

It did. *She* did. And to save him, she'd do it.

Cistine broke open the lightning augment.

Lavender-and-white hues poured through the tunnel. Ropes of molten power warped the air between Cistine's fingertips in a shimmering mirage. It tried to escape her control, to destroy like it always did.

She couldn't allow it to kill Daria, but she couldn't let the spy slip through her grasp, either. So she pulled the augment across her palms like her old favorite rope-shaping game, slinging it tighter and tighter around her hands while Daria steadied, wiping blood from her mouth. The lightning gathered with every pass, taming, settling, crackling in her palms.

Daria scooped up her knife and stepped forward. Cistine cupped her palms together, augmented wind tearing at her hair, the lightning pushing and fanning against her cradled hands.

Julian's death. Maleck's salvation.

She unleashed every bit of augmentation left in her threads.

The power screamed from her grasp, controlled, focused, the way she failed to harness it in Kalt Hasa. It slammed into the tunnel wall beside Daria, exploding in a shower of rock that blew her off her feet and onto the edge of the water, half-buried under a heap of stones. Bone snapped; Daria screamed, thrashing, unable to free herself. In one mighty leap, Cistine landed on her chest, grabbed her collar, and punched her senseless.

"That was for pretending to be my friend," she hissed.

Daria moaned as Cistine sat back on her heels, wiping blood from her nostrils. Strange that her nose was bleeding; she couldn't remember Daria hitting her there. And something else tugged at her mind, something that happened during their tussle; but dazed and exhausted, she couldn't think of what it was.

She was still sitting there, breathing heavily, when the augmented fire disappeared and first Quill, then Tatiana jogged into view. Ashe trailed behind them, Rozalie's arm slung across her shoulders.

Quill slid to a halt, his gaze taking in the buckled wall, the half-buried Mahasari, and Cistine, still pinning her to the stones. A grim smile crossed his face. "I take it you don't need our help?"

She blinked, dredging up words from her burning throat. "If you don't come over here and unbury her, I'll kick you into the sewer."

"You heard her, Featherbrain," Tatiana said. "And you heard Thorne."

Cistine frowned. "What about him?"

"He's scheming something," Quill said. "Apparently, we're not sending this one off to Talheim just yet. Thorne wants her delivered to Tyve's wing."

CHAPTER FORTY-EIGHT

THOUGH HE TRIED to be objective, Thorne's gaze returned again and again to Cistine, slumped on one of a dozen deep blue sofas in the gloomy receiving chamber of Tyve's private wing. Through the low orange ghostlight, she stared unblinking at the Mahasari spy tied to a chair in the middle of the atrium. Rozalie sat beside her, a damp cloth stanching the bloodflow from her brow, and all around them the rest of the cabal clustered. Vassora lined the walls, and the Chancellors stood before Daria's chair.

Bravis scowled. "How long until these herbs take effect, Valdemar?"

"It is not a precise method," Tyve's Chancellor replied. "Sannhet has delicate properties. Too little, and it will not remove the inhibitions or loosen the tongue for truth-telling. But too much can kill."

"She can't die," Cistine said. "We need her alive to return to Talheim."

Tribune Niklause cast her a sympathetic, almost grandfatherly smile. "You trust my methods of administration, do you not, Princess?"

For the first time since she'd stalked into the room leading the others, Cistine relaxed.

Thorne did not. Too much hinged on this; he'd called in every favor and scrap of good will among the Courts to persuade Bravis, Benedikt, and Maltadova to come here; not to mention convincing Valdemar to let them into his private wing. If this went awry, there would be Nimmus to pay.

But for Talheim's sake, his reputation was a worthy risk.

Daria lifted her head at last, muscular arms flexing against the bonds woven between her wrists and the seatback. Her gaze found Cistine, and she launched forward against her bonds, bringing the heavy chair up from the floor. Thorne stepped between them, and Niklause seized the back of the chair, slamming it down to the floor so hard Thorne's teeth rattled at the impact. Cistine winced.

"Tell us your name," Bravis ordered.

Her gaze still fixed on Cistine, the spy hissed, "Daria."

"Tell us your *true* name." Valdemar's voice was silky with anticipation.

A beat of silence. Then she whispered, "Reema." Cursing, she snapped her head toward Valdemar. "What have you *done* to me?"

"Sannhet is an interrogative herb. It makes one prone to truth-telling."

"You should know," Ashe growled. "Your people use something like it, don't they, *Reema?*"

Those furious eyes flashed to her, full of wicked glee this time. "This is a *taste* of what we can do to you. Or don't these Valgardans know you showed us the way into their kingdom? *You* told Kashar of the tunnels."

Ashe lurched forward, and Aden gripped her shoulder, pulling her back and keeping his hand there—a comfort as much as a warning.

"What tunnels?" Bravis demanded.

"Siege tunnels," Ashe muttered. "At the border. From the war."

A flicker of respect shone in the Chancellor's eyes. "Clever."

"But about this one." Valdemar braced his hand on the seatback by Reema's head, bending at eye level with her. "Where do you hail from?"

Her jaw worked, fighting the truth; then she blurted, "Mahasar."

Bravis's gaze shot to Thorne. He worked to keep his expression neutral, not to betray his thoughts.

"Did you present yourself as a woman of Blaykrone to trick your way into my confidences?" Cistine demanded.

Reema's lips peeled back. "You made it so simple, flaunting that bestiary in the tavern, coming to *me* for help."

"And what is a Mahasari doing on Valgardan soil, creeping through tunnels and masquerading as a woman of Blaykrone?" Valdemar asked.

The spy's eyes sliced to Ashe. "Why don't you ask *her?*"

Ashe held her glare. "I think it's best coming from a Mahasari's own mouth."

Reema spat on the dark tiled floor.

"Tell us why you are here," Valdemar ordered.

Reema bowed her head, struggled through several breaths, then slumped. "I was sent to search out whether there is a treaty between the Middle and Northern Kingdoms. And if there was one, to put a stop to it by any necessary means, so my King may do as he wills."

Bravis crouched on his heels, holding her evasive gaze. "You mean to tell me that King Jad of Mahasar sought to control us by subterfuge and spies smuggled into our city? He thinks he can cross our borders and sway our minds about our own alliances and treaties?"

"So you say."

He stared at her, long and hard, and Thorne held his breath. Finally, the acting Chancellor rocked to his feet. "When you go back to that *bandayo* of a king you serve—and you *will* go back, broken leg and all—you can tell him he's made an enemy today he will live to regret. Because the treaty *is* real, and if this King Jad sets one foot north of his own border, he will face the combined fury of the Northern and Middle Kingdoms."

Cistine stiffened, eyes blowing wide. Thorne bit the flesh of his cheek to force down a smile.

"Jad is fortunate we won't consider this an act of war in itself," Benedikt added. "But another toe stepped out of line..."

"He will not survive." Fire and shadow blazed in Maltadova's eyes. "Nor will any who support his warmongering."

Valdemar swiveled to his fellow Chancellors. "I do believe we need to provide proof for King Jad of our treaty, don't you agree?"

Thorne turned to Ashe. "Give us one hour. Then you can take Reema and a copy of the official treaty back to Talheim. And you can tell Jad the alliance between our kingdoms is, and has always been, absolutely real."

CHAPTER FORTY-NINE

DESPITE THE BLOW she dealt Maleck for suggesting it when she visited him in his cell, Asheila Kovar did enjoy a flare of the dramatic now and then. And she could think of none better than how she and Rozalie slammed open the doors of Middleton's meeting chamber and strode inside, dragging Reema with them—bringing every Mahasari and Talheimic to their feet with swears and stunned shouts.

Gripping the spy by the collar, Ashe slung her to her knees beside Jad's chair. "I believe this belongs to you."

The Mad King beheld Reema with furious recognition; then his beady eyes leaped back to Ashe. "You—"

"Be quiet, jester. Royalty is speaking." Ashe strode around the table to stand at Cyril's side. "Or, should I say, the one speaking on *behalf* of royalty. In the name of Princess Cistine Novacek of Talheim, official liaison to the Northern Kingdom, may I present, signed and dated..." she withdrew the scroll and set it before Cyril, "the original treaty as requested, Your Majesty."

He took the treaty, unraveled it, and laid it out, gaze raking over the real signatures—Valdemar's, Benedikt's, Bravis's, Maltadova's, and Thorne's; and below them, Cistine's, legally binding as an emissary bearing the Writ of Nobility.

"Well done, Asheila." He raised his eyes to Jad. "You've now seen our copy, and this original. Do you still doubt?"

The Mad King's nostrils flared with every breath, upper lip twitching. "This could very well be a forgery."

"If you'd like, I could fetch the Chancellors themselves," Ashe offered. "Or we could take you to visit them so you don't assume I just dressed up a few Talheimics to play the part. But I should warn you, they aren't fond of the thought of Mahasari boots on Valgardan soil after they found *Reema* sniffing around."

Jad's scowl promised death for the woman cowering before his chair. Smirking, Rozalie sauntered to Ashe's side. "They also wanted you to know you made an enemy of them by sending a spy into their kingdom. What were Chancellor Bravis's parting words, Ashe?"

"I believe it was that if King Jad and his Mahasari delegates sack one more fort on the southern border, they'll have augmented fire to contend with." She perched her hands on her hips and inclined toward Jad. "That's the sort you can't swat out."

Rion made a strange sound in the back of his throat, but Ashe ignored him. Let him think what he liked of augurs at the border forts; after seeing the state of the sewers when Cistine fought Reema, she was more than happy to turn that power against Jad.

Mahasar's King looked around at his Enforcers, all bristling with uncertainty. Facing Wardens was one thing; facing augurs was clearly another.

"Things being as they are," Cyril's tone was mild, but his eyes blazed with triumph, "I say we've reached an impasse yet again. My offer from before still stands: the chance to leave unscathed. We won't discuss your spy, or the watchfires in the mountains, or Asheila's disappearance—which I think we all can see was not Valgard's doing." He glanced at her in silent question, and she dipped her head; dismissing Mahasar's treachery against her was the least she could give when others gave much more to ensure this moment came to pass.

Cyril turned back to Jad. "In exchange for my *incredible* mercy, you will take your men, every single one in this kingdom, and march back to Mahasar with nothing but tucked tails and the knowledge that this could have gone far worse for you. And we will have *peace* between all three kingdoms now."

King Jad bent forward, bracing his hands on the table's edge, and Ashe tensed. But after several perilous seconds, the Mad King started to giggle; then to chuckle. Then he threw back his head and cackled so loudly even his Enforcers exchanged bewildered glances. "*Well* played, Your Majesty, well played *indeed*! You're beginning to learn how the game works."

Cyril's smile was frigid. "It's no game when my people's lives hang in the balance."

Thumbing his damp lashes, Jad exhaled and shook his head. "That...that is where you're wrong." His eyes shot up, his grin vanishing. "It's always been a game, Cyril. May the best man win."

He whistled his Enforcers to rise. Two lifted Reema and dragged her with them, and a trace of pity scraped Ashe's throat. For her sake, she hoped the woman would be dead by nightfall; better that than subjected to the Mad King's fury.

She followed the Enforcers to the door, leaning heavily against the jamb while they walked away. "Jad!" The Mad King paused at the end of the corridor where he'd threatened her. Smirking, she saluted him without a trace of respect. "Give Kashar my regards."

She slammed the door shut.

For a moment, utter silence.

"Rion," Cyril's curt word broke the pause.

The Commander hauled himself up. "We'll follow at a distance, ensure he gathers all his people."

"Make sure you send a contingent to flush out the Calaluns," Ashe said. "Kashar and his men are still out there."

The other Wardens rose, Viktor with a curt nod to Ashe—perhaps the last show of honest respect she would ever receive from him, but the thought didn't bother her like it used to. Rozalie squeezed Ashe's shoulder and hurried out behind them, leaving only Ashe and the King, who stood, taking up the treaty. "I believe I have a promise to keep to you."

Ashe finally let all her breath tumble out. "How is he?"

"As well as can be expected. How in the world did he grow so tall when he picks at his rations like a finicky child?" Cyril passed her, beckoning with a tilt of his head. "I'll have him brought to my rooms. You and I are going to have a talk."

Ashe followed him, heart thundering, heels dragging.

Cyril's room was obsessively tidy this time, like he'd straightened it to keep his mind off other things. He slid in behind the desk, set the treaty among the scrolls, and reclined in his chair, scratching absently at his thick beard. "Cistine isn't with you." Ashe shook her head, and a slow, regretful smile spread across the King's face. "She isn't coming back yet, is she?"

"She may be of age, but she still has plenty of maturing to do. She can do that better in Valgard than here."

Cyril arched a brow. "Do you think?"

"She's learned and grown more in the past few months than the last several years before them," Ashe admitted. "Talheim is her home, her future...she knows that. But she needs time away from that responsibility to become the woman she wants to be. And I've seen it happening in Valgard. I see the queen she's growing into. Calling her back now won't keep her safe, it will just create strife where there doesn't need to be."

Cyril clasped his hands under his chin and didn't speak.

"She'll come home when she's ready, but you and I both know it doesn't have to be right away," Ashe added. "The threat of war has lifted. She gave so much to make this treaty possible...you should give her this in return. Let her stay with her friends a little while longer."

The King brushed his fingers over the thick scroll, shaking his head. "It's heavier than the truce I carried back from the war."

Ashe remembered that brittle piece of parchment, how flimsy it seemed, able to be ripped apart with just a flirt of fingers—promising nothing but that the wells would be sealed and the fighting would cease. No friendship. No trade. No alliance at all. Simply a vow not to continue the bloodshed.

"If I hadn't been so grief-stricken for my father and desperate to honor him by finishing what he started, we could've had this treaty twenty years ago, and Cistine could've given nothing at all to see it made," Cyril murmured. "I could've handed her peace for her coming-of-age birthday, not a war she felt she needed to prevent herself."

Ashe couldn't find the words to tell him how in some strange way, that threat was the best thing that ever happened to the Princess.

After a long beat, Cyril went on, "But here we sit. And Talheim owes its safety to her. To both of you." He looked up, his face soft. "Where will you go, Asheila?"

"Back to her." A kernel of hope pulsed in her chest; Cistine had been so glad to see her at the gates that for the first time, forgiveness seemed possible. They might find a way back to being friends who trusted each other.

With a quiet sigh, Cyril pushed a different scroll across the desk toward her. "Then you can deliver this. And I hope you'll do what you've always done best and watch over her. She's going to need it."

Grinning, Ashe snatched up the scroll. "On her behalf, *thank you.*"

"I won't say I like it, especially given who she is—*what* she is. The treaty speaks nothing to that." He glanced at it again. "But the girl I arranged to go to the coast for her birthday and the one whose name is on this signing...I don't have to see her face to see the change."

The door creaked open, and Ashe's heart leaped into her throat; she whirled straight into Maleck's embrace, her arms around his neck and his linked at her waist, his breath rushing out against the side of her neck. They said nothing; there was no need. His unfettered wrists, his swords strapped to his back, his hands fitted to her hips as they drew apart and looked at one another—it all said enough.

Cyril rose, clearing his throat. "You'd best be on your way. If I know Cistine, she's already fretting herself senseless wondering what I'm going to say, nevermind waiting for a report on Mahasar."

Maleck's eyes glowed at the mention of the Princess, but he still took a moment to approach the desk and offer a hand. "Thank you for trusting enough to try."

Cyril clasped that hand warmly. "And you. For not begrudging a kingdom that's done you wrong in many ways."

"It's given me far more than it's ever taken away."

Cheeks hot, Ashe nudged Maleck out of the way and stuck out her hand as well. "If you need us, if you need *her*, just send word."

Cyril brushed her hand aside, circling the desk to wrap his arms around her. "From the moment Rion found you following us on the tundra, I have wanted just one thing for you: to live free and be happy, Asheila." He held her out from him, taking her chin in his hand. "I can only give you one. Now go find the other."

He kissed her forehead and released her in every sense, but that no longer felt like free-falling through the dark. In fact, when she left the King's chamber with Maleck at her side, Ashe was climbing hand-over-hand back toward the light.

In understanding silence, they gathered their meager belongings and left the estate, wending through streets where windows opened wide despite the chill, vendor stalls peddling again, the reek of Jad's presence already lifting and no sign of Rion and the other Wardens anywhere. Ashe was grateful for that; there was nothing left to say to her former Commander. He'd banished her, stripped her rank, driven her out...but she was becoming something greater than he could ever fathom.

They'd nearly reached the pike wall when a shout echoed down the dusty path behind them. Surprise jerked Ashe in a full pivot as Rozalie jogged to join them. "Roz? I thought you left with Rion!"

Rozalie shook her head. "I don't need the abuse. He and Viktor have all that time to feed each other's fire about this treaty, and I'm certain they'll be in foul moods. But *I* happen to think it's the start of something wonderful, so I asked for a different assignment."

Maleck cocked his head. "The northern forts?"

Rozalie grinned. "That's right. Anything that happens, you can send for me. Valgard will have an ally at the border from now on...a Warden who will heed any call."

Her throat too tight for words, Ashe hugged her friend.

"May we escort you?" Maleck offered. "The forts happen to be along the way."

"I'd like that," Rozalie smiled, falling into step with them. "I'm glad you're going, Ashe, as much as I'll miss you."

Ashe cocked a brow. "Really?"

"I knew you weren't long for Talheim the moment I found you in the mountains. It's like you told me when you pulled me out of that brothel...life doesn't begin where we were, it begins right now. At any moment, we can choose to be better than we were before." She checked Ashe's hip with hers. "I so admire a woman who can take her own advice."

"Particularly when it's wisdom," Maleck chimed in with a smile.

"Oh, enough, you two," Ashe snorted. "If you plump up my ego, the flight north will be impossible."

Maleck frowned. "Flight?"

Rozalie opened her mouth, and Ashe pushed her ahead through the gate. "Don't say anything. I want to see his face when he experiences it for himself."

Rozalie all but skipped onward, laughing, Maleck wandering on her heels, utterly bemused. But when the pike wall shuttered shut at their backs, a note of melancholy rang through Ashe—a song of farewell.

She slowed, then halted and looked back at the reinforcement around Middleton, the sharp beams that kept enemies at bay...and kept the people inside from seeing the beautiful kingdom around them, its mountains and lakes, the vastness of it all.

Talheim was a fortified place, but it still had much to learn about looking outward. Ashe prayed that under its future queen, and even its present king, that would begin to change.

"Asheila," Maleck called. "Are you ready?"

Smiling, she laced her fingers with his and walked away from Middleton, him on one side, Rozalie on the other, toward the horizon; toward the lake and Bresnyar, toward Valgard far away. Walked with her head high and shoulders back into the light, hand-in-hand with her *selvenar*.

It felt like going home.

CHAPTER FIFTY

HOW ARE YOU, Cistine?" Thorne pressed a mug of orange-blossom tea into his *selvenar's* hands, sitting in her broad bedroom windowsill beside her, the sleek wood warmed by yet another oddly-hot day. She accepted it quietly—as quiet as she was all night while they worked the cipher and compiled the final list of his father's informants in the other courts—and leaned her temple on the glass.

"I thought Daria...Reema was my friend," she said after a moment. "Helping her into Yager made me feel whole again, like I finally knew Salvotor didn't destroy that part of me. But was that all just a lie?"

"You just spent an entire night helping me list his spies," Thorne reminded her. "The day before, you accomplished the very thing you came to Valgard for. There is no doubt of your heart or your capabilities, whatever Reema did."

Cistine tugged the compass pendant around her neck. "That treaty doesn't even seem real yet." Her eyes flicked to him. "I didn't thank you, did I? For bringing Reema in front of the Chancellors. I only cared about sending her home and saving Maleck."

Thorne shrugged. "Pride is important to the Courts. I suspected Jad flaunting our borders would be the last incentive they needed. It made things personal."

She flashed him a smile so tired, yet so warm, it cracked his heart. "What would I do without you?"

He couldn't bring himself to tell her he was wondering the same thing—what he would do once she was gone. "I know what you *can* do with me for now. Training?"

"Yes, *please*." She set aside the teacup and hopped to her feet, dragging him up from the sill.

They were not the only ones in the training hall battling out the tension of the past day; Tatiana and Ariadne dueled with daggers and Aden and Pippet wrestled in their usual spot. Quill, sweaty and shirtless and resting between matches, by the look of him, swaggered up at Thorne and Cistine's arrival, grinning. "Mira's hovering around here somewhere. Looking for you, I think, *Allet*."

Thorne's stomach dropped when he caught sight of her tucked into an alcove. "Give me a moment."

"I'll keep her busy," Quill winked. Cistine socked his arm, and he goaded her on with mock-blows, leaving Thorne to trudge off and join Mira.

"Aden told me about Reema," she said in greeting. "What a ruckus."

He mirrored her posture, arms crossed, propped against the wall. "At least that's over now. With the treaty solved, there's just the trial left to navigate."

"Only that?" Teasing framed the words, but her tone was heavy.

Thorne glanced at her. "I'm sorry there's been no luck finding the thief who ransacked your rooms yet. Quill and Tatiana are doing everything they can."

"I know they are." She shook her head. "The audacity of Salvotor..."

"It's sickening, I know. Every time I think he's showed his last hand, he pulls another card from his sleeve."

"Well, the wonderful thing about sleeves is they only go so deep." Mira shot him a wry look. "Sander says the sentence will be delivered the day after tomorrow, and if you ask me, the sooner the better. We're all ready for whatever comes after." She shifted to face him. "What do you think that means for *you*, Chancellor?"

He watched Cistine and Quill grapple, weight bearing down on his heart. "That remains to be seen."

Mira followed his gaze, smiling softly. "She loves you. It takes a fool or a pack of very distracted Chancellors to miss it."

Thorne leaned his temple against the column to his left. "Some days, that's all that keeps me going. And others...others make me wish she'd fallen in love with Quill instead. Or Maleck. Anyone but me."

"Why?"

He hated that he could never tell whether Mira was speaking to him from a place of profession or friendly interest. Perhaps they were inseparable to her. "I doubt the son of the man who abused her is a good match. Let alone what Talheim would consider proper for its princess."

"Oh, yes. Because that girl currently pounding Quill into the dust is clearly concerned with what's proper."

A reluctant chuckle slid through Thorne's teeth. "Fair point. But that doesn't mean I'm good for her."

"She no longer shies from your touch. Does that not tell you something of the man she thinks you are?"

Thorne shrugged, bending to rub at the deep pain in his calf. Mira watched him, lips tipped thoughtfully.

Pippet's laughter blossomed between the pillars as she finally broke free of Aden's lock on her arms, swiveled on heel, and swept his ankles. When he wavered with a bark of shock, she shoved him down on his haunches and sprang on top of him, foot braced to his chest. "Victory!"

A different chuckle boomed after her shout—deep and livelier than Thorne had ever heard it. A pair of hands clapped and a woman's voice drawled above the laughter, "Oh, I could watch that *all day.*"

Thorne lurched up from the pillar, and the cabal stopped fighting, all turning as the pair of warriors swaggered in lockstep down the hall to join them. Pippet shrieked. "*Maleck, you're home!*"

No sooner did she leap onto Maleck's back, arms around his neck, than Cistine crashed into his front and hugged him with all her might. Then Quill was there, and Ariadne, and Tatiana and Aden, smothering him in a sea of gripping hands and embracing arms. Ashe stood back, fingers tapping her hips, her grin bright as a sunrise. Vision misty, Thorne nodded farewell to Mira and joined them, the clamor of voices all straining against his ears at once.

"I'll kill those Talheimics if they laid a hand on you, *Storfir...*"

"Look at you, Maleck, stars, have you even been *eating?*"

"You've missed much, *Allet*—the trial is nearly over, Siralek's fallen..."

"I grew a whole entire *inch* and you didn't get to mark my doorpost like you always do!"

Chuckling, Maleck carefully extricated himself from the arms around him, pried Pippet off his back, and tucked through their midst to meet Thorne. He held his friend's gaze—his wounded brother, the spine that held them all together—and relief blasted through him so fiercely he nearly buckled. "Welcome home, Darkwind."

Tears glistened on Maleck's lashes, and he said nothing when they embraced.

Cistine broke the moment's silence after they pulled apart, voice soft. "Does this mean the treaty passed with Jad?"

Maleck's gaze cut to Ashe, who stepped forward, took Cistine by the shoulders, and looked deep into her eyes. And then she delivered the words to save and damn it all.

"You did it, Princess. Your treaty stopped the war between Talheim and Mahasar."

CHAPTER
FIFTY-ONE

CISTINE HAD FINALLY succeed—saving her kingdom and sparing her people a bloody, unjust war. Yet she sat on her bed instead of celebrating after she and Ashe stole a moment alone for apologies and a quick catching-up. Ashe's parting token had been a kiss to Cistine's hair, full of sorrow but also healing—and this letter pressed into her hand.

A letter from her father.

This was the moment she'd been anticipating and dreading; for the first time since summer's warmth kissed her face on her balcony the night she hatched this plot, she had no reason to be in Valgard.

She drew in a steadying breath, then flinched at a knock at the door. Thorne stepped inside, looking faintly frantic and almost gleeful. "The cabal is mustering for supper. As soon as Ashe and Maleck finish washing off the journey—*Logandir?*"

The last word hushed, his eyes on the letter in her hands. She bit her lips together, staring down at it.

Thorne settled beside her. "What is that, Cistine?"

"A letter from my father."

His hand brushed her back, light and testing. When she didn't pull away, he rubbed slow circles along her spine. "Have you read it?"

"I'm afraid to," she admitted.

"I can read it to you, if you'd prefer."

She sucked in a damp breath. "I think we both know it's better we don't read each other's letters."

He chuckled. "Fair enough. If you prefer privacy…"

"Stay." She snatched his wrist as he began to rise. "Just be with me."

He settled back at once, pressing a kiss to her temple. "I'm here."

That promise restored a portion of her bravery. She unrolled the scroll and smoothed it out on her knees, tears already gathering at the first glimpse of her father's familiar handwriting.

My dearest Cistine,

May this letter find you well. Whatever Ashe says, I still worry for your wellbeing, especially where you are. But if you are reading this, it means there will be no war, and I can entertain the thought of your return to Talheim ~ knowing that not bloodshed, but peace awaits you here.

What I ought to say is if you're reading this, then you succeeded. You, above us all, sneaking off to the North in search of an alliance that eluded your grandfather and me. While Kion would remind me it's a father's duty to punish such acts of rebellion ~ particularly from his only heir ~ I'm grateful. And, laugh at me if you wish, I'm envious of you. Pursuing that call. Embracing it with your whole heart while I've ignored it these past twenty years.

You have proven yourself a lady of wit and talent, a successor and future ruler I am proud of beyond what words can say. But you've also proven a competent and grown woman of age. And such a woman is capable of making her own choices.

I know you're conflicted. You make friends like most people make breakfast ~ quickly, heartily, and without much effort ~ but I'm sure you feel you should come home now that the treaty's signed. So you're reading this hoping I will give a command that decides whether you come home or stay and celebrate with the friends you've won.

Well, consider it your punishment that I'm not going to make this simple for you. I'm telling you instead that you're a girl of self-reliance, and you can't run from this conflict in yourself. But I will give you a father's advice that may help you choose.

Back in your grandfather's day, the coming-of-age gift from the King to his son or daughter was a year of freedom to explore and travel as they wished, to learn their people and seek out their heart. Twenty years old is younger than it seems, and the crown heavier than it looks, so princes and princesses journeyed abroad to better discover the sort of ruler they wished to be.

Your grandfather Ivan was the last to do this. He took his journey to Valgard, and after a year among them he feared those people and their wells of power so much, it turned to hate. Twenty-two years later, my own coming-of-age birthday was spent at war with the people who opened their kingdom to my father during his. With everything happening in the south this summer, I feared to offer you the freedom denied to me.

Now I will give you better than that. I will give you a year, beginning now — a year wherever you choose, even if it's learning the ways and means of our new allies in the North. Though I will miss you every day, I trust your judgement. Wherever you are, you are precisely where you're meant to be. Know that the Citadel fires will be kept burning, and when you choose to come home, we will throw the gates wide open for you. This is all I can offer, the only way I can express my gratitude for how you spared us this war. How you have, perhaps, saved us all.

You are in my heart and your mother's, a blending that cannot be broken. I love you, Cistine. You are the best of all I am and all I will ever be.

The unsteadiness of his signature showed he finished the letter weeping; she wept, too, when she read it, the parchment fluttering from her shaking fingers to the floor. Thorne wrapped his arms around her and pulled her head against his chest while she cried for a father whose year of freedom became a year of bloodshed, a king who never journeyed, a boy who became a man with a kingdom to lead after a war he never wanted.

She cried for the world she'd saved, and for the choice she'd already made; the question answered the moment Thorne walked through her door.

"I'm staying," she said through her tears. "If Valgard will have me, I'll continue negotiations around the treaty, help lay trade routes and share learnings and—"

"Stay with us." Voice husky, Thorne drew her head up from above his heart. "With me."

She stretched up to press her lips to his. "With *you*, Starchaser."

"She stays!" Quill roared in victory, pounding the table in the middle of their parlor. Beside him, Pippet tossed up both arms and cheered, and the whole cabal raised their glasses in a toast.

Cistine blushed. "As if it's some great surprise."

"It isn't. We're all just that clever," Tatiana smirked.

"I *am* surprised," Aden admitted, stirring his soup. "Your love for your kingdom is no secret even to those who know you least."

"Agreed," Sander said.

Cistine shrugged, tearing her loaf of hot bread in half and reaching around Mira to dip it in Thorne's bowl. "I have my whole life to love Talheim. I only have a year to go where *I* choose, so I choose here. And I choose all of you."

Mira laid a hand to her breast. "Such flattery!"

"It's not flattery. She means it," Ashe said, elbows braced on the table, grinning at Cistine. "I'm glad you're staying. We still have things to discuss."

That was absolutely true; because Ashe was here instead of with the Cadre, Maleck's arm flung casually around the back of her chair, a fiery pendant hanging openly over her heart. And she was already more at ease than Cistine had seen her in a decade. "Whenever you're ready, so am I."

They all returned to eating, and between mouthfuls they took turns bringing Maleck and Ashe up to pace on the trial, the attacks and thefts, and what Rakel and Devitrius were doing. Ashe's calm answer to it all was, "We'll manage this. One step at a time."

When their bowls were scraped clean and Pippet had curled up sideways with her head on her brother's shoulder, Mira cleared her throat, quieting the smattering of conversation among them. "Now that we're all full and relaxed, and a few of us have a bit of mead in them," she shot a playful smile at Sander, ruefully helping himself to a third goblet, "we're going to conduct a small exercise."

"Like training?" Pippet yawned.

"Something like that." Arms braced on the table, hands clasped, Mira stared at one of them in particular. "I want everyone at this table to tell Thorne precisely what they think of him."

Thorne's smile froze and his eyes widened. "I don't think that's necessary."

"I do." Mira's tone was quiet but firm. "Did you really think you could have me watching your cabal for signs of trouble and cries for help, and not see yours?"

"I am a *Chancellor*. A leader—"

"Precisely why I'm not letting this go on a day longer. Thorne, you trusted me with your cabal, I'm not asking anything but that you continue in that faith." When he didn't protest again, a strange desperation in his eyes but his lips pressed shut, she gestured to Aden. "You first."

He frowned between her and Thorne, then reclined in his seat, arms folded. "You've grown from the cousin I was forced to care for to the leader I'm proud to follow. I'm honored to serve this kingdom with you, whether as a member of your cabal or as a Tribune. Whatever you require of me."

Thorne blinked, saying nothing. Ashe, at Aden's side, shrugged. "I haven't always been fond of you, but maybe that's because we're not so different...and until recently I hated myself, too. But you're a good man, Thorne. You helped Cistine achieve the peace she set out for. I look forward to learning more about nobility from you. And I'm excited about your...other prospects as well."

His lip curled slightly, and she shot him a sly smile that raised the hairs on the back of Cistine's neck. But she had no time to ponder that look more deeply before Maleck said, "You gave me hope when I had none, laid a future at my feet in a place where I belonged. I wouldn't be the man I am today without you. For that, I will always be grateful."

Thorne's abdomen lifted in a shallow breath, and he dipped his head. Maleck lowered his eyes in turn.

"Thorne is the *greatest*!" Pippet cried, and everyone broke into chuckles, even him. "He's smart, and he's silly, and I always feel safe with him. And I'm going to be the first female Tribune in Kanslar, so I can't wait to serve under him!"

Thorne arched a brow. Quill shrugged, jostling his sister. "Why wasn't I consulted about this?"

"Because it's none of your business, dolt." Pippet nudged him back.

"*Dolt*? Who taught you *that* word?"

Ashe raised her eyes innocently. Maleck pinched her underarm, and she smacked the back of his head. Laughing under her breath, Mira prompted, "Quill?"

Quill lounged, sliding a cinnamon stick between his teeth. "What is there to say? You've been my brother since we were five years old. When Baba Kallah and my father left us at Kristoff and Natalya's that first time, and I listened to you ordering Aden and me around, playing like you were already a Chancellor. But then you stopped, and you *asked* if we could play that game. You asked me to be your guard, to watch your back. No one ever asked me what I wanted before, not even Helga. But *you* did, the first time I laid eyes on you. And I thought, this little *bandayo*, this gods-loved boy-Chancellor...I'd follow him to the ends of the world." He shrugged and cleared his throat. "Still would, *Allet*."

Tatiana shifted in her chair and bared her palms. "You've never let me get away with anything. No matter how often I hid the drinking and fighting and fear, you always found out in the end. And I used to hate you for it, but you took that in stride, too. You trusted me and believed in me even when I didn't deserve it. So, I'm with Quill. To the end of this world and beyond it, Thorne."

Ariadne leaned forward and spoke with calm ferocity. "When everything I loved crumbled around me, you stood there, reaching out your hand. You looked at someone your father broke and saw a warrior rising from the ashes. There has not been a day since where I have not leaned on you to help remind me of who I am. You honor me with your friendship and trust, and I remember you every day in my prayers."

There were no dry eyes at the table when Sander cleared his throat and rocked his haunches under Mira's pointed stare. "Well, I think it's obvious by now I've long believed in your vision for Valgard's future, even when the whole kingdom was convinced you abandoned us these last ten years. You were a Chancellor worth waiting for...and as Aden says, one worth serving in whatever capacity."

Mira squeezed Sander's shoulder gently. "Cistine?"

Thorne tensed, avoiding her eyes. Heart aching, she wondered if all those days of holding him at arm's length while she battled her own specters had fed his, made him believe he was unwanted, unlovable, unworthy—everything Salvotor and Rakel ground into his heart from his youngest days.

Crying for the third time that day—and resigned to the fact that she might never stop—she pushed back her chair, slipping her fingers over Thorne's shoulder and tugging until he reluctantly turned his seat toward her, gaze still aslant. She knelt, gripped his cheeks in her hand, and forced up his head just enough that he had to look at her.

"I love you," she whispered. "With my whole heart, for my whole life. Maybe I've always been the princess I am now, but I never would've found her if I hadn't found you first. That first day we met, you remember what you told me? That you wouldn't give me respect I didn't earn and you wouldn't hand me my life...I had to fight for it." She brushed away his tears before they reached his half-parted lips, where silent, heavy breaths escaped. "You taught me to fight, you showed me the way. Your father tried to make me forget that, but I fought my way back. Not just for me, not just for Talheim, but for *you*. Because you showed me what true leadership is. The kind of warrior and ruler *I* want to be."

She tapped her thumbs against his jaw, slow and deliberate, three times. Then she leaned forward and kissed him. Once. Twice. Thrice.

After a moment, Mira spoke, her voice so soft it was nearly reverent. "We hold onto the voices of our critics much more tightly than the ones who love us. But we can change that...beginning now."

Pippet beamed at her, sleepiness forgotten. "Can we do this for everyone? I'll start with Quill!"

"Stars help me," he groaned, and laughter broke across the table.

Cistine slid onto Thorne's knees, and he wrapped his arms around her waist and pressed his face into her back, hiding his tears in her armor while Tatiana launched into a sarcastic, eloquent list of Quill's best qualities.

All told, Cistine decided, it was the perfect eve before Darlaska.

CHAPTER
FIFTY-TWO

AT LEAST ADEN had the decency to warn Ashe they were celebrating Darlaska at Cistine's behest; but with only a day to prepare, it was a small mercy at best. Somewhere between the dress shops in the elite district and the forges in the older part of town, she decided Cistine, Aden, and Maleck would receive special gifts from her; the others would have to settle for fairly-priced chocolate.

She didn't return to the courthouse until nearly dark, the satchel over her shoulder considerably lighter than she liked and a storm of nerves rioting in her stomach at the gifts she'd decided on. Tossing up prayers for how tonight might proceed, she crossed the peristyle and slipped into Kanslar's wing, heels stamped with rumors and whispers of tomorrow.

The sentence was coming at last, the long delay explained by Sander after the previous night's emotional meal while Ashe escorted him and Mira, the first of his lovers she'd ever met, back to their rooms: the High Tribunes feared Salvotor's vengeance once they passed judgement. As long as they drew out the deliberation, it all hung in the balance. But Chancellor Bravis gave them until tomorrow; afraid or not, they would finally pass judgement.

Ashe couldn't muster up dread or glee yet. She couldn't think beyond what tonight would bring if everything went according to plan.

The usual parlor was oddly bare for Darlaska, no holly buds or clumps of crimson berries in sight, no silver twine or gold garlands twirled along the walls. The cabal milled in pockets, even Ariadne's silver-haired sister, but they looked better dressed for walking than spending an evening eating, drinking, and sharing gifts.

"So you all agreed to celebrate, but not decorate?" Ashe arched a brow. "Cistine, did you actually teach them about Darlaska?"

"I did!" She glowered at Aden. "But apparently we aren't staying here."

He offered a bland, enigmatic smile, and Ashe's body responded with memories of Blood Hive battle, bracing for pain. "Follow me."

Cistine shrugged helplessly, then took Thorne's hand while they left the parlor. Pippet did the same to Ashe, stealing her fingers right out from Maleck's reach when he brushed by. With a grin to her apologetic smile, he fell into step with Aden instead.

Again, her nervous thoughts danced through the night's many possible outcomes; again, she forced them away.

Twilight swallowed the world, long fingers of shadow interrupted by cold wind and white ghostlight reminiscent of Talheimic festivities. Pippet's chatter filled up the night, interlaced with laughter among the cabal. Watching Thorne and Cistine walk together, Ashe decided it would be a *very* good night, regardless of how things went for her.

It was fully dark when they began to slow at last, the faces changing around her. Though Cistine and Pippet still beamed, Saychelle tossed anxious glances at a stiff-jawed Thorne, Tatiana's heels dragged, and Quill's swagger slowed.

All at once, Aden brought them to a halt; Ariadne's hand clapped to her mouth.

The building would've been utterly unremarkable if not for its carven door: an intricate, tooled portrait of snow and ice with a boquet of flowers breaking through, symbols of new life set deep and smooth into the curved, creamy wood, governed over by delicately-rendered stars in the shape of a compass.

"I hope none of you mind I took the honor of giving the first gift," Aden said.

Tatiana clutched a hand to her throat. "You restored your parents' home? For *us*?"

He nodded. "This was always a place of sanctuary where you could expect a hot meal, a warm bed, whatever wisdom we had to share, and laughter around the table even when we didn't. I thought it might be a welcome relief from the courthouse from time to time."

Cistine turned shining eyes to him. "*This* is where you and Mira had your sessions." He nodded, a half-smile digging into his cheek.

Ariadne slid her fingers into the door's hewn grooves, following the delicate twine of ivy around the expertly-shaped pillars at its edges. Aden stood behind her, not quite close enough to touch, his gaze tracing everywhere her fingers went. "For what's grown from your ruin. For everything you've become."

Her hand fell from the door, swung back, and gripped his. With the other, she opened the way ahead.

Here was where all Cistine's decorations had gone: the wreaths and ribbons, the silver and gold ghostplant buds in glass spheres hanging from the ceiling and strung through archways from room to room. Pippet let go of Ashe's hand and bolted ahead, laughing with delight; the cabal followed more slowly, Saychelle the first to break the awestruck silence. "It's...just how I remember it. Well, besides these gaudy Talheimic decorations." Cistine shoved her, grinning.

"She's right. It does look the same." Quill gestured into the dining room. "How many nights did we sit in there, plotting the glory of Sillakove Court with Nimea and the others, talking about how we'd change the kingdom if not the world?"

"Something was always missing from those plans." Thorne draped an arm around Cistine. "We just didn't know it yet."

They passed through a small tapestry hall and entered a sitting room outfitted in full Darlaska regalia, everything aglow in tones of silver and gold. Pippet sprawled on a sofa already, snacking on an apple from the fruit bowl on the table; Tatiana flopped down with her, and one by one the others joined in, taking sofas and seats, dissolving into conversation. Wine, mead, and hot apple cider splashed into cups; Aden brought a platter of cheese and vegetables from the kitchen, and the cabal relaxed like Ashe had never seen before. From satchels and bags, gifts emerged, piled up into a heap on the center table. Ashe added hers to the mound, pulse kicking at what must've seemed a marked absence of one in particular.

She chafed the starstone along its chain and lowered herself next to Cistine, who brought them all to attention with a clap. "I know we're all dying of anticipation, so let's open these gifts!" Pippet bounced in place and Quill flung his leg over hers, trapping her to the sofa. He sent Faer up to roost in the exposed rafters, eyeing the twine and wrappings for glints of jewel-brightness as Cistine passed two small parcels to Ashe and Maleck. "Everyone else has this gift already, but you should have it, too."

Ashe tore off the butcher's paper and twine, frowning at the vial of dark liquid inside. "Are we supposed to drink this?"

Tatiana burst into laughter, and Ariadne rolled up her sleeves, baring thick, artful patterns of flowers and vines all along her forearms—a design not unlike the front door, but buried under her skin. "It's Atrasat blood...it conducts augments so none of us will ever be without armor again."

Maleck stared at his vial, brow furrowing. "This is a fine gift. But it's not for me."

Ashe cocked her head. "And why is that?"

He raised harrowed eyes to her. "Because of how close I came to becoming like my brothers. It's not that this strategy has no merit, but for me, it's not even a conversation worth having. If I use augments again, I will not be myself anymore. Better if I'm consumed than living on as whatever I would become."

A half-growled protest leaped to the tip of Ashe's tongue, but Cistine spoke first. "Maybe you're right. Maybe, if you used just one more augment, you would become a Bloodwight. But that doesn't matter, because I would find some way to bring you back."

Maleck's smile brimmed with sympathy. "I do not think there would be anything left worth saving."

Cistine's eyes glinted with fighting fury. "What if I said all these things about myself? That the Key doesn't deserve to be saved, because of what it is and how it was made." When he merely blinked at her, she barreled on, "Well, it's true, isn't it? I'm strangely made. I'm...*unnatural.*" Her voice cracked slightly. "So, why should anyone fight to *save* the Key? Why not just open the Doors and be done with me? You'll all see me in the next life, anyway. What do you say to that?"

After a long moment of silence, Maleck murmured, "That we save you in this life, and in the next, we learn to let you go."

"Exactly." She reached across the table and curled his fingers over the vial. "And I'll never let *you* go, either, Darkwind."

The hard planes of his angular face softened, even the scar that bisected his right eye. A flush crossed the bridge of his nose.

"Wear the inkings," Cistine urged, "just in case. So *if* something happens, you'll survive it, and I can find you and make it right."

After another deep, heavy pause, Maleck tucked the vial into his pocket.

The tension broke, and bit by bit the mound shrank. Parcels of jewelry, weapons, and armor met with grins, books and fine teas stacked up next to delicate silk threads and new augment pouches, and Pippet ate half her box of chocolate before Quill noticed and snatched it away. Smiling wider than anyone in the room, he thrust a different box into his sister's smudged fingers. "Open this before the anticipation kills me."

Giddy from sugar and excitement, Pippet ripped apart the fine ribbon and lifted the top off the parcel. Her shriek of delight half-deafened Ashe. "*A lightbox!*"

Quill grinned, spreading one arm on the seatback behind her. "I managed to skim a few augments from a back-alley merch, but just a few, so don't waste them, all right? Take pictures that matter."

Pippet didn't seem to hear him, already fiddling with the device. Ashe's laughter ended abruptly when Maleck set a parcel in her lap, nervousness glinting in his eyes. "For you."

She laid open the paper corner by corner, her fingers recognizing the weight and shape even before she beheld its beauty with her eyes.

The violin was crafted of the finest polished cedar, its design flawless from shape to scent. She knew how silky the wood was even before she lifted it from its case and settled it, bow and all, across her lap. "Mal, I..."

There were no words. Suddenly, her own gift seemed weak in comparison.

Tatiana rescued her from the deafening silence by offering a parcel to Quill. "Here you go. I hope it fits."

Quill took it with the same eagerness as his sister and had the twine off in one deft tug. The paper fluttered to the floor, and he stared at the contents, mouth agape. "You *made* this?"

"If you like it, then yes. Otherwise, Papa did."

"Tatiana." Quill shook his head. "You made me *fingers*."

"Well, Kadlin sorted out the problem with the hinges. Here, I'll show you how it works." She took the device back, and he offered his three-fingered hand. "The strap goes around your wrist here...and this band curves around the side of your hand. The artificial fingers fit over your stumps—don't worry, I measured the circumference. So now, when you wiggle them..." He slowly bent his stumps, and the hinges curled at the knuckles, then extended stiffly. "There, you have your fingers back. Consider this my apology for being the reason you lost them in the first place."

Quill's eyes shimmered. "You're so stars-damned brilliant, I don't know what to say to you sometimes."

She fluttered her lashes. "If you give me my gift now, we'll call it even."

Quill didn't pull from the stack this time; clearing his throat gruffly, he reached into the front of his loose linen shirt, drew out a simple scroll, and passed it to her. Brow creased, she unbound it and laid it open on her knees, skimming it from top to bottom once. Then again. And again.

"Quill. What is this?"

He offered a lopsided smile. "The deed to a house in Blaykrone."

Tatiana's eyes wrenched from the paper up to Quill and Pippet, both grinning wickedly. "You are *joking*."

"You're holding proof right in your hands. It's all paid for."

"I helped!" Pippet cut in, and Quill mussed her hair.

"You absolutely did. With gambling mynts." She stuck out her tongue at him, and he winked. "Our Chancellor was generous enough to offer me a stipend if I help build up the Vassoran presence in Blaykrone. Most of the outposts went to Nimmus in a knapsack when Salvotor pulled them out. Someone has to go fix that."

"And there are schools out there," Pippet added. "Real schools, like the ones in Stornhaz, but everyone's nicer...more like the refugees from Geitlan. I think I'll like them. I'm tired of this big school, anyway."

"It was time," Quill added. "I finally have everything I was afraid to ask the gods for—you, my sister, all of us alive, Salvotor in chains. It's time for you to have what *you've* been asking for, too. I can land on my feet wherever I fall, but you've been the one following *me* since I left school. It's my turn to follow, wherever that takes me...as long as it's with you."

Tatiana dropped the deed onto the table, buried her face in her hands, and sobbed. Pippet and Quill smothered her in a heartbeat, arms around her from either side, and Thorne, mercifully, distracted the others by picking up another scroll and offering it to Aden. "This doesn't really count as a gift—you earned it. But the timing was appropriate."

Aden's breath dropped through him, long and measured, when he read the contents. "This is a Tribune's oath."

Thorne nodded. "Now that Marcel's vouched publicly for my father, I'll be removing his title. Spoek is yours when the trial ends."

"My father's old territory?"

"He would be glad for you to have it."

While the misty-eyed cousins embraced, Ashe glanced over the scant stack of remaining gifts. None for her or Maleck.

She had to do this now, before she lost her nerve.

Rising from the sofa, she beckoned him and slipped from the room.

Laughter and conversation bubbled from below while they ascended a narrow staircase to the upper rooms. She tried to focus on those things and not the itchiness in her face or how shallow her breaths were; or how much this felt like the very first time she did something like it, despite how different it was now.

She chose one of the rooms at random, caring only that it had a door. Once Maleck stepped inside and shut it, Ashe pressed a hand to her middle and prayed for calm.

"What is it, Asheila?" he asked. "Was there something you needed?"

"Yes. To give you your gift."

"Very well," he said with that polite confusion she found equal parts aggravating and endearing. "What is it?"

She took in a deep breath. Let it tumble out. "Me."

She faced him at last, the tremble in her hands intensifying at the shock in his face.

"Me," she repeated, just to hear herself say it. "However you want me. I don't know what that means, and I don't care. If there's anything these last few weeks have taught me, it's that neither of us is walking away from this. We don't want to." She approached him, every step stalking and graceful, and when his back struck the door, she slid her hands up his chest, resting over his scarred heart. "So that means you're mine, and I'm yours. And for the first time in my life, I'm precisely what I want to be."

Maleck's hands stopped hers undoing the first clasp of his armor. "This is the greatest gift anyone has ever offered me," he said hoarsely. "But I will not do it this way."

She frowned. "What?"

He lowered her hands from his collar and took her face instead. "I know you have never been cherished. Longed for. Waited for. You have been a triumph for men like Viktor and a tool for men like Rion. But you are neither of those things to me." He took her chin, slanting his head until his mouth nearly brushed hers. "I will have you when I have earned your trust, your love...when you come to me with steady hands and truly believe what you're giving will be received as it deserves. Until then, what I want is to earn you."

Relief ripped the breath from her chest, and she met his mouth, sealing that promise with a kiss.

It was another gift. And as wonderful as the violin was, this one meant so much more.

CHAPTER FIFTY-THREE

THE CABAL TACTFULLY dispersed when Ashe and Maleck disappeared. While the others examined their gifts and returned to chattering, Cistine slipped out onto the back terrace, a railed patio jutting into the Ismalete Channel. It had begun to snow, almost too fine to feel cold when she folded her arms on the railing and rested her chin in the crook of her elbow. The warmth in her chest went beyond words, as if she'd built up with so much joy over the evening that it simply mellowed and melted. A stack of books and fine shirts, trousers, and tea awaited her inside; Aden had even given her a gauntlet with a hidden *Svarkyst* blade in its seams, unsheathed with a flick of the wrist, and promised to teach her how to use it in the year to come.

So many wonderful gifts, the envy of any Talheimic Darlaska; yet it was the people who made it wonderful, and the knowledge that she wouldn't have to leave them yet. The gift to herself—to choose where she would belong for the foreseeable future—was the best of all.

Still, a pang of homesickness made her think of her parents celebrating tonight as well, perhaps reunited already, walking Astoria's glistening streets together. She prayed Rion and Eboni found a way to feel joy tonight, too, though it was the first Darlaska since Julian's death.

The terrace door whispered open, and she smiled when Thorne leaned against the railing at her side, sleeves rolled up despite the cold, arms crossed. Her gaze fell on the hints of inkings on his muscled forearms—star maps he'd shown her the day before, stretching all the way along his ribs and back and sides; the kind taught by Wayfinders. They were a perfect match for hers: four fine, dark star tails ribboning each arm, one each for Ashe and Maleck, Aden and Ariadne, Quill and Tatiana, Julian and Baba Kallah; and the last joining the trails above her heart, a ninth star for her Starchaser.

"Admiring the view?" His voice coaxed her attention up from his arms to his face. When she stuck out her tongue, he laughed, pushed away from the railing, and slipped behind her, arms around her waist, a kiss pressed to the hinge of her neck. She leaned back into his chest and shut her eyes, savoring his warmth, his sandalwood-and-leather scent. "Tonight went well, I think. Ashe and Maleck are performing a duet as we speak."

Cistine squinted up at him. "Is that a euphemism?"

He laughed harder. "*No.* Aden had his mother's piano restored."

Now that she listened, through the closed glass door she did hear the familiar sound of piano keys being plucked and the accompaniment of a sweet refrain coaxed from a violin's neck. "It's perfect. Everything is perfect tonight."

"That it is."

"Don't think I haven't noticed, though," she teased. "You didn't have a single gift for me. How dare you?"

"I let you bring your garish celebration into my home." He rested his chin on her shoulder. "Besides which, you have me. Isn't that gift enough?"

"Ugh!" She kicked his shin. "I see how it is! Aden gains territory and title, you give Quill a *house* for Tatiana, but me, I'm meant to be content with your presence? *Thorne.* You know I *love* gifts."

"I do know that." He nipped her ear and withdrew. "Which is why I saved the best one for last."

She turned away from the city's twinkling lights, away from the vision of ice and dreams rocked to sleep by the last dregs of Darlaska—and found Thorne down on both knees, offering her a ring.

CHAPTER FIFTY-FOUR

THOUGH THORNE HAD dreamed of this moment for weeks, weaving all the threads together at last with Ashe's advice once she returned from Talheim, he was sweating worse than a man facing the lash now that he was here, staring into Cistine's wide eyes.

"Cistine..." Stars, his voice shook, "it would honor me if you took me as your...husband. Your *valenar*. If we could have more than just a treaty binding us. We could be one, as our kingdoms are one." It all rushed out of him in a single, long breath, and then he was left with just the things Ashe taught him to do, the ring Tatiana and Pippet had helped him choose that morning, and the posture of bended knee for humility.

He'd bent both, just in case.

Cistine stared at him with hands smothering her mouth, eyes glistening with emotion. Her breath puffed out—his name. Just his name. Then she walked to him, crouching in the freshly-fallen snow. Knee to knee, she cupped her hands under his, drawing them closer to examine the ring: a black band and an ultramarine opal, the color of mountain halls and ghostplants lighting up the dark.

"I know how sudden this seems," he added hastily, "after Julian made the same offer, and these tumultuous months since. It wouldn't need to happen now, not even for decades."

"You'd wait decades?"

"I would wait a lifetime. You can have me however I'm needed, wed or unwed, friend or not, *selvenar, valenar,* husband—" his hands dipped, settling deeper into hers. "As long as you're in my life, I'm happy. But I want you to know that for me, there is no end to our story. What binds us can outlast the world itself. So if it brings you some peace about the future, I wanted you to know the place I hope to have in it. And you're free to take this or walk away. If you choose—"

"Thorne, are you going to stop and take a breath so I can say yes?"

"Of course. I'm sorry, I—" Then the words struck. He held her gaze, green eyes dancing with delighted tears. His breath hitched so sharply he choked and coughed. "*Yes?*"

"I'm not saying *yes* as in right this moment. But when I *am* ready...of course it's you. It's been you ever since the Black Coasts. I walked away from the future I was sure I wanted, and you were always part of that choice. So, *yes.* A hundred times, yes, Thorne Starchaser." Her sugar-scented breath stirred joy in his blood like a kicked snowdrift. "For a hundred years and a hundred adventures I want to have with you."

When he slid the ring onto her finger, silent tears sliding down both their grinning faces, relief peaked through him sharp as a spike of adrenaline in battle. He lunged to his feet and swept her up with him, spinning her laughing across the terrace to the railing where he kissed her, blended hearts bringing them closer than breathing, so close neither life nor death could pull them apart.

And then, as if the gods saw fit to challenge that, a loud, cursing cry burst through the terrace doors.

Cistine's hands clenched on Thorne's shoulders as she broke the kiss, her gaze hunting his with the cruelest sort of fear—a silent farewell to peace.

They ran inside the crowded parlor, full of shouting now. Sander stood among the half-circle of the cabal, scarf aslant around his neck, dark curls loose against his shoulders. He'd brought no jacket, his boots unlaced, blood on his knees and palms like he'd fallen while running. He gripped Aden's shoulder with the panicked agony of a creature shot through the liver.

"Iri told me where to find you." He half-swiveled at Thorne's approach. "Thorne, I beg you, *help* me, he's taken her!"

"Taken who?"

"Mira! She was to meet Hana for tea in the peristyle at sunset, but she never arrived." Sander finally released Aden, facing his Chancellor fully. "It's not just her. Taj, Niklause, Kyost, Hallvard...all the High Tribunes are missing something precious, and we've all received ransoms. We're to cast our vote in Salvotor's sentencing as not guilty by reason of insufficient evidence. If we don't, or if we tell anyone of this, then Mira and the others..."

He broke off, straining a hand against his pale lips.

"Why?" Ashe demanded. "Of all your lovers, why her?"

It was Cistine who answered. "Because she's the only one."

Deafening silence crashed over the room. Wide eyes all turned to Sander, who didn't move, or speak.

Cistine slid past Thorne to stand before his High Tribune, searching his helpless, agonized gaze. "The others aren't really your lovers, are they? You've built an army of women between you and Salvotor so he would never do *this*. Take the only one you truly loved."

Sander covered his face with one hand. "Mirassah is my *valenar*, yes, my one and only. The others are well-paid warriors who have protected us ever since I vouched for Thorne's title."

"As if that wasn't obvious," Aden muttered, but no one else looked so composed. Thorne struggled to calm his own reeling mind at the latest revelation of his wily High Tribune's crafty preparations.

"And how did the *bandayo* find out the truth?" Tatiana demanded.

Sander gritted his teeth, jaw leaping. "I had papers signed so in the event of my unfortunate demise, Mira would receive the stipend and all my lands. It's the only proof we've dared keep, and that stars-damned spy stole them from the armoire. And now he *has* her." He shot forward, gripping Thorne by his collar. "Do something, will you? I wanted *you* on the Judgement Seat for times like these. Your people need you! *Help us.*"

Thorne took Sander's wrists and squeezed gently until the High Tribune released him. Then he took the sides of Sander's neck and looked deeply into his eyes. "We're getting her back, and we're stopping my father once and for all." Releasing Sander, he turned to his cabal. "Ashe, call your dragon. Ariadne, Aden, take Saychelle and Pippet back to the courthouse and bring me belongings with the captives' scents. If Bresnyar can locate the hostages, it will spare us having to search the city for them."

Sander slumped, head in his hands. "She could have a fit, and those *bandayos* won't know what to do. She could bite clean through her tongue, she could seize so badly she breaks a limb. You might not find her, or if you do, what if they slit her throat the moment they see you?"

"Look at me," Aden growled, and Sander slowly did. "You know me. You know what feats I am capable of. *I* will bring her back."

Slowly, Sander's face steeled. "Well, not alone, you won't." He stood up from the arm of the sofa. "Lend me some of that Siralek steel, Hive Lord. We'll teach these *bandayos* never to trifle with our cabal again."

CHAPTER
FIFTY-FIVE

WHICH CAPTIVE ARE we looking for?" Cistine's voice felt too loud in the dormant confines of Beryl Avenue, hurrying down its tawny surface with Thorne beside her, his silver hair still windswept from scouting with Ashe and Bresnyar.

"We're searching for Kyost's family portrait," he explained.

She almost slipped on the glass-smooth street. "We're risking our lives for a *painting?*"

"Not just any painting. He gathered his family's ashes after their pyre burning and had them mixed into paint. The portrait is quite *literally* his family."

She scrunched her nose. "That's disgusting."

"I agree, but his attachment to it still means Salvotor has him by the throat until it's retrieved."

Cistine shivered, her quiver and bow rubbing against her spine. Across the sleeping city, the cabal was on the move, dark arrows shooting straight and deadly toward their five targets—all but Quill in pairs. Saychelle and Pippet were back in the courthouse, safeguarded by Sander's lovers on the off chance Salvotor had a contingency in mind for them; the cabal could afford no distractions tonight.

At the end of Beryl Avenue, Cistine and Thorne emerged onto a long wharf jutting directly into the Ismalete Channel, and he motioned her to turn right. "Bresnyar caught the scent a quarter mile north of here."

"The portrait will have to be somewhere not too dry or damp, hot or cold." At Thorne's raised brows, she added, "My mother collects art."

"Well, the harbor air will take care of the damp. As for the dryness..."

"Elevation. It needs to be high above the water. But the heat and cold..."

"Straw for insulation."

Cistine glanced at him. "That's oddly specific."

He cast out an arm, bringing them to a halt where the docks ended in a dark, broad plaza. Unlike the well-tended streets they'd crossed to reach it, this avenue was devoted to labor, not luxury, hosting only a long line of gray storehouses. From the windows of their upper lofts, thin reeds of straw poked loose.

"Dry, dark, and temperate, to keep the wares from spoiling," Cistine murmured. "Thorne, you're brilliant."

He squeezed her shoulder and pushed her down into a crouch against the wet wood. "There."

A man crept toward the third storehouse from the shadows, looking both ways before he unlocked the door and slipped inside. Ghostlight burned around his broad frame; then the door tumbled shut and all was dark again.

Thorne gripped Cistine's elbow and tugged her into an alley beside the dock. "The windows at the top look in through one another. If you position yourself in the adjacent building, can you shoot that distance?"

"I think so. But I'll be firing into darkness."

"Not if you track me. I'll use a fire augment as a beacon, go blade-to-blade with these *bandayos* and give you the light you need."

Cistine nodded. "Then if you break the glass, I'll shoot through the window."

"I'll make it my first priority." He portioned a small ember of a fire augment into his palm, leaving only an inlaid glow along his armor threads, the reflection dazzling in his eyes. "Go swiftly and safely, *Logandir*."

"You as well."

Dark armor blending against equally-dark cobblestones, she raced across the docks and skittered toward the storehouse on the left. It was a risk, moving across the enemy's face, but she wanted the harbor lights at her back—the best chance of seeing what she was shooting at.

Swift and steady, hand-over-hand, she vaulted the ancient storehouse, grateful there were no other windows through which Salvotor's men might spot her besides the one *she* needed to break, and the one at her back when she reached it.

The moment her fingers grazed the sill, fire whipped out, smashing the door of the adjacent building to kindling; then came the shouting and the slick slide of swords into flesh as Thorne went to war. Cistine broke the glass with a crack of her elbow and climbed inside, slinging the bow from across her body and fitting an arrow into the string as she pivoted to keep watch.

Two minutes passed; then the window in the neighboring building blew out under the slam of a man's head, his mop of chestnut hair flopping limply as Thorne dropped him in the broken windowframe and whirled back to confront the rest of Salvotor's men.

Cistine notched, aimed, and fired so smoothly and quickly her muscles burned from the strain, plucking off anyone who came close to her *selvenar's* ember-glowing armor. For minutes, her world was nothing but bow and quiver and sight; she was so focused on bringing down the men around him that she didn't even have time to scream when an arm circled her throat from behind, yanking her from the window.

In her burst of shock, the arrow bounced out of the bowstring; with his free hand, her attacker yanked the weapon from her grasp and tossed it out the window. Cistine finally caught the breath to bellow in fury, and Thorne, blades locked with another enemy, swiveled toward the window. His opponent drew a hidden knife and slashed across his cheek.

Knife.

Cistine's terrified brain revived. As her assailant hauled her away from the window, she freed one of her blades and jammed it into his kneecap. He buckled, howling, and brought her down with him, rolling on top and pinning her smaller frame with his greater weight—

And suddenly she was in Kalt Hasa, Grimmaul's blade at her neck.

A scream ripped her throat so brutally, the man flinched. When his weight rocked back, she freed her arm from under her chest and plunged her blade backhanded into his shoulder, slamming her heel into his groin and cracking her head into his chin all in the same motion. When he slid away, she whirled on him, jamming the knife straight through his eye.

Horror choked her when he twitched and floundered, crumbling backward, dying in spasms. It cost all her strength to tear her eyes from his gruesome, blood-washed face. Gagging, she crawled to the window, gripped the frame in shaking hands, and shouted Thorne's name.

He appeared at once; blood soaked his left cheek, and the fire had gone out of his armor. But he was alive.

"Are you all right?" he called.

She wiped a shaky hand down her face and forced a nod. "The painting?"

"Unscathed. Can you get to Maleck and Ashe and help them?"

She took rapid inventory of herself; her heart throbbed so hard she thought it might fail her, she was nauseous and shaking, her mouth tasted of old meat and salt—but she was unharmed besides the tightness in her throat where the man choked her. "I can do it. Take the painting. And be *careful*, Thorne."

At his deft nod, she grabbed the windowsill, clambered down from the loft, and retrieved her bow. Despite the fall, it remained battle-ready, just like her.

Lashing it around her chest, she ran.

CHAPTER FIFTY-SIX

ASHE FLATTENED HER back against the broad schoolyard arch and cursed as another augment blew a chunk of stone from beside her shoulder. Across the archway, Maleck twisted his head toward her, reflecting her frown; they'd nearly reached the front door before Salvotor's men unleashed fire augments from the open windows, forcing them to fall back this far.

"Almost makes you miss the war, doesn't it?" Ashe called over a pause consuming the half-ruined courtyard.

Maleck's gaze fluttered down from her eyes to her chest. "I was under the impression your dragon flew quicker than this."

"Give him some credit, he's done a lot of flying the past few days."

"Maleck! *Ashe!*" Cistine barreled into view down the street with bloodsoaked hands and bow strapped on, flattening herself against the arch beside Ashe. "Are you two all right?"

"Yes, but Tribune Hallvard's children might not be for long," Ashe grunted.

"*Logandir*, your bow." Over Cistine's head, Maleck and Ashe exchanged a glance.

"Can you shoot the augurs in the windows?" Ashe demanded. "Distract them so we can reach the doors?"

Cistine nodded. "But I need enough light to see by, and I didn't bring a light augment with me."

The hair rose on Ashe's arms, and she grinned. "It's being handled."

A draconian roar pierced the air. Shouts of shock and fury rang like school bells, and Ashe whirled around the arch as Bresnyar descended in a mighty punch of wings and talons, spewing his own fire across the courtyard. "Now!"

Side-by-side, Ashe and Maleck raced toward the door. Halfway across the broken-up courtyard, the air crackled like the atmosphere before a summer storm, then settled when a bowstring twanged; an augur toppled from one of the windows and smashed to the ground, his lightning augment wasted. Then another. Then another. Bresnyar slammed into the building's face and clawed up, reaching inside to pluck out Salvotor's men and hurl them to the cobblestones.

They reached the door at last, and Maleck crashed into it, rebounding and cursing. He smoothed his hands over the frame more slowly this time, then withdrew like it burned him. "It's sealed with an augment from the other side."

Ashe shoved him toward the lowest window, more than a head's height above. When Maleck reached the wall, he put his back against it and cupped his hands. With a running leap, Ashe stepped into his palms, and he thrust her up with all his might. Breaking the glass with her elbow and dropping inside, she turned back to watch Cistine tear across the courtyard; the remaining augurs were too busy fending off the dragon to worry about her.

Maleck heaved Cistine up into the window, and she and Ashe reached down together and helped him inside. The moment his feet touched the floor, they all broke into a run toward the school's central wraparound staircase. As fit as Ashe was, even she panted up its height, her lungs burning and a stitch blossoming in her side when they reached the uppermost corridor—and came to a stumbling halt.

The last augur, blocking the door at the end, had a hostage in his arms.

Hallvard's daughter trembled, gazing at Ashe, Cistine, and Maleck with tearstained eyes. She was so small the man easily trapped her one-armed, his knife grazing just below her ear—one slip away from spilling her throat.

"Drop your weapons," he hissed.

Maleck cast down his sabers and raised both hands. Ashe lowered Odvaya more slowly, keeping her eyes on the girl. "What's your name?"

"A-A-Abitha," she sobbed.

"You hear that?" Ashe addressed the augur. "She's a little girl with a *name*. You don't want to do this."

"And I won't, if we get what we want," he spat.

"Nothing has been done yet that cannot be forgiven in the Courts," Maleck said. "But if you draw that blade against her skin, High Tribune Hallvard will bury you."

The man's mouth jerked in a fanatic smile. "And when Chancellor Salvotor becomes ruler of all Valgard, I will be pardoned."

Maleck went very still. "Unfortunately for you, the only one you will seek pardon from is the Undertaker."

He grabbed Ashe's neck and pushed her to her knees. Cistine's arrow cut swift and silent over them, embedding in the man's forehead. He slammed back against the door, dropping the knife and the girl. She screamed as she fell, a pained, panicked sound.

Ashe scrambled forward on hands and knees, grabbing Abitha, rolling her over. Blood spilled down her neck from under her ear.

Swearing, Ashe scooped her up. "Mal, Cistine, get the other two!"

She soared down the steps, Abitha's body jouncing in her arms, blood soaking her armor as she bolted down the hallway toward the front door. The augur who kept it shut was gone, but the door itself was still sealed, and the girl in her arms was too pale, no longer whimpering.

Then the door burst open in a thousand daggered shards, knocking Ashe on her haunches and sending her skidding back several feet. She shook grit from her eyes and squinted through Bresnyar's golden light, his tail raked bloody where the naked patch had scraped the door. Quill stepped over the wreckage and fell to his knees beside Ashe and Abitha.

"Tell me you have a healing augment!" Ashe shouted.

He was already freeing the flagon from his pouch with one hand, resting the other on the girl's forehead. But when he held the augment aloft, he hesitated.

"What are you doing?" Ashe snapped. "Heal her!"

Quill slowly sank back on his heels, eyes fixed on Ashe's face. He shook his head.

Ashe clutched Abitha's limp body to her chest. "No. Don't you dare..."

"Look at her."

She forced herself to, for the first time since she picked her up in that hall: death-white face. Blue lips. Eyes closed.

She couldn't have been any older than Pippet.

"Gods-forsaken *bandayos*," Ashe rasped. "A *child*."

Quill gripped her shoulder and leaned his temple against hers. They were still sitting that way when Maleck and Cistine found them, carrying the other children—the elder on Maleck's back, Cistine with the younger on her hip.

There was no sound of victory from them. Only the oldest boy's sob when he saw his little sister dead in Ashe's arms.

CHAPTER
FIFTY-SEVEN

So, THIS WAS Darlaska—a night of revelry and fighting never to be forgotten, half of it a blur, the rest popping too vividly in Tatiana's mind. Her body hummed with exhaustion, slumped on the parlor sofa between Ariadne and Pippet. Only the presence of all five Chancellors kept her eyes open, and the absence of their friends—of *Quill*.

Thorne paced, dragging a hand through his hair, and Aden reclined at the wall with his head turned, casting glances out the window; both looked as weary as Tatiana felt, and they had every right to be. Thorne had carried a portrait twice his height all the way back to the courthouse; Aden had fought an entire cabal's share of men with Sander, setting Mira free, then joined her and Ariadne rescuing Taj of Yager Court—its true High Tribune, a crucial gamepiece Salvotor never even knew he held. Tatiana had almost lost a hand in that fight, wrist still throbbing from a *Svarkyst* cut and only still intact thanks to Ariadne's intervention.

Her head shot up when the door opened at last. Eyes red-rimmed, Quill led the others inside. Maleck limped slightly, clutching his side; Ashe's brow was cut, blood running beside her eye; Cistine trudged as if she might faint with exhaustion at any moment.

Thorne stopped pacing, bent with relief. "Report."

"We lost one of Hallvard's children," Ashe croaked. "But the other two are with their mother and father now."

Tatiana swore, and Ariadne shut her eyes, lips moving in silent prayer. Pippet crossed the room and leaped on Quill, and he lifted her to wrap her arms and legs around him, burying his face in her hair.

"Mira?" Cistine asked.

"Safe," Aden assured her. "Being seen to by medicos, along with Niklause's grandchildren and Taj."

"You all did well," Thorne added. "And we'll pay our condolences directly to your High Tribune, Bravis."

The Chancellor rubbed his creased brow. "You should have come to us at the beginning of this."

"There was no time. I believed lives would be lost if we didn't act on Sander's report. If that was offensive to you, then I apologize for the offense. But not for my choice."

"Men like you are impossible to shame."

"But you should *not* be shamed for this," Maltadova interceded. "Your retinue has proven its strength and nobility once again, Thorne. Not only are our High Tribunes indebted to you, but *we* are."

"And if the report you gave is true," Benedikt muttered, "then the rest of Valgard is also in your debt."

"There is no debt," Thorne said. "Not to me."

Cistine rubbed her cheeks and asked quietly, "What happens now?"

Bravis and Maltadova exchanged a glance. Valdemar stroked his beard with long, bony fingers. "We proceed as if it never happened, because that is the greatest retribution possible. Tomorrow, the High Tribunes will decide, based solely on the evidence of the trial, of course, that Salvotor is guilty of a heinous crime. We will do this the legal way."

Quill let Pippet down to the floor, eyes glinting with fury. "He tried to manipulate the entire Court system tonight!"

"Yes, he did," Bravis said, "and I'm certain it will catch up to him."

The Chancellors all smiled like wolves with teeth bared over fresh game. Tatiana had never seen them so like-minded, as if they were sharing a secret no one else in the kingdoms would ever understand.

It was terrifying.

Benedikt stood. "Well, I'm off. I'll see you all in the courtroom tomorrow."

One by one, the others followed him from the parlor—all except Thorne, who shut the door.

For a moment, silence. Then, with a weary groan, Thorne stepped forward and gathered Cistine up against his chest. Aden took Ashe and Maleck by their shoulders and knocked foreheads with them, and Tatiana met Quill's eyes. He offered her the smallest grief-stricken smile, guiding his sister to sit before the hearth. Faer swooped from the nearby windowsill and settled on Pippet's lap, and Tatiana leaned her head against Ariadne's shoulder.

"I don't think I like Darlaska," Pippet said. "Let's never do this again."

Cistine burst into shaky laughter. "I promise it's not usually like this."

"With you?" Tatiana said. "I have a feeling it will be."

Sighing, they all settled onto the couches and seats, and Tatiana shut her eyes. Just five minutes, then she'd drag her aching carcass to her room, bathe the blood from her hands, and try to forget the latter half of the night ever happened.

The next thing she knew, she stirred to the glare of sunlight across her face. Her neck was cramped from sleeping on Ariadne's shoulder, tipped against the sofa's back. Quill and Pippet were sprawled on the floor, Pippet's head resting on his outflung arm. Cistine sprawled in a chair, and Aden slumped against one arm of the opposite couch and Maleck against the other. Thorne and Ashe were gone.

Yawning, Tatiana peeled herself up from the sofa and trudged to the door, scrubbing dried blood from under her ringlets and pausing in the frame to look back at her sleeping friends.

The battle, she wouldn't miss when they went to Blaykrone. But she would always miss moments like this.

CHAPTER FIFTY-EIGHT

E VEN BEFORE THORNE passed the contingent of Vassoran guards in the hall and caught sight of that familiar scarlet door, the sensations struck him: the sting of the belt on his back. The ache of a blow to the face. The sizzle of an augment just barely shocking the roots of his hair, and still turning every thread silver.

His fingers grazing the familiar crimson wood, he froze. That memory never came so clearly before.

Dragging his other hand shakily back along his skull, he shut his eyes. Memories or none, he had to do this.

He opened the door.

Vassora clustered on the walls, fifteen men armed to the hilt and led by Branko, who greeted Thorne with a curt nod. Salvotor slouched at the dining table, shackled hand and foot, yet he still radiated a sense of blistering power that raised the hair on Thorne's arms; or perhaps it was simply being back in this place, more prison than apartment.

But it was not his cage anymore.

Thorne shut the door, and Salvotor looked up, eyes hooded with contempt. "Finally debased yourself to visit? I'm surprised the Princess isn't climbing on your heels. Wasn't she eager for a private conversation with me?"

Thorne breathed out slowly. "I'm not doing this today."

"Pity." Salvotor gestured to the cards on the table. "I was just playing against myself."

"I know precisely what you're playing. But the rest of us won't be part of that game anymore."

"We'll see about that, boy."

The silence was tense, but fracturing. Thorne wondered if his father remembered the beatings, too, the malicious words, all the times Thorne had rushed into his own small chamber, slammed the silver door, and huddled against it to hold it shut, hands over his ears while Salvotor called him unrepeatable names and told him the horrible things he'd do to him when he crawled out—threats that still stalked his dreams sometimes. Or was that door with its glittering black brackets no more than the entry to some storage chamber for him?

Thorne rolled his shoulders, letting the memories slide away. "Your sentencing is today."

Salvotor smirked, his eyes trained on the cards. "So they tell me."

Thorne unclipped the bag from his belt as he approached the table. "*This* might tell you a bit more."

He hurled the bloodstained satchel onto the table, scattering the cards. The burlap mouth fell open, and the head of one of Salvotor's men from the storehouse rolled out of it.

Silence reigned in this place of horror and misery for Thorne and Baba Kallah—even for Rakel. Then Salvotor slowly raised his eyes from the severed head, a glare that promised limitless, unmitigated pain; but perhaps for the first time in his life, Thorne didn't fear it. "It's over. Your manipulations, your games with this trial and our lives. You're going straight to Nimmus where you belong."

"You can't kill me, boy, or else you would have done it on the plains for your grandmother."

The mention of her rocked through Thorne like an augment, quick and fiery, prickling his scalp again and knitting Baba Kallah with that half-forgotten shock to his hair; but he refused to let his father unbalance him.

"I don't plan to kill you. I'm leaving your fate to the law we both swore to uphold. You'll be choking on the oaths you struck by this time tomorrow, and I don't even have to raise my blade."

Salvotor's smirk was void. "And you came to tell me this—why? Are you truly childish enough to gloat?"

"No. I just wanted to be the one to tell you your plan with the High Tribunes failed." Thorne turned and strode to the scarlet door. When he rested his hand on the knob, a tremor of unease skimmed through him, fleeting as a cold mountain wind. He steadied his breaths before he added, "And that you were wrong when we confronted one another outside Jovadalsa that day. I did have a plan. And a promise to keep."

Salvotor scoffed but offered no retort. Despite

Thorne's visceral fear, when he turned the knob, the door swung open without any resistance at all. One last time, he looked back at the man who made his life Nimmus; small and feeble now, stripped of his power.

"You lose."

He stepped from the room and sealed that scarlet door at his back, trapping Salvotor on the other side.

The usual parlor was all but empty when Thorne made his way back. Only Cistine remained, stretched on a couch, reading a truncated Valgardan epic and eating a bowl of berries and cream. She had a habit of licking the cream off the fruit first—one of a thousand small things he loved about her.

For a moment, he lingered in the doorway and soaked in the sight of her so content, a glint of a promise shining on the second finger of her left hand. Like salve on wounded skin, she soothed the ache in his calves and the tightness in his chest, the burn lingering in his scalp.

She was safe and free. They both were.

She tossed her hair from her eyes and glanced up with a smile he never saw her offer anyone except him: equal parts delight and mischief. He leaned his head against the sleek doorframe and held her gaze, letting her see him; how, beneath the relief, he felt raw, like he'd walked on hot coals across Kanslar's wing to reach her.

She set the book aside and sat up. "What's wrong? Where were you this morning?"

"I remember why Salvotor shocked my hair."

It wasn't what he intended to say, but it was the first thing that came out of his mouth. When she frowned and beckoned, he joined her on the couch, staring into the empty hearth. "I was seven. We were locked in the apartment for the evening, as usual, and he was hurting Baba Kallah. I put myself between them...I remember Aden had just taught me how to throw a punch, because Kristoff had just taught him. So I balled up my fist and I punched my father in the groin."

Cistine gaped at him. "You were *seven*."

"And he was screaming in Baba Kallah's face." He shrugged. "I didn't even think before I did it. It must've been the most pain I ever caused him. Baba Kallah tried to pull me away, she told me to run, but none of us could get out. He caught me by the back of my head while I was still trying to tear the door open, and..."

His scalp prickled again. He scratched the feeling away.

Cistine circled his shoulders and pulled him down so his head rested in the hinge of her shoulder and neck. He'd never told her as much, but from the first time she embraced him on the Black Coasts, this was his favorite part of her body: that small dip of muscle and bone that pooled the smell of soap and sweat, where her heartbeat thudded strongest and her skin was pure warmth. All these things brought comfort as he wrapped his arm around her waist and leaned into her.

"I'm sorry both of you had to endure that." Her knuckles stroked from his ear along the line of his jaw and back again. "Baba Kallah would be proud of you for letting the law do its work. For not sacrificing the Judgement Seat just to see him bleed. I don't know who would've ruled if you'd killed him, but...I'm glad it's you."

He relaxed into her touch. She was right; the law he loved would decide his father's future now. And despite the things they'd endured, Thorne could think of no better outcome than that—one where, together, he and Cistine finally had peace.

CHAPTER FIFTY-NINE

THERE WAS ONE more gift for Ashe to give the day after Darlaska.

Bresnyar waited for her at a pond two miles from the nearest barge dock outside the city, and at the sight of his golden glory awaiting in the daylight, some of the grief in Ashe's chest eased. She jogged to meet him, first with her hand, then with her forehead to his, and for a time they stood in the waxing day with their brows pressed together.

"I am sorry about the little one," he rumbled after a time. "Was she precious to you?"

"I'd never met her before," Ashe admitted, drawing back. "But they're all precious. No one deserves to die because of that bastard's schemes."

"Would that I had come to your aid sooner."

"No, you were magnificent. The people were whispering about it all over the city this morning...the golden dragon who wrecked the schoolhouse and vanished again into the night."

"They fear me."

"Actually, they want you to pay for the damages."

Bresnyar sniffed. "They can eat my entire hind end."

Laughing, Ashe gripped his wing joint and swung onto his back. "Let's go see the waves."

They flew to the Black Coasts, silent and sunk in thought. Bresnyar slapped two fish from the water and roasted them with a blast of his breath, and they walked the shore together, eating and watching the white surf crash into the ebony shoals.

"Cold again today," the dragon remarked after some time. "It's strange indeed, this weather we're having. The land and its creatures are all confused. Which does make for easier hunting, granted, but I don't like it."

He was right, it was colder the last two days. Ashe's toes had been all but numb from the frigid courtyard stones at the schoolhouse despite the heat of battle.

Did that make her slower when she ran with Abitha dying in her arms?

She tossed the fish's carcass into the water, her heart dipping. "With any luck, things will get better once Salvotor is convicted."

"Now that my presence is becoming known in this kingdom, please feel free to inform the Chancellors I would gladly eat or set that man ablaze should they wish it."

"I'll keep that in mind." She stooped to skim her hand over the crisscrossing wounds on Bresnyar's bald tail—the arrow mark from Rozalie, the lacerations where he broke down the schoolhouse door. "Your poor tail."

"All is well, I assure you."

"Poor, naked little lizard."

"Are you finished?"

She chucked. "I really am grateful you came last night. You didn't have to fight by my side, but you did."

"It was my pleasure, short-lived though it was. And I would do it again in a heartbeat." He looked off across the crashing surf again, his tail coiling lightly around Ashe's body.

"Good. Because we're likely going to spend the next hundred years fighting—either with each other or whatever gods-forsaken enemies come next." He glanced down at her, naked brows peaking in silent question, and she held his fiery gaze. "I want to be your Wingmaiden."

Now Bresnyar's jaws gaped, his forked tongue flopping between his teeth. "I beg your pardon?"

"What, is that not how it's done? Too informal? Or do you not want the beast-slayer and rain-dancer, defender and trainer of children, as your left wing—or whatever you'll call me?"

His jaw dragged shut, and a low chuckle burned up from his throat. "Do I want you? I have wanted nothing less since that ledge where you fought your captors with the last scrap of your strength. The way you rushed into that building last night to defend what was charged to you, how you wept for a child you didn't know. Leaped before an axe to defend your *selvenar*. Attacked a woman to save me from her arrows." Slowly, he wagged his head. "When I look at you, Asheila Kovar, I do not see a warrior. I see a tide-turner and fate-changer, a woman who could rewrite the paths of the stars if she chose. And I would like to be part of your choices, because a woman like that is someone I can entrust my wings to."

"Well, I trust you, too." And the force of that truth nearly stunned her. Somewhere between shouting and sulking and cliffside conversations, taming the wind together and racing to save Talheim and Maleck's life, she'd begun to see this dragon as an extension of herself: outcasts. Warriors. Survivors. Two broken pieces fitted together by the gods themselves.

She could imagine a future of this—free horizons and a spirit unbound to any kingdom, belonging only to those she chose to share herself with. She wouldn't walk alone on this new path or be ruled by men like Rion Bartos ever again.

That was the future she craved; she would figure out the rest as she went. So she took the greatest risk of her life and said, "Show me what to do."

Bresnyar bowed his head, shut his eyes, and offered his muzzle; with a final, steeling breath, she laid her hand to his snout.

A current of power churned the air between them, different from anything she'd ever felt in her life, raising the hair all along her body, chafing at the surface of her very spirit.

Gammalkraft.

Maleck had taught her that word in Talheim when she asked him how he thought the Key was forged; a power older than augmentation, older than anything else in the kingdoms. Ashe carried a piece of it already: the starstone pulsing in tune with her heart.

And now she opened herself fully to it...and to Bresnyar.

With a flash, that eddy between them turned to a river, sharp and relentless, bearing down from Bresnyar's mind to hers, and Ashe saw the world through his eyes. She saw *herself*, that first time he laid eyes on her, falling with fire in her gaze and a defiant roar in her teeth; the night she woke on the cliff and faced him, fearless and ragged with one foot still in the grave; her gaunt form on the rocky ledge, contours framed in moonlight, desperation blazing in her eyes when she told him she wanted to die.

She saw her own pain that night, but she *felt* Bresnyar's worry; how he would've flown her to the ends of the world and beyond to erase the anguish in her face, because he knew precisely how it felt. Knew what the agony of wishing for death could do to any living thing.

More visions stormed through, glazed in gold: Ashe leaping between Rozalie and Bresnyar; Ashe coming to Bresnyar for help finding Salvotor's captives; Ashe in the courtyard, flinging herself through the wall of his fire, rushing to save Hallvard's children.

A woman with battle in her blood and fire in her gaze, with the power to change the stars.

She heard her own voice cry out in shocked euphoria as the mountains gobbled the sky beneath them; felt the heat pulsing in her own core when they journeyed back to Valgard, Maleck's arms around her waist, his head tipped back into the wind; smelled the relief of forgiveness on her skin as she and Thorne and Bresnyar mapped the city together in search of the captives the night before.

She saw herself turn away from Bresnyar that first time, hoping he'd leave her to die. And she saw herself come back to him this morning, running with a smile on her face to lay her hand on his muzzle—peace storming through her, the fight against life forgotten when she realized she wanted him to stay. That glimpse married with this one, the sight of her right now through his eyes, bathed in the sunrise, choosing the path before her.

Not a Warden. Not a Hive fighter. Not a warrior or a guardian or a mentor. But something far more powerful and true and free.

Jagged, bright pain sliced through Ashe's hand, and she jerked back with a harsh breath, blinking away glimpses of the world through Bresnyar's eyes: trees and mountains and horizons, the school courtyard from above, her and Maleck and Cistine cleaving toward the doors with all their might.

A second pulse in her hand cleared her vision; a black, ember-crusted mark ridged the base of her palm, shivering and sparking faintly, an unfamiliar script she could somehow read, though she couldn't comprehend the meaning.

Ilyanak.

She raised her gaze to him. "The Wingmaiden's mark?"

His eyes glittered. If she didn't know better, she might've thought he was about to weep. "It wouldn't have forged if you didn't consent."

And she had consented. Sigrid was right—the gods had chosen her for a different life, one of music and metal, a destiny of dragonfire and open skies and love given freely; the love she'd fought for from Rion, from her parents, from her fellow Wardens and herself.

It was not the future she'd imagined, but it was the one she wanted now. And the gods had given her a different family to live it with—a family who was waiting for her return.

Skimming her runemarked hand against Bresnyar's hide, she vaulted onto his spine. "Let's fly, Scales. It's time to go home."

With a triumphant roar, her dragon spread his wings and carried her off to the sky.

CHAPTER SIXTY

IT FELT LIKE Sander and the rest of the High Tribunes disappeared into the courtroom's back chamber for days, debating the ruling that would condemn Salvotor or set him free. The spectators adjourned into the outer corridor, the cabal among them, keeping wary eyes on the crowd. Here and there, dotted among them like inkblots on a page, were figures in black robes sprinkled with silver like starlight—visitors from the territories, traveling in to hear the sentence and carry it back to the people. Even the furthest corners of Valgard had their ears pressed to the walls for gossip.

Cistine wished Mira were here today. She missed her friend's soothing, steady presence while she paced away her nervous energy in long loops up and down the corridor, passing in and out of the cabal's conversation while she twisted her betrothal ring around her finger.

"I'll admit, I'm not the most knowledgeable of Valgardan court practices," Ashe said from her place leaning against the wall beside Maleck, "but it seems like a guaranteed victory after Salvotor threatened the High Tribunes."

Aden leaned around Maleck's other side to address her. "The concern is whether the retribution they've feared all this time will still be enough to stay their tongues...particularly men like Hallvard, after his loss."

"Not to mention," Maleck added, "if Salvotor managed to sway any of the High Tribunes in some other way we don't know about. All he needs is to control a single vote, and he walks free."

Cistine flexed her fists and forced herself to breathe deeply as another wave of panic rolled through her. "What's the likelihood of that?"

Thorne shrugged up from the wall. "I think we're about to find out."

Astrid, one of Adeima and Maltadova's guards, stood grim-faced at the mouth of the hall. "Thorne, the Chancellors would like you to stand with them in the courtroom. You as well, Ariadne."

Cistine's heart thundered. Was that show of unity a precaution, or were they trying to send a message to a soon-to-be-free Salvotor that *Thorne* was still Kanslar's Chancellor in their eyes—that they believed Ariadne's testimony despite what was voted?

Nauseated all over again, she followed Thorne and Ariadne into the courtroom, where Bravis already droned on about the rule of law and the necessity for an accord between the five Courts. She barely heard a word of it; she was tired of hearing about laws and reasoning. She just wanted this to be over.

"High Tribune Hallvard." Bravis's tone gentled slightly. "Has a verdict been reached?"

"It has." Hallvard's voice was strained from a night of weeping.

"Step forward and state it."

Cistine's fingers hunted for Ashe's, squeezing with all her might.

"The Tribunal has deliberated." The rough words carried like a boom in the quiet. "We have reviewed the evidence. And in the case of Traisende Court against Chancellor Salvotor of Kanslar, we find the accused—"

Salvotor's chair creaked audibly. Ariadne tensed. The whole room took in its breath all at once.

"Guilty," Hallvard announced, "of the charge of rape of a *visnpresta* acolyte in direct violation of Valgard's laws. The Tribunal recommends ten years' imprisonment, in accordance with the law."

"Let it stand," Bravis said. "The accused will serve the full sentence. Branko, have your men remand him to his chamber pending detainment in the prison."

The Vassora hauled Salvotor up from his chair, and he wrenched an arm free, gesturing sharply at Ariadne. "Not once in ten years did this woman come forward! Now she destroys a man's reputation on baseless accusations from untrustworthy witnesses, and you've all allowed it for the sake of raising up a High Tribune whose title I've not recognized in a decade. There is no imitation of lawfulness in this kingdom anymore!"

"That's enough, you've had your chance to state your piece," Bravis said. "Escort him out."

"I'm not finished!" Salvotor snarled, and Cistine wasn't the only one who flinched. "You all think you need no king, no ruler—that your laws and Tribunals protect you? This is what you have become! Courts allowing foreign emissaries into their very hearts, trials carried out on a decade-old accusation without any scrap of evidence, without—"

"*Hal ulda viy.*"

Salvotor hesitated at the whisper near the windows from one of the many figures in a star-sprinkled robe. Cistine's skin prickled with gooseflesh; a startled, wary hush clasped the room. Then Salvotor barreled on, "This trial has been a mockery of justice. I will contest this sentencing until my last breath. I know my words were never heard, that this liar had you all convinced before you even—"

"*Hal ulda viy.*"

A second woman took up the words near the back wall, her voice a breath stronger than the first. Then another joined in. Then another.

"*Hal ulda viy. Hal ulda viy.*"

Chills spilled down Cistine's arms as the black-robed figures stepped nearer to the fence all at once. Nearer to Ariadne. Nearer to Salvotor.

"*Hal ulda viy!*" The Old Valgardan chant spread among them, linking woman to woman through the chamber. They cast back their hoods, baring faces full of snarling defiance and pure rage angled at Salvotor. But their words they directed at Ariadne: "*Hal ulda viy!*"

We are with you, they shouted.

Ariadne's mouth tumbled open, Iri pressed a hand to her heart, and Saychelle hissed, "*Visnprestas.*"

Ariadne's former sisters all joined their voices together, drowning out Salvotor's accusations, silencing his hate with a cry for their fellow acolyte with her dreams torn asunder, their friend ripped from their arms by this man's cruelty. They stood with her now, women of every color and shape, hoods cast back, eyes blazing, palms striking the wooden railing until it rattled, all their voices as one raising the chant high.

We are with you. We are with you. We are with you.

"Silence them!" Salvotor roared. "This disorder cannot be tolerated in the Courts!"

But no one moved to stop the tide of voices, the pounding hands, the cries in the ancient language soaring to the rafters, rattling the windows and shaking the courthouse to its very foundations.

"*Hal ulda viy, Malatanda!*"

That shout came from Tatiana, hands cupped around her mouth. Then from Ashe, gaze burning with pride. From Saychelle and Iri, tears streaming down their cheeks. And from Cistine's own lips, her fierce joy uncontainable, screaming the words with the others.

We are with you, sister. Hal ulda viy.

At a cut of Bravis's hand, the Vassora dragged Salvotor toward the gate. Still he fought, digging in his heels, spitting at Ariadne, "Thischanges nothing! No matter what they chant, you will never be one of them again!"

She raked him with a long look, the strategist sizing up her enemy as Branko unlocked the gate. "Perhaps not, but that will never stop me from praying. And I will pray for you, because I have what you've never known: healing from what broke me. I'm sorry no one ever tried to heal you."

Salvotor's head whipped back. "I need no healing. I am..."

But the shouts crowded out his words. It was a worthless posture, anyway; perhaps no two people understood brokenness like the boy turned to villainy by his father's cruelty, and the warrior he'd wounded by the arm of his own pain.

He was silent when the Vassora marched him from the courtroom. Aden was the first to break rank and stride out after them; Cistine chased him into the hallway, the rest of the cabal on their heels, even Thorne and

Ariadne. Side-by-side, they all watched Salvotor vanish around the bend in the corridor, flanked by his guards.

After several heartbeats of silence, Tatiana glanced at Ariadne. "Those women. They were..."

"From my acolyte school, yes. From our Order." She turned to Thorne. "You brought them here."

He nodded. "So you would know that no matter what happens, they never stopped believing, just as we've always believed in you. I barely had to ask...every temple I wrote to, anyone who knew the name *Ariadne* sent their reply in a matter of days. They came for *you*."

Her eyes glossed with emotion. She threw her arms around his neck, and for the first time, Cistine's stoic teacher and steady friend burst into sobs. "Thank you. *Thank you.*"

Thorne cradled her face to him, tears sliding through his dark stubble as well. "Laws can't dictate the heart. You are theirs as much as you'll always be ours. I wanted you to know they love you, too."

"And the gods love you," Aden added. "They aren't done with you yet."

Another sob ripped from Ariadne's chest. "I wasn't certain...before today, I could never be sure of that."

"*I'm* sure." Thorne pushed her out at arm's length and took her shoulders. "You are everything it means to truly be a Starchaser, Ariadne. And I'm proud to have you at my side."

Pride raised her chin, drying her tears so swiftly it was like she never cried. "Well, with the irreverent company you keep, someone must hold the balance."

Quill burst into laughter and swooped an arm around Ariadne's shoulders. "*It's done!*" He whooped so loudly Faer took flight to the windowsill with a cross squawk. "That *bandayo's* finished!"

Then they were all shouting and embracing at once, and Cistine laughed as they knocked each other back and forth in a jouncing tangle of arms. She didn't even realize they weren't alone until a throat cleared gruffly behind them.

Silent as shadows, six of Kanslar's Tribunes joined them in the hall—

Marcel no longer among them. The cabal broke apart to a silent, wary line again, regarding these men who'd met them at Thorne's swearing-in with such hostility.

"Chancellor," Njal of Eben spoke first. "Word has spread of how you thwarted Salvotor's schemes against Sander and the other High Tribunes."

Thorne's chin sank slightly. "If you came to bring a warning from my father, walk away."

"Actually, we came to apologize," Tribune Tadeas said. "High Tribune Sander was not as alone as he thought he was. Yes, we voted to have your title stripped, and we followed Salvotor's orders—some of us more willingly than others." The pause allowed for Marcel's notable absence. "But the Valgard Salvotor sought to create was not *our* vision."

"Why didn't you swear fealty to Thorne as soon as Salvotor was deposed, then?" Aden demanded.

"Why do you think?" Njal scowled. "He has our Names."

"What his men did to the High Tribunes is child's play compared to what he's done to us," Tribune Vaclav added. "Threatened us. Compelled us. Used our families as leverage."

"This is what it's meant to be a Tribune of Kanslar Court for more than a decade." Njal fixed Thorne with a piercing stare. "But you know this. It's why you chose to leave."

"A choice for which you all voted to have me whipped," Thorne said slowly. "But I'm beginning to think that may not have been as much out of spite as I once believed."

Njal folded his arms. "We've been watching you closely, wondering if you would become like your father. But last night, you fought for the Tribunes with your own hands. That's something I've never seen."

"It's a shame you haven't, because the Courts should always fight for their own," Thorne said. "I'm sorry your Chancellor never fought for *you*."

Njal eyed him shrewdly. "Something tells me that's going to change."

"Something tells *me* it already has," Tribune Hafgrim added.

After a long, thoughtful silence, Thorne smiled. "We need to have a chat, I think, you six and I. I want to know precisely what my father is holding against you so we can break his grip. I intend to make him fully aware you're under *my* protection now."

Njal dipped his chin. "Chancellor."

Vaclav, Hafgrim, Tadeas, Gunther, and Enar all mirrored him without a flicker of animosity in their faces. Then, as quickly and unexpectedly as they arrived, the Tribunes departed.

"And that," Aden checked Thorne's shoulder with his, "is how you make friends, *Mavbrat*."

Thorne checked him right back. "We'll see how that friendship holds in the days to come, when I remove Marcel from this position and place you on the Tribunal."

"Something tells me they'll be pleased to see another supporter of Salvotor removed from power." Bravis broke in on their conversation, striding from the courtroom with the other Chancellors in tow. "A fitting spectacle to end the utter spectacle of all this. Thank the stars that's over."

"What now?" Cistine asked.

"We'll do the appropriate thing, which is guarantee Salvotor a secure place in the prison. In the meantime, he'll be watched night and day by no less than twenty guards."

"I'd make it thirty," Benedikt grunted.

"I'll take that under advisement," Bravis smirked. "It's only appropriate, too, that we disseminate the verdict as efficiently as possible to the elites. I would think a celebratory feast should do the trick. Let him hear the music while he rots in his rooms."

"A feast it is." Valdemar rubbed his hands together. "And then I'd like to speak a bit more with Talheim's emissary. Now that we are allies, it's time to decide what that means precisely for trade."

"My pen is ready when yours is," Cistine grinned, and to her disbelief, he smiled back, then led the other Chancellors away discussing feasts and litigation; all but Thorne, who lingered with a hand on Ariadne's shoulder until the doors opened again and a stream of black robes flooded out, aiming straight toward them, Saychelle and Iri carried along in their midst.

The hall erupted in a storm of voices all at once, cries of Ariadne's name, prayers and shouts as different hands spun her left and right, and arms embraced her from every side. Above the din, she cried, "How did all of you even secure leave to come here?"

"We told the temples we were going, and if they couldn't make do without us for a few days, they would learn to make do without us forever," one girl smiled wolfishly.

"You risked your place in the Order for *me*?"

"Have you gone deaf?" Another woman knocked her knuckles on Ariadne's temple. "Did you not hear us in there?"

"*Malatanda.*" Someone else took Ariadne's face in her hands. "That will never change. Damn old creeds and ancient laws, you'll always be our sister. And now you're coming with us—we have so much to ask you about!"

Ariadne's head swiveled toward Thorne, and he jerked his chin. "Go. You have some catching up to do."

Her smile even brighter than her Name, Ariadne left the corridor encircled in her sisters' arms. Weightlessness broke through Cistine as she watched them go, the rest of her body finally catching up to what was accomplished. The treaty between their kingdoms was sealed now, Thorne's place on the Judgement Seat secured, and Salvotor only just beginning to pay for his crimes against Ariadne, the Courts, and Talheim.

Suddenly, Cistine could barely breathe.

Julian's *killer* was convicted.

Something small and light and frantic beat along her ribs—a grieving call that demanded to be heeded. She stepped back from the grinning cabal, and when Ashe's eyes cut to her, she forced a smile. "There's something I have to do. I'll see you all later."

At the end of the hall, she broke into a run, and didn't stop all the way to Kanslar's garden.

A hush blanketed the frozen hedges, the paths and fountain, when Cistine finally slowed, quieting her heavy breaths as she wove between the greenery. There was nothing in particular she was looking for, but when she spied a certain tree, it seemed fitting—an orange tree for the boy with the orange blossom tea.

She crouched at its base, cleared away tangles of brittle ivy and fallen leaves, and started digging.

She ought to be making a larger hole than this; a proper grave. There should be a funeral procession, complete with trumpets and standards and pipes, the kind her grandmother received at her interment; the kind that would one day be given for her father and mother, and then for her. Julian deserved that and more, but all she had to give was a small hole barely as wide around as her fist; and in that fist, the lightning-warped betrothal ring he'd given her in Veran all those months ago.

Tilling grave dirt was so different from tending a garden. The soil felt dead, clotted and thick under her fingernails. She yearned for her living gardens in Hellidom and Astoria, even for the box in her room...places of life and growth. But this had to be done.

When the hole was dug, she crouched on her heels and stared into it, imagining if there *had* been a body to return to Talheim to give Julian the burial he deserved; if she would've ever stopped crying, seeing his face so still, eyeless and disfigured and dead. Never coming back.

"I wish I could give you more." The words jarred out so suddenly they startled her. She hadn't thought any would come. "A Talheimic procession. All those banners and trumpets and drums. A few weeping girls for lasting effect. You would've laughed at that forever." She cuffed her face with her sleeve. "When we called off our courtship, I never saw our story ending like this. I told myself one day you'd find a woman to love who fit you perfectly in every way I couldn't. And I'm sorry you never had that, Julian. I'm sorry you never got to ride bareback through the fields at home again, or hug your mother or be a great Warden or rule Practica as one of my trusted advisors. I'm sorry Salvotor took that future away from you. From *us*."

Tears fell in earnest now; she didn't try to stop them.

"We made so many promises to each other. I wish we had a lifetime to keep them. But if nothing else, I'm glad I kept this one: I brought justice for you. The man who killed you will never be free to harm anyone else again. And now I..." Tears masked her lips, filling her tongue with the taste of salt. "Now I have to finish what you died for. I have to set myself free."

She opened her fist to stare at the betrothal band. "The truth is, keeping this never really made me feel closer to you. And I couldn't understand why when it was all I had left. But now I do."

She hesitated, letting out her breath on a sad, wondering laugh. How strange and unfair that it was easier to speak to Julian when he was dead than in those last few weeks they'd had together after Veran.

"It's because this ring was from the worst part of our courtship," she whispered. "I'd rather remember us when we were happy and everything made sense. That's how I'll honor your memory...by remembering the Warden you were going to be, and the man who served his princess to his dying breath. The man who made his kingdom proud."

She pressed a kiss to her knuckles, then dropped the ring into the shallow hole and slowly scooped the dirt back over it. As the dull glimmer disappeared, a strange weight lifted from her chest, different from all the other griefs she carried. All that remained of Julian was this ring, and it was right that it should live among the growing things, like a seed planted in the heart of Valgard, watered with her tears, sprouting a legacy of memories.

"You and I are Talheim's children. You are Talheim, Julian Bartos. And I'll carry you with me for the rest of my life." She scooped her hair back and bent down to kiss the mound of dirt—a last goodbye.

Someone said her name quietly from among the hedges, and she sat up, wiping her nose on her sleeve again. Ashe appeared through the dead foliage, kneeling at Cistine's side and smoothing her palm over the packed earth. "He was a good man. I think in time, he would've been a great one."

"If Rion had let him be, you mean."

Ashe shook her head. "He would've chosen you. If he lived long enough to see Rion with us in Keltei, if he faced the choices I did, he still would've chosen you. He always did...he proved that in the end."

Cistine followed Ashe's gesture, sweeping her hand over the soil where the last piece of Julian was laid to rest. "I couldn't keep carrying that part of him with me. It just felt like it was time to let go."

Ashe's hand covered hers gently on the mound, rough patches of her skin scraping against Cistine's. Frowning, Cistine snatched Ashe's wrist and flipped her hand over.

Her stomach plunged. There was a shape branded on Ashe's palm like a slave mark. "What is this?"

"A Wingmaiden's rune, apparently. You're not the only one who's allowed to swear unbreakable vows to wild things, you know."

"Bresnyar made you his left wing?"

"I chose to be."

Cistine blinked at Ashe's steady calm. "You're all right with this?"

"Better than all right. I always thought I was happy in the Cadre, but it was no more real than the love my parents claimed to have for each other." Ashe drew the starstone gently along its chain, her gaze fixed on the sky. "This is happiness, right here, right now, after everything we've learned and fought for and *won*. Bres and Maleck are the ones I want to share it with."

"And me?"

"Always you."

Cistine laid her head against her friend's. "I'm happy for you. And I'm glad you're home."

Ashe pressed a kiss to her hair. "It's good to finally be here."

They leaned against each other's shoulders, waiting for the sun to set on Salvotor's final day as a man of title, sharing the last of the daylight with the memory of Julian sitting beside them—three Talheimic wanderers in the wild north, watching the stars light up the night sky.

CHAPTER
SIXTY-ONE

THERE WAS RELIEF in escaping the courthouse chaos, visitors streaming constantly through its doors after the sentence came down. Already word traveled out to the territories of Salvotor's fate, concluding the most influential trial in recent memory. Even within the city where opinions were divided on the subject, there was a tinge of liberation on the air—and nowhere stronger than in Kadlin's house, where Tatiana, Quill, and Pippet joined her and Morten for supper two days after the trial ended. The household bustled with chattering servants still packing things for their departure, and Kadlin wore a wildcat's grin.

"Good riddance," she toasted over a platter of braised beef and potatoes, and they all raised their cups. "To sentencing the greatest stain on the Courts' reputation in a century or more."

"And to whatever comes after." Morten flashed Tatiana a smile.

"Quill, I see that hand is working marvelously for you," Kadlin remarked slyly as he spooned broth into his mouth.

"Oh, this?" He shot a fond look at the device. "It's a gift. Watch this."

He snapped his hand to the back of Pippet's neck, and she squealed, scrunching up. "*Cold!*"

Tatiana rolled her eyes. "That's exactly what I designed it for."

Pippet pouted. "Why do you like it when I suffer?"

"Because I'm a cruel sister. You thought brothers were the worst?"

"She's right, you know." Kadlin nodded sagely. "Sisters are of the Undertaker."

"Must we invite death to the table?" Morten stirred his soup moodily, and Tatiana shot him a fond smile.

One of the servants swept into the dining hall and spoke in a rapid whisper to Kadlin. She nodded and rose, a sliver of sadness in her smile. "Tatiana, might I borrow you for a moment?"

"As long as these three can behave in my absence."

To a braiding of protests from Quill, Pippet, and Morten, she followed Kadlin from the room, pausing only once to look back at her father, her *valenar*, and her sister all tackling their portions at an inventor's table. There was rightness to it, in the way of new beginnings.

They crossed the home to Kadlin's gallery, and on the way she explained, "I received a private commission for a specially-enhanced blade. It was expensive enough to buy our crossing to Blaykrone."

Tatiana whistled lowly. "Elite?"

"A Vassoran guard, actually, the very one who trained me: Branko. Do you know him?"

"In passing."

"Well, if you pass him again, I hoped you might deliver it to him." They entered Kadlin's rooms, a cave of cloth-wrapped delicates and dismantled display mounts. "I'd do it myself, but as you can see, I'm up to my elbows in all this."

"I can't imagine." Even in Hellidom, Tatiana had never owned so many things, and she left it all behind anyway when they raced into the wilds to find Cistine. She'd had precious little her whole life to move with her.

Perhaps that would change in Blaykrone, with her own house.

A harsh quiver of delight and nervous energy racked through her as they reached a writing desk on the far wall. Kadlin reached into the drawer and withdrew a cloth-wrapped parcel, laying its folds open to reveal a blade black as night. "Be sure to deliver this to Branko directly."

Tatiana took the weapon, marveling silently at its strange weight—

heftier on the blade than she was used to—then sheathing it in her belt. "Consider it done."

Kadlin leaned against the desk, facing her. "There was something else I wanted to discuss with you, but you've been so absent lately."

"I know, I know," she grimaced. "Cabal duties."

"It's all right. That's part of it, actually." Kadlin waved a hand. "About the investigation...I think it's time we laid it aside."

Tatiana stared at her. "But my father's schematics..."

"They're long gone by now." A sad smile crept over Kadlin's face. "I've arranged to tell him. The night of that feast everyone's discussing in the markets, we're going to have one of our own...a farewell of sorts. I'm going to apologize to him, and stars willing, salvage our friendship despite my carelessness."

"But—"

"Tati. It's all right." A hard note crept into Kadlin's voice. "It's over. The guild is leaving soon, and I don't want my last days with your father marked by secrets. It's time to let this go, do you hear me?"

Tatiana studied Kadlin while she rubbed her temples, a picture of dejection. "I was just going to say, maybe it doesn't have to end when you leave. Maybe I can help sort it out *after* we reach Blaykrone."

Kadlin's head snapped up again. "*We?*"

"That's assuming the thief wasn't one of Salvotor's spies, already snatched up in Bravis's dragnet. You haven't noticed anyone from the guild going missing, have you?"

"Tatiana!" Kadlin laughed. "You're coming with us?"

"We all are. Me, Quill, Pippet...and my father."

Kadlin pressed a palm to her mouth. "Stars...are you *absolutely* certain about this?"

"I've never been so sure of anything...well, except swearing the *valenar* oath with Quill," she grinned. "With the trial over, all I want now is peace for my family. And Blaykrone might as well be home. I can't think of anywhere I'd rather begin a new life."

CHAPTER
SIXTY-TWO

FOR THE HUNDREDTH time, Cistine reminded herself this was her choice. She'd talked with Mira for hours, taking her fears like battlefields, until all that remained was the decision itself; and knowing what hung in the balance, it was far easier to make.

She'd picked an armored, spidersilk dress for the feast and wore reinforced leggings beneath—a careful compromise. The modest neckline didn't suffocate and the sheer sleeves allowed no chill on her skin; the thin chain around her hips could serve as a weapon if needed.

It was all about control. Tonight, in this dress, she had it.

She was focused so hard on keeping her eyes closed while Tatiana lined her eyelids with kohl that she nearly jumped when a knock came at her apartment door. "Are you two ready yet?"

"Perfection takes time, Thorne," Tatiana sang back, patting Cistine's cheek to signal they were finished. She opened her eyes to behold her friend dressed in a plunging dark blue gown, Atrasat marks curling along her arms and down her back in the form of a raven's outstretched wings. She was a gleaming vision of night, a perfect complement to Cistine's daylight glow.

She stood from the edge of her bed and gave a twirl. "What do you think?"

Tatiana backed away, tapping the kohl stick against her lower lip.

"Flawless. How do you feel?"

Cistine smoothed her hands over the fabric. "Nervous. But I can't think of a better way to celebrate Salvotor's sentencing than in a dress."

"An armored one, no less. It's a spit in his face, and I love it." Tatiana kissed her forehead. "We'll be right there with you, *Yani*. Every step."

Smiling, Cistine dragged her out into the hall where the rest of the cabal assembled: Aden looking just a shade uncomfortable in his silver-fletched emerald jacket and trousers, Pippet with her hand looped into his elbow, her dress a stunning sky-blue chiffon that made her look far older than she was. Ariadne and Saychelle were mirrored contrasts, dark hair and a pale dress, silver hair and a black gown. Ashe wore cream trousers stuffed into polished boots and a silk shirt with the sleeves rolled up, baring the day-old inkings on her arms: twists of fire on one, curls of shadow on the other; the same as Maleck's, leaning against the wall beside her. Quill lounged on his other side, chewing a cinnamon stick, Faer roosting on the shoulder of his casual vest-and-shirt. And next to him, Thorne, dressed in a sleeker, more sophisticated version of his usual dark shirt and pants, the collar undone through several buttons, baring a slip more of his chest and star-charted inkings than Cistine could bear with dignity.

She swallowed and focused on his face instead, but that was worse. He wore a stunned expression like she put her knee into his groin.

"Cistine, you look..." He trailed off, shaking his head. "You look happy."

"I *am* happy." She grinned at them all. "And you all look wonderful."

"Don't we always?" Ashe pushed up from the wall, slinging a tooled brown leather jacket over her shoulder. "Ready, Princess?"

"I'm ready. Let's show them Valgard and Talheim united."

They followed chatter and distant music into the courthouse proper, where the stream of foot traffic thickened, almost bottling in the lower market and again near the steps to the fifteenth floor. Cistine's heart thudded so loudly she was certain everyone could hear it when the tall doors of the feasting room came into view, a string quartet wafting from the other side. She slowed, letting the tide of people move past her. Even the cabal kept going, swept up in the crowd.

The last time she wore a dress in this courthouse, she was so sick she fled—and some dark voice warned her it could happen again. At any moment, she could lose control.

No. Not tonight. Tonight is ours.

She twisted the ultramarine betrothal ring around her finger with the pad of her thumb, anchoring herself in the moment. They were celebrating a new season of life, and Cistine was defining her place in the world, taking back every last piece the former Chancellor peeled away from her.

There would be no more running. Not for her.

She stepped up to the doors, and the Vassoran guards nodded in passing recognition. "Ready for the feast, Princess?"

"Yes," she said. "Yes, I am."

She pushed forward into brilliant ghostlight, the phosphorescent plants crushed inside jewel-studded chandeliers that multiplied their glow. Red tones flirted with amber; green and gold married in beautiful swathes against the tiles. Blue and purple danced along the walls, a dreamy echo of her birthday celebration a lifetime ago, the night a princess's destiny forever altered. When Cistine Novacek decided to change the stars for her kingdom—and for herself.

Across the room, elite faces swiveled toward the steps. Eyes found her at the top: the princess. The emissary. The daughter of their new ally. The one who'd helped bring Salvotor to his knees and raise up a new face for their kingdom.

She lifted her chin, pressed her palms to her legs, and met their stares with a smile and a wolfish slide of teeth. She was just like them—a pretty thing wrapped over steel. Equal. Strong. And never to be trifled with.

She nearly jumped when Thorne's hand slid into hers. "They're not looking at that dress, you know. They're searching for a queen."

Cistine squeezed his hand three times. "Then let's show them one."

She tugged him down the steps to the floor, straight into the dance.

CHAPTER
SIXTY-THREE

SEVEN SONGS PASSED and Thorne could barely feel his feet anymore when Cistine declared her need for food. They wove toward the sitting tables dragged off to the sides of the feast, each with its own platter of stuffed boar, apples, and cheese. The cabal was already gathered around one; laughter perfumed the air, loudest of all from Sander and, to Thorne's surprise, Tribune Njal, who took up the seat between him and Mira.

Cistine flopped down next to Maleck and toed off her flats. "It's finally happened. I think I prefer boots over slippers."

"Perish the day," Ashe deadpanned. Cistine threw a shoe at her head, and she caught it, laughing.

"I'd forgotten what Stornhaz celebrations were like." Saychelle sagged in her seat, head on Ariadne's shoulder. "I'm too old for this excitement now."

"Much to my relief." Ariadne flicked her sister's ear.

"You're one to talk. Have you slept at *all* since the trial?"

Ariadne sipped her drink, brows peaking. "Here and there."

"She does have ten years of catching up to do with the other girls," Iri interceded with a glance around the dancing floor, where the visiting *visnprestas* celebrated the downfall of the man who stole their sister's future.

"What's that been like?" Cistine asked. "Seeing all your friends again."

"Painful." Ariadne's lips twisted. "But also healing. The divide between us was not as deep as I thought. In fact, I've been meaning to speak with you about that." She addressed the table at large, but her eyes were on Thorne, so he sat forward to pay her his full attention. "The *visnprestas* have a request to make of the Courts. They wish for training to defend themselves."

Saychelle straightened, blinking. "That's news to me."

"Me as well." Iri frowned. "But I won't say I'm surprised. What happened at Nygaten was bound to shake the other temples."

Ariadne nodded. "Not only that, but what happened to me...I am not the first, nor was I the last. There are many who do not know the law, or worse, do not fear it. As a woman who understands both the sacred and the sword, they want me to strategize a course for new acolytes to defend themselves and their temples. And to oversee their training personally, here in the city."

"I thought the gods protected the temples," Pippet said. "That's what they teach us in school, anyway."

Quill ruffled her hair. "Maybe the Order is catching on that the gods offer protection by gifting people like Ariadne with a talent for steel."

"I think that's wonderful!" Cistine squeezed Ariadne's hand. "You must be so happy, having the chance to serve with your friends again."

"I am, but not like I thought I would be. This doesn't give me purpose, I already *had* purpose." She turned her smile to each of them, lingering on Mira the longest. "I suppose that's the answer to a question, isn't it? The chance to use my blades and my knowledge to help others."

Grinning, Mira raised her glass. "To prayers answered."

"Whatever help you require, it's yours," Thorne added.

Ariadne's smile was radiant. "Thank you, Chancellor."

Tatiana flicked water at her. "Let us know any help we can be from Blaykrone."

Quill nodded. "I'm ready to have my haunches handed to me dueling *visnprestas*. Besides, my current student hardly needs me anymore."

"I'll always need you," Cistine yawned, helping herself to more apples.

Their words were a melancholy reminder that after tonight, things would change. Tatiana, Quill, and Pippet wouldn't linger long. Ariadne might travel to the temples, perhaps even with Iri and Saychelle when they returned to Keltei. And there was little guessing whether Ashe and Maleck would stay or go, with a dragon who could carry them anywhere. The firm foundation of five warriors in the wilds was slowly breaking apart, everything Thorne leaned on for ten long years coming undone around him.

And yet Sander was here, and Mira, reclining in his embrace; Njal, who'd come to Thorne's chambers the past two nights to discuss the needs of Eben; and Aden, on whom he'd come to rely again like brothers fighting their way back to one another across an impossible warground. And for the next full year, he had Cistine.

Life was changing, but that was no reason to give up hope. This was what it was to be Chancellor—to put the people's needs before his own and make the most of the time he was given with the ones he loved.

Pippet pushed back from the table abruptly, clapping her hands. "Tonight has been so perfect. I want to make a picture of it!"

Quill narrowed his eyes. "I told you to leave that thing in your room."

She swooped under her chair to retrieve her lightbox. "I know, but I didn't listen. It could be worse, I could be gambling! *Please*, Quill?"

All it took was a bat of her eyelids, and he gave way.

"All of you, up!" Iri laughed, and they pushed back from the table with varying degrees of halfhearted protest. "I'll take that box."

"Everyone, around me!" Pippet ordered, and they crowded in, arms flung around necks and backs, all tilted forward and sideways to fit. Quill circled his sister's waist with his brawny arms, and when Iri gave them the count of three, he swept her up, her squeals of laughter shattering like the light that bloomed from the box. Thorne's eyes watered, but his face hurt harder from laughing. Maleck didn't let him go right away, giving him a sharp shake before he released him; then the cabal was off, tugging one another into dances, the light waking them up from their drowsy contentment—all except Cistine. She stood rooted where they left her, one hand to her stomach, the other clinging to the back of Pippet's empty seat.

A flutter of pain crossed her face.

Skin prickling, Thorne stepped nearer to her. "Cistine?"

She sucked in a breath and pivoted toward him. "What? I'm sorry, did you say something?"

He rested a hand on her shoulder. "What is it? A memory? My father?"

"Not that." She smoothed her hand uneasily over her middle. "I'm sure it's nothing, just...the crowd. It makes me anxious after a while."

"Do we need to leave?"

A determined frown sliced into her brow. "Not a chance. Dance with me, Thorne."

There was something different in her grip when she dragged him into the middle of the room this time, her hand a cage around his, her face full of anger. Like she was taking, not a dance floor, but a battlefield.

Thorne danced with her long past the point of pleasure and into pain, when his fine boots bit into his toes and his calves ached in a way that for once had nothing to do with the course of his thoughts. Yet he danced on, following her steps, trusting her needs, letting her guide him from song to song until they were both sweat-soaked and panting.

Still, the peace didn't return to her face.

"I'm going to get a drink," she announced between one song and the next, and slipped off into the crowd without a backward glance, leaving him bemused in the sea of dancers. Dragging a hand through his damp hair, he gazed after her, at war with himself over whether he should follow.

But if she wanted him along, she would invite him. So he returned to the cabal's table instead.

A few of them had drifted back for more food and conversation: Mira and Saychelle bent on the arms of their seats, chattering away, while Maleck sat next to Pippet and rubbed her back. Chin in her hands, she nodded off with every stroke of this knuckles down her spine.

Thorne braced one hand on each of their seatbacks, taking the weight off his throbbing legs. "I think this one needs her bed."

"Not tired," she slurred, eyes still shut.

"And I'm not a Chancellor." Thorne drew out Pippet's chair, jolting her when her elbows slid off the table. "Come on, Hatchling."

She scooped up her lightbox with a yawn and bent to kiss Maleck's cheek. "Goodnight, Darkwind."

His smile as relaxed as the rest of him, Maleck leaned into her kiss. "Tracking lessons in the morning. Don't forget."

Beaming sleepily, she sagged into Thorne while he steered her along the edge of the dance toward the staircase. He caught Quill's eye through the crowd, mouthed *Bed*, and gestured down to Pippet. Quill saluted and sucked his lip in, whistling; the sound barely cut above the music, but Faer swooped from the rafters, alighting on Pippet's shoulder with a gentle pinch of talons. With a smirk, Quill went back to spinning Tatiana across the dance floor.

It was mercifully quieter in the halls; ten years in hiding had worn down Thorne's already-scant interest in festivities. The tension eased from his muscles the moment they stepped into the deserted courtyard robed in shadows from the high walls and statues, not so much as a guard in sight.

"I'm going to miss parties like this." Pippet's tone was forlorn, her gaze wandering around the courtyard like it was the last time.

"Blaykrone is plenty capable of hosting a good dance," Thorne assured her. "And if they're lacking, you can teach them. Host parties of your own."

Pippet blinked up at him, eyes shining. "Do you really think I should?"

He flicked her nose. "With your brother's permission, yes."

She stuck out her tongue, then hugged his waist and slumped against him again. "I'm going to miss *you*, *Allet*."

"And I you." Thorne tucked her tightly to him, careful not to disturb Faer from his roost. "But you'll come back to visit...and you'll have to return on your own eventually to begin training as a Tribune."

Pippet grinned, nestling her head under his arm.

They entered Kanslar's wing in silence, and Thorne savored that pause, the world holding its breath, only the faintest hint of the faraway dance whispering in the walls.

Then they stepped into the bedchamber corridor and spied a figure, hooded and cloaked, picking the lock on Pippet's door.

Thorne slammed to a halt, limbs going taut, but Pippet spoke before he could silence her. "*Excuse* me, what are you doing? Those are *my* rooms!"

The man froze, gnarled hands going still, and Thorne knew—even before he pivoted and straightened, turning back his hood, revealing his scarred, bald head and perpetual leer.

Devitrius.

Faer croaked a warning, and Thorne swept out an arm, pushing Pippet behind him. "How did you get in here?"

"If I told you, you'd wet yourself." His father's man stalked toward them, hand drifting to the whip belted at his waist. "Did you really think by sealing your own creeping holes to and from this city, you were ever safe?"

Thorne gave ground one step at a time, shifting Pippet closer to the hall where they'd entered. "It sounds like you had it all plotted out. But unfortunately for you, my father is not in that room."

Devitrius scoffed. "*I'm* not here for him."

There it was—the faint tell in the flicker of his accent. He wasn't alone. "Then why are *you* here?"

Devitrius flicked his gaze past Thorne to Pippet.

Icy dread and hot fury braided together in Thorne's chest. He settled his stance, bracing his feet; he wouldn't give one more step before his father's most powerful ally. "Then you came to die."

"We'll see."

Before Devitrius's blades left their scabbards, Thorne dropped to one knee and spun, kicking his ankles out from under him. Two fingers in his mouth, he whistled a command to Faer; the raven lifted off, shooting down the corridor, and Devitrius rocked to the side and aimed his knife. Screaming, Pippet cast her lightbox aside and dove at him, slamming into his knife arm—but too late. The blade sang out, ripping across Faer's back. The raven floundered, collided with the wall, and flopped across the rug, blood streaking his wake.

Pippet ran to him, and Thorne leaped on Devitrius, scooping up the thrown blade as he went. His father's man met him knife-for-knife, a wicked dance of metal spitting sparks as they spun down the ghostlit hall. Cold air bit into Thorne's face when Pippet flung open the window at the end of the corridor and sent Faer out, repeating the whistle to dispatch him for aid—sounding the alarm.

In the brief heartbeat Thorne was distracted by them, Devitrius winnowed in. Their blades locked at the grip at chest-height, and his elbow, thick as stone, slammed into Thorne's chin, snapping his head back so hard blackness blotted his vision. He crashed against the wall, hand springing open around the knife, all the air gushing from his lungs at once. Devitrius lunged for the discarded weapon.

But Pippet was already there, fearless like Ashe and Aden and as mad as her brother, kicking the knife down the corridor and spinning in a dancer's pirouette with the same movement, cracking her knee into Devitrius's jaw. He stumbled, swearing, and she was after him like a wildcat, kicking and hitting and clawing at his face. Thorne choked down air and pushed up from the wall, gasping her name, but it was too late; by the time he reached the knife, Devitrius had overpowered her. In two blows, he set Pippet's nose bleeding; then he caught her by the mouth and spun her around, pulling her against his chest and pressing his own serrated blade to the leaping pulse at the side of her neck.

Thorne froze, panic sparking in every nerve, chest heaving, the knife an unbearable weight in his hand.

"Drop it," Devitrius ordered, "or I'll spill her throat."

Thorne measured the distance and how quickly Pippet could break that hold with her nose broken and tears swimming in her eyes; how long it would take his blade to soar and lodge in Devitrius's forehead and whether the drag as he fell would end Pippet's life.

Then, cursing, he hurled the knife down, embedding it in the floor.

Pippet's eyes blew wide, a muffled shriek bursting from her chest. She thrashed and bit down on the hand covering her mouth, twisted her head free and screamed his name—not in terror, but a warning.

Thorne pivoted.

A *Svarkyst* blade pierced down above his clavicle, into his chest. Crunching bone. Tearing sinew. Setting loose a torrent of blood down his front, *inside* him, so swiftly and deeply he didn't even feel pain.

And over the hilt of that dagger, his father's eyes, cold, merciless, boring into his. Behind him, Rakel, her stare as void as Salvotor's was ruthless, unchanged while her husband twisted his black blade deeper into their only son.

Thorne's mind ordered him to strike—this close, he could wrap his hands around Salvotor's throat—but talons of pain held his limbs in a vise. He couldn't move, couldn't draw a full breath even to give voice to the agony bellowing in heaves through his body.

Salvotor jerked him close by the back of his neck. "Actually, boy, I *win*."

He cast him to the floor. The impact jolted fresh pain through Thorne's body that numbed too quickly, telling him everything he needed to know about this injury, about that blade and what was happening to him. But he grabbed at the carpet anyway, soaked with his blood, and tried to get his feet beneath him when Devitrius roared and cursed again. Then there were hands on Thorne, scrabbling at his back, trying to drag him up to his elbows. Pippet sobbed at him to get up, get up, *get up*.

He tried, but he broke down again and again, choking on blood, on her name, while her hands tore against his shoulders and then peeled away.

Her sobs turned to furious screams. His name. Over and over.

Salvotor had her, his arm around her waist, hauling her away. Pippet kicked and flailed, drilling elbow jabs and kicks into his body precisely how they'd trained her; but against his reinforced flesh, it did nothing at all. Devitrius, bleeding from Pippet's punch to his mouth, and Rakel, tall and wicked as a sheathed blade, flanked them up the hall.

They were escaping. Taking Pippet with them.

Panic sliced through the pain-addled fog, and Thorne made one last valiant effort to crawl after them, gasping Pippet's name. She gave up fighting and reached for him, tears streaming down her cheeks.

He reached back with everything he had left. He was still reaching for her when the darkness claimed him.

CHAPTER
SIXTY-FOUR

THE FEELING OF darkness returned with the flash of Pippet's augmented lightbox; after nothing but tendril traces since Nygaten, its vicious reappearance shook Cistine to her core. She tried to ignore it by dancing and eating and drinking, but nothing helped. It festered deep in her throbbing middle even when she curled up in her chair at the table, trying in vain to focus on the story Ashe was telling about Maleck dressed up as a vendor, giving a rose to the Queen.

She should've been in stitches about it, but something was wrong and growing worse. Even pressing on the compass pendant, visualizing Darlaska, and turning her betrothal band around her finger did absolutely nothing to distract her. A piece of her was separating from the rest, drifting off into some dark void—stealing her attention with it.

She flinched when Quill and Tatiana flopped down at the table, her on his lap, his arm slung around her waist. "Did we miss anything?"

"Maleck in a hat," Aden chuckled, sipping his mead.

Quill slapped the table. "I demand to hear this tale *from the beginning*."

Ashe groaned. "God's bones. I forgot how much I *didn't* miss you."

Tatiana toasted with a mug of water. "The feeling was mutual."

Ariadne bent away from her conversation with Mira and Saychelle, a frown sketching her brow. "Cistine?"

She blinked rapidly, trying to come back to them, reaching for her voice buried deep under her straining ribcage.

Up by the steps, someone shouted in surprise, disgusted gasps following a shrieking knot of black feathers that shot down from the door; the whole cabal leaped to its feet as Faer plowed into the table, knocking dishes everywhere. Quill bellowed the raven's name, panic rending his voice, and scooped him up. A gouge on his back dripped blood on Quill's bare hands, and Tatiana's when she helped support him.

"What *happened* to him?" Cistine shouted.

"I don't know, something must've attacked him! A hawk, maybe?" Quill bundled up a discarded cloth napkin and pressed it to Faer's bleeding back. "I sent him out with Pippet and Thorne, he was supposed to stay with her! Someone get us a healing augment!"

Cistine stared motionless at Quill, his words dropping through her one by one like stones loosed from a great height.

Faer had gone, but he'd been sent back to them—a warning.

"Cistine?" Ashe growled.

The drumming in her chest, the fraying sensation in her spirit—

Salvotor. She didn't know how she knew. But she did.

Not only that. Thorne was in danger. Thorne was *dying*.

Louder than the call of the Doors, louder than anything she'd ever heard, his name roared through her—love's last defiant scream in the face of death.

Cistine hiked up her skirt and ripped the wind augment from the pouch belted around her thigh, then hesitated.

It might be a trap. Salvotor might take her again.

She didn't care.

She shattered the flagon between her palms. At the force of its unleashing, the torrents of power howling loose to her summons, every window in the room exploded outward, a deadly constellation touched by the power of the gods. And Cistine let that power carry her away.

She had just enough control to know when those gods-sent winds bore her out of the courthouse, into the courtyard, and through the arched doorway into Kanslar's halls. Dispatching the augment with a snap of her wrists like slowing a downhill descent, she skidded and slid on her heels, slamming to a halt at the mouth of the cabal's bedchamber corridor—all closed, all untouched, every ghostlamp dimmed.

But still she saw him.

Thorne was sprawled on his chest halfway down the hall, a discarded knife just out of reach stained in blood, his arms akimbo as if he'd dragged himself after his attackers. Pippet was nowhere to be seen, but her lightbox lay broken in half on the floor.

Cistine registered all of this before she reached Thorne, before she tumbled down, fingernails stroking from his shoulders down to the small of his back, searching for wounds. A thin trickle of blood seeped through the back of his shirt, but that was all.

When she maneuvered him onto his side, she found the puddle below him. The shredded strip of his shirt showed blood plumping from his collar, close to his heart. Too close.

She screamed for help, even knowing if there had been anyone nearby, this couldn't have happened. There was no one, just her and Thorne, his eyes shut and breath rasping slowly from his lips. She ripped his fine shirt apart, baring the injury to what little light remained. Balling up the hem of her dress, she pressed against the wound.

"Thorne." Her voice shook, yet her hands held steady. They had to. No one else was here to help. "Thorne, I know you can hear me. Look at me, Starchaser!"

At his Name, a tinge of consciousness crept in. His breaths hitched, and he moaned, a shattered sound of pain that tried and failed to become her name.

"There you are." She peeled back the wad of bloodsoaked fabric and fresh panic screamed through her. There was something wrong with this wound; the blood wasn't coagulating, and the edges pulsed a sickly, purulent yellow-white. But it couldn't be infected, not in mere minutes.

She rubbed her bloodstained fingertips together and found grit to the substance.

Poison.

Silence clanged through Cistine's head and stilled her hands. She stared at her *selvenar's* face, his flickering eyelids as he fought to stay conscious. Another scream built in her throat, but she swallowed it back. She wouldn't sit here and cry for help while he bled to death. She'd sworn she would never be helpless again when a friend was poisoned.

She could mend this. She knew what it was, the texture, the color: bloodroam, Niklause had called it the night of the Tribune's dance—a Tyve poison often forged into blades to create unclotting wounds not even a healing augment could close. The counteragent was a poultice of sweetsap...a northern delicacy to drink, a fragrance used in potpourri. Thorne had planted it in her bedroom garden.

She ducked under his arm and yanked him forward, sitting him up on his knees. His head lolled, his body arching in a pained spasm as she pressed her hand uselessly to the bloodied slit on his chest. "Thorne, I need you to help. I need you to get *up!*"

She heaved with the last word, and his weight barreled into her, knocking them both against the wall. Muscles throbbing, she dragged him the six agonizing paces to her door and crashed inside, hauling him onto the bed. Then she fell to her knees beside her garden, uncovering the sweetsap and tearing it at the root. She crushed it in her mortar and pestle, gaze flying between her work and Thorne splayed on the bed, his chest rising and falling weakly.

Chanting prayers under her breath, she drizzled in the sap from the leaf and lunged back to the bed. When she grabbed Thorne's shoulder, his hand crawled up to meet hers and squeezed three times.

"*No!*" Her shout jerked his eyes wide open and yanked his breath in so deeply, it sounded like a death rattle. "I forbid you to say that if it means goodbye! I'm not letting you go, Starchaser. You made me a promise—you still have to marry me!"

She packed the poultice over the wound while she rambled, pressing down on the tacky leaves with all her might and praying with everything in her that it would bond and draw the poison out. Aloud, her rambles turned to a desperate mantra: just his Name, over and over, a tether to reel him out of the darkness when his eyes started to close and his stomach lurched—two quick flutters of pain tightening his abdomen for every breath he took.

The door slammed open, and Maleck barked her name. He and Aden filled up the doorway like twin storms, death and rage embodied.

"Healing augment!" she cried, though she didn't yet know if the sweetsap had pulled out the toxins enough for the wound to knit shut.

Maleck's weight landed on the bed, Thorne between them, and he cursed quietly. "He needs a blood augment as well."

Then he was gone again, Aden sliding into his place, and the radiance of a healing augment broke open and spilled from his hand. He laid his palm on his cousin's wounded chest, the other brushing through Thorne's hair like a child sick with fever, not a man dying of bloodloss. He murmured under his breath, words blurring together, long seconds passing before the harsh syllables made sense.

Don't you leave me, don't leave me, don't leave. A cry Cistine's heart echoed, that her lips took up as another prayer.

Finally, Maleck returned, throwing a deep crimson flagon to Cistine. The moment she broke it, she felt the difference in its power. Violent—not in the way of battle, but in the way of altering things. Energy forced itself from her fingertips and shoved brutally into Thorne, joining them like marionette strings twined around her knuckles. It sizzled in his bloodpaths, forcing through every crevice, kicking his heartbeat into a reckless cadence. His breaths heaved, but Cistine didn't pull back. Tears dripped from her jaw as she and Aden worked over Thorne in tandem, her blood to his healing, and Maleck sank to his knees at the bed's edge, hands clasped, eyes fixed unblinking on his Chancellor.

At long last, the bleeding eased. Thorne's breaths deepened beyond those terrified staccato heaves, and his eyes opened wider and focused. He rasped Aden's name. Maleck's. Then hers.

Cistine could've flung her arms around him, but she was too frightened to let go of the blood augment yet. She held the flow between them, ebbing in and out of his body, restoring what he lost until Aden reached over and clasped her wrist. "Enough."

She called the augment back and shook out the power like tongues of scarlet lightning. Then she hurtled into Thorne, wrapped her arms around his neck, and held on with all the strength she had left. His arm struggled around her waist, gripping her to him while he lurched upright, steadied by his friends. It was a full minute before he caught his breath enough to speak.

"Pippet."

The relief shattered, and Cistine yanked back, looking into his hate-stricken eyes as footsteps pounded down the hall. Quill, Ariadne, and Ashe slid to a halt inside the room; Tatiana swore profanely out in the hall.

"Where's my sister?" Quill snarled.

"Salvotor has her," Thorne panted. "Devitrius and Rakel are with him."

Ariadne's brows knitted. "How did they enter the city? The Vassora are watching every way in and out, even the sewers!"

"Check those patrols. I'd bet every dress in my closet they were redeployed." Tatiana's voice ripped between their ranks, and they parted to frame her in the doorway, her shaking hand clutched around the blood-soaked knife Cistine had left in the hall. She stared down at it, lips pursed like she might cry. "Where did this come from?"

Thorne's arm tightened around Cistine. "My father stabbed me with it. It's inlaid with poison."

Tatiana's eyes flashed to him, then dropped again. "I have to go."

"Tati!" Quill snagged her arm when she turned. "He has *Pippet!*"

She shook her head. "Go save her, Featherbrain. This is for me to do." She ripped from his grasp and vanished into the hall.

"Let her go," Thorne ordered when Quill jolted a step after her. "We'll find Pippet. Is Faer fit to fly?"

Quill whirled back to his Chancellor, jaw clenched. "Healing augment. He's in good shape."

"Then send him out to track her," Thorne ordered. "All of you, gather your weapons. We hunt. *Now.*"

CHAPTER SIXTY-FIVE

TATIANA DIDN'T WANT to believe it. With every pounding footfall carrying her through the dark, empty streets, she tried to conjure up some excuse, an explanation that didn't break her heart. But she knew, even if she couldn't accept it...otherwise she wouldn't be here when Pippet was missing.

She had to stanch this hidden bleed before it killed them all.

Her lungs seared and her chest felt shrunken to a needle's point by the time she reached the familiar home and burst inside, not bothering to knock for once—and entered to the sight of her father with Kadlin in his arms, bending his face to kiss her.

"*Stop!*" Tatiana shouted, and they startled so badly they staggered opposite ways, breaking apart. "Get away from her, Papa, she's not who you think she is!"

"Tati!" Morten's face colored. "What's gotten into you? What are you *doing* here?"

"I said, *get away from her*." Tatiana stalked toward them, and Kadlin backed away, palms bared in surrender.

"Tatiana, whatever this is, if I've offended you in some way by my feelings for your father—"

"As if I give a damn about your *stars-forsaken* feelings! If you truly *have* them!" Tatiana snarled, still advancing. "What did you *feel* when you lied to me all this time? How did you *feel* when you made me deliver the knife Salvotor just used to try and *murder* my Chancellor?" She hurled the black blade down, embedding its tip in the low table between the sofas.

Silence descended, dizzyingly thick, as they all stared at the weapon.

"Was it Salvotor's idea?" Tatiana hissed. "Yours? Branko's? How long has that *bandayo* been sending messages in and out of the city to Rakel and Devitrius, telling them where and when to strike? Or was that you, too?"

Kadlin didn't take her eyes off the blade. "It was both of us. First the Chancellor to Branko, and then through me."

Tatiana lunged at her, but Morten caught her around the waist and dragged her back, eyes fixed on Kadlin's anguished face. "You—but *why*?"

"Because she's a spy!" Tatiana shouted. "She's a traitor, one of Salvotor's loyalists—"

"No! I despise that *bandayo* for what he did to this city, to Blaykrone," Kadlin cried. "That knife was the end of it, he was supposed to set me free!"

Tatiana stopped struggling, that familiar word echoing every hope she'd ever held at bringing Salvotor to his knees. Morten echoed quietly, "Free?"

"You remember your schematics?" Kadlin's voice rolled with unshed tears.

"Of course I do. You've been looking over them for me."

Kadlin slowly shook her head. "I haven't had them for months. They were stolen, so I employed Tatiana and Quill to help me find them. But Branko admitted he stole them during one of our monthly suppers. When he realized we were searching for those missing plans, he told Salvotor." She thumbed her lashes dry. "That *bandayo* threatened to have me tried for treason, and when I didn't yield, he threatened *Heimli Nyfadengar*, every member of my family...he threatened both of *you* unless I agreed to courier the communications to Devitrius. Then it was ransacking High Tribune Sander's room. Then deciphering the journals and reporting on the High Tribunes. Then forging the knife. But he swore that was the end of it, he *swore*..."

Tatiana wrenched free of her father's hold, but not to attack. Not yet. "What was in those plans? Why would he try you for *treason* over them?"

Morten answered, barely louder than a whisper, "It was a siege tower."

Tatiana whirled on him, shock prying her jaws apart. "You were building *battle* plans?"

"For Thorne. I thought perhaps one day he would need a way into the city. Kadlin was lending her insight as a former Vassoran guard."

Tatiana turned back on Kadlin. "That's why you wanted to stop the hunt after I came back from Siralek, isn't it? Salvotor got to you while I was gone."

Kadlin nodded. "It was my cooperation or the end of everyone and everything I ever loved."

"Why didn't you just *tell* me? I would've done anything to help you!"

"And I you." Kadlin dashed more tears from her lashes. "When you agreed to come with us, I thought perhaps I could redeem myself by laying the world at your feet. By being everything you and your father needed."

"I don't need anything from you! Your knife was in Thorne's chest tonight! Pippet was *taken* because of you!"

Kadlin's eyes leaped wide, horror hollowing her cheeks. "*Taken?*"

A guttural blast of sound rattled the rafters. They all looked up at once. "What was that?" Tatiana breathed.

Morten paled. "The city's siege horn. It's never been blown before."

Tatiana lunged for the steps leading up to the roof, Kadlin and her father on her heels. They burst out onto the flat, railed span, and Tatiana skidded to the edge, staring at the city wall. Her stomach plunged, her mind screaming that what she saw was wrong, unnatural, impossible.

But it was there nonetheless, defying all reason.

The siege tower emerged like a specter from the shadows, higher than the wall itself—so high there was no need of wind augments or ladders or barges to enter the city. And not just one. They were everywhere, appearing around the wall at the north, south, east and west, then between those points, each one so close it should've been spotted already, the alarm raised *hours* ago.

But there'd been no warning.

The first tower slammed its piked bridge atop the wall, unleashing dark shapes onto the walkway who rammed against the Vassora posted there like a battering ram and broke them down. Their ranks were spread so thin by the attacks on Detlyse Halet, Siralek, and Nygaten Temple, precious few remained to defend the city. And Branko commanded those who remained.

Morten's head jerked in disbelief. "This was not in my plans, not like this. Not this height, and not this...this *invisibility!*"

"They found some way to enhance them." Kadlin paced like a caged wildcat beholding the siege. "Look at them, Mort, they're using mirrors and light augments!"

"Bending the light around the towers," Tatiana said through clenched teeth. "That's why no one raised the alarm...they couldn't *see* them."

"Not my doing," Morten whispered. "But who—?"

A blast of fire smoked the sky. Ice ripped down the wall, cracking nearby homes off their foundations. Familiar sensations of power swiveled together on the air, a precise taste of cruel might. Something she'd only ever tasted once before.

Tatiana caught her breath. *Oh, stars, no. Not here, not here...*

But there was no denying what was coming. She should've known.

Sliding the knife from her thigh-scabbard, she stepped to the edge of the roof. "Go. Get out of the city, both of you, while you still can."

"Tatiana." Kadlin's voice broke. "I'm so sorry. Salvotor already had the city, I didn't think he would ever *need* to—"

"He isn't. It's not just him."

She gripped the railing and crouched to spring, but her father caught her arm, desperation burning in his soft brown eyes. "No, *Tatiyani*. Come with us. *Please.*"

She looked into his face, perhaps for the last time. "I love you, Papa."

Then she kissed his cheek and vaulted over the edge.

CHAPTER
SIXTY-SIX

C ISTINE THOUGHT SHE knew fear before; but when that horn blew, when the windows flew open on countless homes and shops throughout Stornhaz's streets and the screams and prayers rose like smoke, terror dragged her down to new levels and flung wide the doors of her panic, revealing a horror she'd never yet danced with. And against a sky burning with darkness and stars, black towers shed the cloak of shadows that carried them this far and loomed into sight, one by one, each silhouette jagged-tipped like a crown of volcanic glass higher than the wall itself.

"How did Rakel and Devitrius have all these built?" Aden snarled while they ran. "They're only two!"

"No. They're far more than that," Ariadne said grimly. "They have the criminals of Siralek and Detlyse Halet. Hundreds of men."

This was the plan; every move and countermove across the weeks had dredged up an army at Salvotor's command, furious criminals with years of hatred boiling in their blood. They hadn't just come here tonight to take their Chancellor back; they'd come to take the city by force.

The sensation of world-ending doom soaked these streets, sucking at Cistine's heels as she fought to keep pace with the cabal, following Devitrius, Rakel, and Salvotor's trail. *Pippet's* trail. Somehow Thorne led them without faltering, halting only occasionally to spot Faer tracking above them. Then he turned the cabal's course, and they were off again.

They rounded a corner through one of the elite districts, and from above there came a tremendous crash as the first siege tower unleashed its ramp, pikes slamming into the stone and digging deep. Shards of rock sprayed down, some fist-sized, others as large as a man. The cabal scattered and dodged, Thorne's shout pulling them together again when the shower ended, leading them on.

All but Cistine.

The foreboding sensation stopped her, staining the multicolored avenues dark as ink, a strange rottenness clinging to the buildings and hugging the tips of her boots in liquid shadow. She turned away toward the source, stepping into a long, narrow alley off to one side and calling over her shoulder, "*Thorne?*"

Not answer but the resonation of cries from above, rage and agony as guards fell.

They needed to find Pippet. They needed to stop Salvotor, Rakel, and Devitrius before this scheme played itself out.

And yet...

Come. The familiar sensation, gentler now than ever since they came to Stornhaz, beckoned down the alleyway. *Come and see.*

Teeth gritted, Cistine heeded the call.

At the alley's opposite end, smoke hemmed the air in a thick curtain, shrouding an inner plaza ringed with homes and shops. Everything wood had already gone up in flames; a statue of Kanslar, the Conquering King, watched with emotionless bronze eyes as the city of his descendants fell under siege. Shivering beneath his dead stare, Cistine followed the thread of darkness up a broad set of steps to a tall, steepled building, the largest and last standing in the stone yard.

The interior was magnificent caramel marble, colonnades and pillars and arches chiseled in sharp relief, and at the aft of the atrium, wider than it was deep, a span of shallow steps led up to another imperious statue, this one hewn of stone glittering white like new snow. The figure faced its back to the world and its front to the rear wall mosaiced in color-stained glass, arms spread low in benevolent warmth—an embrace welcoming the world.

Cistine caught her breath at the glory of the firelight glazing through the window, texturing the marble with flames reflected in every color known to man—and at the man himself, if he could be called that, who stood between her and the statute. His black shroud contrasted in every way with the carving's light, from the heels of his boots up the impossible nine-foot height of him, all the way to where his hood ended and a tangle of antlers grew up another several feet.

Two realizations jammed through her like blades.

She'd seen this man before—in Nygaten Temple. She hadn't realized how tall he was, and he hadn't had the antlers then, but it was him. Because now, just like then, he was the source of the decay soaking the air.

"You shouldn't be here." The words leaped from her lips—an accusation.

The man didn't stir.

"I remember you," Cistine added, pacing toward him on silent feet and blessing the marble that muffled her flats with every step. "You were at Nygaten Temple...you killed the *visnprests,* didn't you, when they wouldn't help you with this...this *siege?*" The words tumbled out as quickly as her mind made the connections. "Who in God's name do you think you are? What gives you any right to kill these people, to kill *visnprests,* to come into this city like—"

"I have the only right."

His voice was death and cruelty, freezing her in place.

The door slammed shut under the force of an augmented wind. A low chuckle, familiar, hated, filled the atrium. "You see? I told you they would leave the courthouse for the child. And I told you *she* would come to us once she felt you. Painless as can be."

Cistine whirled, heart in her throat, pulse kicking in her wrists and temples as Salvotor swaggered into view. Hatred drove out her fear as she fisted her hands, gauntlet creaking—the only piece of armor she'd had time to fit on before they chased after Pippet.

It was too familiar, too much like Eben's plains. This had always been the cabal's weakness, and once again Salvotor exploited it masterfully.

"Where is she?" Cistine growled.

"Rakel and Devitrius have already delivered the girl." Salvotor's gaze flicked past her. "A good faith gesture to our new friend."

Cistine sidestepped twice so she could turn, exposing her back to neither man.

"You lied to me, Wildheart." Salvotor's voice curled around her Name, sliding into her mind like poison, stopping her again. "You were a very good little performer, but my ally here informed me of the truth." He took a step toward her, and she fought not to shrink back from the cold rage in his eyes. "There never was a ritual for the Key. I could've forgone all that mess with Thorne and simply slit your throat the day I killed the Butcher's son."

Cistine's gaze leaped between them—Salvotor, eyeing her like a wildcat with prey, and the man gazing up at the statue who somehow revealed what Cistine hid in Kalt Hasa: the sham ritual, the trinkets and pieces that helped save their lives.

"Did you hold him?"

Salvotor's question drew her focus back to him. "What?"

"Thorne." Salvotor spat his name like a filthy word. "Did you reach him before the end? Cradle him while he died? Did you know the knife was given to me by a friend of Tatiana's? She's been sniffing at the heels of all this for too long...that tinker's daughter always had a knack for interfering, ever since she was a girl. I hope she knows her ignorance delivered the weapon straight into my hand."

Rage reddened Cistine's sight. "You won't taunt me into a fight, *bandayo*."

He flushed at that word—then attacked without warning, augmented wind curling around his fists. But Cistine had anticipated him, the corners of that whip of air crawling toward her while he postured. So when he struck, she was already moving, banking off the base of the steps in a spinning dodge and launching herself at him. She formed a fist, thumb outside her fingers, knuckles driving in; and Salvotor, wicked, pain-pleasured fool that he was, didn't retreat. He braced and smirked, welcoming her to break her hand on his cheek like she did the very first time they met.

But not again.

At the last instant, she flicked her wrist; the mechanisms in Aden's gift made no sound at all, launching the thin, sleek *Svarkyst* knife from the gauntlet's hidden seams. And she would never forget the sound or the feeling as it jammed to the full length straight through the flesh of Salvotor's cheek, so flush that his weeks of stubble scraped her palm.

Howling profanely, he smashed her away with a kick to the stomach, knocking the air from her lungs; but when she went, the blade went with her, ripping clean down his teeth and out the side of his mouth, shrieking over his molars hard enough to spit sparks. Cistine cracked against the stone, her head snapping along the steps, and black splotches bloomed across her vision. While she struggled to cling to consciousness, Salvotor slammed his foot on her gauntleted wrist; bone snapped audibly, and if not for her training, she would've vomited. White fire screamed through her arm up into her head, and then *she* was screaming in agony until Salvotor struck her across the face, splitting her lip and knocking her head to the side so she spat blood on the steps.

"Enough," the other man spoke suddenly, his tone harsher than before. "Do not waste one drop of that sacred blood."

Salvotor ripped his foot from her arm, and light flooded back into the world too fast. Gasping, fighting not to retch, she watched through pain-slitted eyes as Salvotor jerked a healing augment from his cloak. He shattered it against the unhurt half of his face with a wobbling hand, and those warm white threads spread across his body—but it didn't heal properly. Too much of the man was replaced with the machinations meant to protect him from attack. The healing augment bucked across his skin, stitching and unbinding, knitting the edges askew so that what emerged was not pinked flesh but a jarring mound of scarred tissue and still-weeping gaps along one half of his ravaged face, teeth peeping through.

Salvotor glared down at her. "Nevermind that, she's going to bleed anyway. Let's get her to the Door, shall we? Then you take your augments and your companions and go. Once the disloyal are routed, I'll reshape the remnants of this city into something fit for a king."

"We will not leave the city." His voice full of an ancient hunger and hate, the man still didn't turn from the statue.

"But that was the arrangement." Salvotor's tone darkened. "You would tell me the secret to opening one of the Doors. In exchange, you could take your fill of augments before we parted ways."

"That agreement was the only way to solicit your aid in taking this city. We have no interest in braggart Chancellors who think themselves kings, and we will not share our rule."

"Rule? Since when do you care for rulership?"

"Since he who rules the city rules the well. And he who rules the well rules the world."

Cistine pried herself up on the steps and slowly dragged herself backward, clutching her broken wrist to her body, scooting on her heels and feeling along her thigh with her other hand.

"I grow tired of this." Every imitation of amicability vanished from Salvotor's tone. "We struck a bargain. My *valenar* brought you the plans you needed. These siege towers and the people who helped build them are ours."

"I think you will find what we offered them was enough to sway their loyalty from your banal dreams to our broader vision." The man flicked a long-boned hand, casting off Salvotor's mustering shout of protest. "This city is ours. The prisoners that your woman and your spy freed are ours. And the augments will be ours, too. You and your spies and messengers served your purpose of distraction. If you humble yourselves before us now, we might have more use for you."

Silence again as Salvotor's schemes crumbled before him.

"Kneel," the man purred. "And I will spare you."

Salvotor's lip curled. "I kneel before no man."

"I am not a man. I am your new god."

Thunder boomed as Salvotor unleashed a lightning augment, spanned it across his palms, and stepped forward to battle the ally who'd betrayed him. At that torrent of power set free, the man finally pivoted to face them, a slow, lazy swivel on heel revealing his long antelope-skull mask, sharp teeth forcing the mouth into an unnatural grin. Empty eyeholes dripping with shadows, he snapped both hands, shattering a flagon in each: wind and blood. Stirring together, they shot across the atrium and slammed into Salvotor's chest.

He froze, trembling, then jerked to one side—head aslant, limbs contorting, his entire frame tangling into an unnatural rictus. His reinforced skin rippled, violent heaves traveling up his arms, across his scale-plated cheekbones. The stench of unbearable heat corroded the air, and Salvotor cast his head back and bellowed in agony with a voice so like his son's.

Then he evaporated.

There was no other word for it. Cistine's tormentor, Thorne's abuser—the cabal's greatest nightmare and seemingly-unkillable foe—turned to vapor. Bone, muscle, sinew, marrow, and flesh all became a fine red mist hanging suspended on that augmented wind.

Then it all dribbled onto the marble.

Mouth filling with vomit, Cistine stumbled to her feet as the creature turned to face her. "I know what you are. You're not a god, you're a criminal who kidnaps children." She swallowed the surge of panic in her throat. "You're a Bloodwight."

"I am called the *Aeoprast*." He turned back toward the white statue. "This was my first house of schooling. Before we fled to Azkai, I came here every day for a month, a fresh and pious acolyte. I prayed at this statue so fervently my body ran wet with sweat. I prayed for some answer...some sign of my place in this world. Swore I would atone for every theft, every murder, every defilement if only I was given purpose. I received silence in reply."

He circled to the statue's front, and Cistine fingered the augment pouch on her thigh, mapping the course from the steps to the door. With all her might, she avoided glancing at the stain of Salvotor spread on the floor.

"We are not bidden to render their faces, you know." The *Aeoprast* looked up at what must've been the statue's blank countenance. "Yet still we're expected pay tribute to them with the labor of our hands and the lay of our minds. A faceless honor for a faceless God."

Clamminess spattered Cistine's palms. The sick feeling in her stomach steepened and bile rose up her throat.

"The silence was the reply, I realized. I have no need to atone. The True God will atone to *me*. I will march to his realm and lay claim to what is his. And *you*," his head snapped toward Cistine, augments rising around him in a torrent. "Your blood will pave my path to the stars."

Cistine shattered her own flagon, and fire burned up the wind he sent toward her. She lunged back from the steps, sending one blast of flame toward him and sheathing her arm with the other, tight tendrils to stabilize her broken wrist. The blinding pain dimmed so she could think while he moved, a vicious shadow melting through the wall of fire and gliding toward her like a nightmare given flesh.

Cords of flame sailed from his cloak; Cistine's fire broke them. He feinted from the right, and she pivoted on heel, dispatching another gout. This one he caught backhanded, bringing it up along his cloak, and for a moment as his shadows and her flame braided together, she was back in a cold sewer tunnel, facing Reema, not him. Cold wind sailed over her, then heat, moving in tandem like two heads of the same beast.

Two augments as one.

Her focus scattered and reformed as his shadows did the same, anchoring her boots to the marble so she couldn't retreat when he leaped toward her, hands grasping for what wasn't his to take.

He didn't expect her to brace for their meeting; nor had he seen the earth augment gripped in her weak hand, hidden up the fiery sleeve wrapped around her wrist; so he didn't expect the power that rallied and boomed out from her; perhaps he didn't even sense that it was not just fire, but earth as well, that scythed out from her body.

And when they did, the acolyte temple exploded around them.

CHAPTER SIXTY-SEVEN

THE SCREAMING DRAGGED Cistine back from oblivion, many voices raised like figures gathered around her crib, like warm, white light and a hand on her brow.

There *was* light, not white but red, bathing her face from above, interrupted by flirts of shadow and so much *screaming—*

Cistine, Cistine, look at us. Look at me, *Princess! Say my name!*

"Ashe," she choked.

Her Warden swore in relief. "I've got her, she's here! Over here, Thorne!"

Another curse. Then Thorne plunged down next to her on his knees, his hands curling around something, and he moved it with a grind of rock and rock and a burst of strength beyond reason. The heaviness lifted; air rushed back into Cistine's lungs, and hands looped under her arms and slid her backward on mud and marble, propping her up. No questions came before the healing light stole over her body, mending hurts just as she became aware of them: in her hips and legs, in her stomach and chest, and at last in her broken wrist. The last of the terrible pressure released from her lungs, and she croaked Thorne's name.

He knelt over her sprawled legs, yanking his armored jacket off and hurling it around her ripped dress. Then his bloodied hands felt along her shoulders, her arms, and her sides, seeking any injury the augment didn't heal. "Are you all right? Cistine!"

"We have to *go*," she wheezed, and the arms around her tightened. At that, she knew them, and gripped the elbow locked across her body. "Ariadne, *please...*"

"She's right. *Now*, Thorne," Ariadne hissed.

And then above the wreckage Cistine had created with her power, Maleck screamed like a man being burned alive. Ashe shouted, Aden roared, and deep in the belly of the decimated structure, stone groaned and shifted.

The *Aeoprast* was moving.

Cistine yanked forward in Ariadne's grip, seizing Thorne by the shoulder to brace herself when her head tipped and spun. "Help me. I have to get away from here!"

He reacted to her desperation without further pause, the thunder echoing her lightning. He swooped her up in his arms and was out of the hole in three precise jumps, broken rock to broken rock and then out. He staggered when they landed and settled her on her own feet, Ariadne lunging out behind them.

Breathless at the carnage she wrought, walls folded and floor caved in, Cistine saw at last how her augments sundered the acolyte training grounds to their barest foundations and leveled half the plaza—and in that ruin the cabal had fallen together. Ashe grabbed Maleck's cheeks as his unfocused eyes darted, seeing and sensing what Cistine had trapped under this ruin.

But it wouldn't be held there forever.

Something snapped under their feet. Thorne wrapped both arms around Cistine's waist and slung her toward the alleyway, and Aden and Ashe pulled Maleck up and shoved him after her. He buckled with every step, grabbing his head, and when Ashe tugged him upright again he cried out at being touched, pulling away.

They hurtled into the city, crashing past broken Vassoran bodies, more stone and ruined buildings, clots of ice and unnatural fires licking up the city's edges, and too many dead to number. Elites rushed by with weapons, ready to fight for the first time in twenty years. Ashe yanked up the necklace she wore and screamed for Bresnyar, and Cistine's ears rang with all the yelling, the gasping, the weeping in the streets around them. Thorne hauled her with his hand locked around hers, her feet dragging at the stone road like a drunkard, the call almost loud enough to consume everything else. Understanding slammed again and again into her head, making sense at last of all she had felt, pursued, and endured from the moment she stepped onto that Door beneath Stornhaz when she set all of this in motion.

Nazvaldolya. A name for what she'd been running toward all this time.

"Bresnyar!" Ashe's voice cracked from shouting. "Wherever you are, *please—*"

She broke down without warning, slamming her hand into the nearest building and rocking back and forward like a sailor reeling on her sealegs. Maleck dug his heels into the road and twisted, reaching for her; Cistine screamed, "Ashe, what's wrong?"

"I just saw..." She dug the heel of her hand into her brow, then snapped her head up. "*Bresnyar.*"

Gold flashed and flickered across the fire-soaked sky. With a bellow to rend the world, the dragon plunged from the smoke and crashed into the nearest siege-tower, ripping into it with his mighty talons and gutting it with his hind feet. Inside, men screamed, and outside mirrors cracked with concussive bursts.

Ashe yelled again, this time in warning.

Lightning shot out from the siege-tower slats, bursting across Bresnyar's scales. He roared, released, and plunged backward; Ashe sobbed his name and staggered into a run toward the wall, though she could never scale it—nor was there any need. The dragon vaulted back into view seconds later, faltering and angling, forgoing the tower for the city streets this time. Homes and shops fractured under the drag of his tail, the slam of his feet, but no one cared—if they were even left alive to see.

The cabal skidded up to Bresnyar's side, and his pain-dimmed eyes raked over them. "All of you, climb on."

"Wait," Quill panted, stepping back. "Tatiana."

"I know where she is, I can scent her. Now *climb up*, will you?"

Cursing, Quill gripped the dragon's hinge joint and swung onto his back. Ashe flagged the others up, streaked her rune-marked hand over Bresnyar's side, and leaped on last. Spinning in place, he bashed more buildings to rubble, clearing a way for himself; then he lunged and clawed up the wall to the walkway and streaked down it at a dead run, teeth and tail sweeping enemies to their deaths on both sides.

Lightning arced from the towers, rippling whips of pink, white, and lavender. Cistine cringed against Thorne's chest as a tine shot out past Bresnyar's nose, far too close. Then Quill coiled up at the front, straining forward on Bresnyar's back. "*I see her!*"

Tatiana was fighting for her life at the top of the Channel gate, battling six men at once, a wild fury in her movements Cistine had never witnessed before. Every blow precise, no strength spared, she was a death-god in a cobalt dress. Fury raged in her face, embers flocking the tips of her hair as she hurled men down with honed blows and snapped their necks left and right, clearing a path; then she slammed her boot into the hauling winch that ran up the gate.

"What is she doing?" Cistine screamed. "She'll let them all inside!"

"She's letting our people *out!*" Aden's voice was nearly lost to the wind.

He was right; the Channel had clogged with fleeing Valgardans clustered on docks and barges. But the Vassora who manned the winch and chains were splattered on the stone far below; there was no one to free the city except Tatiana, running to the second chain and activating the winch with flying fingers. She whooped in relief as the gate groaned and started to rise, then whipped down the wall to face another pack of enemies dismounting from the nearest siege-tower, moving straight toward her.

Quill's shout of her name cracked with anguish. Tatiana swiveled half-toward them, eyes glinting, then looked back at the men. Quill yelled for her again, warning and a plea woven in his tone.

Bresnyar tore down the wall, picking up speed as he went, and Tatiana drew the knives from her thigh sheaths and hurled them with all her might, picking off the two men at the lead. Then she turned and hurtled toward the golden dragon running to meet her.

As they neared the gate, power built on the air again, turning static as lightning gathered at their backs.

"Bresnyar!" Ashe cried out.

Roaring, the dragon lunged sideways from the wall toward free skies. Tatiana changed course and hurtled after him, flinging herself to the mercy of the empty air. Quill jerked his feet under him and leaped with all his might, gripping Bresnyar's wing joint in one hand, the other reaching out wildly for his *valenar*. His fingers caught hers at the very tips, and he swung her toward the dragon's back and Ariadne's waiting arms. Aden steadied Quill's graceful, brutal arc, landing again on Bresnyar's spine where he clung on for dear life, panting and shaking. Then Bresnyar gathered what remained of his strength and shot into the darkness—away from the Bloodwight siege.

When Stornhaz was little more than a speck on the horizon, burning across Eben's plains, the dragon finally slowed, descended in tight spirals, and struck down on a small hilltop. Cistine tumbled from his back and whirled toward the others. "Is everyone all right?"

Quill shook his head.

"Pippet?" Tatiana croaked.

"Gone." The word ripped from Aden like a knife, agony shining in his sweat-damp face. "Faer couldn't keep her trail."

A tear slid from the corner of Tatiana's eye. Quill stared at her, jaw feathering with tension. "Where were you?"

"My father. Kadlin. She was the thief we were looking for, the knife came from her, she broke into Mira and Sander's rooms—" Tatiana wiped her nose on her bare arm, looking back at the city. "The siege towers were my father's plans. Branko smuggled them out to Devitrius and Rakel months ago. One we started digging, he reported to Salvotor. They used Kadlin's family against her as leverage."

At the word *family*, Quill's fists loosened and he staggered forward. Tatiana caught him in her arms, and his wrapped tightly around her. "I lost her. I tried, I *tried*, Tati, but I *lost* her..."

"Maleck." Thorne stumbled across the hilltop and fell to his knees beside his warrior, a dark, braided slump cradling his head in his hands. "Darkwind, look at me!"

Maleck spasmed with terror, gasping for breath. Ashe crouched beside him, gripping his wrists. "Mal, *breathe*. Look at me, come back..."

"It's the Bloodwights." Aden stared down at his friend with heartbreak and fury blistering in his gray eyes. "They've returned."

"We should've known," Tatiana seethed as she and Quill drew apart. "We should've *known* as soon as we faced that thing in Oadmark..."

"We've known about the Bloodwights in the north for years!" Quill snapped. "They've never come this far, they should've *stayed there!*"

"Never." Maleck's voice was raw, his head wobbling up at last. "Not since she stepped onto the Door. It's all happening again...the reason they took Pippet—"

"No." Quill cut in sharply. "*No.*"

"It makes sense," Tatiana croaked, laying her singed curls flat to her scalp. "They were doing the same thing in Oadmark...taking whoever they could."

"Children are easier to turn into Bloodwights," Aden growled. "But grown men and women make better augurs."

"That explains why the *Aeoprast* took Salvotor's army right from his hands," Cistine muttered.

Thorne stiffened. "How do you know that?"

It occurred to her then that none of them knew—but they deserved to. "Salvotor was there, in that place where you found me. He's...he's dead. The *Aeoprast* turned him to blood mist with a pair of augments."

Her voice faltered, hands twitching with memories of fire and wind, fire and earth together. Twice, she'd done the impossible, too.

"What do they want?" Ashe demanded.

"*Nazvaldolya.*" Cistine spoke the word aloud at last, matching it against what she sensed all along: a world out of balance. The unseasonable storms and angry creatures, the ransacked strongholds, the blight Tatiana, Aden, and Sander had faced in Siralek. The moment she stepped on that Door and rang the knell, she all but summoned these enemies to take vengeance on their old kingdom.

After several silent moments, Ashe shoved to her feet. "All of you, stay here. Keep each other safe."

"Where are you going?" Cistine demanded.

"Back to the city." She swung astride Bresnyar's shoulders, and he struggled up without complaint. "If we're going to win this fight, we need numbers."

Maleck turned his head slowly. "Asheila. Be *careful.*"

Quill surged up suddenly, dislodging Faer from his shoulder. "I'm going with you."

Ariadne stepped into his path. "You aren't. Your head isn't clear. This will only make things worse."

"I don't care! That *thing* has my sister. I'm not letting it turn her into some stars-damned addicted, augment-hungry—"

"Quill!" Thorne's gaze cut to Maleck, still down on his knees, staring at Quill with stricken eyes.

He followed that look, and his rigid jaw softened. "I didn't mean it like that, *Storfir*, I—"

Before he could finish apologizing, Bresnyar took wing straight into the sky. A blur of gold and red, the woman unclaimed by any kingdom and the dragon cast out from his flew back to save what lives they could.

Quill took one step in their wake, then fell, knees cracking the rock-riddled dirt. He slumped, shoulders drawn forward, chin to his chest, and stared at his empty hands. Tatiana knelt beside him, winding her fingers between his. Slowly, Cistine lowered herself on his other side and did the same.

In silence too stunned for weeping, they stared toward the horizon and waited for death or dawn to come.

CHAPTER SIXTY-EIGHT

THEY STILL KNELT on the hilltop long after Cistine's knees numbed and the others broke apart—Thorne with Ariadne, Aden keeping close to Maleck. Then, at long last, Bresnyar's roar rent the thick air like an echo from a dream, and Aden swore with relief as the dragon landed below the hill, staggering from exhaustion. Thorne hurried to meet the five retching figures who slid from his back with Ashe: Bravis and Benedikt, Adeima and Maltadova, and Valdemar.

"They were being rounded up for slaughter. Or imprisonment, maybe." Soot streaked Ashe's face like war stripes, her voice a smoke-choked rasp. "They were the last ones we pulled out. Bres is done, he can't carry anymore. The rest are coming by foot."

Bravis stared up at the dragon with a mixture of awe and unease. When Thorne said his name, the acting Chancellor tore his gaze away at last, features hardening with rage. "Those were Bloodwights sieging our city. With a gods-forsaken army of criminals."

"This was what Salvotor plotted all along," Maltadova said bleakly. "What he swore would come if we didn't surrender our Courts to him."

"Then all of this," Benedikt muttered, "Detlyse Halet, Siralek, Nygaten..."

"Why?" Adeima cut in, her gaze on Ariadne. "Why that temple?"

"Mirrors," Tatiana said flatly. "They needed a way to move the siege towers here without being spotted. They must've found plans for cloaking mirrors in Nygaten's designs."

"So they have augments," Valdemar said. "*Many* augments."

"Apparently they raided the temples for far more than were marked missing after the war with Talheim." Ariadne folded her arms, scowling. "Which is of little surprise. So much was dismissed as collateral...books, artifacts, flagons as well."

Bravis wiped a hand down his face, then looked at Thorne. "We should've taken this more seriously after your swearing-in. I'm sorry."

"What *really* should have been done was executing those *bandayos* twenty years ago," Benedikt growled.

"It's pointless to argue what should've happened then," Maltadova said. "What will we do *now*?"

"We will fight." Adeima took his hand. "For our territories, for our brothers and sisters, we will go to war."

"I agree," Benedikt said. "We can send the surviving Tribunes to their own territories, shore up defenses and rally the people. Build an army of our own."

Their steadiness struck Cistine so sharply tears jumped to her eyes. It was true, what she'd learned all those months ago: ever since the war, Valgard had not known a peace worth protecting. Struggle was a way of life for them—and they were wholly prepared to step into the deeper, blacker waters of it to save their kingdom now.

"What of Talheim?" Valdemar asked. "They begged us to come to their aid against Mahasar. Now will they come to ours?"

They all stared at Cistine, and she couldn't muster a single word past the knot of shame and panic lodged in her throat. She had made that treaty to deliver her people *from* war, not to it. She couldn't imagine her father's face, his hurt and rage, if she came to tell him she'd consigned their Wardens to die on another kingdom's killing fields for a cause that was not even theirs.

"Cistine and I have discussed this," Thorne cut in. "Talheim will give aid the way only they can." The focus swooped back to him, and Cistine struggled to rally her wits in the face of his smooth lie. "We know what the Bloodwights want: the wells, and every augment inside. There's only one means of opening them, so Talheim must rally within its own borders. While we push the Bloodwights back, they hold firm. Protect the Key."

No one spoke. Cistine couldn't breathe.

After a moment, Adeima nodded slowly. "Wise. The Bloodwights forged the Key. They know precisely what it is, what it looks like, and how to use it. If we brought Talheimic Wardens here, its location might be tortured from them. It isn't a risk worth taking."

"But we'll hurt for the numbers," Bravis argued. "Will we receive supplies, at least? Rations to aid our warriors?"

"If you want to draw attention to Talheim." Thorne's eyes narrowed. "The last the Bloodwights knew, we were bitter enemies, our feud lulled by a truce that barely held the peace. If we keep up that ruse, we keep their focus away from the Key."

Another pause. Distantly, screams floated on the wind.

Then Adeima turned to Cistine. "The Key was entrusted to your family. Do you vow to guard it with your life?"

Hysterical laughter clawed at her throat. She barely nodded and choked out, "I will."

Bravis dipped his head, a show of respect Cistine didn't deserve. She and Thorne were liars, and she was a coward withholding aid from an allied kingdom. But she couldn't betray Talheim; so she let the Chancellors turn from her and huddle up to discuss the night's horrors among themselves.

"Cabal." Thorne's voice was quiet. "With me."

They came down from the hill and crossed nearly a half-mile of open plain before Thorne stopped, the others forming a circle around him and Cistine. He turned to her then, drew a pale blue flagon from his augment pouch, and held it out to her. "This will be enough to carry you past the border."

Cistine flinched back. "I don't want that. I'm not—"

"Cistine." His voice was soft, but relentless. "There's no point to this ruse if the Key remains in Valgard."

"He's right, *Logandir*," Ariadne said. "It was a lie, but there is truth to it. You *must* protect the Key at all costs."

She shook her head sharply, tears scattering from her lashes. "I'm not leaving. I can fight this war!"

"But it's not where you want to be, or where you're needed most." Thorne's voice gentled, his eyes beholding her too reverently—like it was the last time. "I swore an oath long ago that I would always fight for your right not to be forced into a battle not your choosing. You found peace for your kingdom, Cistine. Let me give it to you now. One last gift."

Sniffing back tears, she raised her chin. "We'll put it to a vote. No," she added at their quiet groans, "we *vote*. Like the Court we are."

"Then I vote you go," Quill's voice was no louder than a breath. "If we fall, we fall. But I'll die happier knowing Talheim has you to pick up the sword after I'm gone."

"Go," Maleck murmured. "There is nothing for you here but death, *Logandir*."

Tatiana blinked away tears. "I know you'll hate me for this forever, but it's what's best. Go home, Cistine."

"It's your blood that will win them this war," Aden said. "If not for your own sake, then for ours...go. We will fight better and stronger if we don't fear for you."

"Talheim needs its heir more than Valgard needs one more body on the battlefield," Ashe agreed. "I vote you go."

"Go home, *Malatanda*," Ariadne said, "and live out the freedom we won together. Live it for all of us."

Cistine looked around at them, betrayal and disbelief, heartbreak and gratitude warring in her chest at their determined faces and unbending will. Then she looked at her *selvenar*. Her betrothed. The last to vote.

Thorne still held out the augment to her; silent tears tracked his bloodied face. "I gave you the only chance I could to keep your people from dying for our mistakes. That's all I have left. If you ever loved me, you'll let me live and die on the battlefield knowing I saved your kingdom. I saved *you.*" He took her wrist, turned over her hand, and pressed the wind flagon into it, curling her fingers around its precious, pulsing power. "Go home, Wildheart."

At the sound of her Name, that last vote sealing her fate, a furious sob jerked from her chest. She threw her arms around his neck. "I hate you."

His arms looped around her waist. "I know."

Terror pounded through her at that, twisting her fingers sharply into his hair. "No. I love you, Thorne. I *love* you."

"I know that, too."

The others closed around them, arms wrapping shoulders, a storm of embraces closer and hotter than the flames engulfing Stornhaz on the horizon. Then they took hold of her, one by one; Tatiana's hug around her neck tight like a noose, Ariadne's lips to her brow a blessing from the True God. Cistine slipped the compass pendant back over Aden's head and kissed his cheek, held Maleck's face to her shoulder and told him over and over it would be all right, though that was a lie. She closed her eyes to soak in the smell of cinnamon and steel when Quill kissed the top of her head, then wept when he offered his own augment pouch in the narrow crook between their bodies.

"Just in case," he said.

She drew back, dashing her face on her sleeve. "Thank you. For everything."

He sucked in his bottom lip and whistled; despite the healing augment that had saved his life, Faer still wobbled slightly when he drifted from Quill's shoulder down to hers. Quill patted a hand over his heart. "Make sure you tuck him into your jacket. Protect him."

She looked desperately between the raven and his warrior. "Quill—"

"I can't lose him, too. You look after each other."

Faer shimmied when Quill stepped back, but quieted at a stroke of his hand. Cistine had no time to argue before Ashe stepped forward to wrap her up in a hug. She held her the longest, the smell of rosewater and embers wafting from the crook of her neck, and Cistine knew without asking—Ashe would stay. She was a creature of battle, and Valgard needed her.

Maleck needed her.

"We never seem to say anything but goodbye these days," Ashe laughed hoarsely when they parted. "Whatever I regret about my time as a Warden, I'll never regret serving you. It's been an honor."

She offered her hand, and Cistine clasped it. "The honor was always mine."

At last, she walked to Thorne. He'd retreated further down the plain, and there was no hiding the agony in his clenched jaw and bright eyes when he watched her walk to him for the last time.

"This is one of those moments," he said when she halted before him. "One I'm going to remember the rest of my life."

"Me, walking away from Valgard?" she asked wretchedly.

He took her chin. "You, walking toward me with love in your eyes."

He kissed her under a veil of smoke and shadow until she forgot her fear and sorrow, until she was only Wildheart and he was only Starchaser, the crescendo of all their struggles and trials, triumphs and adventures rising to a wailing echo of grief and love—their final parting. When the kiss broke and his arms were around her, she drank in the strength of his grip and the heaviness of his hands and the way his heartbeat sounded under her ear.

"I would've loved you for a hundred years. Two hundred. However long the gods gave us," he murmured. "I would've wedded you in front of everyone we know and love. Maybe even a few we hated."

A strangled laugh burst from her. "I would've worn white. You would've worn black. It would've been very fetching."

"A dress?"

"Just for you." She drew back, taking his face in her hands. "Anything for you, Starchaser."

Even this. Even goodbye.

He bent his brow to hers, shutting his eyes. "Wildheart."

The word bathed over her, soft and sweet and aching. She wished she'd made him say it a hundred times before now, so this wouldn't be the only way she remembered it.

As goodbye.

~~~

On the plains of Eben not far from where Julian gave his life for her, Cistine Novacek turned back for a last glimpse of her cabal who stayed behind to do the same. They all stood together, watching her go: seven warriors strong and true, framed against the glistening golden body of a dragon and a sky running red with flame, red like blood—like a half-forgotten nightmare.

Either you stand alone, or you fall together.

The wind augment hummed in her fist as she raised it toward them— a parting salute. A silent cry to hold the line. And a show of gratitude no words could ever touch.

One-by-one, the cabal sank to their knees in reply, arms across their chests. A salute in turn; homage fit for a queen.

They didn't rise even when Cistine broke the wind flagon. Even when it carried her home.

CHAPTER SIXTY-NINE

ASTORIA WAS JUST as Cistine remembered it, as bright and beautiful this dawn as the one she left. The winsome Darlaska decorations hadn't come down yet, the four bridges from the city to the Citadel plot still strung with garlands of silver and gold dancing in a breeze half of her making. The wind augment brought her and Faer alighting on one of the city rooftops; her aim was precise, her control perfect.

Quill would've been proud.

Cistine unzipped her jacket, freeing Faer in this strange new world. He landed on her wrist and croaked a single long note, then tipped his head, listening for an echoing whistle that never came.

Cistine pressed a kiss to his head. "It's just us now, Faer."

With a short note, she sent him up to the Citadel towers to explore, eyes stinging while she watched him go. Then a gnawing need set her scrambling down the handholds of the shop's side; the moment her feet struck the familiar cobblestone way, she started running.

South Bridge rose and fell beneath her feet, its grueling arch digging welcome pain into her thighs. Over and down she went, flying toward the southern doors into the Citadel, shouting at the Wardens to make way for the Princess; they obeyed, startled eyes watching her burst through the doors and keep running.

Down familiar halls, past familiar windows throwing familiar squares of sunlight where she used to grab her maids by their hands, twirling and laughing, dresses floating and flower crowns on their heads; up and down staircases, through the glass parlors, while servants and distant relatives and commoners drew back and whispered behind their hands. She didn't hesitate once on the way to her parents' bedroom, where the Wardens jerked back and gaped at her more in shock than reverence or recognition. She grabbed the bronze knockers and pushed with all her might, barging inside.

Her parents were seated by the fire just like the last night she sat with them here, sipping tea and discussing her coming-of-age ball months ago— someone else's birthday, another girl's life. Now she was this woman in the shreds of an armored dress and a man's jacket, clinging to the door handles and breathing her family's names.

Cyril looked up from his book and Solene from a pile of citizens' requests—first with alarm, and then, after a fleeting moment, with shocked recognition. They came to their feet together, eyes wide, mouths agape.

A sob rolled from Cistine's chest, and she closed the distance to them, crashing into her mother's arms, the safe harbor she'd yearned for so many times since she went to Valgard. Solene staggered backward from the impact, her grip keeping them from falling into the fire; Cyril grabbed them both, his tears hot on Cistine's hair when he kissed the crown of her head. They folded down on the rug in a heap of fine clothes and armored threads, and Cistine wept bitterly—for the joy of seeing them and the misery of leaving Valgard. For Pippet, for Quill, for Maleck, for the devastation in Thorne's eyes when he said goodbye. For the ring on her finger and its promise that might no longer come true. For the fear of what was certainly coming for her cabal; what might still find them here in the Middle Kingdom if the ruse didn't hold. Then she wept simply because she was exhausted, and had seen too much night—had held her *selvenar* and prayed he wouldn't die, fought Salvotor and seen him fall, felt Pippet slip through her fingers, and let the cabal go.

Her parents held her, grieving the known and unknown until there was nothing left but their arms around each other and the fire popping quietly.

Only then did Solene loosen her hold and peel back gently to assess her strange attire, her new scars, the crusted blood on the side of her face. "My beautiful, brave girl. Look at you."

Cyril said nothing, but his hand tightened faintly on her shoulder and his gaze dropped to her waist, where Quill's augment pouch hung. Cistine's grief coiled up and faded into a dull, hard lump in her throat, letting other feelings free when her father's gaze snapped back to hers.

She was not the same Princess who left; and she didn't see him as the same King she loved back then.

"We thought you would stay." Solene's voice broke the silent war of thought between her husband and daughter.

"I was going to. Something terrible happened, Mama. The Bloodwights...the *visnprests* who sealed the Doors. They're back." Cyril's face drained of color at that; softly and with all the articulacy of a hereditary archer from the wild plains, Solene cursed their enemies. "I wanted to stay and fight, but my friends voted against it. They sent me home."

"To spare you rather than open the Doors?" Solene demanded.

"I can't imagine why," Cyril said blandly, taking Cistine's hand and exposing the ultramarine opal to the firelight.

Solene covered her mouth, eyes darting from the ring to her daughter's face. "Did you—*Cistine*. Did you make a *marriage alliance* with the North?"

"It wasn't for alliance. Not that it matters anymore." The words emerged bitterly. "I don't know what will happen to him now. How long he'll even live." But she would never stop praying, as fervently and wholeheartedly as Ariadne taught her, until she felt the *selvenar* bond give way. And even after, she would pray Thorne stepped into Cenowyn and found Baba Kallah and Kristoff there, and that they'd wait for her.

"Oh, Cistine." Her mother's voice cracked. "I never wanted this life for you. The fear of war, seeing the man you love ride off to it while you stay behind..."

The man you love. "You're not angry with me?"

"I think you've made it clear by now you're a woman of your own choices," Cyril said. "Besides, you're here, when you could've been bled out on a Door. When you could've been their entire salvation, he chose your life over his whole kingdom. I need no other proof that this Valgardan, whoever he is, loves you with his entire heart."

Cistine had never heard truer words. Nor had they ever hurt so much.

Solene took both their hands and rose. "Up, both of you. We need to be prepared if they break down Valgard's defenses." Though her words were calm, fear was plain in the slant of her mouth, the tremble of her hands, for her husband and daughter—the two Keys, the greatest prizes in a war just beginning beyond their kingdom.

With a swift nod, Cyril was the King again, focused and firm. "Muster the Wardens, love. Have Viktor bring his best to the throne room."

"Not Rion?" Cistine asked.

"He and Eboni are on their way back to Practica. I don't think his council is required for matters like this. Do you?" The question was honest, Cyril's expression vulnerable. If she said Rion was needed, he would send for him in a moment.

"No, not for this. And not Viktor, either," Cistine said. "I'd choose Rozalie. She can be trusted when it comes to Valgard."

Cyril nodded to Solene. "Rozalie it is, then. Send for her at the northern forts. Let her select who she thinks is best to help shore up our defenses."

Solene cast a last look of fondness and worry over her daughter. "Welcome home, my little love."

Cyril beckoned with a tilt of his head when his wife departed. "Let's get you into better clothes before your report."

Cistine glanced down at her scant attire and flushed. "I suppose we should."

They walked the corridors they'd traversed so many times together, Cistine often with her nose in a book or her eyes out the window, daydreaming while her father told her about legislature and swordplay and other things she didn't care for. But today she was focused, waiting for the inevitable question.

"How many people know what you are?" Cyril asked at last.

And there it was.

"Only a handful." And fewer still if Sander and Mira, Saychelle and Iri were dead. The thought shoved sour sickness into her mouth.

Cyril nodded. "The less, the better. Will the *visnprests*—?"

"Bloodwights."

He grimaced at the name. "Will these Bloodwights sense you're here? Sense *we* are here?"

"I don't think so. Not from afar." Not like she'd sensed the pestilence of their presence; mercifully, that stream seemed to flow mostly one way. "I'm sure Thorne and the others will spread a rumor that I'm still in Valgard. Gods willing, that will be enough."

"Thorne," Cyril mused. "I assume it's his ring you're wearing?"

Cheeks hot, she nodded.

"Well, I'm proud that you made the difficult choice," Cyril said after they crossed another hall in silence. "Leaving Valgard was one of the most difficult things I've ever done. I could barely put one foot in front of the other. I thought it was war-weariness at the time, but it didn't abate. It never really has, it's just gotten easier to manage."

She glanced up at his drawn face. "You can sense the augments I'm carrying, can't you?" He nodded slowly, and a fresh ache pounded in her heart. "Papa, why didn't you ever tell me about Valgard? That the augments still existed, that the Doors were sealed with *Gammalkraft*, that I was a Key?"

"I was afraid you would leave us and travel north if you knew you had some claim in those lands. And I was ashamed I saddled you with that burden. I thought if you knew, you would despise me. And especially after we lost your brothers, I couldn't bear to lose you, too."

She shook her head. "You should have prepared me better for this. I had the right to know."

"I realize that now, far too late. I'm sorry for the lies and compromises that came between us. I hope you'll forgive me."

"I do. But if I'm going to succeed you, we have to be honest with one another from now on."

"Is that what you want? To succeed me?"

There was desperate hope in his voice, as if she offered him a dream beyond reason. "Yes. I want my birthright so I can help our kingdom. I won't neglect my duties from now on, I give you my word. But I want yours in return."

"You have it, Cistine."

"Then start by telling me this: do you think I'm worthy of the throne, or did you always want a different heir?"

He halted outside her bedroom door and took her hands, dragging her around to face him. "I have *always* wanted to see you on that throne. It's all I've ever wanted."

She bit back more tears at the small, delectable tug of an old wound in her heart slowly stitching itself shut. "Come inside. I want to show you something."

The sheer normalcy of her bedroom was almost breathtaking, everything exactly as she'd left it—except for the mound of birthday gifts on the dining table and chairs, spilling all over the floor, forgotten in her wild rush to the North.

But they weren't the presents that mattered. Not now.

She opened her augment pouch, reached for the white-gold whisper of light, uncorked the flagon, and poured a kernel of the augment into her palm. Its warmth and weight no longer surprised her; she let it climb to her elbow in streamers, bright enough to illumine her body and nothing more. Cyril watched it dance with yearning in his eyes, brighter than tears—a desire Cistine knew like her own name. That insatiable call.

"Come here, Papa," she urged, and when Cyril stepped closer, she added, "don't be afraid of it. It's just a weapon. You can control it if you don't fear it."

His hand opened just below hers, and she dropped the kernel. The moment it touched his palm, the gods-gifted light bloomed like a lotus, furrowing out across his fingers and wrist, twining along his arm. It ate away at his clothing, but not his skin; just like her, he was impervious, even unarmored and uninked.

Tears slid down her cheeks as he pivoted on the balls of his feet, tracing the augment's unfettered journey across his shoulders and down his torso, singeing away his shirt and crossing the scarred contours of his body...scars like hers, too; scars of war. He was just like her in every way.

The light spent itself and faded, and in the drape-drawn dimness of the chamber, father and daughter stared at one another.

"You have no idea how glad I am to have you home," Cyril said hoarsely. "I meant what I said in that letter, but I'm glad you came back before..."

Before the battle. Before the storm. Before she shared her grandfather's fate—or worse.

Miserable energy stirred in her chest, and she pushed Cyril's shoulder. "Go and put on a shirt, Papa, you look ridiculous."

Chuckling, he went to the door. "I'll see you in the throne room in one hour. We'll prepare the Citadel while we wait for Rozalie's arrival."

When he was gone, she flung the balcony doors wide, coaxing a breeze into the stale room, lifting the drapes like mourning banners. Then she wandered to the stack of gifts; there were dozens to look at, and with gratitude but no profound joy, she stacked them into smaller piles. Some were clearly dresses, others jewelry. The tallest heap was books, and she wished battle didn't preoccupy her thoughts so she could muster an ounce of excitement at the prospect of reading them.

Her mind wandered so far from the task at hand that she was all but floating, her body in Talheim but her mind in Valgard, when the clock tower in Astoria's center chimed midmorning, startling her so badly she jumped, elbowing the last gift from the table. It dropped to the floor with a dull clap, and she cursed, bending to retrieve it. But when she laid eyes on the note pinned to the trappings, her heart skipped.

That was Julian's handwriting.

For a moment, she simply stared at it; if even the sight of that half-forgotten scrawl made her chest ache, she couldn't begin to imagine what reading it would do to her heart.

She opened the parcel itself first. That seemed like something Julian would've wanted her to do.

It was a journal of medium size, its soft leather cover tooled with running horses, clearly handmade in Practica where horse husbandry was a common way of life. She unlooped the cord from around it and found blank pages inside—nothing to distract her from picking up the note and reading Julian's voice back into her life for the first time since Eben's wetlands.

I know you've always loved reading your books of adventure. I thought maybe you'd want the chance to start writing your own. Whenever you do, I hope I'll be there to read it. And I hope I'll always be a part of your story.

Forever your friend, whether close or apart,

-J

A tear plopped onto the note, and she swept it away with her thumb. "Oh, Julian."

The wind in the drapes dropped suddenly, the fabric settling still as a corpse's veil. Far away, so distant it was like God's breath whispering, thunder stirred; she didn't have to look to know it came from the north.

A rustle of wings, and Faer drifted in through the window to perch on the bedpost. He cawed and groomed his feathers, then fixed her with that beady, expectant gaze, wondering what would come next.

What, indeed?

She went back to the balcony doors, gripping the ornate handles as she gazed across her city toward the distant horizon—toward the kingdom, the friends, and the war she left behind.

"I'm sorry," she whispered. "I love you all."

The only answer was another hiss of thunder.

She turned away from the call in her spirit, shut the doors, and dressed quickly in pants and a shirt—the closest thing to armor she had left. She hesitated a moment, hand hovering over the last piece of her raiment, wondering if she invited more pain by this. If it even mattered anymore.

But it did. It always would, even after they were all gone.

So she picked up Thorne's jacket and slung it across her shoulders, fluffing out the seams and breathing in the scent of sandalwood and leather from its fibers. The smell of him, of the home she left behind.

With a sharp whistle, she summoned Faer to perch on her shoulder. Then the Princess of Talheim went to do her duty—to prepare her kingdom and herself to hold the line.

EPILOGUE

L ONG into the morning, people streamed out to join the cabal and the Chancellors on the plain, wounded, drenched, trembling from cold and the night's trauma. They moved like Hive fighters after their first match, surviving with blood on their teeth and terror in their hearts, uncertain of what they'd become and what would become of them now.

Aden wished he could gather them all together and offer some hope. But they were too many by now—too many even to be on the plains. They would draw attention as their ranks swelled; they had to disperse, and soon. Already the Chancellors had rallied what Tribunes remained. Orders were being given, a plan enacted as hastily as it was sketched.

Aden didn't like it. His father had taught him and Maleck that acting with too few options to consider, having no choice but to move and do it quickly, was as good as inviting disaster to dance.

But Thorne had dismissed him from that conference—to tend the cabal, he claimed. He'd dismissed Sander as well. So it was to Sander that Aden went, and Mira, sitting on the backside of the hill a ways from the others. He heard them arguing before he even arrived, their hushed tones full of aggravated affection.

"I'm all right, Sander, I told you, it's just a wounded hand."

"You are not all right, you were fortunate to have escaped the city at all! First your capture, and now this..." A rip of cloth punctuated Sander's harsh tone as he tore his opulent scarf in half and bound Mira's bloodied knuckles. "Of all the reckless, mad, dangerous things..."

"I'm told those were once my most attractive qualities." Mira angled a tired smile up at Aden when he halted beside Sander. "Hello, you."

"You're hurt?"

"Just a scratch."

"A *scratch*. She nearly broke her knuckles beating off criminals in the courthouse," Sander snapped.

"They would've taken Saychelle and Iri if I hadn't!" Mira's calm tone showed a rare fracture; even when they'd freed her from Salvotor's men, she had maintained that levelness, soothing Sander more than he soothed her while he carried her out of that abandoned house. But fury gleamed in her gaze now, as if she'd attack all those criminals again if given the chance.

"They were after the *visnprestas* in particular?" Aden asked.

Mira nodded. "They were taking captive as many of Ariadne's friends as they could corner. Children as well."

Aden glanced over his shoulder at Quill, sitting atop the hill with legs cocked and arms loosely linked around his knees, staring at the stomped-flat grass. Maleck, crouched beside him, was still as stone. Ashe had an arm around each of them, spine raised like a wildcat guarding her den.

Mira followed his gaze, then squeezed Sander's hand. "Go find Thorne. Shove into his conversation if you must. You're High Tribune, make him appreciate what you bring."

"My place is at your side, Mira."

"Your place is with your Chancellor, and if you keep spewing this protective nonsense, it's going to send me into a fit, which will be all your stars-damned fault. Now *go!*"

Grumbling, Sander tossed a clipped nod to Aden and stalked off to join Thorne, the Chancellors, and the other Tribunes. Aden wondered if he ought to go as well, force himself into that discussion just like Sander; but it was not lost on him that Mira didn't send him away.

He settled onto the hillside next to her, folded his hands under his chin with elbows braced on his knees, and shut his eyes. He tried not to wonder why Thorne didn't want him there; Sander made sense, he'd escaped the city only recently and had Mira to think of. But was this really about Aden caring for the cabal? Or was he not wanted in that council, still not trusted after all this time?

And did he even deserve to be? He'd lost Pippet. He'd nearly lost Thorne last night. And he felt himself losing Maleck already, pieces chipping away at the horror of his brothers' return.

"We'll go west," Mira broke into his thoughts. "Hana, Kendar, and me. There's a place called Holmlond, known only to a few medicos, Vassora, and elites. I intend to hide Saychelle and Iri and as many other *visnprestas* there as I can. Something tells me we'll be in desperate need of them soon."

"And in short supply, if the Bloodwights have their way." Aden let his eyes flutter open, taking in Mira's wan face. "We'll be sorry to see you go. Yours is the sort of help we'll need in the days ahead."

"Not mine." She shook her head. "Yours."

He snorted. "That, I doubt."

"I don't." She twisted toward him, planting one hand on the grass. "Aden, do you realize how precious and rare men like you are? Men who know both battle and honor, who know what it is to fight for their survival day after day, who have not grown complacent since the war?" Her lips thinned as she stared off at the red-ribbed horizon. "I watched the elites try and fail to fight last night. They've grown too soft, too sure of things in our unbreachable city. I fear for what will happen to those who haven't kept their minds and weapons sharp. They'll need men like you to lead them."

"You think me capable of that." He meant to tease, but the words emerged honest and quiet. Stars help him around women like Mira and Ashe, who always reeled the true heart out of him.

"I do," Mira said. "You are a pillar, not a burden. You must be their strength like your father once was yours."

His hand drifted to the compass pendant around his neck—Cistine's parting gift, a farewell and a promise from a princess worth waiting for. "I'll do what I can."

"That's all any of us can promise in the days to come." Mira pushed herself shakily up from the hill, and Aden helped her straighten. "Look ahead, not behind. Not to the things you didn't prevent. The only way we survive this is if we keep our eyes on the horizon."

Aden gritted his teeth as heat flooded his throat and ebbed into his eyes. It still hadn't become real for him yet, that Pippet was gone—that he couldn't simply turn on this hill and see her cheering up the survivors, couldn't give the summoning whistle they practiced so often in training and see her come running to spar or duel or wrap her arms around him.

Was she trapped in that city, begging the gods for him to find her? Did she think he'd abandoned her like he walked away from his cabal five years ago, bound for Siralek?

Mira touched his arm, drawing him out of himself, faith bright in her eyes. "Look after your friends. And Sander. And yourself."

That much, at least, he could do. And he told her so.

They walked back to the hilltop together and found the assembly broken up, Chancellors and Tribunes scattering. With a nudge from the hip, Mira went to find her *valenar*, and Aden veered off toward Thorne.

His cousin had taken up post at the farthest-forward hill; the foul, hot wind dragged his hair and clothes, but he was otherwise motionless, hardly breathing while he watched Stornhaz burn.

Aden halted beside him. "Orders?"

Thorne's shoulders lifted and fell in a deep breath. Inhaling the warrior; exhaling the elite. "Most of the Tribunes are dispersing to the territories to spread word. Others will watch the Vey. The rest will lead these enemies on a chase."

"A chase to where?"

"There are more Bloodwights than these, Maleck is certain. That they aren't here suggests there's more to their strategy than just taking the city. We need to flush out their support wherever it lies."

"Do we travel to our own territories, then?"

"Not you and Sander. You stay with me."

He didn't explain his reasoning, nor did he need to. Thorne, balanced and mindful, who withstood a lifetime of abuse and betrayal from those who should have loved him better, even Aden himself—he couldn't bear another farewell. Not with his augment pouch lighter by one, his last act of love to send his *selvenar* to safety while they stayed and fought.

So Aden said, "I'm with you, Thorne. Whatever comes."

Thorne's head bobbed. "We travel to the northern mountains first, spread rumor of Cistine's movements there to keep the Bloodwights off her trail."

"To the north it is."

But neither of them moved. Thorne went on staring at the City of a Thousand Stars, the crackling cinder of a home they dreamed first of changing, then returning to, the brighter future they fought to build consumed now in flames. The only hope left was its people, what they had proven they could accomplish together—and still would.

Footsteps brushed the grass, and the rest of the cabal joined them. Every step was familiar, from Quill and Tatiana's tandem strides to Ariadne's steady march, Ashe's feline grace and Maleck's shadow-softness, Sander and Mira in lockstep, gripping hands behind them.

"We heard what you said," Quill rasped. "North, *Allet*."

"Then we fight," Ariadne murmured. "To the last breath, to the very last of us."

Aden gripped Thorne's shoulder. "We will stop this, Thorne. We will."

Gently, Mira's fingers slid into Aden's as she stepped up shoulder-to-shoulder with him. On her other side, Sander still held her hand. Then Ashe took his. Then Maleck. Ariadne. Tatiana. Quill. A silent, unbreakable chain, the cabal watched their home go up in smoke and listened to the echo of thunder, of cracking roofs and sundering stone ringing across the plains like the beating of bone drums.

Like a song summoning the world to war.

End

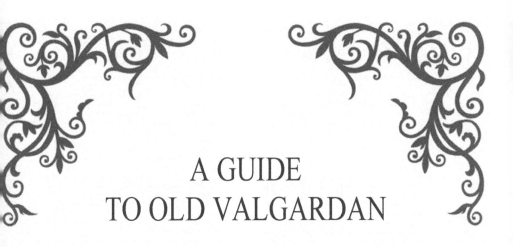

A GUIDE
TO OLD VALGARDAN

Words:

Allatok – Heathen

Slynar – Bitch (roughly)

Bandayo – Bastard (roughly)

Nahdar – Uncle

Allet – Brother

Malat – Sister

Tajall - Infant

Storfir – Big One

Stornjor – Great Love

Banjor – My Love

Yani – Sweet

Sillakove - Starchaser

Selvenar – Blended hearts

Valenar – Blended blood

Creatures:

Atrasat (CEPHALOPOD)

ACKNOWLEDGEMENTS

WORDS CAN HARDLY express the unique journey of *LIGHTFALL'S* becoming. I always knew it would be a turning point in the story, but over the course of the hardest year in my life, it went from being a draft I skimped on and hated, to a full rewrite, to one of my favorite books ever!

First, as always, to God: for answering my prayers and showing me the story I always needed to tell, and for healing me from the brokenness that made it impossible to tell it right the first time. I am humbled by Your patience with me, letting me tell it my way first so You can prove Your faithful love by teaching me how to tell it *Your* way. There is no me without You.

To my family: for never asking why I do this crazy writing thing, just rolling with it. To Mom for the proofreading, Dustin for the alpha-reading, Dad for the necessary kicks in the pants, Danny for the endless love and reorganizing the whole kitchen by yourself so I could work on this book and all the others, and JD just for being. You are all my reason. Always. <3

To Cassidy and Miranda: for asking "What if there was Mira?" and birthing the idea of the counselor and confidant, the missing piece the story always needed. Thank you for encouraging, loving, and supporting me through the trenches of bringing this story back to life.

To Katie and Meaghan: for your enthusiasm, your friendship, your love, all the songs (SO MANY SONGS!) and for crying, cheering, laughing, screaming through this whole book, and doing LIFE with me.

To Savannah: for teaching me how to be a better author, a better businesswoman, and a better person overall. Your friendship helped me through the peaks and valleys of this rewrite. I am so grateful for that one Instagram post that brought us together, and all our adventures since!

To Annelisa and Meagan: for the Florida adventures and magical nights when I thought rewriting this would be the death of me, and always being such an amazing support, distraction, and sanctuary.

To my incredible cover artist and partner-in-crime, Maja, for going over round after round of colors on this one to get things JUST RIGHT! We did it—we always do!

To everyone who gave me the Hamilton treatment, asking me why I write like I'm running out of time and telling me to TAKE A BREAK. It was very needed!

To every one of my followers and friends on social media, but especially: to Lina, Sydney, Dani, Katie, Kay, Stephanie, Piper, the Brittanys, Allie, the Hollys, Heather, Sammie, Gee, Stephanie, Sania, and every other person who has made an impact. I wish I could list you all, but I would take up a whole book with it! My love for you knows no bounds.

And of course, to you, reader: for experiencing, for adventuring, for loving. I hope you found peace and power in these pages. Thank you for reading the books of my heart and also sharing your heart with me in turn.

See you in the next one! <3

Read On For a Sneak Peek at
THE STARCHASER SAGA
BOOK V

CHAPTER
ONE

I T MIGHT HAVE been a lovely day, bright, full of thawing spring sunligh and birdcall melodies. But inside the princess's mind, it was always smoke an scarlet skies, a warmth which did not belong in winter and sickness festering i the air.

This is one of those moments. One I'm going to remember the rest of my life.

Me, walking away from Valgard?

You, walking toward me with love in your eyes.

A kiss that blinded. Shadows that consumed.

I would've loved you for a hundred years. Two hundred. However long the god gave us.

They had none of that time. Because she had walked away—because h *begged* her to.

Anything for you, Starchaser.

Wildheart.

Wildheart...

"Cistine?"

She jolted, head rising from her fist, focus returning to the Citadel's counc chamber. It was indeed a bright day, the meeting table splashed with gold dappl tumbling through the glass roof, and a league of councilors stared at her—lor and ladies of Talheim from estates far and near. Plainsmen and desert dweller fishers and mountaineers.

Cistine felt like she'd been all of them, in another world her mind stole away to whenever she wasn't careful. On days like today, the heat of the room's twin hearths and the monotony of the reports lulled her back to a dream where there was never too little to do; when she was the fulcrum upon which meetings like this hinged. When it was only her standing for Talheim's interests—not her and her father, whose voice drew her back to this meeting.

Cistine sat away from the table, smoothing her hands down the scarlet dress spilling across her knees. It was still difficult to wear gowns like this, even with long sleeves and high collars, at a table full of men; but each time she did, it was to honor Mirassah, her bright-eyed and sharp-witted counselor. She could only imagine how Mira would smile to see her now, dressed in trousers under a full dress, a tiara woven into her hickory hair...conducting royal business like the future queen she was. How proud they would all be. How Thorne—

The thought of him was a blade driven straight through her, wrapped in vines of slick darkness, dread and despair and *illness* tunneling deep into the very bones of the world itself.

Nazvaldolya.

Clenching her molars against a surge of bile that never lessened no matter how many times that sensation came and went, Cistine forced a smile. "I'm sorry, the warmth has me drifting. You were saying about the southern border forts, Lord Petr?"

The elderly lord flashed her a cautious smile. "That there's been no sign of unrest. So far, King Jad remains within Mahasar's borders."

"He'd be a fool not to." At Cistine's left, King's Cadre Warden Rozalie Dohnal cinched her arms and tossed her honeyed hair over her shoulder. "I think we proved well enough in Middleton we won't stand for provocation."

"Be that as it may, we keep the watch on the southern border." Queen Solene Novacek leaned against the table's edge, the softness of her face not in the least belying her piercing green eyes. "We don't need Jad seeing a lapse in our attention as an excuse to start prodding again after the harsh winter we had."

It *had* been harsh, the worst Cistine could ever remember. She wasn't certain if she was simply too distracted to notice them before—wrapped up in books and tea and suitors—or if the vicious snowstorms and shortage of game and plants was a creeping down of the blight from the north, an echo of far more perilous dangers beyond their borders. Whatever the case, she'd spent much of the last three months helping ration out supplies to the neediest towns in Talheim...when she wasn't researching fortifications and sieges, or writing in the tooled leather journal tucked into her belt, never far from reach.

She traced the dimples of horses artfully etched into the cover now, and her heart clenched. If the boy who gave it to her were still alive, he'd either take faint at the words within, or beg to be part of everything she was plotting. Perhaps she was better off not knowing which it would be.

King Cyril Novacek cleared his throat, bringing every eye at the table to him—including Cistine's, to whom he spoke: "Suggestions?"

The direct solicitation no longer made her palms sweat. This was a dance they had mastered by now. Trapping her hands together on the table, she held his stare. "I agree, we don't give ground at the southern forts. But I think we should offer the Wardens there a well-deserved rest. Pleasant as the southern warmth must be compared the snow we've had, I'm sure they're missing their families."

Cyril nodded curtly. "Viktor, see to it."

Viktor Pollack, the acting Commander of the King's Cadre with Rion Bartos retired back to his estate in Practica, dipped his head and offered a fleeting glance to Cistine from the Queen's right. She held that stare when she added carefully, "I think it may be time to offer the Wardens at the northern barracks a reprieve as well."

A hush gathered up the table, as it always did when she mentioned the north. She tried not to blame them—for two decades, her kingdom was mandated to keep silent about Valgard, and none were as comfortable discussing it now as her—but it was an effort not to bristle at those uneasy looks.

"The North has been quiet," her uncle Filip mused, "aside from that gods-forsaken storm. We're left weakened at both sides if we rotate our ranks all at once."

"But the ranks haven't changed in nearly three months." At Cistine's own behest, but Filip didn't need to know that. "It's long past time those Wardens saw their homes again."

"I agree." The shock at Viktor's flash of support was nearly enough to rend Cistine's focus. "Most are exhausted, homesick, and restless, especially at the northern barracks."

All her doing, because Cistine had insisted they be kept there from the moment she returned to Talheim. She shoved away a prickle of guilt that sizzled in her fingertips, reciting a silent mantra to herself: *Wartime necessity. Wartime necessity.*

The chant floated like words off a musty page, ink and old paper soothing her frayed senses. When her focus returned, her father was nodding—both to her and to Filip. "I agree, a rotation in the north is necessary. But it's also true we don't want to change shifts at the borders all at once. We'll compromise— move the southern ranks now, the north in a fortnight."

Cistine fisted her hands in her skirts.

Another fortnight. She could endure it.

When both Cistine and Filip dipped their heads, the King rose, bringing the rest of the table with him. "It's been a long day, my friends. Let's reconvene in the morning, and I'll see about having the hearths stoked less often tomorrow."

A few chuckled, and Cistine shot her father a dry smile he met with a wink—carefully covering for her distraction.

The room slowly emptied, Solene escorting a flock of ladies to the tearoom with a parting kiss blown to Cistine. She returned it, glanced at her father's face again, and stilled; he had that look in his eye, the sort that once heralded discussions of successorship and her duty as future Queen. These days, it lent itself far more to conversations she enjoyed even less, because they required too much delicacy of tongue that erred close to lying. And she did not like to lie to her father.

"I really am tired," she said quickly. "I think I'll nap before supper." A meal that would, thankfully, be attended by every lord and lady from across the kingdom, keeping the conversation shallow and cordial.

She feigned ignorance to the King's heavy sigh when she all but dragged Rozalie from the room, yanking the doors shut behind them. Rozalie offered a grimace while they walked. "That went better than expected."

Cistine kneaded her temples. "Thanks to Viktor's support, of all people."

"I'd rather have the support of a snake sleeping in my bed, but in this case, I think we take it as it is: we're getting the rotation at the northern barracks. It's finally happening."

Excitement veined Rozalie's voice, and Cistine dropped her hands and met the Warden's gleaming stare. "Two more weeks. That's manageable."

"I'd believe you better if you didn't have that murderous look in your eyes."

Cistine stuck out her tongue, and she and Rozalie carried on in silence the rest of the way to the Princess's rooms—not the same ones where she'd lived for her first twenty years. She'd tried to stay in the chamber of her childhood, its balcony stretching above her beloved inner garden where the comforting scents of winter berries and pine waited to embrace her during these long days. But after so many difficult nights reading and writing in her new leather journal—after restless slumber when she woke in cold sweats, sobbing Thorne's name into the darkness, aching for her *selvenar* who was not merely across the hall anymore, but a kingdom away—she found the restlessness was too much, the surroundings too familiar.

The call was too great.

It whispered to her now when she and Rozalie entered her new rooms in the north-facing tower, inhaling scents of lavender, jasmine, and cinnamon from the bouquet on the breakfast table. Shutting the doors and leaning her weight against them, Cistine breathed in until air struck the bottom of her lungs, trapped there while she listened to that quiet growl deep in her spirit.

Come, it urged, as it had all her life. *Come and see.*

But she couldn't. Not yet.

A throaty caw greeted their arrival, and Cistine flashed a tired smile at the sleek black raven roosting on the back of her dining chair. "Hello, Faer."

"*Hello, Cistine.*"

Rozalie shuddered. "I still think it's horrible you taught him to mimic your voice."

"He's a battle bird. He needed something to occupy that clever mind...didn't you, you handsome bag of feathers?" Cistine fed Faer a scrap of beef from her cold breakfast plate. "Besides, it was this, or let him keep stealing necklaces from all the courtiers until Viktor went mad searching for Astoria's newest jewel thief."

"That was a good week." Smiling, Rozalie dumped herself on the bed. "Just don't teach him to say *my* name."

Cistine laughed. "I give you my word."

Rozalie was silent. Cistine turned from feeding Faer, and her heart lurched, then sank like a dropped stone. Rozalie had peeled back the lumpy quilts Cistine ordered untouched by the servants, burying stacks and mounds of books frittered out of the royal library. She should have stashed them under the bed before the council, but after another restless night of bad dreams, she'd slept so late all she could do was throw down a few bites of cheese and run to the meeting hall, leaving the mound where it fell.

"Bit of light reading before bed?" Rozalie's tone tried and failed for mirth. "I didn't think you were researching *this* deeply on battle tactics, Princess."

"I couldn't sleep last night."

Rozalie turned to her, scooping one book from the buried heap. "What is *this* all about?"

"Arithmetic." Cistine sank into the dining chair, and Faer settled on her shoulder. "The average war in Talheimic history consisted of anywhere between six and ten thousand battles, did you know that?"

"I didn't. Nor would anyone who hasn't had their nose buried in books on war theory for the past three months."

Cistine couldn't muster even a smile at her wry tone. "The Bloodwights depleted their store of augments over the last twenty years in the wilds, but they took Stornhaz, which means they have all the flagons the Courts couldn't steal out during the siege. Besides that, they don't need flagons for every battle, they have Blood Hive fighters, too."

"Your point?"

"Let's say the Courts fled with five hundred flagons, generously. If they skirmish with the Bloodwights even twice a week and use as few as five augments every time, they'll only have enough to last a year."

Rozalie shrugged. "Maybe they can win by then."

"Maybe. Except most wars have historically lasted eighteen to twenty-four months."

Now Rozalie set the book side, frowning. "It's not enough."

Cistine slumped forward, resting her head in her hands. "It's nowhere *near* enough. They'll be fighting with steel alone while the Bloodwights still have plenty of flagons to spread around."

"So, what are you thinking?"

"What I always have: that they can't win this war without help." And help was something her father wouldn't be quick to send, something the lords would never agree to. She'd tested those waters her first week back in Talheim and found them fathomless, full of doubt and suspicion.

But then, this wasn't truly a war of able bodies; it was a war of augments. And in such a skirmish, there was no one to plead Valgard's cause. Nothing could be done, except...

Cistine furiously clamped down on the thought, shoving it aside as she did whenever it arose; as deep as she'd stuffed it last night before it manifested once more in her nightmares. "You're free to go, Rozalie. Spread the word to the Wardens and prepare a note for Viktor. If you need to, let him know the names on your roster have my personal support. I'm not certain what his angle was today, but let's use it for all it's worth."

"Consider it done." Rozalie stood and stretched. "I'll see you at the dinner tonight."

The moment she was gone, Cistine latched the door and hurried to the bed. Beneath it, she chiseled a stone loose and opened a cavity in the floor where she'd hidden the last gift from her mentor, Quill: an augment pouch with six flagons inside.

Too dangerous to leave them exposed in a citadel full of those who didn't yet fathom that the augment wells in the North were truly gifted by the gods— the powers within them mere weapons, not the abomination Cistine's grandfather Ivan claimed them to be; those who still believed forcing the Northern Kingdom to seal the Doors to the Gods, depleting their augment stocks dramatically until these six precious flagons had become a gift without measure, was justified. Those like Viktor, tutored to prejudice by Rion Bartos, who might destroy them—and devastate the city and Cistine's heart.

If she was wiser, she wouldn't touch these augments at all. Quill had given them to her in case Valgard fell to the Bloodwights—the twisted and cruel Order of former *visnprests* who keyed the Doors shut and sealed their craft into the Novacek blood—and it was left to Cistine alone to ensure they did not spill her blood or her father's on the Doors and summon enough augments to enslave the world. But handling the flagons calmed her, quieted the call, soothed the ache in her chest. It made her feel powerful again. Training always did.

She perched on the edge of her bed and cradled a flagon in each hand, their separate calls weighing differently on her mind: fire in one, ravaging darkness in the other. She breathed deeply, in and out through pursed lips; then she uncorked the fire, releasing the smallest kernel into her palm.

It bloomed like a flower, not so much as a tendril of heat escaping her command. She let it burn back her sleeves just enough to bare the beginning of the Atrasat inkings that girdled her wrists, extending up along her arms and meeting above her heart. The winking stars flickered in flame, one for each member of her cabal: Quill and Tatiana, Maleck and Ashe, Aden and Ariadne, Baba Kallah and Julian, and Thorne. Every name a blow, every one welcomed for the love that came with the agony. Bringing them back in moments of solitude was the only way she kept them alive.

Sucking in a deep breath, she let the fire bracelet her wrist. Wiggling her fingers, she thumbed open the shadow flagon, its murky purple contents roiling like that deep night when she'd fled Valgard to protect the Key and let the war against the Bloodwights be waged without her.

She poured a seed of darkness into her palm.

The separate augments surged like hounds baying at their leads, racing up her arms, tugging at her will with a violent threat to destroy the entire northern tower in darkness and flame. Pressure built in Cistine's chest, a mixture of panic and power braided together, but she ground her teeth, stopping it in its place with a silent command barked inside her head; at that unspoken word, the storms abated. The fire crawled back down her arm, the darkness returned to sulk within the cage of her fingers.

Sweat sliding down her nape, chest shuddering, Cistine held an augment in each hand.

She'd begun practicing this her first week back in Talheim, when memories of facing the *Aeoprast* in the acolyte temple and a Mahasari spy in the sewers below the City of a Thousand Stars kept her awake long after dark. Curious and still grief-stricken enough to be daring, she had ridden out deep into the heart of the plains one night, halfway to the Calalun Peaks where no one would see what happened next. Then she did what she'd managed twice before, purely on luck and guessing both times: wielding two augments at once.

It should not be possible; the power ought to rip her apart from the outside inward, armored flesh or none. Yet here she sat with a strength she only saw Bloodwights possess, or heard in stories Quill and Tatiana told of treacherous Oadmark and the time they fought the *Aeoprast* there. And while it chipped away at her stamina far more quickly than a single augment, she could cling to them both, and more: she could command them.

Rallying her strength, she rose, cupped her palms, and wove the augments together, an undying heat and a darkness so deep the light did not penetrate it. She watched their hypnotic dance a moment, then spread them out between her fingers and started sparring.

It was strange to do it with the empty air, fire-and-darkened fists leaving glowing paths, then snuffing them out. But she did as Quill taught her, mustering the power and bending it to her will; and while the sunlight climbed down the walls and night beckoned the capital city of Astoria, steadiness filled her middle, soothing the quivering tension of another day spent in long councils that felt like such a waste when war breathed at their backs.

Training reminded her that she *was* doing something for the good of her kingdom. Of *all* kingdoms.

When sweat dripped down her back, her dress destroyed and the augments all but spent, Cistine relented at last. She dispatched the fire into her bedside washbasin with a hiss of steam and scattered the darkness against the stone floor. In the silence, she heaved for breath and twisted her thumb against the black-gold band of her betrothal ring, setting moonlight dancing along the ultramarine opal; a promise from Thorne, a vow for a future he gave up to send her home and keep her safe. She wielded it like an anchor now, kedging her mind back down the channels of question that had distracted her in today's council meeting.

Had the cabal found Pippet yet—Quill's younger sister, ransomed off to the

Bloodwights? If they hadn't, how were Quill and Tatiana faring? What of Maleck, facing his brothers on the battlefield again, those masked manifestations of his greatest fears and failures; and Ashe, always a sword and shield, at Maleck's side no matter how terrible things became?

What of Ariadne, the cabal's light and soul, helping shoulder the weight of their spirits in dark hours like these? And Aden, a newly-minted Tribune, taking his position in a war which had to echo so vividly his years in Siralek's Blood Hive arena? They would be perhaps the most focused, the most reliable in the fight, but what if the weight became too great for them to bear?

And what of Thorne, a man who fought for decades for a better future and instead inherited conquesting *visnprests*, stolen children, and the city of his birth set aflame?

Fear licked her insides, and she forced it down. All was not hopeless. She was doing *something*.

Two weeks. Just two more weeks.

A heavy weight banged against the inside of the glass balcony doors, startling Cistine so badly she yelped. Faer picked himself up from his impact with the shimmering surface and strutted before his reflection, offended croaks taking on a deeper cadence—the first name Cistine had taught him to mimic. "*Quill. Quill. Quill. Quill.*"

Pain speared through her chest. "Oh, Faer." The raven squirmed when she crouched beside him and lifted him in both hands, brushing her nose against his skull. "I miss him, too. But we can't go back. Not now."

Outside, a faint toll of thunder rattled the Citadel mortar, as if the True God and his vassals agreed to the danger. And yet the very core of Cistine's being—that wild heart of fire reduced to embers but not entirely foundered—ached to go anyway.

Just two more weeks.

ABOUT THE AUTHOR

Renee Dugan is an Indiana-based author who grew up reading fantasy books, chasing stray cats, and writing stories full of dashing heroes and evil masterminds. Now with over a decade of professional editing, administrative work, and writing every spare second under her belt, she has authored *THE CHAOS CIRCUS,* a portal fantasy novel, and *THE STARCHASER SAGA,* an epic high fantasy series. Living with her husband, son, and not-so-stray cats in the magical Midwest, she continues to explore new worlds and spends her time in this one encouraging and helping other writers on their journey to fulfilling their dreams.

Find Renee Dugan online at:
Reneeduganwriting.com

And on social media: **@reneeduganwriting**